Forged in Rome

Books by Conn Iggulden

CONN IGGULDEN

Forged in Rome

INK AND IRON: BOOK I

MICHAEL JOSEPH

PENGUIN MICHAEL JOSEPH

UK | USA | Canada | Ireland | Australia
India | New Zealand | South Africa

Penguin Michael Joseph is part of the Penguin Random House group of companies
whose addresses can be found at global.penguinrandomhouse.com

Penguin Random House UK,
One Embassy Gardens, 8 Viaduct Gardens, London SW11 7BW

penguin.co.uk

Penguin
Random House
UK

First published 2025

001

Set in 13.5/16 pt Garamond MT Std
Typeset by Six Red Marbles UK, Thetford, Norfolk
Printed and bound by CPI (UK) Ltd, Croydon CR0 4YY

The authorized representative in the EEA is Penguin Random House Ireland,
Morrison Chambers, 32 Nassau Street, Dublin D02 YH68

A CIP catalogue record for this book is available from the British Library

HARDBACK ISBN: 978–0–241–68955–4
TRADE PAPERBACK ISBN: 978–0–241–68956–1

Penguin Random House is committed to a sustainable future
for our business, our readers and our planet. This book is made from
Forest Stewardship Council® certified paper.

MIX
Paper | Supporting
responsible forestry
FSC
www.fsc.org   FSC® C018179

To Toni D'Urso – eighty years young

Foreword

By AD 37, the Roman Republic has become a true empire, stretching from Egypt to the sea coast of Gaul. After Julius Caesar's death in 44 BC, his great-nephew Octavian ruled first as part of a triumvirate, then as Emperor Augustus for over forty years. That long reign was both expansive and prosperous. Augustus consolidated Roman rule, establishing the empire as a stable power. As he said on his deathbed, he found Rome in clay, and left her in marble.

Augustus' adopted son would become emperor after him, in AD 14. At fifty-six, Tiberius came late to power – and was already jaded and utterly corrupt in his pleasures. He spent a great deal of his twenty-three-year reign on the island of Capri, leaving Rome in the hands of a friend. Rome deserved better.

AD 37 is witness to two events that change the path of history. Emperor Tiberius is finally killed – smothered in his bed. We cannot be sure his successor gave the order or was present, but it fits. That tormented young man is still best known by his childhood nickname: Caligula.

The second event will eventually affect the lives of everyone in Rome. In AD 37, another child is born. His mother is Agrippina, great-granddaughter of Augustus. Sister to Caligula, she was a ruthless, intelligent woman, famed for her beauty. She named her son Lucius Ahenobarbus. We know him better as Emperor Nero.

This is not his story. I have told that in the trilogy *Nero, Tyrant* and *Inferno*. This is a very different character, one captured as a slave of Rome and sold to a noble house. Cormac has neither power, wealth nor status. However, in Rome of the first century AD, with skill and ambition – and luck – perhaps such things can be won.

Conn Iggulden

PART ONE

ROME

AD 37

I

Cormac could feel his heart beating. He pressed a hand against his ribs on the left and felt a pulse. It seemed fast, as if he had run a mile. He wondered what it would feel like if it suddenly stopped. He'd heard of one boy who had died in the middle of the exam the year before. It might not have been true, he didn't know. There were always stories.

The schoolroom smelled of some combination of the magister's armpits and sour breath, mingled with old wax, pine and dust. Cormac looked over the little collection of items he had laid out on the desk before him, touching them one by one for reassurance. He had sat at that very seat for years, seven mornings at a time until the nundinae, when he was expected to continue studies on his own. He tapped the inkstone with its bowl, one he had ground himself. He had mixed black dust to a paste with drops of water from a tiny phial, filled in the river Tiber on a previous visit. Any water would do, of course, but this was the Gradus Scriptorum. It was good luck to have the Roman river in the letters, everyone knew that.

The city bustled outside, a clamour of carts, steps and cheerful talk as people headed home for lunch. Cormac tried to shut it all out. The desks had been placed in neat rows, the afternoon sun shining gold in the dust. He could feel eyes on him and a slow flush prickled his neck. That gaze came with a silent pressure. If he did not look up, he would pay for it later.

Marcus Junius Silanus was known as 'Plato' in the estate house. The original name of the greatest philosopher ever to have lived meant 'broad-shouldered'. That part was true enough. Though Marcus was just sixteen, he had been trained with sword and shield from a young age. It showed in the width of him, only slightly spoiled by eyes that were a touch close together. In the right light, they seemed almost to meet, leaving odd expanses of face with no feature at all. It made him look stupid – and that was a fair assessment, at least in Cormac's view. Not that he would ever say so. For a boy without any great imagination, Marcus had a sort of genius when it came to causing pain. Cormac remembered the metal box only too well. It had been designed to carry live birds to market, so had holes punched in the top. The previous summer, Marcus had lit a candle inside and made the younger estate boys sit on it. The shameful part was how they had competed with one another. Cormac had held on as long as he could, though he could smell burning hair. Marcus had congratulated him on his endurance, he remembered. Somehow, the memory of that hurt more than the blisters.

The magister turned away from glaring at the row of boys and two girls. Cormac tried not to stare at those rare birds, though they intrigued him. Women were not allowed to draft wills, of course, nor do half the tasks of a scribe in the city, not when a poorly written word might mean an entire estate going to a different branch. They had all heard the stories – such as the man who referred to his wife as 'mother' all through their marriage. On his death, he had left all he owned to that wife, only to see his actual mother dispute the will and win. Terms of affection caused all sorts of trouble for the scribes, even the elite caste employed by the imperial treasury. That was Cormac's dream, to sit in splendour there one day, with great houses like the Junii and Furii coming to him for his skill.

He felt a thrill pass through him. He was *ready*, his mind swimming in verse and the Twelve Tables of Roman law. When this day ended, he would have a piece of white parchment, of polished sheepskin in his hand. It would be his ticket to a different life. He flexed ink-dark fingers and smiled.

Stretching a leg across the narrow aisle, Marcus kicked his chair so hard it moved. Cormac saw the phial of water fall and grabbed for it. If he ran out of water or ink, there would be no help. A good scribe tended his own tools.

He missed. The bottle skipped and bounced on pine planking, but did not break. It came to rest closer to Marcus and of course the other boy put one large foot over it. His sandals were studded with iron and the threat was clear. One quick press and the glass would shatter. Cormac would take the blame and no doubt the whipping to follow. The Silanus house had only lent its tools that day, investing in him. They would demand an accounting.

He looked over at Marcus Junius Silanus. 'Plato' raised both eyebrows in silent question and Cormac was forced to give a sharp nod. The sandal was removed and Cormac snatched up the fragile thing. He would leave his exam papyrus on his right side, though it cramped him to write on the left. All the hard work he had put in would be stolen like coins from a purse.

In that moment, he hated Marcus with a sort of heat that flashed behind his eyes. It filled him, making him strong. He was no thin-fingered scribe, not then. He had grown taller over the previous year, he was sure of it. Though he had not increased in strength, he could roll his own shoulders and imagine knocking 'Plato' down, he with his little pig eyes.

It was a fantasy. He and Marcus came into the city in a fine chariot each morning. Two drivers whipped powerful horses and expected right of way on the approach. Guards either sat above or loped alongside as protectors of a Silanus son. Marcus was the adopted heir to one of the great branches. The boy's uncle had no sons to inherit the estate of Cedri Magnae. The deal had been done a couple of years earlier, with the lad brought down from the north to learn about his inheritance. Marcus was already promised to some wealthy daughter of another family. It was how the senate kept their power, as far as Cormac could see. They took it from the earth in crops and ingots, or they married more. Not all the crops were green, either. Some of them were taken from villages by white cliffs, bound and sold at auction, their own farms lost to view.

Cormac made himself breathe, touching each of the items on his desk once more, moving the water bottle from the edge. He tested the point of the reed with his thumb, nodding and breathing through his nose. He was just a few pages away from leaving the school for ever. When he had his gradus, he would never set foot in that room again. It was a joyous prospect, one to start him dreaming.

He found himself smiling. When he glanced over, Marcus was scowling, looking almost afraid.

Cormac forced himself to concentrate. Being stupid was its own punishment, he supposed. Marcus Silanus was free, rich and Roman. He was destined for the army or the senate, or both. Yet he would never understand the things that mattered. In the small hours sometimes, as Cormac stole a few extra moments in bed, he felt he could see the whole empire, from the western coast of Gaul to Judaea. There was a temple in Rome with a map on one of the walls, made from thousands of tiny pieces of coloured stone. Cormac could name all the regions and even the major families marked in gold: the Furii, the Fabii, Aemilii . . . the Junii, from whom the Silanus family claimed descent. If he focused enough, if he made the world still, he thought he could feel the city that ruled, half a million people rising and eating and working together. It was a vision he could not share with anyone else. When he had tried, the other boys just looked at him or tapped their heads.

'The gradus scriptorum for this year, 790 ab urbe condita is as follows . . .'

Cormac had to stop himself thinking about the founding of Rome, almost eight hundred years before. He preferred to take his dates from each emperor, as was becoming more popular. That would make the year twenty-three of the reign of Tiberius . . . He bit his knuckle as the magister droned on. It was good news.

'. . . for penmanship, Horace will be our guide. You will produce the first eighty lines of his Odes, without error. I will collect those and issue new papyrus for an analysis of his relationship with his father – as discussed in Satire VI,

book the first, lines sixty-five to one hundred and nine . . .
For arithmetic, you will discuss Euclid and his rules for the
formation of triangles.'

Cormac tensed. If that was it, he wanted to get started.
There was a shadow stick on the wall with hours carved into
the wood. All the pupils had studied it on summer afternoons, when the line seemed to slow or cease to move at all.

'Finally . . .' the magister continued.

Cormac swallowed and Marcus shifted in the chair next
to him. They both saw something bad coming in the man's
pleasure.

'. . . for your exploration, you will discuss the three paths
of Parmenides, with particular concern for the example
of mortal opinion.'

The magister allowed himself a thin smile as the class
groaned. Fourteen boys and two daughters of a noble
house sat there blinking. Cormac glanced at his companion and saw Marcus Silanus looking utterly blank. He
wracked his own memory, trying to recall a text he'd found
so convoluted he'd thought the author might have written
it for spite.

The magister sighed to himself, his arrow flown. Almost
in irritation, he waved a hand to begin and in moments the
scratch of reeds filled the little room. Cormac took a long
breath. Horace was a favourite of the magister and he had
prepared a number of his texts. He was much less confident about Parmenides. Should he write down all he could
remember of the Greek's arguments while he was fresh?
He could do that and finish the penmanship at the end.
He knew those lines well enough, he was sure. Though his
hand would be a claw by then.

He felt Marcus glaring, waiting for him to produce

something that could be copied. Had the big ox learned nothing at all? Cormac hated him, for his sullen gaze, for his strength, for his cruel laughter. Still, this was the gradus scriptorum. This was the door that would give Cormac value in the world. For one like Marcus, it meant being able to understand the speeches of his peers. For Cormac, it was his entire life. He would not fail, no matter what obstacles they put in his way.

He touched the point of his reed to the ink, letting black threads creep up. This was his day. He put all his worries aside and wrote the first line of an ode. Horace had been a genius, there was no doubt about that. He was also the son of a slave – a man who had made himself of value to his masters and *bought himself free*. That freedman had believed in education and sent his clever son to the best tutors in Rome. Cormac wondered if the magister had chosen the text with that in mind, or simply for the complexity of thought. He glanced up, but the magister appeared to be asleep, leaning back in his chair with eyes shut. Cormac smiled, feeling confidence swell as he wrote with a sure hand. He could see lines before him, unrolling like a scroll in the air.

A clatter of boots on wood was one more thing to ignore at first. Cormac felt his lips thin as someone opened the door to the schoolroom and the magister jerked awake from his drowse. There was some indignant whisper-ing and Cormac could not resist glancing up, though he feared losing the thread of his thoughts. He had finished the Horace; it was the serpent coils of Parmenides that strangled him then. Yet his reed dried in the air as he saw the magister pushed firmly aside and a pair of armed men enter. They had not bared their blades and there was still no alarm. Cormac knew them for Silanus guards. Urban was a free man, recruited to serve the Silanus estate after retiring from work in the Circus. He was fiercely loyal to the family – and to Marcus in particular. The other was less imposing, one of a dozen new recruits over the previous year. Cormac knew Albanus from the carriage that brought them to the city each morning. Of course, he knew each face from the Cedri Magnae estate, exactly as he might have learned every son, daughter or cousin in a village. Besides that, both Urban and Albanus wore the ornate armour the Silanus family favoured, marking them as private guards rather than legionary soldiers. They sported wristbands of leather that had been dyed and painted creamy white, with the same colour appearing on shield rims and in bands of ivory on sword hilts. The Junii Silanus clan owned the Whites, the chariot team that raced in the Circus. As far as Cormac could tell, they owned the colour itself.

The two men crossed the room with eyes on Marcus. As the rest of the class stared, Urban dropped to one knee and bowed his head.

'Speak,' Marcus said, though his voice shook. He watched as the ex-gladiator rose, standing with him so that they faced one another, his scripts forgotten.

'*Dominus*, a message has come from the estate. I . . . I have orders for you to return immediately.'

Marcus paled as Cormac blinked. The term 'dominus' was one for a man in authority, never a boy. It meant the impossible. It meant the elder Silanus they had left that morning was dead – and Marcus Junius Silanus was at that moment master of a noble house.

10

Marcus glanced down at tight black lines of writing, his mouth opening and closing. Cormac still sat and he could feel time slipping away like water. He too rose and the guard glanced over, giving him a nod.

'Can we not . . . finish here?' Cormac asked desperately. He knew better than to challenge an order, but he had given too much to this just to see it forgotten in a crisis. What did another hour matter? His eyes pleaded with Marcus, though the great sheep seemed lost, stunned by his new responsibilities.

'It is not far from the end . . .' Cormac pressed on, 'and we have worked hard for the gradus scriptorum. It will be another half-year before it is held again and . . .'

Urban held up a palm, frowning. He was around forty and still trained every day. There was no weight on him and the muscles of his legs were astonishingly distinct. In some ways, Urban had the wiry frame of a boy, though he had won sixty bouts in the arenas, so Cormac had heard. Either way, the man looked disgustingly fit, still capable of enforcing his authority. The threat in just that open hand made words dry in Cormac's mouth. Though his heart broke, he waited for the axe to fall.

Marcus Silanus gathered himself. He shook his head as if to clear it of confusion, jaw muscles clenching visibly as he digested the news. He looked at Cormac, then at the papyrus sheets piled at his right hand.

'Come,' Marcus said nobly, gesturing to the door. 'Duty takes us away.'

Cormac moved in a sort of daze, gathering up inkstone and water bottle, settling his finished sheets in a neat pile. His sight blurred as he was taken from a world he knew, without the prize he had worked to win. It was unfair, monstrously so, but he dared not say a word. He was a slave – and his worth had just been reduced to match the lowest ranks. Without the gradus scriptorum, without that mark of scholarship, he could not set out his stall on festival days to produce wills and contracts for the people of Rome. He could not save coins he might earn with that work until he bought himself free. He could not apply to the treasury as a freedman, rising in status to serve praetors or senators. He could not take a wife, nor have sons to follow him. His entire life was in ruins.

He stumbled as he followed Marcus and the house guards out of the schoolroom, blind with tears. Urban saw, but chose to ignore it. The magister too said nothing. He just stood with head bowed, a man of low estate and no wealth, preferring to be unnoticed by a Silanus.

Outside, the carriage was the one sent to the city that morning. Two drivers sat on the high bench, sharing a long whip and ready to send the team trotting east down the long road to the estate. Urban opened the door for Marcus and Cormac climbed in alongside him, still mute at the change in their fortunes.

As Urban began to close the door, Marcus Silanus put out his hand and stopped its swing.

'Is my uncle truly dead?' he said.

Urban winced, looking up and down a busy street. This was news to fly across the city. There would be members of the senate who might profit from it, snatching up businesses or selling their own concerns before the price collapsed. Rome was a trading city and so Urban leaned very close and kept his voice to a whisper.

'He is, dominus. You'll hear all when we get you safely home.'

Marcus raised his voice as his man began to step away, understanding instinctively that Urban would have to remain close. Sure enough, Urban leaned in once more.

'How?' Marcus hissed. 'He was in good health this morning. Are we under attack?'

Urban chewed his lip as he considered how to answer.

'I don't believe so,' he said. 'Though Albanus and I will give our lives to keep you safe. The doctor will tell us more when we return . . . That's all I know, dominus.'

Urban vanished from the side opening before Marcus could think of a response. The young man slumped onto the padded seat. It was forty miles to the estate. Cormac knew they would be shaken until their bones were sore, just as they had been that morning. He had watched the sun rise on that journey, full of hope and confidence. All that had gone. He sat in numb silence as the carriage turned and both Urban and Albanus swung up to their seats. Cormac saw they had drawn their swords, keeping them ready. Whatever they had said, they believed there was a threat. He found himself staring out, looking for assassins as they clattered across stones, heading for the road home.

2

The sun was low on the horizon and the horses covered in salt rime by the time they reached the gates to the estate. Cormac wondered if Marcus saw them with new eyes now. The big lad had been brought to Cedri Magnae two years before, then fourteen and a strange mixture of arrogance and innocence. Cormac understood he was the third son of a different branch, but they would not have expected Marcus to inherit so quickly, raised above his brothers. He had no advisers around him and even his guards were retired men. Cormac assumed Urban and Albanus would be replaced, reflecting the young master's new status.

If Cormac had won his gradus, he might even have dreamed of advising Marcus Silanus himself. He sighed as the carriage drew to a halt. Urban jumped down to exchange words with the gate servants and they passed over a package of letters. Those men looked ruffled somehow, tear-stained, no doubt reflecting the entire staff as they reacted to the loss.

Cormac tried to feel grief, but it passed over him, almost

like birds overhead. Instead, he found himself wondering whether Marcus would let him retake the gradus. Somehow, looking at his sullen expression, Cormac doubted it. A leaden mood had settled on them both over hours of silence on the road. Cormac's fate was not in his own hands – that had been made very clear. He had been a fool ever to feel it had.

Urban tossed the packet into his lap as he climbed to the high step once more. Cormac riffled a thumb over the edge. It was one of his tasks to distribute letters when they arrived at the estate. Life went on, even in the midst of tragedy.

From the gate to the main house was over a mile further, rattling along a wide tree-lined road of dressed stones. Sheep and goats munched the edges while a dozen gardeners clipped and fed the soil. They bowed their heads as the carriage passed, showing respect to Marcus. He frowned, lost in his own thoughts.

Cormac could not help the way his heart lifted as the house came into view. This was the world he had known since his earliest years, after all. He may have been a slave, but he was home nonetheless.

The staff of the house, fully six hundred men and women, all perched or leaned in the great hall, crammed in and waiting to hear whatever they would be told. A few dozen had found a spot on the balcony that overlooked the rest, climbing stairs of black and ancient oak. It was rare to have so many up there, Cormac thought. Wood creaked and dust spilled, catching the lamplight in threads.

Cormac could hear sobbing. A few of the older ones grieved openly; others stared at nothing or shook their heads, fearing the way their lives had changed.

He'd woken in a perfectly ordered world that morning, confident as he'd emptied his bladder into a bleaching vat and wet his hair down to something like order. To sit in that hall with the sound of choked tears was as if he had stepped into someone else's life.

He knew everyone there – from the Gauls who tended the olive presses to the weaver families, to the divorced stonemason and his three lads. When Cormac was not at school, his work kept him in the house. He only saw men like the threshers at feasts and holy days, when they were given wine from the master's own store. He nodded to them even so, though they looked pinch-faced.

At harvest time, the entire household turned out to beat olive trees with long whips, dislodging the fruit that became bright green oil, the stuff of life. Out of season, Cormac knew the lads tended herds of estate sheep, living in huts far from the main house and driving their charges back and forth to streams and distant hills. The estate was a wealthy one, but it was not mere ornament. He'd seen the accounts.

Cormac realised he could recite the names of every man, woman and child there. He had written each one a hundred times, noting time off for sickness, or loans and earnings lodged in the estate coffers. He knew the carpenter Plautius sold carved figures of wood made in his spare time, saving the profit each month. Plautius would buy himself free soon, Cormac was certain. He knew them in ink as much as for kindness or bad temper – the few who might slip him an apple, or cuff his head as he passed. Yet that evening, nothing was the same.

For ten years, Cormac had woken at the same pre-dawn hour, heading to his ablutions and to dress for school. He never ate then, not until the kitchen staff were up and coddling eggs still warm from the hens. No, it was his first duty to walk to the gate before dawn, waiting there to stare down the road to the city. He'd learned to remain until he heard the first bell sound in the stables before he dared to return. That was if he didn't want a whipping. The way old Antoninus told it, it was always his choice. Cormac could complete all his chores and work with a good heart and no complaints, or he could laze about like a Gaul and accept the lash as a punishment well earned. It was completely up to him, Antoninus said, a free decision.

Antoninus had found a snake in his bed the month before. The thing had writhed around his arm like a rope – though the bite had not been much. The lads in the fields suffered those same bites and always lived, so they'd told him. Yet Antoninus had made such a shrieking, he'd woken the whole house. Cormac had struggled to hide his laughter then.

He looked across the room, to where Antoninus waited near the door. The scribe's white hair was combed and oiled, Cormac noted, the man's tunic belted neatly. He looked in turn to the doorway, his jowly old face towards the light. It was like a painting of an expectant man, Cormac thought. He imagined a frame around the scene and smiled, before bitterness surged back. This was his home, but he was meant to have a new scroll of parchment in his hand. They would all know he'd come home without it. The shame burned.

On mornings when a herald did come from Rome, it was Cormac's task to collect orders and sealed letters and then to distribute them. Some he left for Antoninus to copy into the estate record. Personal letters always went to the outer rooms of the dominus, while anything marked with the Silanus seal went to the old man's bedside, to the little tray there.

Cormac had always put on felt slippers to enter that part of the house. Silanus senior did not like to hear little mice, so Nartius claimed. The man's seneschal treated his master like a god walking the earth, as if Nartius was the only one who truly understood the needs of the dominus. Sleek with plump flesh and somewhat over forty years of age, Nartius had been a terrifying presence in Cormac's life since he had arrived at the estate. It was worrying not to see him in the hall with the others. His absence meant decisions were being made somewhere else.

To his very marrow, Cormac knew he should not be sitting idle at that moment, not while the sun set. In earlier years, he might have been spending that last hour of light greasing sandals, filling lamps or just copying lines of Horace while Antoninus nodded off in his chair. The senior scribe had been appalled in the beginning, as if Cormac's lack of letters was an offence against nature. He had laid on hard with the whip in those days, apparently under the belief he could thrash knowledge into a boy.

It had been two years before Cormac had even understood Antoninus too was a slave. The scribe may have had his airs and robes and bushy white eyebrows. He may have written with the fine hand of a scholar and spoken both Latin and Greek as well as his native Syrian tongue. Yet he was owned, just as Cormac was – just as Nartius was, for that matter, or Sophia, who ran the kitchens and fussed like a mother hen over the whole staff. Her own children had been born as little red scraps, passing out of the world as quickly as they came in. Cormac vaguely remembered her husband. Cephas had managed Silanus estate horses and been a bright-eyed fellow, always ready to laugh. He'd been taken in some summer flux or other and yet in her grief, Sophia's affections had only grown, encompassing all the young ones on the estate. When Cormac thought the word 'mother', he thought of Sophia.

His own true family was barely a scent. He had a memory of white cliffs and red blood on the ground. He still dreamed of that sometimes. The slavers had seemed giants, men who laughed and shouted orders he could not understand. Cormac knew he had been taken on a ship that moved without wind. There had been crystals of salt on his skin and wood that creaked like a voice. He wished he could remember his mother and father as well, but all that was gone. With thousands of his people, he had been sold on some muddy dock in Gaul. Factors for the Silanus family had checked his mouth and groin and armpits for signs of disease, then paid bright silver coins for Cormac and sixty like him.

They'd been made to walk for a month after that, heading south from the coast with the rising sun on his left shoulder. Eight of them had caught some fever and been found cold. Four more had run and been hunted down, killed as an example to the rest. Cormac had known he wasn't the weakest then. It was a strange comfort, even in memory.

He had been a skinny little thing, with all his growing still to do. He'd plucked road grasses as he went, choosing ones he knew would be sweet. Those, with dry bread and a little salt fish, had kept him alive. His lips had cracked and his skin had burned, but he'd survived to reach the Silanus estate.

There were times when some drift of kitchen smoke would form the shadow of a woman singing softly, cooking for a man she loved . . .

Cormac looked up suddenly over the great hall. He'd been drowsing, he realised. The hall was warmer than usual with so many crammed in. No, it wasn't that. It was a sort of torpor in his thoughts, a heaviness that had weighed on him since the schoolroom. He slapped his own face suddenly, to keep him sharp.

The stable lads saw his movement. One of them kicked him in the back for spite. They were both a year or two younger, but they didn't look away when he glared, all red knees and rangy limbs. They already said he had taken on airs, that he thought he was better than them. He couldn't deny it.

Silence and stillness entered the hall, spreading like oil from the great doors to the rest of the household. Cormac knew a fountain burbled out there, water drawn from lead pipes that narrowed to the width of a child's finger. In the sudden silence, he could hear it. Household slaves were meant to draw their water from a well in the back field, but they had all risked the whip to taste that cold spring, a wonder of the world that splashed over green bronze fishes.

The Silanus atrium was one of three, all ringed in columns of white stone. The walls there were painted to let visitors look onto scenes of slaves labouring in the fields. They looked strong, those workers, Cormac always thought. Strong and happy. The men laughed as they lifted great sheaves of wheat, while full-breasted women gathered lambs around their feet. Cormac liked to gaze on those images in stolen moments, usually rushing from the stores back to his little alcove, where his desk and his copying waited. He . . .

He blinked as the household rose to greet whoever was sweeping in, through that atrium, into the Silanus main hall. He'd drifted off again! He could not slap his face without drawing more attention, so bit the inside of his lower lip, hard enough to make his eyes water. What was this sleepy state? To have a chance to appeal his gradus scriptorum he needed to have his wits about him. He could make a claim to have his unfinished sheets collected and marked, to have the extraordinary events of that morning taken into account. They would grant it to a Silanus, he was certain. Marcus knew what it meant to him.

'Rise for his most august honour, Senator Decimus Junius Silanus, Gens Junii Silanus, Censor of Rome, beloved friend and most trusted of Emperor Tiberius.'

Cormac felt another kick between his shoulder blades as he came off the bench and stood. He didn't dare turn as a senator's retinue came into the hall. Nartius entered like their herald, Cormac saw, the man swollen almost to bursting with his own importance. The old master's seneschal took up a position just a few paces in front of Cormac, head bowed and hands clasped as if at prayer.

Silanus slaves and staff edged back there, leaving the centre stones free. Cormac watched in awe as legionaries in full armour took up positions where they could glare at that crowd. If they were at all nervous in the presence of so many working men and women, it did not show in their expressions.

Scribes too were coming in, strangers with ink-marked hands. Watching them, Cormac thought to slip his left thumb between the next two fingers, so the tip poked out.

He held that up behind his back, waggling the thumb so that the stable lads would see. It resembled female parts, so he had been told – a terrible insult to men. He wasn't entirely sure how accurate the gesture was, but it provoked a hiss from behind. He dipped his head, satisfied with that small rebellion.

On the main floor, the staff of the estate watched as an actual senator came among them. This was a man who had talked with consuls, even the emperor, a man who strode the halls of the Palatine. His father warmed a second seat in the senate, as *his* father and a dozen generations had done before.

Those calm eyes had witnessed legions on the march, perhaps commanded them. Cormac felt his heart racing. This was Marcus' own father, come to oversee the inheritance fate and foresight had granted his line. Cormac had to crane to see the wide-shouldered son standing abashed in his father's presence. Ahead of him, Nartius rocked up and down on the balls of his feet. The seneschal's hair was combed into a great slick, like crow wings that met at the back.

Cormac had known his master was not of the main line of the Silanus family. It hadn't mattered in any real sense. It would have been like comparing one mountain peak with another, while standing in foothills far below. Yet the one who looked around at six hundred slaves resembled the man whose letters Cormac had distributed. This Silanus was the eldest of three brothers and a sister. The senator still had dark in his hair, though it was fading to an iron grey. The gaze too had a certain hardness. From the way his son Marcus stood with downcast eyes, Cormac was suddenly pleased to be a few rows back, with Nartius blocking sight of him. If this was the oldest son of the Junii Silani, he was a god amongst men, commanding more wealth and power than Cormac could imagine.

'You will all have heard the sad news,' Decimus Silanus said, nodding as if answering his own words. 'My dear brother has passed from the world. As you know, your master had no children of his own loins. He adopted his nephew Marcus as his son and heir, though we had hoped for more years . . . It falls to me to arrange his affairs, as the most senior of my father's sons. This estate will pass therefore into my hands, in accordance with statute and natural law . . .'

The clipped voice broke off as one of his own servants shifted, touching a hand to his mouth as he made a soft, throat-clearing sound. Cormac watched as the senator became rather more human in his visible irritation.

'What is it?'

'There is a sealed will, dominus,' the man said. 'I found it in the private rooms, in the desk there.'

He held up a scroll, marked with a broken coin of blue wax. Cormac knew it was the real thing. He had seen Antoninus prepare copies over the years, consigning older versions to the fire.

'I will attend to it this evening,' Silanus said, waving it off like a fly. 'I don't doubt my brother intended some minor bequests. As head of the family, I will decide which ones to honour.' He spoke with certainty, but still paused, Cormac saw, a question hanging in the air.

His personal servant shifted again, uncomfortably.

'There is the seal of the imperial record house on the copy, dominus,' he said at last.

Cormac watched the senator frown. The news of an

official copy did not please him, that was clear. Whatever they were, the old man's instructions could not just be ignored. Cormac was somehow pleased about that. Perhaps it was rare for the senator to encounter some obstacle to his authority. Cormac could hardly imagine.

The servant who had spoken was one of those with ink-darkened fingers, Cormac noted. He felt an odd sort of pride to see one of his own standing up to a senator, an anointed member of the nobilitas! Yet the law bound all men, whether their estates were high or low. The thought gave Cormac a feeling of warmth in his chest. This was Rome, he thought.

'Very well,' the senator said, his mouth even tighter than before. His son actually flinched when that gaze fell on him.

'And where is the one who found my brother?' the senator added, casting his voice across the hall.

Cormac expected Nartius or one of the others to raise their hand. Yet he saw the seneschal looking around with the rest.

On his return to the estate, Cormac had taken the last batch of letters into the rooms where the master had been laid out. The bedchamber had been very still and he'd only glanced at the figure lying there, breath caught like a briar. The flesh had been yellow, he recalled, a dark ochre that had no great resemblance to life. The mouth had sagged, with eyes that looked sunken. Something had been taken from the man Cormac had called dominus for ten years.

Cormac felt a hand take his arm. He pulled away from instinct, making Nartius grunt in anger. He didn't let go though. Instead, Nartius dragged him from the crowd as if landing a fish. In a single motion, Cormac was plucked to the front, half-sprawling and rubbing his elbow.

'You are the one?' the senator snapped at him. 'You discovered your master? You found my dear brother dead?'

Cormac had never spoken to one like him. He shook his head in awe.

'No, I was in the city, d-dominus,' he stammered. 'I came back this evening, w-with your s-son.' He glanced at Marcus, but the boy stared at the floor.

'Come closer,' the senator said, beckoning.

Cormac did as he was told. Should he kneel? Old Antoninus knew the rules of how to address his betters. None of them came to mind as Cormac stood before a man of severe Roman dignity. He felt his tongue cleave to the roof of his mouth.

'You are a house slave?' the senator asked.

Cormac nodded, his throat too dry.

'And you attended my brother?'

Cormac shook his head, quite unable to make a sound. On normal days, he had brought the letters, but he had not been there when the dominus died. It seemed too complicated to explain with this man glaring like an accusation.

The senator looked to his servants in frustration. Cormac reminded himself to breathe when he realised he had forgotten. He drew in a lungful, feeling his face redden. He might have answered then, but an impact from behind made him stagger forward. He glanced back in dismay to see Nartius had stepped in. The big man had always been free with his hands. The unfairness stung as much as the blow.

'I am a scribe, dominus,' Cormac managed at last. 'I carried letters in this morning and this evening, but in between I was taking my gradus in the city . . .'

The senator waved him to silence.

'And you are the one who discovered my brother? Who found him in death?'

'N-no, dominus,' Cormac replied. 'I just c-carried the letters.'

The senator was perfect, somehow. From the man's new sandals to the kilt of leather over cloth that he wore, to a tunic woven to a design . . . of a boar. The house crest in white, of course. The face too had a sort of nobility, showing no marks of disease or starvation. Many of the house slaves had pockmarks or scars from some old abscess or ulcer. They lost teeth and suffered through the agues of childhood, usually until something burst. It left a few cruelly marked, but there was no sign of anything like that in the senator. This Silanus was clear-eyed and noble in aspect, taller than most and still strong despite his years. Cormac knew in that moment that he could follow such a man into battle, that he would give his life for one glorious moment in defence of the Silanus family. It would be an honourable death and . . .

'The last letters, was it?' the senator said, trying to understand.

Cormac nodded once more, though he didn't see how it was relevant.

'Very well. Take him up,' the senator went on. 'I'll attend as he is put to the question.'

Cormac felt his mouth open in confusion. He saw Marcus turn as if to object, then look down at his feet once more. His father allowed no opposition, that was clear.

The senator gestured to the six hundred men and women gathered in that place, looking faintly exasperated. 'Until then, continue your usual duties, whatever they are. Understood? Good. I will cremate my brother tomorrow, then read his will.'

The head of the Silanus family looked at Nartius, accepting the man's bulk and strength as useful.

'Show me to some private room. I'll need a fire. Bring the boy.'

Nartius bowed in reply, pulling Cormac along in a grip as implacable as Roman law. Cormac didn't struggle. He saw Sophia from the kitchens standing by the door, fingers over her mouth and eyes shining with tears. He wanted to speak to her, but Nartius was shoving him past. What was happening? Put to the question? Who *had* found the body? He had been in the city! Cormac had only ever known one estate, with a master who hardly intruded on the life of the scribes working for him. Nartius was a greater presence in Cormac's life than the old Silanus had ever been. The grip on his arm felt real enough, but he could not understand what was happening.

3

Cormac remained silent as he was taken out of the hall. Every year he could remember had been spent in that house. For all his dislike of smooth-faced Nartius, he still trusted the man as one of the senior household, a member of the adult group who carried authority in their every glance and action. Nor was it particularly strange to be grabbed and hurried along so quickly his feet barely touched the ground. That sort of handling had been part of his life from his earliest recollection. If a pot of soup spilled in the house, or something valuable was knocked over, Cormac found himself dragged or cuffed to see to the mess. He was usually left alone then, with a broom or a bucket and cloths.

As he'd reached manhood, he'd hardly noticed how long it had been since something like that had actually happened. These days when a pile of fence posts toppled over, a dozen other boys were set to work before anyone came looking for Cormac. With the approach of his gradus scriptorum, he'd moved up in the hierarchy of the estate without being fully aware of it.

Nartius shoved him into a chair and Cormac blinked around. This was one of the storerooms, with stoppered amphorae of wine all along one wall. It wasn't a spot he knew well as his duties rarely took him there. He sneezed as dust got up his nose.

Cormac watched as two slaves he knew carried in a brazier on wooden poles. He supposed they'd been told to fetch it from the kitchens, but the room was already warm. One of the senator's scribes splayed his hands before it even so, warming black fingertips over the iron. The kitchen boys did not look at Cormac, vanishing like mice as soon as they were dismissed. The heat made the air shimmer, Cormac noted. He could feel it on one bare leg.

Another stranger peered down at Cormac like a hawk examining prey. This one wore a skullcap and a belt set with pouches. Cormac wrinkled his nose and knew him for a doctor before he even spoke. Men went to those when they were ready to die, as he'd heard it. Or to have rotting teeth pulled with pliers of black iron. Healthy men stayed away from the caste, with their powders, prayers and chants. That was what Antoninus said, anyway – and he was old enough to know.

Before a word could be said, Senator Silanus came into the storeroom, looking round in distaste. Bare-armed and brown-legged, he brought a sense of sunlight, a clean scent of new oil or pine sap. The noble Roman seemed to bustle even when he came to rest, as if Cormac's very existence was one more thing of a thousand for him to deal with that evening.

'Well?' Silanus said. 'Let's get *on* with it.' He waved vaguely at the fire. 'Manus! Stop your fussing.' He addressed the one Cormac thought of as a doctor. 'Use the irons, so I can say I followed the law. Oh, by Jove, I am surrounded by fools! Here! Like *so*!'

He crossed to the brazier and took two rods out of the coals, examining them and putting them back. Staff used them to stoke the fire, Cormac knew. Those born in Rome seemed to feel the cold more than he ever did. It was a strange inheritance, but he could bear winters better than almost anyone on the estate, even the Gauls.

The senator's other hand rested briefly on a pair of tongs, then left those in the coals. Cormac watched it all with a sense of rising apprehension.

'Dominus? I don't understand . . . what is happening,' he said. Odd how he couldn't quite take a breath. He felt light-headed from the effort of forcing words out past a blockage in his throat.

'Summon courage, boy. You are to be tortured. Ah, you understand that! Good.'

'B-but . . . I have done nothing wrong!'

The senator sighed and pinched the bridge of his nose between finger and thumb. Cormac hated to vex such a man, one so clearly important. The gods alone knew what matters of state had been postponed for him to be in that little room. Yet, he had to interrupt. There had been some sort of mistake, that was clear.

'A slave is a ward of the estate,' Nartius said suddenly, obsequious in his desire to please. 'Like a child, though of any age.'

Cormac craned his neck to see.

'I don't need to be tortured though . . .' he said, braver with the bully he knew.

'You have no say in it,' Nartius said with a shrug. 'If you were a free man, it would be different, but the law says slaves must be compelled. It says they *have* to be tortured and made to speak the truth.'

Cormac felt his mouth open in fear. His gaze slid to the fire, where the irons were still heating.

'There is no need. I will speak only the truth, I promise,' he said.

Nartius shook his head, but it was the senator who replied.

'Slaves don't make promises, boy. I see my younger brother kept a slack house! Whatever you say, whatever you believe to be the truth, you are still Silanus property. You have no honour on which to base an oath, no more than the chair you sit on. No, you will be compelled with fire, until I am satisfied you have told all you know and held nothing back. Do you understand?'

Cormac began to rise and Nartius laid a meaty hand on his shoulder, pressing him into the seat. When he glanced up it was to see the seneschal was sweating. Was Nartius the one who had discovered their master? Cormac wondered. There was fear in his eyes, right enough. The seneschal's voice was sickly sweet when he spoke again.

'He will sit quiet, dominus. Though he may flinch from it. I would have him bound, if it please the master.'

The senator nodded and Nartius drew a cord from under his tunic. He produced an eating blade, cutting the string in two. The big man knelt then to bind Cormac's wrists behind the chair. He came back to the fore and slapped Cormac's ankles together.

'Sit still,' Nartius hissed when Cormac tried to rise once more, an animal resistance despite his bonds. The senator was inspecting the irons again and Nartius moved with quick efficiency, tying knots hard and tight.

'I don't know anything,' Cormac whispered, pleading.
Nartius rolled his eyes.

'Don't curse, or lie. Don't accuse another, or say anything the master might take as an insult. Or you won't leave this place. Underst—'

The whispering voice broke off as the senator returned with an iron in each hand. The tips were gold, crusted in black. The doctor reached to take one and Silanus swayed aside, making the man flinch. He was like a child with a new toy, unwilling to share.

'Bare his chest,' the senator said.

There was an unpleasant gleam in his eye and Cormac could only stare and breathe, fast and shallow. There was no one in the world who could come and save him. The old dominus would have stopped it, but that Silanus was dead and open-mouthed, his flesh being wrapped and doused in sweet oil for his own flames.

'Ask me anything, dominus! I won't lie, on my oath!' Cormac said desperately. 'The master lived when I left the morning letters. He had passed when I brought the evening post. That is all I know. Please!'

'How full of yourself you are!' the senator said in wonder. 'My father always said his middle son ruined slaves, treated them too gently so that they spoiled. I see no tattoos on you, even! That can be put right, at least. I see now what my father meant. Boy, slaves make no oaths. You'll take me through every detail, but at my convenience, not your own. Like . . . so.'

He jabbed with an iron that smoked as it moved through air. Cormac screamed as it touched. He looked in horror at the thing trailing across his flesh, making skin split and sizzle. Then the pain hit and he stopped screaming, stopped breathing, just stared beyond that room, every tendon showing like wires under his skin.

The sun rose in a clear blue sky the following morning, as if nothing had changed. Cormac sat on a bench dragged out from the main house, feeling ill. When they had released him at last, Nartius had taken him to the kitchens. Dawn had lit the house as Sophia poured sour wine on his wounds, then dabbed on goose fat. Those white curds melted back to oil from heat still in his skin.

Cormac winced as he tried to raise his face to the warmth, feeling something crack and bleed. He'd never known pain like it, not in all the whippings, cuffs and boots helping him on his way. Yet in the midst, he knew he'd lost more than just hair or skin and blood. He did not yet know what it was exactly, only that it had been in him – and it had gone. He would have answered any question in perfect truth, but they had still hurt him.

Not a dozen paces from where he sat, the funeral pyre was lit. Cormac shrank away as flames sprang to life and wood spat and crackled. His chest could not bear even a whisper of heat, not then. Yet he made himself watch as priests of Jupiter and Pluto sacrificed animals and implored their patron gods to welcome a great man to Elysium. Those slaughtered bulls and geese would become the feast that afternoon, Cormac thought. Priests were always well fed.

Some of the household were sobbing by the pyre, shedding tears for a man who had always treated them with kindness. Cormac felt his lip curl for them. He whispered how much he hated them all, his pain like the oil that fed the flames. It gave him comfort, though his hands trembled and he could hardly breathe.

33

When they had finished their vigil, when the old man's flesh was left to burn to ashes, the new master had given word for them to assemble in the hall, where the will would be read. After that, Cormac knew another evening would come. The estate would sleep and rise, the rain would make the fields green, but it would not be the same. He had been blind before. The burning irons had woken him. If he'd had a blade . . .

He felt a cuff across the top of his head, perfectly judged so that his vision flashed white for an instant. He began to rise, though his tunic stuck and tore free, making him gasp.

Antoninus was there, the senior scribe. Cormac hesitated, confused. Were they all his enemies? Was his entire life a lie?

'Look away, boy,' Antoninus breathed by his ear. 'You were staring at the senator. If he sees that anger in you, he could order you whipped or castrated – even killed. I could not save you then. Understand? Keep your gaze off your betters.'

The corpse on the pyre was revealed as logs burned, a dark figure at the heart of the flames. Cormac shuddered, knowing the advice was good. He felt tears come and it was more that Antoninus had thought to protect him than anything else. He hardened himself with an effort. If he accepted kindness, from anyone, his shield would crumble and he would have nothing. The old scribe leaned over to look him in the eye, but Cormac just stared at the ground, until he felt the presence leave.

Smoke stretched to clouds overhead, thick and black with oil. The body dropped from sight as branches beneath gave way. It would be reduced to ash and someone would have the task of collecting the residue and scraping it all into a pot for burial.

The crowd was heading back into the house, still exchanging memories. The one he thought of as 'the dominus' had been a good master compared to some. Cormac heard that said more than once as he rose to go with them. No one stood too close, though they nudged one another and pointed him out. He folded his arms over the burns, feeling his tunic stick to melted skin.

In groups and alone, every member of the Silanus household took places in the great hall. They blocked enough light to make an unnatural gloom, one he found comforting. Cormac wondered if he would run away as he waited. Not while his wounds made it hard to move. No, he needed to heal, to grow strong. By summer though.

There were men in Rome who hunted slaves with dogs, so he'd heard. They followed a scent and tracked those who ran, across field and stone and even river. Every slave had heard the stories, of the terrible punishments that followed. Some of it had to be true, surely? Perhaps it was all a lie, as his life had been a lie before. Perhaps they were chained only by fear and there were no dogs and brutal men to chase them.

The senator's presence brought silence once again. Cormac wondered how he had ever seen him as a god amongst men. This Silanus was cruel, he understood that. Not noble, not some better clay. Just a man. He did not seem to be in a good mood either. Cormac watched as the senator waved for his clerk to go ahead. The entire staff grew still.

'The will has all the correct seals from imperial records, witnessed and recorded there . . .' the man began. 'There are a few private lines intended for his heir, Marcus Junius Silanus, son to Decimus Junius Silanus . . . the entire estate including all holdings, and property . . . the mines, the house in the city . . . Here, this part applies: "It is my final decree that my slaves are to be freed on my death. By my will, they shall be released in that moment from all debt owed to me or the Silanus family. I ask only that they light a lamp to me on the anniversary of my passing, each year. Freedom is a trial, but it is also a glory. Rome understands – and you will understand. Freedmen and freedwomen can rise in our city, as they never can in Assyria or Parthia or Egypt. Use this gift well – and if you would, I ask only that you pray for my soul." '

The words were read in a monotone, almost as a dirge. Cormac felt as if he'd been punched. There was a murmur of astonished reaction in the crowd as they looked to one another – husbands and wives, stable boys and sewing women. Cormac saw Sophia bury her face in her hands, shaking. He could still feel fever rising in him, let in by the burns he had endured. Yet his thoughts sharpened. He stepped forward and Nartius was a moment too slow, though the seneschal hissed at his back for him to stop.

'We were free from the moment the old master died?' Cormac asked.

The senator looked as if he'd eaten a bad olive, a flush spilling up his throat. His scribe began to reply, but Senator Decimus Silanus spoke over him, addressing them all.

'Free to starve? Yes. Though you have all enjoyed another meal and shelter since then. I should demand payment to settle that account! This was . . . unexpected. My brother was not usually a sentimental man. Perhaps his mind was deranged in his final days, I cannot say. It does

36

seem to have the force of law and I will not dispute his intentions. However, I am loath to leave my son's estate to go to ruin and weeds without a proper staff either. I have therefore decided to make an offer, a generous one to reflect the terms of the will.'

Cormac wanted the man to stop talking, to just give them time to take in what had happened. He was *free*. He was a freedman, like Horace's father. The words had no meaning for him, not really. The estate of Cedri Magnae was his world, along with the schoolroom. He knew no other. What could possibly . . .

'As freed slaves, you hold your own worth in your hands and backs,' the senator went on, his voice breaking through Cormac's thoughts like a heated iron. 'You will remain free until such time as you amass debts you cannot pay, or are convicted of a crime. For some of you, I expect that to be a short interval.'

The man's gaze flickered over Cormac and passed on.

'Despite my brother's odd idea of mercy, you do have value to the Silanus family, not least in this place. I have been convinced it would be cheaper to retain your service than to train new slaves to do your work. Accordingly, I will offer each of you one half of your value at market, the price agreed as a reflection of skills and service with my factors, a sum to be retained by you. The offer is in exchange for your continued slavery here, under the law. I will give you until noon to make a decision. After that, I will arrange for new staff to take up any empty positions that remain. Is that understood?'

The crowd murmured, still abashed in his presence. Cormac might have spoken again, but Nartius had his large hand on his neck, pressing down with clear threat.

Yet he was free, wasn't he? The unfairness of being burned for his testimony when he had not even been a slave was eating at him. He struggled from the grip of the seneschal, though the man stepped close and covered his mouth with his other hand. The fleshy palm crushed his nose and lips so that Cormac could not breathe.

At the other end of the hall, the senator was discussing something with his staff, moving out to the atrium. He would return to Rome, their lives of no more interest than an anthill. Cormac stopped fighting. There was no justice, not for him . . . He paused, glaring at Nartius as the man stepped back, wagging a large finger at him in warning.

'You'd better show a little respect,' Nartius muttered to him. 'He could have your balls just for answering back.'

'Are *you* the one who found the old dominus, Nartius?' Cormac asked. He saw fear flash across the other man's face. 'Should I tell him?'

'I'm not a slave, am I?' Nartius said. 'Not any longer.' He said the words slowly, as if tasting them. The same wary awe was spreading across that hall. They had all been slaves. They whispered in shock.

'Oh, I think you are,' Cormac said. He tapped the side of his head. 'I think you're still a slave up here. But if you take the offer, they might put hot irons to you yet, don't you think? Difficult, isn't it? You'll be a slave again, but this new master isn't like the old one. He wanted to tattoo me, like the ones I see in the city. How would that look on you, Nartius? "Take me up, I have run away" written in ink across your face? You won't like that, I think.'

In his anger, he used words like a knife, looking to hurt. Cormac wanted to wound the man who had threatened and bullied and lectured him on his responsibilities to the old master, then sat without a word while they burned him. He hadn't given Nartius up either, not even when he could smell his own flesh like cooked meat. Somehow, pride had risen to stop his mouth. It was all he'd had left by the time the questions ended. He'd said 'I don't know' about a score of times and they could not make him add a word.

Just a day before, Nartius had been the cockerel in the yard of the estate, sending all his hens scurrying. He'd had the arrogance of a trusted man. Yet that world had vanished, lost in a heart that stopped. Cormac wondered how old Nartius was. Fifty? It was hard to tell with that big, smooth face and meaty hands. The man's cheeks were flushed and lightly veined, but it was the eyes Cormac watched. There was guilt there. There was also dislike in the curl of the seneschal's lip. Perhaps he saw Cormac's youth, or heard the quiet rebellion in his voice. A man like Nartius would hate him for that alone, he realised. Nartius was the dog at the door, loyal and mindless. What would a free dog say to one like him?

He matched Nartius' gaze until the man made a disgusted sound and moved away. The seneschal sought out more senior members of the house staff then, like Sophia and Antoninus. That little group became a murmuring centre as others drifted close, looking for guidance, for someone to tell them what to do.

Cormac winced as a scab split on his chest. 'Half his value' was not what it would have been if they'd let him complete the gradus scriptorum. Yet they could have offered twice as much and he would have thrown it in their faces. He could imagine doing it, as clear as a memory. No, if he was free, he could walk away ... He stopped breathing. He *was* free. He could leave the hall and walk to the main gate at that very moment.

He shook his head. Perhaps it was his training, but he knew some things as well as anyone there. As chief scribe, Antoninus would know it as well. It was one thing to read a man's will and declare his slaves free, another to prove it. No, the ones who left the estate that day would need a written deed of manumission, sealed and witnessed. Or they could be taken up as an escaped slave by anyone with a mind to make their lives difficult.

Cormac patted the belt where he had his little cloth pouch, invisible inside the leather. He had a spare reed flat against his muscles – and he had a stone seal of the Silanus house. With a scrap of parchment, he could make the whole manumissio himself and scrawl the name Silanus. It wouldn't do, of course. Senior scribes would know it was a forgery in an instant. Better for him to wait, to bite his tongue and be patient. He saw the staff gathering in groups, gesturing and discussing, shaking their heads. For the first time, Cormac was apart from them. Something had changed and they were *not* his family. He felt an ache, but it passed.

One thing would remain true. He would walk away from the estate the very moment he had his release. He swore that on the gods. Rome was just forty miles away. He could walk that far – and he would. He'd shake the dust from his sandals and never look back. He would. Even if he was the only one.

4

The world he knew, the closest thing Cormac had to a
family, split into two groups in front of the house. Senator
Silanus had not come out to witness the result of his offer.
He was still somewhere inside, no doubt tallying deeds and
counting silver spoons.

Out in the yard, Cormac shook his head in answer to a
question. The scribe was a stranger, busying himself with
reed and ink, applying a Silanus stamp. When it had been
blotted, the man rolled parchment into a tube and tied a
white ribbon with quick skill before holding it out. Cormac
reached for it and the man drew back a touch, noting his
ink-stained fingertips.

'Are you sure, son?' he said quietly. 'There's still time to
take the money.'

Cormac could feel the heat of his burns like a sickness. He did not blink as he waited. The man shrugged
and handed over a document that changed for ever
who he was, who he could be. The ribbon was the Silanus
colour, he noted. Cormac might have spoken then,

but his brother in ink had moved on to another in the queue.

With trembling fingers, Cormac tugged the ribbon loose. Not many in that yard could read, but he was one of them. He had to see the words, to make sure it wasn't some senate speech or receipt mixed in with all the rest. That sort of confusion might suit the cheap playwrights, but it mattered too much not to check. Cormac tried not to think of another scroll as he read, his gradus scriptorum. With that and this manumissio, he could have walked into the treasury in Rome – or set up a stall in some street near the forum and begun to earn rent and food.

His sight shimmered. It was strange to see his own name and he brushed a thumb over the letters. Though it was in his gift, the senator had not troubled himself to append the family name, not to those who had rejected his generosity.

Cormac was freed. He could vote, but not involve himself in politics. He could make money, but not as a member of a noble house. The Silanus name had protected him from the moment of his purchase ten years before, over half his life! He felt himself trembling at the thought of being without it. Where would he sleep that night? By the gods, what would he *eat*? Who would look after him? He whispered questions, drawing out shock and grief, forcing himself to face his fears.

The senator's staff didn't care what he did, not really. At that moment, Cormac knew he could still cross over and stand with the ones who chose to stay. With the gaggle of kitchen women, Sophia was sobbing there, her voice rising until she muffled it in a cloth. The threshers too remained, along with all the stable lads. The work they knew was out in the fields, with horses and willow fences, in crops they had sown. Cormac wondered if it hurt those grim-faced men to stay, whether they would ever think back on those hours of freedom and wish they had made a different choice.

He'd thought they might at least look happier. Their place in the world hadn't changed much, but they had a pouch of silver for their trouble – half their value at market. Yet they could see a choice drawn on dusty ground, a line that separated freed from slave. Perhaps they would lose those tight expressions when those who had refused the offer had gone.

It was not an equal split by the time the scribes reached the end of the queue. Over five hundred would stay in the house they knew, choosing to be slaves. The ones who stood apart were a much smaller group than Cormac had expected. A few dozen. So few? It made him ashamed for the rest.

As he looked across a closing gulf, he saw there was no real pattern to it. It wasn't just the old and broken who remained, staring like geese. He was not surprised to see Antoninus among those. The senior house scribe would doze through long afternoons for a new master, that was all.

Cormac shook his head. To turn their faces away from freedom was not something he could forgive. No matter how gentle the net, they were still in it. To have been free for just a morning should have stirred more, he was certain. Yet they seemed resentful of his smaller tribe, scowling like *they* were the traitors. He could not have forgiven himself if he had remained behind. To accept his manumission had been his first choice as a libertus of Rome – a freed-man. He swallowed nervously.

The larger crowd suddenly turned their heads, sheep in the presence of a wolf as the crunch of sandals sounded. It was the new Silanus coming out to them, the man who had hurt Cormac as if it was some legal chore. So he had said. Cormac had looked into the man's eyes as he leaned in, pressing with his irons. Whatever the law required, Senator Decimus Silanus had *enjoyed* that much power over another.

Two guards walked behind with his son Marcus – dominus of the estate now, Cormac realised. Urban glared around, alongside one of the legionaries who guaranteed the life of the senator. There was no triumph in the man's heir. Marcus looked scuffed and humiliated, stumbling on dusty ground.

For the first time, Cormac wondered how the old master had left the world. The room had been very still when he'd entered, carrying the letters everyone else seemed to have forgotten. There had been a strange smell in the air, he recalled. He'd assumed it was some oil applied to the dead, myrrh or lavender to hide the odour of decay. He'd been distracted by the body itself, his gaze drawn to that open mouth in horror. Yet he knew that scent from when they killed rats in the stables . . . A word came to him in a whisper and he frowned.

Sophia gave a great wail then in the larger crowd, a sound that dragged Cormac back from his thoughts. Some of her kitchen staff tried to comfort her, perhaps to quieten her in the presence of the senator. Yet Sophia grieved for the old master and Cormac knew some believed it honoured the departed. In that place, with a senator pursing chiselled lips in irritation, it seemed suddenly false.

Silanus conferred with his scribes, learning the tally. He

seemed pleased enough, with so many choosing to stay. Cormac could see the fortune in silver meant little to him. It was an interesting idea. To a slave, coins meant owner-ship: horses or a house in the country, perhaps men and women bought on docks in Gaul. For the first time in his life, Cormac understood it was more than that. Wealth was convenience. It was time saved, the labour of others on your behalf. He tucked away the insight for later on, as the senator addressed them.

'You have made a choice – and I will honour it. Those who have accepted my price are from this moment once again slaves of the Silanus household, with all the pro-tection, honour – and duty that bestows. No doubt there will be changes ahead, but for today, you will resume your old positions and labours – though for my son, your new master.'

The senator nodded to Marcus Silanus, but the one Cormac secretly called 'Plato' didn't look up. The father's face darkened, as if he had been promised a speech. Denied that, he looked over the huddled crowd, then the smaller group. A frown marred that perfect brow and Cormac felt the man's spite. This was one who knew legions, he reminded himself, a noble breed. If Cormac had not hated him as an enemy, he might have looked away.

'Those of you who have chosen to leave, know that you have refused Silanus honour and protection. If you are attacked on the road, I will not send men to raise you up, either to bind your wounds or to avenge you. Freedom . . .' He smiled, though it was a wintry thing. 'Freedom means free to starve, to freeze, to sell your flesh to live. You will learn the price sooner than you know. For now, take your manumissio and leave. When your stomach aches for food, perhaps you will try to eat the sheepskin on which it is written. Until then . . .'

Cormac turned and walked away. He heard the man's words break off in astonishment, but Cormac had not been able to bear another moment, not even if it meant losing his life. None of the others moved and he noticed some of them staring in horror as he passed through. He almost missed a step when he saw Nartius was among them. Of all the staff on the estate, Nartius was one Cormac had expected to stay behind. Yet there he was, red-faced and sleek, his hair combed in a dark wave.

At his back, the senator continued to speak, though anger now clipped his words. Perhaps he thought it beneath his dignity to shout after a slave, no, a *freed* man. Cormac still expected him to roar an order and his guts dissolved in panic. Would he run?

'. . . you are dismissed the service of my family,' the senator snapped. 'Though we gave you shelter and salt and bread. Though we lent you honour. You are not fit for it. Leave.'

The rest of Cormac's group turned away then, just a few paces behind him. He sagged in relief, glancing back at Nartius as the man glared in cold-eyed fury. What was eating the seneschal? Nartius had not said a word, as far as Cormac could tell. His half-share would surely have bought him many comforts, but he had not taken it. Cormac noticed the man was dressed for the road, in good sandals with a cloth bag slung across one shoulder. He had spent the morning preparing, of course. Nartius was a man of plans and order – which made it all the stranger to see him leave the world he knew.

The senator's voice carried across the yard, echoing

from the house as he continued to instruct the remaining staff. Cormac slowly left all that behind, until a phrase caught him like a fish hook.

'. . . my brother kept a lax house, but my son will not make that mistake. You will be tattooed with the words "I have run away, return me to Silanus".' As Cormac looked back, the senator drew one finger across his forehead to show what he intended. 'In that way, there will be no confusion after these . . . unfortunate days.'

One of the stable lads suddenly broke, sprinting after the group that had chosen freedom. Cormac grinned at the sight of the senator twitching and pointing after him. Nartius hissed in dismay and Cormac suddenly understood, his stomach dropping as if he'd missed a step on the stairs. They were a long way from the outer gate. Worse, the stable lad had already accepted half his own worth. In that moment, he was both a slave and a runaway. There was nothing they could do for him.

The smaller crowd of freed men and women leapt back as the young man came through. It was as if he carried disease and they did not want to feel his touch.

'Go back, you fool,' Nartius growled. The boy heard but it was already too late and he was lost in terror.

Two men came after him. One was Urban, the guard Cormac knew well enough to fear. The other was the legionary from the city. Perhaps it was his chestplate of shaped leather that slowed him, but Urban led the way. Cormac felt the oddest touch of pride at that, though it came with a twinge of loathing. They were not his family. If he had run, it would be Urban coming after him.

The stable boy made it a fair way before Urban brought him down in a tumble of dust and kicking legs. Cormac watched as the estate guard took a grip on his tunic and dragged him all the way back. The lad was blubbering by then, snot running from his nose as he tried to say he didn't want to be tattooed, not across the face.

Cormac watched, frozen, while Urban took his capture to the feet of the senator, throwing him down to weep and apologise. They were too far away to hear what Silanus said then, but the stable boy gave a great shriek. He might even have run again if the legionary hadn't stepped forward and knocked him out with one massive blow. If that man felt he had been little use in the chase, he redeemed himself then.

'It'll be castration,' Nartius said at Cormac's shoulder, suddenly there. 'If he doesn't take a fever and die, it'll mean he doesn't want to run again. Yes, I'd say it'll be castration.'

There was a sort of relish in his voice and Cormac was suddenly sick of it.

'Why are you here, Nartius? I thought you loved the old master.'

The older man looked on him as he might a dead dog.

'I know things, son. Like when it's time to move on.'

'You saw the tattooist heating his needles,' Cormac guessed.

Nartius chuckled and reached out to ruffle his hair. Cormac swayed back, though he gasped as scabs on his chest cracked. Nartius didn't seem to notice. He was staring into memories and looked both older and more miserable. He shook his head, casting off the mood.

'Quick lad, aren't you? But I know more than that! Things that would curl your hair for the shame of them. No, I'd have stayed if I could . . .' He looked back wistfully

48

as they started to walk again. 'But the wind changed. I'm just one who sees it coming.'

Cormac sneered. Nartius was taking on graces again, pretending to knowledge he didn't have. He had done it all Cormac's life and yet for the first time they stood as equals. A week before, Nartius had been personal servant to the master, a man of rank and responsibility in the household. Perhaps he hadn't understood all that was at an end, not deep in the bone. Cormac mulled it over as they made their way to the outer gate. They *were* free to starve, it was true, but not one of them stood higher than the others. He looked around and saw determination and strength. *These* were his people, not Sophia and her wailing, nor Urban with his rough courtesy. The ones who had taken a chance and just . . . walked. He felt he loved them all in that moment, even fat Nartius.

The road lay just beyond a gate of wood and stone. There was no wall in that part of the estate, so the posts had been raised as a symbol of Silanus holdings rather than any real barrier. The little group slowed even so as they reached the boundary. It wasn't hesitation so much as awareness. They were leaving all they had known. The whole world lay beyond that gate and it was a strange and frightening place. It also meant the end of the strange kinship that had sprung up between them.

They had been Silanus slaves. On that walk, they had been equals, freedmen and freedwomen. Yet on the road, they would surely go separate ways. Some would head to Rome, others to family or friends, or some promise of work in towns further south. A few had savings they'd earned over years, while young ones like Cormac owned nothing beyond the clothes they wore, not even a bag or spare tunic. The road stretched flat and empty into the distance and it was no small thing to set foot on it.

Cormac saw some of the crowd taking an exaggerated final step. He did the same, feeling a smile rekindle. He was free. The sun was hot and he felt the first touch of thirst . . . and the worry that came with it. He watched as Nartius drank deeply from a water bottle he produced from his back, an ornate thing of silver and leather. The older man noticed him staring and grinned.

'I know things,' he said, tucking the flask away.

The sound of hooves froze their little group then, the habit of fear and obedience still strong. Awareness of freedom vanished to rags and Cormac found himself bristling as he recognised Marcus Silanus. New master or not, if 'Plato' tried to bring him back, Cormac knew he would fight. Hidden by the others, he slid the tiny thumbnail blade from his belt pouch. He could stripe a face with that – and he would, if they thought to make him a slave again.

The small crowd looked on the son of the house with a new awareness, one the young man slowly understood. He did not have his father's certainty, not yet. Marcus Silanus saw the way they stared and he swallowed, aware that he was one and they were many. He held up open hands in a quick gesture.

'I just wanted a word with one of you . . . Cormac, there you are.'

The strange tension broke and without another word, some of them began to drift onto the road, clearly determined to put miles behind them. Nartius remained nearby, Cormac noted. The man was still a Silanus slave in his heart.

Cormac resented being made to stay, but he could not help his own curiosity. There had been so many changes to his life, so quickly, it made him feel slow and stupid. He needed time to think it all through, as he preferred. In the days ahead, he knew he would tease out all the meanings, examining words and gestures until he was sure he understood, right to the bitter dust of them.

'I'm not going back,' he said firmly.

Marcus nodded, wincing in grim memory at whatever he had just witnessed.

'I know. I just wanted to say I'm sorry. I didn't know about my uncle's will. I thought, when we left the city, that you would be *protected* – that you could take the gradus again, when there was time. I tried to find you before, but my father made me stay and listen to all his plans for the estate.'

Cormac blinked in confusion. This red-faced boy had more power and wealth in his control than an entire town. His words, his manner, made no sense. Was he really concerned about the gradus they had left behind on their desks?

'Don't worry about that,' Cormac said. 'I'll find a way.' He furrowed his brow, searching for something to say that would let him head out.

'I don't blame your father,' Cormac said.

Marcus raised one eyebrow, his flush deepening.

'You don't ... blame him? What would you blame him for?'

In answer, Cormac held his tunic open, wincing as the cloth unstuck from his burns. Marcus looked at him in the sort of dull confusion that had earned his nickname.

'Slaves *have* to be put to the question. You remember the Twelve Tables better than I do. It is the law.'

Cormac remembered sitting in pain on an iron box, determined to show how brave he could be. After a while, he could only close his mouth and nod. There was no arguing with truth.

In the stillness, Marcus Silanus glanced aside. He frowned in recognition.

'I thought you at least would have stayed, Nartius,' he said. A new coldness came over him then and for the first time, Cormac saw a shadow of the senator in his son. 'I hope you will remember the secrets of our house are not yours to share. Or to sell. I think you are the most senior to have chosen to accept the terms of my uncle's will. If I had known his plans, I would have asked him to keep . . . senior men and women in the household.'

'I am deaf and blind, dominus,' Nartius said.

Marcus Silanus stared unblinking for a time.

'I hope so. Or I will make sure you are,' he said.

Nartius bowed, accepting his authority. Cormac could see the older man was trembling and struggled not to show his own fear. They stood just a little way from Silanus land and he didn't feel free then, not in that moment. There were currents there Cormac could not understand and he just wanted to get away.

'Will you head to Rome?' Marcus asked, gesturing with a tilt of his chin.

Cormac didn't want to share that with him, but found himself nodding.

'It's a long way,' Marcus said, 'forty miles or so. I could fetch the carriage for you. Come on. It feels like the least I can do.'

'That is generous,' Cormac said, 'but I'll walk. Thank you.'

Nartius made an exasperated sound, but they were not

together. In that moment, they were just three men standing on a road.

'It wasn't for me,' Marcus said suddenly. He spoke as if the words could no longer be held back, as if he spat them like poison. 'I won't inherit, I mean.'

Cormac paused, unsure whether he had to listen or not. The one he still thought of as 'Plato' had gone red with effort or shame, it was hard to tell.

'My father has plans, but he needs vast wealth to bring them about. This estate is part of that, do you understand? Even for us, even for my family, the amounts are impossible. His brother had no children and no . . . interest in them. Do you see? He was worth millions, but he wouldn't make a loan, or even see anyone from the family. I had to be forced on him, and that against his will! He only took me to keep grandfather quiet. My father will probably sell this place now. I just wanted you to know. It wasn't all for me . . .' Marcus trailed off at last, perhaps finally aware he had said words that could not easily be recalled.

Cormac shrugged. He felt a pang of sorrow for the old master. The great families were ruthless, everyone knew that. Still, it was not Cormac's business, not any longer. It no longer mattered.

Almost in a daze, Cormac began to walk, feeling muscles loosen. Rome was forty miles away and he had neither food nor water. Yet he was sixteen years old and he was free. In that moment, there was nothing else.

5

The road to Rome was not a safe place, not when the light failed. It had seemed a fine adventure at first as Cormac set out. He walked without anything to eat or drink, but he'd felt a sort of shine in his blood, at least while the sun was high. He had even found a tiny fountain for travellers, a shrine to Minerva and wonder of device that brought fresh water bubbling from pipes below. He'd scooped with his hands and drunk dust from his throat, spilling water down his chest and not caring.

The sun had been hot then, a lash across his neck. Still, he'd felt free. As the summer's evening darkened, he realised he was starving. Unlike clever Nartius, he had not planned for this walk. Visions of kitchens at the estate tormented him as he went. The slaves would be preparing an evening meal for the new master round about then, perhaps the senator as well if he had decided to stay. Cormac's lips had dried and grown sore, no matter how often he licked them. Back at the estate, he would have gone to Sophia for a dab of grease, but there was nothing he could do on the road. He longed to sit down, to rest, but he could not. His legs ached and he had a blister on one heel that felt like it had worn through to the bone. Every step sent a spike of pain shooting up his calf. Worst of all was that he was being followed.

He'd been passed a dozen times that day, usually by the carts and oxen of farmers, on their way to the city to sell whatever they had grown. Not many families could afford a carriage and guards of the sort Cormac and Marcus had known. These were men scratching a living from a family plot, taking whatever they could to markets in Rome. Every last one had waved him off, even threatened him with the whip if Cormac looked like he might leap up amidst their sacks. Some of them had a boy to protect the wares, hard-faced lads with knives ready to stab a thief. Despite his youth, they saw a threat in him. Some of the farmers even called apologies as they went by, but they didn't stop.

The ones he met on foot were a more varied sort, as far as Cormac could tell. He made a point of speeding up when he saw one of those ahead, rangy-looking fellows on their way to Rome for work or some opportunity. If they'd had coins, they would surely not have been walking, not so far out from the great gates and walls. Those men watched him warily as he passed. If they spoke or greeted him, Cormac only went faster. It pleased him to make them dwindle behind, as if he had beaten them.

One of them had refused to grow small and instead kept up for hours. Cormac had seen the rat-faced, skinny man a long way ahead originally, bare-armed and with one flopping sandal that slapped the sole of his foot with every step. Cormac had set out to draw him in like all the others, closing the distance until the fellow became aware and started glancing back every few paces. Despite his tiredness and the pain in his heel, Cormac had put on a burst of speed to leave the stranger in his wake. He'd felt the man's gaze as he came abreast, frowning at the horizon, lost in his competition.

'Going to Rome, are you?' the man had called out. He'd smiled even, though it looked an unaccustomed expression. Cormac had repressed a shudder when he saw the man was missing his top teeth. It meant his upper lip folded in and yet he was not so very old. His skin was seamed in dust, lines spreading like claws around his eyes. Yet he was no more than thirty, at least as far as Cormac could tell.

'I have to meet my master,' Cormac called over his shoulder. He knew not answering the question properly might be taken as an insult. He just wanted to make an excuse for not slowing, for avoiding the company of strangers. Yet the words he'd used were those of a slave.

The man had scowled.

'The road markers say there's sixteen miles yet to Rome, so your master will be waiting a while.'

He'd laughed at his own wit, though Cormac couldn't see any humour in it. He just nodded and tried to open up a little more distance between them. To his dismay, the skinny man increased his pace, swinging along easily to match him.

'You look nervous, son. You a runaway? Maybe I should fetch one of the vigiles when we get to Rome. Might be a little reward in it for me.'

Cormac had felt rising irritation. He'd studied the Twelve Tables of Roman law for his gradus. He knew the vigiles were a sort of city watch, some combination of thief-chasers and men who put out fires. The rumour was they'd take anyone into their ranks. He'd even thought of applying to join them if he couldn't find work anywhere else. He didn't want to start by being reported, but he suspected the man was playing with coins he didn't have. There was weakness in his face, Cormac thought. Something about him said he would walk a mile rather than speak to one of the vigiles.

Cormac hadn't imagined having to show his manumissio so early – and the idea of this toothless sort fingering the parchment was not something he could bear. Instead, he'd snapped a phrase he'd heard Urban use when one of the horses kicked him. It was just two words and had a nice bite to it. The man's face had wrinkled so much his eyes disappeared, as if he'd inhaled pepper.

Cormac had lengthened his stride even further, though his legs burned and trembled. In his youth and will, he'd been sure the angry man would fall behind. He had at first . . . but then remained, doggedly close, somehow hanging on though another dozen miles passed beneath their blistered feet.

The hills of Rome appeared as light faded. Cormac found himself almost breaking into a trot to reach the city before nightfall. His legs had gone so stiff he could hardly feel them. Even the blisters had numbed. He had an idea that they closed the gates at night and he was afraid. He didn't want to be left outside, not with some angry stranger on his heels. He almost wished Nartius had stayed with him then, but the older man could never have matched the pace he'd set. A mile – a mille passus – was a thousand paces. Forty miles was forty thousand. He'd counted down to pass the time, marker to marker along the road.

It was a sort of mindless comfort and it had brought him to the city. Like the Silanus family, Nartius had been left far behind.

The last half mile seemed to go in a flash. Cormac stopped beneath the open gate, panting, suddenly unsure. Should he just walk in? The Silanus carriage had always been waved through, the men exchanging greetings with the city guards. For the first time in his life, Cormac was on foot and road-stained, looking like any other vagabond.

He could feel the guard's attention settle on him like a fly. The man waved a cart full of cabbages into the city and then sighed at the boy standing like a post in the centre of the road. Others walked in and a couple more guards began to work iron rods set in stone, ready to close the gate. Cormac risked a glance over his shoulder and saw the skinny man staring just a few paces away.

'Can I enter?' Cormac asked the guard.

'That depends, doesn't it?' he said. 'What's your name? Your business here? Can you work? We don't need any beggars.'

Cormac felt the man from the road edging closer. He didn't want to answer those questions with him listening. He lowered his voice as much as he could, his face growing flushed.

'I am freed,' Cormac said. 'First day, but I trained as a scribe. I can work.'

'Oh! You have your gradus?' Cormac shook his head and the guard sighed. He seemed a great one for sighing. 'There won't be much work without that. You can read and write though? Add up?'

'I can,' Cormac said with pride.

'How many coppers in . . . one denarius, two sestertii and three asses?'

'Twenty-seven,' Cormac replied.

The guard shrugged.

'Hope for you yet, maybe. You might try one of the temples, or the vigiles, perhaps. Show me your manumissio.'

Cormac passed it over and the man took his time. Cormac realised the guard wanted him to know he too could read. He rubbed the pad of his finger along each line, nodding to himself. It was the finest sheepskin, stretched and dried and polished on the estate under the supervision of old Antoninus. None of that was useful, so Cormac kept his mouth shut.

The guard's eyebrows shot up once more as he traced the seal and initials of Silanus.

'There's a name,' he said softly.

Around them, a cart was creaking past. Another of the guards took a quick look under grubby cloth, then waved it in. The skinny man from the road hadn't moved, waiting his turn and of course listening to every word. Cormac wanted to use the curse phrase again, but he was too intent on getting his manumissio back. He held out his hand, but the guard wasn't finished.

'You'll need to find work tomorrow or leave the city, do you understand? We don't let people beg here, not unless they were born in Rome anyway.'

'I'm not a beggar,' Cormac said.

The guard nodded, though his lack of belief showed on his face.

'Come back tomorrow night and tell me you have found work. Or you can try your luck somewhere else. Ostia, maybe. They always need crew on the ships there.

Or find a legion recruiter. Don't make me look for you, understand? "Cormac, freed slave of the Silanus family." If I have to find you, you will regret it. If you embarrass the ones who owned you, they'll find a way to take the skin off your back – freed or not, understand?'

'Thank you,' Cormac said, though his hand shook as he took the sheet and rolled it once more. He could tie the white ribbon later, when he found a quiet place to sit.

'If you do find work, you might like to buy one of these,' the guard said. He pointed to himself and Cormac saw a band of silver on the fourth finger of his right hand. His frown cleared as he understood.

'Like Horace's father,' Cormac murmured.

'Who?' the guard said, suspicion suddenly back on his face.

'A freedman, I meant.'

'Ah, right. Yes. It helps to have a ring. Slaves aren't allowed to wear silver.'

Cormac felt something important in the man's gaze, but he was unsure of what else to say. He shifted uncomfortably, wanting to move on.

'Thank you,' he said.

On impulse, he held out his hand, one freedman to another. The guard took it in a quick, hard grip before he'd even thought about it.

'What is your name?' Cormac asked, emboldened.

'Quintus Lanuvium,' he said, after a moment. The name showed where he had been born rather than a family line. The older man grunted then, turning back to the tower where in a few moments he'd put his feet up and brew a tisane or a mulled wine.

Darkness had come as Cormac stood there on the

boundary. The Rome he knew as a place of light and bustle looked very different in the twilight. Some of the stragglers on the road were already being waved off, told to wait for morning. The great gate was being drawn shut and Cormac made sure he stood inside the line.

He thought he could feel eyes on him and glanced back as he walked away. The skinny man too had made it inside. He was talking to the same guard, Quintus, perhaps answering the same questions. With no warning, he suddenly pointed in Cormac's direction, stabbing the air angrily.

Cormac broke into a loping run he hoped did not look too guilty. It was late, after all. The darkness would hide him from whatever that madman wanted. Rome had half a million people, or so he'd been taught. There were slaves and freedmen working there, from those who dug through blockages in sewers to scribes of the treasury, trusted with the wealth of nations. He could find work there, he was certain.

He walked deeper and deeper into the city, relying on memories from previous visits. He could not recall ever having been in Rome at night and it wasn't long before he realised he was truly lost. He turned a corner and instead of the square he had expected, with benches and a fountain, it was another narrow street, with alleys stretching into such thick darkness he hardly dared look into them.

The first thrill of arrival faded. His feet were aching and he stumbled, catching a stone. He muttered the curse words once more, taking obscure comfort. He had not known how dark the city would be. The moon had to have risen, but the light didn't extend down to the alleys between buildings, four or five storeys high some of them. He licked sore lips nervously as he heard voices in rooms above. There were people up there, speaking to one another, arguing, pleading, whispering. He had thought the city would swallow him up and it had. In the darkness, he was suddenly so tired he just wanted to fall down.

The sound of steps brought his heart into his mouth in sudden panic. Two men were walking towards him and he had nowhere to hide. He turned to hurry in the opposite direction, but saw another pair cross moonlight at the junction behind. While he had stood there like a newborn calf, they'd marked him, cut him out and surrounded him.

He used his thumb to slide the tiny reed-sharpening blade from his belt, holding it ready to slash. He'd never struck in anger, but he would if they laid hands on him, whoever they were. He'd stripe a face or gash a finger and hope to break free. Cormac readied himself as they closed. He had never been trained to fight, but he knew he was quick, lizard-along-a-wall quick. It was all he had against thieves and grown men.

One of the first pair reached for something that emitted a faint gleam. As Cormac stared, he eased an iron slide across, revealing a flame in a tin lamp. Light spilled across that little lane, gilding trash and scurrying things trying to get away.

To Cormac's surprise, the man with the lamp held up a brass disc, marked with a laurel wreath like a copper coin.

'Vigiles, son. What brings you out on such a fine evening?'

Cormac dropped the hand to hide the tiny blade. He considered letting it fall, but it was almost all he had, so he just closed his fingers over it.

'First night in the city . . . dominus. I'm looking for a place to sleep.'

Cormac was pale and exhausted, swaying slightly as he stood there. He had no more reserves and the man seemed to believe him.

'Not a lookout then? For the gangs?'

'N-no, dominus. I've just come in the gate, an hour or so back. I'm lost, I think. If you could give me directions to Magister Apicellus, he has a school on the Quirinal. I thought I would ask there about being allowed to take my gradus. I was taken out before . . .'

One of the others spat a curse. 'By the gods, let His Majesty go back to selling himself, Terentius. He talks like a whore. Let him earn his living.'

Cormac didn't respond. He'd heard worse and he knew the man was trying to goad him. At the estate, Antoninus said that sort of talk was for those who lacked a good upbringing.

'Maybe,' the one called Terentius growled back. 'Or maybe he's the sort they use to put us off the scent.'

He leaned close enough for Cormac to smell the onions he had eaten with his dinner. His voice became a whisper and Cormac had to resist leaning forward himself.

'If they're watching now, son, you could just dip your head in the right direction, understand? We'll find them anyway, sooner or later, wherever the bastards hide themselves.'

'I don't . . . truly, dominus, I . . .'

The vigile raised his voice then, speaking to anyone else who might be listening.

'They'll learn what *happens* then, to *thieves* who go bothering the good families of Rome! Who lack the sense they

63

should have got from their mother's wrinkled old tit! Or they'll lie low for a while and not *risk* my coming back! They might have the sense a child is born with and not *force* me to kick in every door around here until I find them!'

Cormac could only blink at the man's anger, directed at the whole city, or at least the streets in earshot.

The one called Terentius straightened up, apparently satisfied he had delivered his message. As Cormac stared, he slid the panel shut on his lamp, covering the flame. Darkness returned to that narrow street and the sense of threat lessened. The vigile wiped his nose with the back of his free hand.

'What's your name, anyway?' Terentius said.

'Cormac . . .' He thought of the guard at the gate. Cormac had been born in Britannia, the land named for some painted tribe of the south coast. Julius Caesar had landed on shingle where the Cantii lived, so it was said. His people. 'Cormac . . . Cantii?' he added.

'Funny sort of name. I'd choose another, if I were you. Something less foreign.'

'Thank you, dominus. I'll try and think of one.'

'See you do. Now piss off.'

'Thank you, yes. I-I will,' Cormac stammered.

The other vigiles chuckled at that and moved on, continuing the patrol Cormac could only assume they kept up all night. He slumped against a wall, suddenly exhausted. He'd walked all day and eaten nothing. His stomach was making creaking noises and on top of that, he'd been terrified. The muscles in his legs were fluttering in the oddest way, completely beyond his ability to control. The desire to sleep had vanished while the vigiles surrounded him, but it came back with a vengeance. He had to rest, he just

64

had to. He came away from the wall with a curse when he felt wet seeping through to his skin. Wonderful. First sleep, then he would find food in the morning.

He glanced inside the closest alley. It looked dry enough there, but so dark he could only tell by touch. There was something like a wooden door further in. He put his ear to it, but there was no sound. If anyone lived there, they were sleeping.

There was no help for it. He emptied his bladder a little way along and then eased himself down the doorway, leaning back and drawing in his knees. He grinned to himself then, just for a moment as he hugged his legs close and shivered in the night's cold. He had come to the city on those two feet, at no one else's call. He would rise the next day as a free man, with every hour his own. His stomach may have been empty and his legs numb, but he felt a sort of giddiness rising in him.

He closed his eyes, still smiling. The city was quiet at that hour, but it was the heart of the world even so. It was a place where he would dream of becoming . . . what? He could almost see it. An image of the Silanus senator flashed into his imagination, making him wince. There was the face of Roman power. Cormac promised himself he would never go back to the Silanus estate, that he would not waste the chance he'd been given . . .

He had no sense of time passing. He woke from dreams of addressing the senate, lurching awake as something opened behind him. Hands dragged him from the moon light into darkness, leaving the doorway empty.

6

Cormac struggled mindlessly. He heard the scratch of iron on flint and saw a flash of light fill the room for an eye-blink. It meant he dodged a piece of wood coming down on his head and struck out in turn, rewarded by a grunt. There were at least three of them, though when the flint sparked again, they used the chance to grab his flailing arm. An unseen assailant thumped a blow into his ribs. The world spun and Cormac would have been sick if there had been anything in his stomach.

The wick of a tiny lamp sputtered into flame on the third try and darkness lifted. What had seemed like madness came to an end and there he was, pressed into a chair as they tied his arms. He tried to stand up before they could finish and someone shoved him back.

A beanpole of a youth unfolded from the other side of the room, light spilling across him. He brought the lamp and settled it on a shelf. Cormac looked up into a face marked by scars or disease. One entire nostril was gone, as if he'd been burned to the bone. One cheek too was open at the centre, wide enough to put a fingertip inside. Cormac could see teeth through the hole. Breath hissed from it though the lips were pursed over a jaw that leaned to one side. It might have been broken and healed like that, Cormac supposed. When the young man spoke, the lower teeth overlapped oddly with the row above.

'We saw you talking to the vigiles,' he said. 'An informer, are you? Sneaking around in the dark . . . What did they offer? A few coins to point us out? A hot meal and the commander's bed, was it?'

'I was just looking for a place to sleep,' Cormac said desperately. 'I don't know *anyone* here. I don't even know where here is! I just wanted to find the school on the Quirinal hill, where Magister Apicellus takes classes. I thought I'd ask if I could take the written exam again, if he'd allow it . . . maybe if I pledged part of my pay in exchange.'

He knew he was babbling, but there was something feral in the face that loomed over him. The vigiles had been frightening enough in their way, but they'd still had rules and official brass discs. They'd still had honour, or at least respect for the law. This little room smelled of sewers and Cormac felt he'd fallen in with wild dogs. They'd tear him apart in a moment and he had been through too much that day. He'd lost track of time and for all he knew the sun was rising outside. He whispered a prayer to see it again and heaved against the bonds in fury. It consumed him, making lights flash across his vision. He was actually surprised when he could not free himself.

'Look at the fight in him!' another of them crowed suddenly. 'Go on, son!' Two or three more crowded in, blocking out the gleam of the lamp. 'Oh, he didn't like that! Aw, is he going to cry? Is he missing his mother?'

Cormac let his head sag, his misery complete. He was too tired to struggle and his thoughts thickened like ice on a river, moving slowly. Even the pain from his blisters and sore muscles faded away. He blinked, drifting . . .

'Has he passed out?' he heard the tall one ask. Cormac felt his cheeks being slapped, his head lolling back and forth.

'You still with us?' his tormentor asked. 'Did I hear what I thought you said? You've been schooled, have you? You know your letters?'

'What does that matter?' one of the others said with a sneer. 'We've never needed the fancy stuff, have we?'

A yelp sounded alongside a thump of bone and flesh. The one with the open cheek and offset jaw came back into view and there was a complicated gleam in his eye. He spoke as he stared at Cormac, but addressed the others more than the one before him.

'There are things we might do with ink and paper that we can't do any other way. There are opportunities. *Can* you write? Might be we could be friends if you can. Or were you lying? If you were lying, I think we'll just cut your throat and put you in the sewer to be washed out with all the other shit. Understand? Don't lie to me now. I'll be needing proof.'

'He's not worth the trouble, Malvo,' the other one said.

Cormac glanced at him and saw he was rubbing the side of his head. The one he called 'Malvo' only had to look at him and he flinched. Cormac understood. Though he was barely the same age as Cormac, somehow Malvo was the leader in this little group. Despite the cruel puckering of his face, the lad's eyes were alight with intelligence. It made him dangerous.

With an effort of will, Cormac pressed down his exhaustion.

'In my belt,' he said. 'There's a reed . . . a fragment of inkstone. And a scroll, flattened down.'

He thought better of mentioning the tiny blade to sharpen the reed point and just hoped they wouldn't find it. Rough thumbs ran around his waist as they searched him. There was a hiss of surprise as they saw the still-weeping marks on his chest. One of them brought the lamp closer, making Cormac shrink away. He could not bear heat on that melted flesh.

'Here, I can feel something,' said the one Malvo had punched before.

He took the lamp and it was Malvo who drew items from the belt pouch. One was the Silanus seal he had no right to carry, a stone oval no larger than a silver coin. The other was the flattened scroll, his manumissio. Cormac felt his heart thump at the sight of that. It was his most precious possession and he was helpless.

The tall young man peered at the carved stone. If he knew what it was, there was no sign of awareness in his expression. In the end, he shrugged and put it into a pouch at his waist. Cormac shook his head a fraction as Malvo tugged the little ribbon on the scroll, running the strip of cloth between his fingers, marvelling at it. He unrolled the manumissio then, watching Cormac all the while.

'These are important things,' Malvo murmured. 'I can see that much. Read it to me, would you? Don't lie now. Vittore here can read some, can't you, Vit?'

Another boy nodded, wiping his nose with the back of a hand.

He held up the scroll and Cormac blinked at it, reading in a dull tone.

'"Be it known, in accordance with the terms of the will and testament of Severus Junius Silanus, as ordered by Senator Decimus Junius Silanus, the slave known as 'Cormac' is freed by the hand of his master on this date, the eighth day of July, the year seven hundred and ninety from the foundation of Rome. No debt remains, nor responsibility of this house, its . . ."'

The sheet was whipped away once more. Malvo looked to the one called Vittore for confirmation. The boy sniffed and nodded, wiping his nose once more. His eyes were very dull, Cormac noted, the mouth set in a permanent sneer. Cormac wondered if the nose-wiper could read as well as he claimed.

Malvo shook his head in wonder.

'A "freed" man, is it? And what was that date?'

He brought the paper back, but Cormac could see he wasn't looking at the letters, not really. He could not read. For reasons Cormac could not understand, Malvo still pretended to, showing his memory was sharp.

'Ah . . . there. The eighth of July. Isn't today the ninth?' He was showing off his knowledge and his audience shifted and chuckled, grinning in the dark. 'So this was recent, then? You were a slave up to a day ago?'

Cormac nodded and Malvo made a strange sound. In a whole face, it might have been a whistle of surprise, but with his misaligned jaw, his lips would not form the right shape. Instead, a dribble of saliva appeared, making his chin shine. He rubbed the spot with his hand, angry that Cormac had seen.

'And here you are on my patch, with no coins and

nothing to show for it. What a shame, eh? What a crying shame. It feels like this little piece of paper is your only proof, isn't it? Not even a silver ring, or one of those little cloth caps some of them wear. Just . . . this.'

One of his gang still held the lamp. Malvo waved the scroll close to the flame as he spoke, enjoying the threat. Cormac could not help following it with his eyes, though he knew it was exactly what they wanted.

'Looks like you're one of us now,' Malvo said. 'As you can read and write. I'll vouch for you if anyone comes looking. Just say "I am with Malvo" and they'll leave you alone around here. Most of them anyway. So . . . you won't be needing this paper.'

'Please don't,' Cormac said, forcing the words out. He could see the lad's gaze flicker to the little flame, followed by all the others watching. They wanted him to do it, but he didn't really understand the stakes.

'"Please don't",' one of them repeated, mimicking his voice. Malvo chuckled.

'How nice you speak, my free slave. Don't do what though? Don't put your fine words in the flame?'

As he spoke, he drifted the scroll towards the lamp. His companion was chuckling and holding it up, increasing the threat that they would set it alight by accident. Cormac watched in horror as his future swung in the balance. They hadn't found his little blade. If he could somehow get that out of the pouch, he might cut the cords around his wrists. He might free himself and grab the manumissio and break for the door . . .

He froze as the young man touched the scroll to the flame. Sheepskin crackled and blackened immediately, giving off a foul smoke. Malvo swore, pinching at the flames and cursing as he stung his fingers. He hadn't meant to do it, Cormac realised. Not like the one who held the lamp. That one was giggling as he jumped, demented in his desire to please.

'Perhaps I *should* burn it,' Malvo said irritably. 'I don't want you free, do I? Not when you can work for us. No, I think . . .' He broke off as a crash sounded somewhere close, followed by yelps of pain. Cormac watched as the young leader crushed the scroll in one hand and snuffed the lamp with the other. They were pitched into a dark so absolute it might have been a pool of ink. Cormac could see nothing, but somewhere nearby, he heard grunts and men's voices raised in anger or struggle.

'*Vigiles!*' someone hissed.

The voice seemed to come from nowhere, the dimensions of the room already lost. The mind played tricks in darkness and Cormac was afraid one of them would cut his throat unseen. There were people creeping around him like mice in a roof, heading for a way out. Someone kicked his chair leg and swore by his ear, making Cormac gasp. He bit his lip, heart thumping hard enough to burst.

Light flooded when a door was battered in from the outside.

'More of them here!' a man's voice roared.

He came in without waiting and there was a great spasm around Cormac as the gang scrambled. He gave a yell when his chair went over. It loosened the ropes that bound him and Cormac struggled madly, fearing being trodden upon or stabbed. Light swung crazily, a new lamp in the hands of a man trying to grab another of the gang, even as that one kicked out and roared. It was Malvo, Cormac thought with satisfaction. He hoped the vigiles gave him a proper beating.

Down on the floor, his cheek pressed against slick, damp wood, Cormac heaved with his shoulders and the chair itself gave way. He realised he smelled something burned and began to search the floor with his hands. The leader of the gang was getting a kicking from at least two vigiles on the other side of the room and the single light swung in flashes. Cormac suddenly saw the burned scroll and could have wept to see it so reduced. He snatched the charred thing, crumpling it in his fist as hands grabbed him.

Cormac looked up into the face of the vigile he had met before. Terentius? The name came back to him. The man grinned like a cheerful uncle, but there was no kindness in it.

'I *knew* you were one of them,' the man said. 'I smelled it.' He tapped the side of his nose.

'I'm not,' Cormac said desperately. 'They had me tied up. Look at the rope there! Please, I haven't done anything.'

'That will be up to the magistrate, son,' the man said, shaking his head in mock regret. 'You've certainly "associated" with them. That will get you a whipping and a fine, with all the crowd howling fit to burst. They love it, you know.'

The man was panting, Cormac saw. As he stared, he saw Terentius' eye was swelling. It seemed Malvo had given back at least a part of what he'd received. In that moment, Cormac was glad.

'I can't pay a fine,' he said.

The vigile rose to his feet, his grip tight on Cormac's filthy tunic. There was no mercy in him.

'Then you'll be indentured, son. Made a slave again. Perhaps you should have chosen your mates with a little more care. Take him to the cells, with the others. Praetor Gracchus likes to deal with the dregs as the sun comes up.'

'I've done nothing *wrong*!' Cormac said. Panic was rising in him. He knew very well what being a slave meant. He tried to stop his voice trembling, but it betrayed him. The vigile shrugged as he handed him over. His hands were bound once more.

'That's what they all say.'

In the grey light before dawn, Cormac was tied to a dozen strangers and stumble-marched through the streets. The vigiles were yawning by then, looking forward to sleeping through the morning. They were the night shift, Cormac learned, and more than pleased with the tally of prisoners. There might be a reward, one of them told the others.

Even at that hour, Rome was waking. In summer, Cormac knew a lot of men started very early, then slept through the afternoon before beginning a second shift in the late evening. It was a place where the strong and fit could flourish while others withered. He'd thought he was the first sort the day before. Yet there he was, a failure. More than a few of the early workers made gestures or called out curses Cormac had not heard before. He committed them to memory, even the ones he did not understand. 'Catamitus' he could guess at with a twinge of disgust, but 'landica' was new and 'cunnus' made no sense at all, even combined with other words.

The prison known as the tullianum or the carcer was not

a place for men to languish, not for long. Cormac shivered in the morning cold as he and the others were brought inside a great gate. Only with it closed behind them were the ropes removed, though he saw armed guards strolling about, starting their own shift. There was some mummery with the vigiles, accepting responsibility. Terentius nodded to the prisoners like a proud father, stopping on his way out to address them.

'You'll go before Praetor Gaius Gracchus in a little while. I suggest you plead guilty and hope for lenience for all your thievery and murders.'

The prisoners grumbled and one or two even grinned, as if Terentius had made a joke of some sort. Cormac looked around in astonishment. Some of Malvo's gang were hard-looking boys, battered and filthy. One had lost an eye, though he left it uncovered. The one Malvo had called Vittore was missing fingers on one hand, an old wound made shiny by time and grease. Together, they were a rough crew and yet they were still children, for the most part. They looked to Malvo to show them how to react, though he could not have been much older than the others.

Cormac saw Malvo stood unbowed and wondered if it was just a show. There had been intelligence in those eyes back in their den, he was certain. He was almost sure Malvo hadn't meant to burn the parchment. Not that it mattered.

As Malvo glared around at their captors, Cormac wondered again if the cheek and nostril were the result of disease. He'd heard of whores where the nose rotted. At the estate, Antoninus had warned him about such things once, on a summer's day. He'd hardly understood the old man's fond recollections, but had been left with a fear of parts swelling or even falling off.

One by one, they were shoved into cells. There was no chance of escape, Cormac could see that much. Even if the guards had been careless, he had glimpsed archers lounging on the walkway around that little yard. Prisoners were held for an hour or a few days, taken to court and straight to punishment, whatever was decreed. A single magistrate would sit in judgement in the lesser courts – juries were rowdy and it was better to have serious men who could not easily be swayed. It had seemed a fine system to Cormac when he'd learned about it for the gradus. Faced with a cell himself, he suddenly wasn't so sure. He only hesitated for a heartbeat on the threshold, but one of the guards kicked him from behind, launching him onto straw and nameless wet things.

Three more of the gang were shoved in after him. Cormac was displeased to see Malvo among them, as well as the one who'd held the lamp to burn his manumissio. He hated them both for what they'd taken. He could feel the burned piece still in his fist. He didn't dare look at it, for fear it would be just the lower part, with nothing written at all.

The guards were quick with their work and efficient enough, though they didn't seem to search anyone beyond a quick pat-down. One big knife was taken away, but they never looked at the belt Cormac wore, not to run a finger around the inside anyway. He wondered if any of the others had little blades like his. He kept an eye on them as he moved away to a corner, where a dim light shone from gratings above.

Too many things had happened too quickly. Cormac

needed time to think before he was sentenced as a vagrant and a thief, with a return to slavery ahead. With no manumissio, he wondered if he could still call on the name Silanus, without it drawing even worse punishments down on his head. No, he was cast off, the senator had made that clear. Cormac could imagine the man's relish at finding one of those who had refused his offer in trouble so quickly. He'd have Cormac tattooed or branded and back on the estate before he could say his own name. It was hopeless.

A slow anger began to burn as he put his back to a stone wall. The others found their own places and there was a little low conversation as they muttered to one another.

Cormac unfolded his hand, then the burned scrap of parchment. He'd hoped against hope that it might have been the empty half of the page that had gone into the flame, but no, his luck stayed bad. He peered at a blank scrap, barely wider than his thumb. All the words above had gone to ash, along with the ink stamp of the Silanus household that lent them authority. He was reminded then that Malvo had stolen the little stone seal. Cormac looked to where the gang leader sat. Malvo's head was lowered to whisper to one of the others, but he sensed that glance and looked up in challenge. Cormac scrambled in the straw for a stone, but then remembered his blade. Once again, he slid it from his little belt sheath. He could feel the scrap of inkstone still there, along with one good reed. Without that seal or a piece of parchment, they were no good to him . . . He stopped glaring at Malvo and thought for a moment.

His whole life had been lived by rules. Laws and restrictions applied to slaves more than anyone, more than freedmen, certainly more than freeborn citizens. That obedience had brought him to the cell, with slavery threatened once more. It was too much and he found himself thinking in new ways, for once in his life without caring what anyone else might want. He'd been burned and tied up, knocked around and put in a cell. All he had to show for his years as a slave were a couple of bits and pieces of no worth to his old estate. Well, he could use those.

He looked up again at the twist-faced gang leader. Unfortunately, he could not escape alone. Cormac glanced at the light overhead. The vigile officer had said something about the magistrate sitting at dawn. The sun was rising and they could be called out of the cells at any moment. Cormac could suddenly hear footsteps outside and the rattle of chains. He swore under his breath, beginning to sweat as he scrabbled to get the reed out of his belt.

7

Cormac used the tiny thumbnail blade to shave a strip from the burned vellum. It was no wider than the first joint of his thumb, but he cut away the charred paper and was left with something that might still be used. He spat on his tiny piece of inkstone and dipped the reed point into the smear, letting the fibres draw.

Malvo watched all that with a frown. He could see something was going on, but not what Cormac was doing. His eyebrows rose when Cormac gestured for him to come over. The deformed youth sprang up, fists ready for a challenge. His face scowled in an expression Cormac might have found frightening if he'd actually looked up. Instead, he was concentrating, scratching neat letters on the strip of vellum.

'Hold this edge down, Malvo,' he murmured as the young man loomed. He could hear chains clanking as the jailers readied manacles outside. Cormac had seen lines of men on previous visits to the city, shuffling along miserably to hear their fate. Now it was his turn. They'd all go

79

to the court chained together, at the mercy of a praetor's judgement.

'What are you *doing*? They're coming!' Malvo whispered furiously.

'I'm getting us out,' Cormac whispered back. 'Just put your finger there and stop it curling back on me. I need to let the letters dry.'

Malvo frowned, but his curiosity was kindled. He crouched down and put one dirty finger where Cormac had pointed, leaving a dark smudge.

'There?' he said.

Cormac nodded, blowing on the strip as he wrote.

'What are you . . . writing?' Malvo said. He hesitated as he remembered his claim of being able to read. In truth, letters were just chicken scratches to him.

Cormac read aloud as he came to the end of the line.

' "The bearer and his companion are mine. Aid them in my name . . . Senator Decimus Junius Silanus." '

Cormac heard his companion draw a sudden breath as he understood.

'You'll get us both killed,' Malvo hissed.

He might have pulled back then, letting the tape spring into a curl and smudging the letters. Cormac gripped his arm, holding him in place.

'Give me the seal you took. You put it in your pouch. Come on! That will *make* it true and keep us from the mines or the whipping post. If you return it right now. I've included you, haven't I? Or would you rather be tattooed or branded as a slave?'

Malvo looked close to panic, his gaze flickering to words he could not read, brows heavy with suspicion. He thought it was some trap, Cormac could guess that much.

He had no more coins to throw. He had spent them all and he could hear the jailers coming.

'Take a risk,' Cormac growled.

Malvo heard his scorn and worked his tongue inside his cheek, so that the pink tip suddenly showed in the hole.

'Fine! Gods curse you if you betray me!'

He produced the tiny oval of carved stone, passing it over. It had been set in a ring once. Such intaglios fell out in the heat of baths or just when their soft gold surrounds wore away. Cormac had found that one forgotten in a drawer at the estate. If it had ever been missed he hadn't heard. Another would have been carved into bloodstone like the first, or perhaps a ruby, marked with the symbol of the Silanus house. To have it in his hand was to hold a key to many locks – and Cormac felt a wave of relief. He knew his idea was dangerous, but against being made a slave once again, even his life was a small thing. He clenched his jaw. If he stopped to think, he knew he wouldn't go through with it.

The guards were at the door. Cormac smeared ink from his thumb to the tiny disc and pressed it against the end of the vellum tape. He slid the intaglio back into his belt as the cell door opened, letting the vellum spring into a tight roll, small enough to hide in his fist. As he rose, he scuffed the charred pieces he'd cut away with his foot, grinding them into the straw.

Malvo stayed with him like a shadow. He may not have been able to read, but the words 'The bearer and his companion' were not something he had heard before. He feared the court's ruling as much as anyone, more if his scars were anything to go by. Malvo was a young man who knew something about suffering. Cormac nodded to him, the two of them bound together in prickly cooperation.

The guards gestured them over one by one, closing manacles around one ankle and hammering an iron peg through the parts, far beyond the strength of fingers to wiggle out. If Cormac had been given a day, he thought he might have loosened them, but the court was just a few hundred paces across from the prison.

He felt Malvo's hand on his shoulder as the guard hammered the manacles. The gang leader cleared his throat almost by Cormac's ear. His eyes were on the fist that held the scrap of vellum.

Cormac shook his head. He needed actual authority, someone who might know the Silanus family and how far they could reach. Cormac swallowed nervously. He needed the magistrate himself, the praetor who would sit in judgement on them. More, he had to find the right moment to use the scroll without rousing the man's suspicion. He didn't dare think what would happen if they were caught. Once again, the threat of a Silanus loomed like Malvo at his shoulder. The scabs on his chest itched. He'd only been free for a day and he was battered, chained and light-headed from hunger and thirst. When had he last eaten? He swayed as he considered, thoughts growing thick. He needed to be sharp and yet the day was shimmering.

With a strangled curse, he gripped the front of his tunic, twisting the skin there. The pain was instant, like a bucket of cold water thrown over his head. It would not last, but his thoughts cleared. Malvo was looking at him as if he'd gone mad, which was fair enough. Cormac grinned as the guards gave a whistle and the line shuffled forward, out of the darkness into light.

Cormac found his gait immediately checked by the length of chain, so that he stumbled and almost fell. Early as it was, there were free men and women on the street. Cormac blinked as he realised they had been waiting for prisoners to emerge. They gave a ragged cheer and he wondered if they had come to support the downtrodden. For a single beat, he stood as straight as his hobbled steps allowed. Then something foul hit his chest and slithered down to his hands. He looked in horror at a huge, smashed lemon. He could see the thing was rotten, its insides black. Yet he was starving, so he raised it to his mouth and sucked while the crowd howled. The bitter juice stung his lips, but he was so thirsty he could not bring himself to care, not in that moment.

The air filled with rotten things, even some stones. Others in the coffle called out in anger or pain while the guards just chuckled and bantered with the crowd. They had known it was coming, of course. It wouldn't have surprised Cormac to hear those men took a collection in payment for the entertainment, a perk of an unpleasant job.

He kept his head as low as possible, bunching close with one prisoner ahead and Malvo behind. Instinctively, they protected one another, shuffling as quickly as they could. Some man in the crowd was yelling, Cormac saw. The fellow was so red-faced with hate Cormac wondered if he knew one of them.

The sun was not high enough to warm the skin before the shuffling line entered the outer vestibule of the courthouse. One of the prison guards walked the line then, tutting as if in disapproval, using a foul old cloth to remove the worst gobbets of fruit or mush. No doubt the praetor would be annoyed if they let such things inside, Cormac supposed. He shook his head at the unfairness of it. His tunic had been filthy enough before. Between the cell and the rotten fruit, he looked like a beggar. His hands were black with muck and he could feel his hair sticking out at angles he could not smooth down. He felt his eyes prickle, tears of self-pity threatening. He thumped himself on the chest again, letting pain and anger crush any sign of weakness.

Justice in Rome seemed a slow process, at least after the frantic dash across the forum. Cormac could only stand and wait while officers of the court drifted in. He had never been inside that building before and when the doors opened, he wanted to look up at the beamed ceiling and around at the painted walls. He and his companions were made to sit on a bench that would face the magistrate, while other free men and women took up seats behind and to the sides, frowning on the prisoners as if they too sat in judgement.

This would not be a matter for a jury, Cormac was fairly sure. He recognised two or three vigiles from the night before, including Terentius, who seemed to be the most senior. Cormac could remember the man's cheery manner in the street, all smiles and winks before he'd come back for his ambush. The man had shaved and changed his clothes, Cormac noted. Terentius looked refreshed, but he was at the end of a long shift or the beginning of a new one. The vigile yawned hugely as Cormac watched him.

The magistrate entered at last, trailing clerks like leaves in his wake. He ascended a few unseen steps behind an oak rostrum, appearing above them all and arranging his papers as if unaware of every eye on him. Perhaps two hundred Romans had crammed into that room, taking every seat. Cormac didn't know whether it was some proof of civic interest, or just a morning's diversion.

Silence fell like a drumbeat on the air as they settled.

The magistrate nodded to his clerks and one unrolled a sheet of vellum Cormac would have given his eye teeth to own. It looked like proper calfskin, square and very white. The man's ink holder was an ornate construction of silver and polished wood, with a place for a large block of ink, a tiny water bottle and a reservoir for the liquid. It was a thing of beauty and Cormac longed to examine it.

Another of the clerks stood from his desk. 'Rise,' he bellowed. They all did – including the coffle of prisoners. Cormac found himself wondering what it would take for men to ignore that order. 'The court is in session, on this year, seven hundred and ninety, the tenth day of July, under the authority of Emperor Tiberius, blessed of the gods and beloved in Rome and all her territories. Praetor Gaius Gracchus Aemilianus presiding. Let the gods see all we do. Let Justitia bestow her wisdom – and Jupiter grant the judgement to sift the good grain from the bad.'

The entire crowd sat as one. Cormac could feel Malvo staring, waiting for him to move. He shook his head again, though the truth was, he'd hoped for an opportunity before everything was so very public.

'First on the list . . .' the praetor muttered. He turned to his clerks and one of them whispered, pointing out the line of chained prisoners and then the vigiles. The praetor nodded and shrugged.

'Vigil Terentius Pariola? You are to testify, I understand. Approach.'

Cormac watched as Terentius stood at a second rostrum. He pressed his right hand over his heart and repeated an oath:

'I swear I shall speak only the truth, in the sight of the gods and at their judgement, in this court of consular authority, on the fate of my immortal soul. I give this oath freely and without dissembling.'

Cormac felt his lip curl. He had not been allowed to give an oath on his honour, not as a slave. Had it been just a couple of days back? His chest throbbed and he felt light-headed once again, this time with anger.

The officer of the vigiles was flushed with pride under the attention of the court. Cormac watched in disgust as Terentius described his movements the evening before. He used words oddly, as if he was telling a story or reading aloud.

'. . . I was proceeding on my usual patrol of the area, when I was approached by a merchant of my acquaintance. He informed me as to the location or whereabouts of a gang I knew to have been stealing and outraging the local markets. That very day, I had been called to secure justice for three stallholders, after theft of their goods. I then proceeded on foot to the house basement indicated to me – and entered, with force. My companions and I discovered the miscreants and thieves in their den and removed them *thence* to the tullianum, there to be held for trial and justice for all their wrongdoings.'

'Excellent work, as I have come to expect,' the magistrate said, smiling as if to a favourite.

No doubt they had encountered one another many times, Cormac imagined. He looked around for someone to speak in their defence. According to the Twelve Tables, an imperial court could appoint an advocate to argue on their behalf. No one else was rising, however. Though Cormac had been swept up in the raid, he supposed the rest of them probably were the very gang of street urchins and forgotten men Terentius had been seeking. He had no idea of their guilt or innocence, if it mattered at all. The lads themselves were all slumped, staring at the floor as they awaited judgement. They didn't believe anyone was coming to help them.

Cormac stood up. He heard Malvo hiss in dismay and his stomach squirmed. The sound of moving chains was loud in that place and the praetor's expression of goodwill froze as he looked across.

'Praetor Gracchus,' Cormac said loudly, 'may I ask if any of the stolen goods were found in that basement? I saw none.'

He sat down again and had the satisfaction of seeing the vigiles mutter to one another. The skinny one from the night before was shaking his head and Terentius was scowling in Cormac's direction as if personally insulted.

The magistrate could hardly believe his ears.

'*Stand up*,' he said in icy fury.

Cormac rose once again, swaying in exhaustion.

'By what right do you address this court? You stand accused of crimes that carry a sentence of ten years in the mines and a fine of twelve denarii – or slavery if you are unable to pay. Yet you assume such airs as to speak unbidden? To me! How *dare* you rise unasked in my court! What have you to say for yourself?'

Cormac had had enough. Though he knew it meant his life, he was a freedman, no longer a slave. He'd been burned and knocked down, chained and pelted with rotten things. He was so tired he wanted to weep. Instead, something snapped in him.

'The Twelve Tables allow a defence, dominus,' Cormac said firmly. 'These vigiles have gathered a group of men and called them thieves, yes, but on the word of an unnamed informant? Was this "merchant" summoned this morning? Where is the evidence? What proof have these vigiles of any crime? If they had collected the stolen goods, that would serve this court, but must we take the word of one man?'

'You . . .!' The magistrate could not believe his ears. 'You dare to question the honour of a servant of the city? A man of long-standing dignity and . . . and service!' In his fury, he was spluttering.

Cormac dropped back to his bench as if his legs gave way. He felt ill with what he had done. It had made things worse, he could see that.

'I will see you *whipped* for your insolence,' the praetor shouted, his voice breaking in the emotion that over-whelmed him. 'Unchain him, jailer! I will watch him lashed before this trial continues. In all my *years* I have never seen such a display! The arrogance of this common man, to stand before me, in this august place . . .' He was almost frothing and Cormac could actually see white spit gather-ing in both corners of his mouth.

One of the jailers from the tullianum came trotting up from the back of the court. The man was visibly embar-rassed, as if he felt some personal responsibility for the outburst. He knelt to tap out the iron peg, staring at Cormac as if he were a two-headed lamb. He was almost gentle as he removed the irons, leaning in close.

'You've done it now, you madman,' the jailer murmured. 'He'll talk of bringing you back in after, but I've seen this before. You'll die on the post, mate. I'd make your peace with the gods, while you can.'

He took Cormac by the shoulder and began to walk him past the praetor. The man was following every step with malice in his gaze. The timing had to be perfect. As Cormac came within a step, he raised his blackened hand, opening his fingers to toss the scroll tape onto the rostrum.

The magistrate recoiled as if from a weapon, but then snatched it up. Cormac struggled in the grip of the jailer as he was rushed out even faster. He saw the magistrate opening the tape in a pale strip. He waited another beat as the light grew. Some of the people were still there, outside. There were iron posts set into the stone by the courthouse and on a good day they would see a man lashed, or better still, a woman. The light was blinding him when he heard the praetor's voice once again.

'Wait. Bring him back.'

Cormac felt his eyes sting and told himself it was just the sun. There were bells sounding, he realised. In a temple off the forum, he could hear low notes tolling over and over. A second one began like an echo. He hardly had time to wonder what it all meant before he was dragged back inside.

The magistrate had risen from his chair and loomed over the court as Cormac was brought to stand before him. He held the grubby tape in his hand, the edges curling. His expression was still flushed, but he was frowning as he looked down, as if he could discern truth by sheer force of will.

'Bring him behind, to my chambers,' he said suddenly. 'The court will remain. This won't take long, I am certain.' He turned to go, then bit one lip in thought. 'Who is your "companion"?' he growled.

Cormac pointed to Malvo and the young gang leader flinched at being identified in that place. Malvo would clearly have preferred to remain anonymous, but the praetor only let his gaze rest on him for a beat.

'Bring him as well. And you, Vigil Terentius. You will accompany us. I will have the truth of this, before this hour is at its end.'

8

The room reeked of sickness, of rot. It sat in the air and in the cloths of the bed like the aftermath of a fire, too deep to cover with lavender water or even the waxy myrrh used to anoint the dead.

Women of the imperial household laid out the body with arms crossed over the chest. The old man had been emperor in Rome, pharaoh in Egypt. They had stripped away his clothes to clean him, wiped the product of emptied bowels and oiled his withered skin. It shone as it began to stiffen. The most senior matron of the imperial household had even welcomed a quaestor from the treasury, summoned as the sun rose. He had brought an aureus coin marked with Tiberius' own face in profile. It was a Greek custom, but the emperor had been known to favour it. If the gods demanded a coin to cross the river, they would see this one was gold, a metal that did not tarnish or corrode. They would know this soul had been that of an emperor.

Maryam observed the coin being placed just so on the

dried tongue, then used a little glue to seal it in place. Her companions eased the lips back and she added a single stitch to his gums, over the exposed roots of his teeth. She tutted to herself then. Not many men lived almost to eighty years old, but Tiberius had been iron-willed, right to the end. He had come home to Rome from Capreae, with that strange boy in tow. Maryam knew Tiberius had completed some unpleasant business since then, dispatching a rival grown too big in his authority. Sejanus, that had been the name. She'd heard the emperor had ordered the man strangled and thrown down the Gemonian steps. Her master had never been one to suffer fools, she thought. No, Tiberius had been a strong emperor, a man to rule the world.

Maryam was only pleased his breath had fallen still at last. It had always been obvious which rooms Tiberius had graced with his presence, sometimes hours after he had left. The memory might linger even longer, she imagined, still turning her stomach though the man himself had gone to the gods.

When they were finished and Maryam had brushed his hair, the dead emperor looked completely at peace, his flesh clean and the delicate yellow of a primrose. Maryam wondered if she should bring a cosmetician in to add colours of life, but decided on balance against.

The man on the bed kicked suddenly. Six women had been standing looking down on him in silence, thinking their own thoughts. Almost as one they gave a shriek at the sudden movement, stepping back to run. If Tiberius lived, they would know his wrath! If he discovered they had shoved wadding up his back passage, that they had stitched his mouth shut to keep the coin safe, to stop his jaw from sagging!

One of the emperor's eyes opened, staring blind at the ceiling. A woman dropped bonelessly to the floor when she saw that, thumping her head on the rug in a dead faint.

Maryam frowned. In forty years of service, she had witnessed babies born and bodies made ready for the tomb. Old men who passed in their sleep did not often twitch like that. Death already had such a hold on them they just slipped across without any great fuss, at least in her experience. No, the ones who jumped – she shuddered at the memory of one who had sat up suddenly, hours after death – those men had all died with violence. The body fought to live then and could tremble or twitch, long after the soul had fled its cage.

The emperor's physician came running in, summoned by the high voices.

'What is it?' he demanded, looking in fear to the corpse on the bed. It *was* still a corpse, Maryam saw with relief.

'Just a twitch,' she said. 'The girls must have disturbed his parts while they were cleaning him.'

Another man entered, so that Maryam lowered her gaze. Naevius Macro was prefect of the praetorian guard, a new appointment settling into his role. He was short and wide of shoulder, powerfully muscled and seeming to fill the room as he glared around. Maryam almost smiled as the man glanced at the emperor and froze.

'Why is his *eye* open?' Macro said. His voice shook with horror and Maryam took pity on him.

'Eyes do open,' she said gently. 'He cannot see us, not now. Here, I'll stitch it closed.'

Prefect Macro blanched at that, which she thought ungrateful. The Greeks put coins on the eyes sometimes, but they tended to fall off. The lids would then ease open, a very disconcerting expression in the dead. Maryam gathered her needle and thread and put a quick stitch into each drooping eyelid, almost invisibly. There was little dignity in death, she thought. She wondered if Tiberius would be declared divine. Both Julius Caesar and Augustus Caesar had been. Of course, they had turned the republic into a great empire and been beloved – by legions, the praetorians, even the fickle people of Rome. Tiberius had spent rather too long away from the heart of empire, preferring his palace on the island of Capreae. More, there were rumours from that place, of deaths and parties and broken souls. Tiberius had not been divine, Maryam was almost sure. She shuddered at the thought of his smell once more. No god would smell like that.

A door opened wider at the rear of the room, so that she felt air move. Maryam looked over her shoulder, to another private chamber she'd thought was empty. It was still dark in there and yet as she glanced, a young man came out. She felt her eyes widen, wondering how long he had been listening, what secrets he had heard while they cleaned the body. Maryam winced at the blunt talk she recalled, common between women, at least those engaged in unpleasant work. She stood back from the bed as he approached, careful to show respect. He would understand, she thought. Emperor Tiberius had died hard, in pain, but all that had been smoothed away by their labours. She wondered again about the twitch, but he had been an old man and this was a new world.

Maryam watched from under lowered lashes as Gaius Caesar stood to look down on his mentor and adopted father. He was very beautiful in his youth, a fine figure of a young man. He had been six years on Capreae and she wondered what he had seen there. A slender lad of eighteen had been taken away, returning to Rome at twenty-four. His eyes were much older than his years, she thought. Maryam did not like to meet that gaze.

She remembered him best as a little boy. His father Germanicus had been a famous general and one of the legion smiths had made a tiny set of armour for the son who would follow him. Maryam could remember young Gaius marching up and down when they returned to Rome, standing guard and patrolling with the praetorians. They'd called him 'little boot' for his pride in his legion sandals, a sweet nickname from a time when the world had been innocent.

Maryam felt a tear begin and wiped it from her cheek. It did not matter in that place. In fact, she encouraged the young ladies on her staff to weep. It honoured the passing of a great man. At that very moment, word would be winging out as far as Syria and Gaul, carried on galloping horses, by a thousand pigeons released from the dovecotes of Rome, by ship and on foot, all bearing the news.

She watched as Gaius Caesar reached down and kissed Tiberius on the lips. Maryam was grateful then that she had used the most expensive myrrh oil. The slender young man seemed to shudder at the contact. The flesh would be cold, of course. Maryam had felt it growing heavy and still as death took its hold. She realised she was witness to a moment of wonder. One emperor was dead, but another stood in his place.

Slowly, Maryam dropped to kneel. Her girls were quick to follow and the physician and Prefect Macro sank down in turn. When Gaius Caesar straightened up, it was to see bowed heads.

'Rise, all of you,' he said. 'I know you have done your work well. I heard you. I know he would be proud.'

Maryam blushed at the compliment. His eyes met hers for a moment and she looked away, suddenly afraid. Gaius Caesar was beautiful, but also terrible, like a forest fire. She found herself wondering again if Tiberius had died as peacefully as she had been told. Some men could not wait for their inheritance. Perhaps this slender youth was one of them.

'The emperor is gone from the world at last,' he said, his voice like a breath. 'Sound the great bells in every temple – the dolorous notes. Let the people hear Tiberius is dead, that they may grieve and pray for his soul – and for me.'

His order was taken away and Maryam busied herself packing up fallen cloths and oils with all the rest. She left Gaius Caesar alone with the prefect of his praetorian guard standing vigil. As she glanced back, the sunlight lit the bed in a great bar of gold, filled with dust.

At the rear of the courthouse, the magistrate passed through a door, entering an office that was sumptuous in comparison to the benches outside. Cormac stared through large open windows that looked up the Palatine hill. It might as well have been gods who lived on those heights, so far removed were they from lives below. Cormac knew the name of the emperor, but the fate of great families or politics in Rome had not been of much concern to a Silanus slave, even one training to be a scribe.

As the door closed, the noise of bells was muffled and the praetor lost some of the snap and vigour that had characterised him before. It seemed his role as magistrate was in part a reflection of his surroundings. Cormac watched warily as the man rubbed his eyes with both hands. The gesture made him seem older – though still exasperated. The man nodded to the vigile officer, handing the little tape of vellum over to him. Terentius could read, Cormac saw, which was interesting. They were clearly friends and Cormac could only watch. His life hung in the balance and he could feel his own heart beating.

'May I question him, Gaius?' Terentius asked.

The praetor waved a hand in permission and Cormac felt the weight in the air shift as the older man came to stand in front of him.

'Where did you get this?' Terentius asked in a low, gruff voice.

'I was given it by my master,' Cormac said. He made himself frown, as if in puzzlement at being asked. He would lie, he had decided. His feet were on the path and he would lie for his life, giving no sign it was false.

'I see – and your name?'

'Cormac, as you read on my deed of manumission.'

'Answer quickly now. The name of your master?' Terentius pressed, glancing at the tape in his hand. A simple memory test, but Cormac had written those words in the cell just a few hours before.

'Senator Decimus Junius Silanus,' he replied without hesitation.

The praetor grunted at hearing the name spoken aloud.

'You are "the bearer", are you?' he said. 'And this . . . ill-faced gentleman here is your companion?'

Cormac did not dare look at Malvo, for fear of what might be obvious in his expression. They were both so far out of their depth it should have been terrifying, but Cormac felt a strange confidence. His *words* were written on that scrap of polished skin! Yet it had stopped a praetor in his tracks, one of just a dozen to hold that post in the whole empire. Cormac met the gaze of the vigile with the appearance of calm, while his bowels turned to water.

'My master allows me some freedoms,' Cormac said. 'Leaving my companion unnamed is part of that trust. For today, yes, Malvo is important.'

Cormac could feel thoughts whirring like little fly wings. He knew houses like Silanus employed hundreds, even thousands as their clients. Those men and women took a stipend each month to support the family in all endeavours. It was a shield the nobilitas built around them. Surely, this vigile could believe Cormac was one of the less savoury parts? He would have to be cautious, he reminded himself. Terentius was used to dealing with liars.

'And what is that work, that brought you to a known thieves' den in the middle of the night?' Terentius said, raising his eyebrows. He had adopted a friendlier tone and instinct made Cormac even more cautious. This man was an enemy. Terentius would smile as he was nailed up, he was certain. One wrong word would bring it all down around his ears.

'Little fishes,' Cormac said, remembering a phrase Sophia had used in the kitchens once. 'I cannot say all the details of my work, only that I was after more than just a street gang.' He remembered his outburst in court and improvised. 'I . . . tried to move the court against finding them guilty for that reason.'

He felt Malvo shift in surprise and prayed he would keep his mouth shut. Malvo was the weak thread in the rope

Cormac was weaving. If he broke and denied the tale, they were both done. Cormac felt the vigile's attention turn to the deformed man and spoke quickly to head him off.

'Work you have interrupted, dominus, by bringing me to the tullianum cells, by delaying me here for half a day. I do not think my master will be pleased if I tell him how you questioned me, seeking details that are not your concern.'

That seemed to strike home. Cormac kept his face carefully blank as Terentius exchanged a glance with the praetor. He imagined Senator Silanus was a bad enemy to have, for anyone. Cormac had looked into the man's eyes while skin burned, while he experienced more pain than he had ever known before. Yes, a bad enemy.

'You are very young to have such trust rested in you,' Terentius said, almost gently. 'You are a Silanus slave, are you? On the senator's personal staff?'

Cormac clenched his jaw, as if in anger. Yet it was the first truth he could speak.

'As you know, I am freed,' he said, lifting his chin a fraction.

Terentius nodded. He grunted again, turning back to the praetor. Terentius shrugged.

'That much is probably true. As for the rest, you saw the seal, just as I did. I can't say for certain.'

Cormac felt a line of sweat drip down his cheek. They would see the droplet and wonder, he was certain. Yet the body sweated more when it was denied food and sleep. He might explain it away as mere exhaustion. When had he last eaten? He could not remember.

The praetor sat up straighter in his chair, his expression suddenly more alert.

'There is a Silanus property not far from here. Can you describe it?'

Cormac frowned, hiding his relief. He'd been coming into the city for years to study for his gradus. The carriage of his master had stopped at a grand property on the Quirinal hill more than once to pick up letters. Each branch of the clan was like a small island, but they all communicated and planned together. That was how young Marcus Silanus – Plato – had been sent to a childless uncle to be adopted.

Cormac shook his head, letting something like irritation show. He had never been inside and felt a little bluster was needed.

'That house with the red porch columns is indeed the property of my master, but you are wasting my time – and his. You have already seen his instruction. If you wish to know more, you should approach Senator Silanus and see how well that goes for you.'

Terentius chuckled, though it was more at Cormac's irritation than the prospect of questioning a senator. The authority of vigiles tended to stop at the senate door, or some way before it.

'If he lies, he does it well,' Terentius said. He shrugged once more.

The praetor made a wincing expression, still unsure.

'That is a famous house, though,' he said. 'I think . . . yes. I will send a runner. I don't like this . . . It cannot be too hard to have Senator Silanus claim his man – or perhaps someone on his staff.'

'I'll use one of my lads,' Terentius said.

'Immediately, please,' the praetor said. 'I have a dozen cases to hear today. Just ask them to confirm a "Cormac" is in the senator's household.'

The man sat back as Terentius went to the door and passed on the news to one of his waiting men. He went off at a fast run.

Cormac could feel sweat trickling down his back. He found himself staring, but it was at the brightness of the morning. Malvo shifted once again and Cormac slid his gaze to the deformed youth. There was terror in him. Malvo had faced only years in the mines before. In trusting Cormac, he'd raised the stakes a lot higher – and failed.

There was a soft knock at the door and the tension was broken. Terentius crossed to it and saw his own man standing there once more.

'What is it?' he asked.

'I heard news outside. Thought I should come back and let you know. Palatine has fallen.'

'Palatine has fallen?' Terentius repeated. The phrase clearly meant something to him, Cormac could see.

'What is it?' the praetor demanded, rising from his seat.

'The emperor is dead,' Terentius said.

'The bells . . . I see,' the praetor replied. He had paled. 'And who is the heir?'

'Gaius Caesar,' Terentius said immediately. 'The one they call "Caligula".'

'He still lives? I thought he'd been killed along with his brothers. A most unlucky family.'

'I believe he does,' Terentius said. He was uncomfortable discussing such things in the presence of strangers, which the praetor seemed to have forgotten in his shock. Terentius indicated Cormac and Malvo, still standing almost to attention.

'I will be called back to duty, Gaius,' Terentius said. 'What do you want done with these two?'

The praetor cast his sour gaze over them. He fastened on Cormac.

'Describe Senator Decimus Silanus to me.'

'Dark eyes, cropped hair, grey at the temples,' Cormac said quickly. 'Tanned and healthy. My master is tall, with a sharp nose. No fat on him. He has the bearing of a military man. With this tragic news, I should go to him for new orders. Is there anything else?'

'No,' the praetor said grudgingly. 'Very well. I will say that I do not enjoy my court being host to this sort of . . . *acting*, these masks and messages, whatever you call it. There is no honour in such things. So take a word of warning – I do not expect to see you again.'

Cormac held out his hand for the strip of vellum Terentius still held. The man handed it back with the utmost reluctance.

'I hope not, dominus,' Cormac replied. 'Good day to you both.'

His voice came out well enough and the vigiles stepped back to let him through. He knew they had marked him in their minds. Terentius would certainly remember his face.

With a sigh, Cormac realised he had to put aside any thought of joining the vigiles himself. He needed to disappear from the view of men like Terentius and the praetor. In some ways, Rome was a vast city; in that moment, he wondered if it was even large enough to hide him.

He and Malvo came out into the morning sun. The crowds had scattered as word spread. Bells now sounded across the city, the deepest notes that called a warning of war or the death of an emperor. Praetorian guards stood in pairs on every corner, glowering and ready for violence. They would allow no riots or public unrest, not in a time of crisis. Palatine may have fallen – but Cormac was free.

Malvo had not said a word in court or the office, though he'd experienced mindless terror for most of it. He looked around then in a sort of wonder, breathing as if he'd thought he might never know free air again. The gang leader looked back into the shadowy courtroom they'd left. There was no one close enough to hear.

'I thought we were done then,' Malvo muttered.

To Cormac's surprise, the taller man put out his hand and Cormac took it briefly. The grip was strong, as if they held on for support.

'What now?' Malvo asked.

Cormac had expected him to just walk away the moment they were safely out.

'I'm starving. I need to eat before I pass out,' Cormac said. Malvo nodded.

'I know a place. I meant later on.'

Cormac gave it a moment's consideration.

'My school. They have what I need.'

Cormac saw a strange hesitation in his companion as different needs pulled him one way and then another. Apart, they were both alone. Cormac was not quite ready to be alone again.

'Are you coming?' he said.

Malvo nodded and they shared a shy grin. They had both survived the tullianum and the threat of much worse. They set off together, bustling along at a good speed, nodding to a pair of praetorians as if they were late and could not stop.

9

Cormac eyed his companion as they walked. With the missing nostril and the hole in his cheek, Malvo drew glances from passers-by, all hurrying along through the clamour of bells. He would always be remembered, Cormac thought, if anyone ever came asking. That was a problem that needed to be solved.

Tiberius had been emperor as long as Cormac could remember. He had no idea what the official processes were. Would there be a period of mourning for the city? Parades of legions in slow step, with sombre music? The thought of a great feast laid on in the emperor's honour made his stomach twist. Cormac had passed hunger by then into pain. It was not something he had known before, but his stomach ached badly, worse every moment. His thoughts spun and his mouth and tongue were like dust. All he wanted to do was sit down and sleep. The Silanus estate he had known had always fed him well. In the kitchens, Sophia baked flatbreads and sliced cheese for any hungry boy who might come by. He groaned, rubbing his sore gut.

Cormac had a rough idea where the school was, in a back street near the Quirinal hill. It meant he knew the northern half of the city much better than the south. Below the Palatine, Rome was a mystery. He knew enough to keep the afternoon sun on his left shoulder to head north, but the rest was flashes of memory, usually from a carriage while Marcus Silanus chatted about some new horse he was getting, or what daughter of a noble house he might be told to marry. Cormac shook his head free of those memories. Like the smell of flatbreads on a hot stove, they were from a different life.

He pointed down an alleyway as if directing himself, then stopped in surprise when Malvo put a hand across his chest. Even that light touch was enough to make Cormac wince as scabs broke.

'Not down there,' Malvo said. He looked apologetic as Cormac raised an eyebrow. 'There are . . . territories in the city, places I can't go. The gangs around here won't come much further south. They will know me though, unfortunately.' He indicated his face and Cormac understood.

'What about the rest of your . . . gang?' Cormac said.

A shadow crossed Malvo's face at that. He shrugged, trying to pretend he didn't care.

'Nothing I can do for them lads, not now. They'll do some time in the mines, or be lashed in the forum. I suppose I would have been with them . . .'

He shook his head, unsure what to say to the one who had saved him. Cormac walked in silence for a time. He'd never had a friend before, not someone of his own age. Old Antoninus didn't count, or Sophia in the kitchens. Malvo knew the city and he felt less helpless in his company. That was part of it, but not all.

'So you're on your own then, for now?' Cormac said.

Malvo snorted, but he didn't reply for a while as they stepped over an open sewer, bustling along an empty street.

'There are some of the older firm who'll want to hear from me when they find out we were taken. They'll come looking if I don't turn up. Not today, maybe, but soon enough.'

'I thought you were the leader. They looked to you, didn't they?'

Malvo kicked a loose stone as he walked. He took on a mulish expression as he thought of his life. Cormac was regretting asking when he suddenly spoke again.

'Some of the lads do what they are told, for food and a place to sleep. Vittore was one of those, as well as Salvus and . . . it doesn't matter, you don't know them. They looked to me because I fed them and told them where to go, because I made the deals for which roads we could use. I deal with the older firm. There's a . . . ladder, right? At the top are the ones who used to be street boys in the old days. Hard men. You don't want to meet any of those, believe me.'

He touched one finger to the hole in his cheek, his face grim with memory.

'They didn't get you out of a praetor's chambers though, did they?' Cormac said.

Malvo looked up and saw Cormac walking like a cockerel for a few steps, chest out. Malvo chuckled.

'That is true . . .' He considered for a moment and Cormac saw again the quickness that had raised Malvo over a dozen others, despite his youth. 'Though I had that little carved seal you needed. You saved me to save yourself, as I remember it.'

'Maybe, though I *did* save you. And you kept your nerve when I thought you would tell that vigile everything in the praetor's chambers. That counts.'

Malvo was pleased at that. He clapped Cormac on the shoulder as they walked, making him stagger.

'It does. So what now?'

'Well, we need to find a bath-house,' Cormac said. 'I can't go to my school looking like I've been dragged through a sewer. I remember a place on the way to the Quirinal, I'm sure. I saw it from the . . . I saw it a few times before, when I came into the city.'

'I know that place!' Malvo said. 'Just a few streets over. The gangs will be quiet today, anyway. Probably. There are too many praetorians around to cause any trouble.'

He seemed to be convincing himself as much as anyone, but Cormac let it go. As they reached a busy crossroads, Cormac began to really look around, to mark the faces of everyone who turned to watch them. He realised he had been oblivious before.

The great families employed vast numbers, he already knew that. He imagined the vigiles paid informers as well – and then, of course, there were the thieves and street gangs, all jostling for advantage. It seemed on that day of terrible news that half the city was observing the other half, with more eyes on Cormac than he wanted. He hurried along with Malvo, keeping his head low.

The bath-house was not the place Cormac remembered. That had been a minor establishment, the sort used by market traders and messengers. For a copper coin, they could empty their bowels there each morning, be rubbed with used oil and scraped clean, perhaps with a dip in the steaming pool before work. Those who could not afford even that made their own arrangements, filling pots and emptying them into the street sewers before heading out.

Cormac looked up slowly at huge columns crowned with stone acanthus leaves. This bath-house had the look of a place senators might visit – or consuls and emperors, for all he knew. He swallowed, more aware of his own filth than he had been to that point. He needed a new tunic, food and a long soak, but had not a coin to his name.

'Do you have any money?' Cormac murmured to Malvo.

'Not here,' the young man replied defensively. 'I thought you would. Come on, the praetorians have spotted us. We can't stand in one place, not here – not today.'

Cormac saw Malvo was right. His companion had a good instinct for knowing when he was observed and there were indeed two grim soldiers in black plumes watching. One of them seemed on the verge of coming over and Cormac thought furiously.

'Can you read, Malvo?' he asked.

'Of course . . .' Malvo said. As Cormac watched, he gave it up and shrugged. 'No, I never learned. I'm not a scribe.'

Cormac nodded.

'Come on, then,' he said. 'Though you might want to think of something to say. You can't just stand there like a bag of washing while I do all the talking.'

He strode towards the entrance to the baths. The praetorians moved to intercept them, one of them holding out a flat palm. The other was on his sword hilt, Cormac noted. He could not remember his life ever being threatened before coming into Rome as a freedman. Since then, it seemed to be a regular experience.

'No beggars or slaves here,' the soldier said with a certain amount of malice.

Cormac stood still, his brows drawn together in apparent confusion.

'My master Senator Silanus sent me to this place,' he said. 'The senator expects all his staff to be clean, as he made clear.' He winced as if in memory and the soldier's expression eased, enjoying the young man's embarrassment. The two praetorians lost the tension they had shown before, exchanging a glance.

'You'll need a silver sestertius to go in there, son. Did your master give you one of those?'

Cormac unrolled his little vellum tape, holding it up for them to read the words.

'He gave me his permission, as you see here,' he said. He held his breath while one of them appeared to read the words, his eyes moving. The other looked away, checking the road for anyone about to cause trouble.

'I see,' the first said. 'In you go, then. You'd better be quick though, or you'll get your backside striped.'

Cormac hid his delight. Reading was a rarer skill than he had known. He bowed his head and walked in through the columns. Malvo went with him and he thought he really would have to teach his companion what to say if they stayed together. Malvo could not just stand wide-eyed like that. People would remember.

In the entrance hall, an attendant heard the door open and came out. His expression did not change as he took in the filthy state of the two young men. It was an interesting display of control, Cormac thought. He swallowed when he saw the fellow wore a silver ring. One of his new clan, it seemed.

'Read this,' Cormac said, handing over the scroll. He felt relief when the man took it upside down and made no attempt to turn it round.

'You'll see we have permission to use your baths to restore ourselves,' Cormac added, pointing at the words. The freedman nodded and clapped his hands. Two more slaves appeared, bearing towels and robes.

'Have you been here before, dominus?' the freedman asked, handing back the grubby scrap. It seemed he would not comment on their filth and battered state, not in such a fine establishment. Perhaps discretion was part of the service.

Cormac shook his head, trying to hide his shock at being addressed in such a way. He felt a twinge of shame at having to lie. It seemed he was good at it, but it did not fill him with pride.

'My first time,' he said, his voice tight.

'Then you're in for delights. The staff here will look after you. I'm not sure I caught the seal you showed me. Shall I send the bill to . . . ?'

'To Senator Silanus, yes,' Cormac replied, as if confirming what the man had read. He made himself say the name, though his heart raced. He felt like someone who had stepped off a cliff and could not go back. Instead, he was falling, faster and faster. He smiled as the freedman relaxed and nodded, impressed.

'We'll need food for two and new clothes as well,' Cormac said quickly. 'Is that all right?'

'Of course! I will have a tray made ready and arrange for new tunics and . . . undergarments?' Cormac nodded. 'Very well, I will send a boy out.' The freedman closed one eye as he estimated their sizes from experience, then smiled. 'Welcome to the Balneae. I believe Senator Silanus is in the steam room.' The man looked again at the level of dirt in the pair. 'Would you prefer to bathe first, or shall I have these lads show you straight through to him?'

Malvo made a sound that was not quite a word and Cormac spoke before he could.

'No, there is no need to bother the senator, not at the moment. I will, er . . . bathe and change first.' He turned to Malvo then, warning him with wide eyes. 'We really must eat.'

Malvo only raised his gaze to the ornate ceiling. Cormac swallowed a lump in his throat and followed the two bath slaves down a long corridor, walking as if to his own execution.

Once past the gatekeepers, Cormac might have been able to relax, if not for the news that his apparent patron and master was in the same building. He should have known the Balneae was the sort of bath-house the nobilitas might favour. For all its size, Rome could be a small city. No doubt families like the Furii or Silani used the same establishments, just as they met at the senate house and the great temples. He imagined they all knew each other as well. It was vital information and Cormac stored it away as he lay down. He knew his survival would depend on how fast he could learn the rules and expectations around him. To those born to them, they were invisible, present but unnoticed. He was in the same fine net, but unaware, thrashing in the cords.

In an outer room, he stretched his battered body on a raised bed as Malvo clambered awkwardly onto another. Two strangers were already present, attended by staff of the Balneae. Cormac and Malvo settled on sheets of reed matting without a word, ready to be scrubbed with soft brushes and cloths from head to foot. The attendants wore only loincloths and sandals in that place. The one who approached Cormac had a chest of thick white hair. He felt that touch of bristle as the man leaned over him, trying not to show distaste. Copying the others, he and Malvo turned like ducks on spits as each side was done. Cormac could see dark streams dribbling into a drain. He did not think he'd ever been so dirty in his life – nor, after a while, as clean.

He sat up to have his ears explored and for the gruff male slave to apply fresh olive oil. The man ladled it on liberally, then worked big thumbs into the muscles of Cormac's arms and legs, digging into each rib and knuckle of his spine. The pain was excruciating, though it eased after a time.

Both Cormac and Malvo had left their loincloths on. Malvo's was grey with old dirt and his slave tapped it in silent question. They both shook their heads, not quite sure what was being offered. Cormac knew he could wash that part himself, when he had a moment.

Malvo remained quiet as they took his tunic and sandals from where he had made a pile, though he leaned over to try and see where they would be placed. He had struggled against the brushes, making incoherent sounds as his slave worked to remove ingrained grime, perhaps for the first time. The men worked ivory needles under black fingernails, then trimmed them with a knife not much larger than the one Cormac kept hidden. He'd managed to snag his belt before they left with that, hanging it himself from a different peg on the wall.

The white-chested slave peered closely at the burns on Cormac's chest. The man looked up then and Cormac held very still. It was the worst moment of the day as he thought one slave might recognise the torments of another. Instead, the man left and returned with a pot of thick unguent. He applied it so lightly, Cormac felt very little pain. His skin lost some of the sting he had felt ever since and he breathed more easily without that tightness. He saw Malvo slap a hand away as his man reached for the hole in his cheek.

'Let him take a look,' Cormac ordered.

Malvo almost replied, but then gave up. He said nothing, just scowled as the same pot was opened and applied to his oldest scars.

That full oiling was followed by rods the slaves took from their belts, this time shaved flat and smooth like shallow spoons. Cormac watched as they were applied to his legs, drawn down the long muscles and coming away with a slick of black oil. He could hardly believe how much filth still came off him. Malvo seemed to be doing even worse, as he exclaimed in shock. The slaves grunted with effort, but the truth was, Cormac could feel muscles relaxing and old pains vanishing.

Someone brought a huge platter of sliced meats, cheeses and grapes, with a jug of wine and two cups. Malvo and Cormac devoured it all and if the slaves thought it was bad manners, they just waited until they were ready, sighing and belching as they climbed back onto the tables.

By the time the whole process was finished, Cormac was fighting sleep, despite his fears. He knew it was dangerous, but an old ache in his lower back had gone and he had eaten cold grapes and drunk wine. His head swam and he yawned, feeling himself drifting.

His attendant yawned in reply and Cormac saw the mouth had no tongue inside it. His thoughts sharpened then, with that reminder of his situation. Presumably, the best bath-houses needed to provide discretion in their staff. They had to be places where men could discuss business and their private lives without having anything repeated. When the slave turned to pick up a fallen cloth, Cormac said, 'Are my feet clean?' to see if they could hear. Neither reacted. Instead, his fellow returned to buff a cloth along his shoulders, so roughly it was almost painful. Deaf . . . and made mute.

He felt a chill. Cormac had been a slave himself, just a few days before. He wished he had a coin to give his attendant. Though what joy the man might find in buying himself free without ears or a tongue was not clear. Cormac shook his head. At least they worked in the warm. The room was heated underfoot, the ceiling domed and fluted, so steam would collect in the runnels and drain away. The whole place was a miracle of Roman ingenuity, the product of clever men. There was nothing he could do for one slave of the Balneae.

Cormac bowed thanks to his attendant when he finally finished and stepped away. The strangers had already moved on, heading deeper into the bath-house. When the slaves trooped out as well, Cormac was left alone with Malvo. They sat back against the tables in a sort of wonder as two more slaves entered with armfuls of clean cloths. One of them reached for his loincloth and Cormac made himself give it up without a fuss. He did not want to draw attention and he had already seen the others thought nothing of nudity. No, his main concern was bumping into the senator.

Malvo copied him, letting fall a rag that had seen better days, or better years. He seemed to have the same worry as the slaves bowed to them both, indicating the way into the bathing rooms.

'What if we meet . . . your friend?' Malvo breathed.

Cormac thought. It was hard to explain why he wasn't as worried as he might have been. Even the prospect of the Silanus household being presented with a bill for the Balneae's services didn't make him sweat. He had an idea how extensive Silanus holdings were. Both father and eldest son were senators. Between the one who had burned Cormac and the Silanus brother he'd watched cremated – along with a dozen other cousins, siblings, uncles and aunts – Silanus holdings were simply vast. The bills and goods flowing in and out of even one of their establishments were too many to count, never mind read. Cormac was sure his little tally would just be added to a score of them, waiting on some spike at the Balneae to be settled at the end of the quarter. In the meantime, he walked naked through a doorway, along a little tiled cloister and through another door, held for him. Steam billowed from it and he entered a caldarium pool, heated as high as a man could bear. Cormac had to bite his tongue not to cry out as he went down steps into the waters, Malvo following his lead like a lost pup.

Cormac thought he would have to retreat from the deepest part when the level reached the burns on his chest. They had only begun to heal and yet the unguent had numbed the skin somehow. He felt the barest of stings as water reached that part – and further, until he was able to dip his whole head. He ran his fingers through his hair as he came up, gasping in awe. Malvo sank himself completely, folding his legs and sitting down. The gangly young man held his breath, though bubbles issued from the hole in his cheek.

They should get out. Cormac knew they should get out. He had no idea how large the Balneae was, but it was a private establishment for members of the nobilitas. He thought it was unlikely to have many rooms of this sort. Yet he had never been submerged in hot water before and he could feel it unclenching parts that had always been tight. For the first time in his life, Cormac understood what Rome could mean. Malvo surfaced at last, lying back with just his face out of the water. They lingered – and that was a mistake.

Cormac heard a voice he knew, accompanied by steps. His sandals had been taken away, to be cleaned or more likely burned. These men had retained theirs to walk on slippery floors, the clack of iron studs unmistakable.

'Of course, I must find the boy a wife now, to secure his inheritance,' Senator Silanus was saying.

Cormac tapped Malvo on the shoulder, but he was already moving. They were naked as the day they were born, but that didn't matter. Both young men moved at a speed no one older would have risked, not on wet tiles. They both skidded as they left the pool, keeping their backs to the party entering from some other part. Cormac's fear was that the senator would not stop at the pool but come straight through, looking for the exit with the fine marble columns.

Behind them, he heard a splash as the senator stepped off the side and plunged into the steaming water. The air was thick with heat and moisture and no voice rose in shock behind them. No one called out and demanded to know what they thought they were doing there.

Naked, Cormac dared not stop in the massage room. Two more strangers were handing togas to the attendants. One of them glanced across and Cormac met his eyes for a moment, seeing a piercing gaze. He dipped his head in greeting, hurrying on before the man could do more than look.

He and Malvo made their way back down a corridor to the entrance. It seemed their movement was not completely unobserved as a door opened and the attendant came bustling out once more. He had garments in his arms and he was red-faced with the suddenness of their appearance.

'Here! Gentlemen, please. There are women guests in this part of the Balneae. These are the clothes you asked for. Please put them on. Your sandals have been cleaned and repaired.'

'Loincloths?' Cormac asked.

The freedman clapped a hand to his forehead and vanished for a moment. He returned with clean ones and they tied them on, sitting on a bench to lace the sandals. As they did so, the freedman looked nervously to a flight of stairs leading to another part of the building.

Cormac grinned at Malvo in private amusement. It almost felt strange to wear clothes again after such a brief time in the nude. Yet he was clean – and he had eaten. He could have managed that same massive platter again all on his own, but his thoughts had sharpened and he knew what he had to do. He had taken small risks before, risks that could easily have meant his life. For such high stakes, small risks were not a good bet, not for him. No, what he needed was a *huge* risk. All or nothing.

10

Seeing the school on the Quirinal was like stepping back in time. It was hard to resist a sense of nostalgia as Cormac stood before the door. The past was *there*, almost within reach. Yet impossible, far beyond his touch. Cormac had been a slave, yes, but a slave with prospects and security – a slave of a vast clan represented in the senate. There were some who said the Silanus family might one day wear purple on the Palatine, if they married well and were both clever and patient.

Cormac could recall the pride he'd felt, even as he scorned his previous self. What did it matter whose slave he had been? Yet he had considered himself better off than most. The ones who laboured in mines or cleared fields hadn't been given rooms with clean parchment and the scratching of reed nibs as their companions. Perhaps that was it, he thought, blushing. He had seen the hard labour of others and assumed airs because *his* work kept him indoors, with no master's brand or tattoo across his face. He grimaced at the innocent he had been. His tattoo had not been visible, but it had still existed. In a way, that was worse than one they could see.

He stood on a quiet street, looking at a small door set inside a larger one. There was no one else around and he reminded himself he had turned up at that spot a hundred times without giving thought to being noticed. He needed to find that same blithe confidence, his first defence against the city.

'Is this the place, then?' Malvo asked.

Cormac jumped, still lost in memories. He nodded firmly, stepping forward and putting his hand on the little bar that had to be raised to gain admittance.

It didn't move, as he'd half-expected.

'Come on, we'll try again later,' Malvo said in a low voice, glancing left and right. He looked like a criminal, Cormac realised. There was just something shifty about him, never mind his memorable face. Any honest house-holder would keep an eye on Malvo the instant he turned up in their street. It was a wonder he hadn't been sent to the mines years before.

'The magister sleeps late sometimes,' Cormac said quietly. 'I found . . . if I jiggle the bar like this, the locking peg . . . can be made to . . .' he heard something drop on its cord and grinned, 'fall.'

The door creaked open and Cormac went in as if he owned the place. That was what Malvo failed to appreciate. Innocent people walked like they didn't care who saw. The trick to not being innocent was doing things the same way. No nervous looks up and down the street, no turning away or hunching of shoulders as vigiles passed by. Cormac real-ised he would have to explain all that to Malvo, before his suspicious ways had them thrown back into the tullianum.

Once inside, putting the peg back in the bar was a calculated choice. Cormac did not want to be surprised by anyone else trying to enter, not then. Though he supposed any arriving pupils might jiggle it free as he'd done, or even bang on the door. Cormac smiled as he heard the magister snoring in the schoolroom. The day's lessons would not begin for a while and the man was a dependably heavy drinker. Cormac had smelled sour vomit and old wine on him more than once. He remembered too the times he and others had crept in, then let a chair fall with a crash, startling the magister from sleep. *That* remained funny, even in memory.

Cormac walked with no caution at all across the little yard inside the street door. It wasn't much and there was a line of washing strung across it. Tiled roofs formed an open square above, enough to let in air and sun. It was a peaceful place and Cormac felt his fists clench. He had been happy there, despite everything. Did everyone know their old school well enough to steal from it? He wondered.

The storeroom was where the magister kept his most valuable supplies. Cormac tried that door as well, but was not surprised to find it locked. This was no simple bar and peg either. He could see an actual keyhole. Cormac thought he could kick it in, but that would mean noise and, worse, proof that someone had robbed the school. The theft would be reported to the vigiles and perhaps they'd even start looking for a boy with cause to resent the magister, one who had been denied his gradus scriptorum. Sweat ran cold in Cormac's armpits. He just wanted to slip in and out, with no one the wiser.

He glowered, then crossed the yard once again, peering

in a slot window to where the magister snored with feet on the table. The key was on him, Cormac knew. Malvo pressed against his shoulder, trying to see. Cormac raised his eyes in frustration, or silent prayer.

'Stay here, all right?' he whispered to Malvo. 'If someone comes . . . or anything happens, just get out and meet me back at the bath-house.'

Malvo began to shake his head, but Cormac was already moving. If he stopped, he knew his nerve would fail. Only his easy familiarity with the school let him enter, though his hands trembled and he could taste metal in his mouth.

The desks were exactly as he remembered. That shouldn't have been so strange, he knew that. *He* was the one who had changed, or been changed, over a very short time. He was the one in that room to steal, risking fresh-minted freedom to gain an advantage in a city that cared nothing for his success or failure. Somehow, as he crept to where the magister sprawled, Cormac still felt the sting of being denied his gradus.

The teacher's mouth was open. Cormac could see his teeth, including missing molars on one side at the back. A wineskin flopped across the desk, something Cormac had seen many times before. Some Romans drank from cups and clay amphorae. Others preferred the Greek style, a skin they could squeeze, directing a line of liquid to the back of their throats. The thing looked flaccid, Cormac noted. He hoped the magister had enjoyed a skinful before passing out.

He froze as the man scratched himself in sleep, smacking his lips but not quite waking. Cormac was like a statue as he waited for him to settle. This was madness, but he could see the cord around the magister's neck. Cormac knew there was a key on the end, hidden under the grubby tunic. As a trusted student of the Silanus estate, he'd been sent to fetch slates or papyrus half a dozen times. The key had been tossed to him and he'd snatched it from the air with pride at being trusted. The memory was like sitting on the candle box for Marcus.

He reached down and hooked the cord with a finger, holding his breath as he drew it up. The key was revealed and Cormac could feel his face reddening with effort. The magister's eyes were closed, but it was too easy to imagine them opening, rheumy and dazed, then furious.

The key hung in the air, polished by time and touch so that it shone gold rather than the dark brown of older bronze. Cormac inched forward, easing it up and up, peeling the cord from the man's neck.

It came free and he folded key and cord into one hand before moving. If those eyes opened now, he thought he could pretend he had come to ask for another chance to take his exam. He even wondered if the magister might actually be open to such an offer, perhaps against a part of his future income. It was an idea to think on.

Step by trembling step, he retreated from the little room, pressing his back to the wall of the courtyard outside. He was hidden from the road there and just breathed for a time, while Malvo stared.

Children's voices startled them both. Cormac had the horrible thought of being discovered by some new crop of slaves and freedmen, or worse, sons and daughters of nobilitas families. He felt a clutch of fear at the thought that he might even be recognised. He could imagine them asking the magister and the man discovering the key had gone. He was sweating again, he realised, though at least he was moving.

He used the key to open the storeroom, reaching in as someone began to rattle the bar outside, exactly as he had done. He grabbed a pile of vellum sheets, shoving them under his tunic where they sat next to the skin. Cormac looked longingly into the gloom for a moment. There was ink in there and reeds and papyrus – everything he could possibly need. No, he was out of time. He turned the key in the lock and stood back as the peg fell and a new class began to charge in. They had to be in the last year of preparation for their own gradus, he thought enviously. Some of them had moustaches and the swagger of young men. They were incredibly, unthinkingly noisy after the silence before! Cormac strode across the courtyard just in front of them, passing into the schoolroom without missing a step. He leaned over the magister and used his body to block the view as he draped the key back around the man's neck.

Cormac straightened up and breathed in relief, just as one of the grinning young men let a chair fall. That crash made Cormac jump and when he glanced down, it was to see the magister awake and staring in confusion. Cormac could feel the sheets he had stolen then, hot against his skin.

'What are *you* doing here?' the man said, rubbing sleep from his eyes as he sat up. He spotted the wineskin and swept it from the desk, hiding it from view.

'I am sorry to disturb you, magister,' Cormac said quickly. 'I wanted to ask if you'd let me sit the gradus again. I am freed. I can't pay right now, but I could promise a tithe of my income, after. For six months, perhaps.'

The man scratched his jaw as he considered.

'I might say yes, though it would be for a full year to be worth my while. I do not set the task though. The treasury choose the texts. They are the ones who decree each pass and fail as well. I'm sorry. I could use the extra money, but there's nothing I can do until the next exam. Come back then and I will let you sit a few lessons before. You'll pass then, I'm sure.'

'I would have passed this time,' Cormac said, his frustration showing. 'I was taken out before the morning was half over.'

'Ah yes, of course. Well, perhaps. Nothing is certain. Still, that is my offer. You were a clever one, I recall. Return to me in six months and I'll let you sit – in return for . . . a lien of a tenth part, on two years of future income.' He saw anger rising in Cormac's eyes, but shrugged. 'Or you can pay. If you have twelve silver denarii, I would be happy to enrol you as a private student for the entire course.'

Cormac clenched his jaw, suddenly pleased he was not truly asking for help. He knew he had seen that figure of twelve denarii before, on a scroll of accounts at the estate. The numbers then had meant nothing to him – just as they had meant nothing to his old master. A denarius was pay for a week of work, he knew that much. Each one could be exchanged for four sestertius coins, or sixteen coppers. It had been the currency of Rome and her territories for over two hundred years. Cormac had seen a small locked chest of them just once, when Antoninus had paid craftsmen to set a mosaic.

Cormac had to revise his assessment of the magister's poverty. If the man accepted twelve denarii from each of his students . . . He shook his head, irritated by one who drank away a fortune, yet still seemed angry at the world.

'I will consider it,' Cormac said, trying on confidence like a cloak. The magister looked amused. Perhaps he saw a boastful young man, but there was nothing Cormac could do to make his words ring true. He wanted to knock the smile off the man's face, but the vellum sheets crackled when he folded his arms across his chest. He needed to leave.

Cormac turned to see the desks had filled while he and the magister talked. There were at least twelve boys there, shoving one another on the long benches. Cormac glanced across those without interest. If anything, they were a painful reminder of everything he had lost. It wouldn't . . .

His thoughts skipped as he sensed different eyes on him. He was almost at the door and would have gone through it if not for that prickling awareness. When he looked to the corner of the room, it was to see a young woman of about his age or a little younger. She was dressed in a stola robe so layered it must have weighed as much as she did. He could tell almost nothing about her height or shape in that mass of cloth. Even the throat that might have been open to the air was covered by some inner garment. She wore the uppermost folds raised into a hood, covering all but a finger's width of black hair. Some sort of fine stones glittered along her forehead there, like spots of blood.

Her eyes were very dark as she watched him in turn, a silent appraisal he had felt for some time. Had she seen him place the key around the magister's neck? He didn't think she had been in the room then. He felt his testicles creep at the thought. If she'd been early and sat in silence, he thought she might have seen it all. By the gods, he hoped that wasn't true. His focus had been completely on the snoring man. He wouldn't have missed a single young woman sitting in a corner, surely? If he had, she would have denounced him!

He stood still, holding her gaze. Her eyes widened slightly as she realised he had caught her staring. Yet she did not look away. Cormac felt his mouth dry. He felt a wild urge to slide along that bench and ask her name. The magister was handing out wax slates for the rest to practise their letters. The man was clearing his throat, his impatience increasing for a petitioner who hadn't yet left.

'Class has begun,' the magister announced primly.

Cormac blinked, the spell broken. He saw the girl flush, a delicate colour along her jaw. Her hands appeared from somewhere in the cloth, laying out little items he knew as well as his own name. An inkstone and reed, a phial of water. He wondered if she also carried a tiny razor to trim the reed.

The magister cleared his throat with more emphasis and Cormac shot him a look of pure venom. Her skin was lightly tanned, burnished almost gold by the sun. Her hands were paler, perhaps more often hidden. Her jaw was a little wide and her nose had a small bump on it, either natural or because it had once been broken. He did not think she would be considered beautiful to all men, but still, his feet had taken root.

'Master Cormac! I wonder if I may be allowed to begin today's lesson? Or will you stand there making calf eyes for the rest of it?'

The magister was amusing himself, but he had also told her Cormac's name. It saved him from being knocked down when he laid a hand on Cormac's arm and tried to turn him to the doorway. Cormac smiled and when she smiled back, it was as the sun rising. He sensed the teacher bracing for a big push. Cormac bowed – to her and not to him – then left, the hand across his chest preventing the sheets from dropping out at his knees.

Malvo was still peering nervously in, denied the chance to see whoever had caught Cormac's attention by the angle of the door.

'Come, we have a great deal of work to do,' Cormac announced. He wanted his voice to carry to the one who had stared at him so. He had never wanted to impress anyone before, not like that. Yet he did in that moment and he could not resist beaming as they went out and he felt the cobbles of the street under his sandals. He could not have explained the rise in his mood. Malvo looked at him as if he'd gone mad.

They left the school behind, slipping into streets even busier than before. It seemed the city did not slow for an emperor's funeral. Whatever those arrangements would be, it felt as if someone had kicked an ant nest and sent them all scurrying.

When Cormac had been a slave, the Silanus carriage had always waited to take him back to the estate. It actually waited for Marcus Silanus, but Cormac had sat with him, forty miles in and out of Rome. He'd never had to walk city roads before and set against those memories, he was surprised anew at how many people there were. Some of them pushed past rudely, while others took one look at Malvo's glowering face and gave them both a wide berth.

'What now?' Malvo said, panting slightly as he was forced to keep up.

Cormac put aside thoughts of the mysterious beauty

back in the class. In such fine cloth, she had to be the daughter of a noble family, so far above him in that moment as to be another mountain peak. For the first time he could remember, he felt that distance as an evil thing. He grinned then, amused at himself. He had not put aside thoughts of her at all.

Cormac took a moment to reach inside his tunic, using his thumb to judge the vellum sheets. True calfskin, smooth and thick. He'd left many more than he took. The magister might not notice a few missing for months, or even for ever. There was no damage left behind, no hue and cry or vigiles searching for them. Cormac was trembling with exhaustion and . . . yes, hunger once again. His stomach ached.

'I need a quiet place, Malvo, a place where I will not be disturbed for a few hours. With these sheets and my own reed and ink, I think I can make something of them – a new life for us both even.'

He saw something like awe in the twist-faced young man and realised he had just included Malvo in his plans. A note of caution forced its way into his thoughts and he wondered how he could bind Malvo to him. He needed loyalty, or they would both be destroyed.

'After that,' he said, 'I had a thought about changing your face.'

Malvo leaned back as if he'd been slapped.

'What do you mean "changing"?' he demanded. 'I'm not paying to be cut, not again. It is the way it is.'

'You frighten children and dogs, Malvo,' Cormac said. He was looking ahead as they walked, moving around a cart that blocked that part of the road. He didn't see the hurt he caused, not in a big, callous youth he thought could never be wounded by mere words. 'Let's see if we can do something about that.'

They passed through what had once been a gate in a stretch of ancient city wall. Though Rome sprawled through into the field of the Campus Martius, that part still stood. What had once been an old guard's watchtower had become some merchant's house, with flowers in terracotta tubs on stone windowsills. Cormac looked at it with envy.

'I will own a place like that,' he said to Malvo. 'I swear it, on . . .'

He had been about to invoke the household gods of the Silanus family, the lares who had protected him for ten long years. He set his jaw. Ahead was a small temple that looked almost deserted. He saw a figure in painted marble stood at its door. Twin bearded faces looked out on the passing crowds. The door was his symbol, of course – Janus, the god of change and gates and endings. Cormac nodded. The first month of the year was named for Janus, but he had never attracted a large following, not like Jove, Venus and all the rest. Those were gods with roles and purpose. Soldiers prayed to Mars, messengers prayed to Mercury. All men whispered to Asclepius or Apollo when their loved ones fell ill. Janus, though, was a god for those who feared change, or more rarely, for those who sought it out. It was a more subtle thought than the desire to win a lover or destroy an enemy. The temple was as old as the piece of wall, a remnant left behind as the city grew past old boundaries. Travellers would have stopped there once, centuries before. Cormac found he was smiling.

'Janus,' he said. 'There is a suitable patron, wouldn't you say? It looks quiet, anyway.'

He led the way and Malvo trailed behind. Cormac passed through an ornate bronze door, with symbols of the seasons in relief. The clatter and noise of the street dwindled and he took a longer breath. This place suited him well for what he needed to do. He could not stop, he told himself. If he stopped to rest or think, it might all fall apart.

There was no priest inside to challenge them. Cormac had begun to prepare a few words, a desire to learn of the god who had presented himself in his moment of greatest need. It did not have to be a lie if he took Janus as his patron, he assured himself. No one offended the gods lightly, for fear of what fate might bring down on their heads.

In an alcove away from prying eyes, Cormac set Malvo on guard against interruption and brought out his fragment of inkstone from his belt. It was no larger than his thumbnail, smaller than it had been. He wondered if it would be enough. With utmost care, he spat on it and used the reed to mingle compressed black dust and spittle, forming an ink they called 'Atramentum Librarium'. Cormac had seen scrolls of vellum that were centuries old, the letters as black as the day they were written.

He counted the sheets he had taken once again, wishing he had more. His hands trembled and he could not afford a mistake. There were just three and in that place, he prayed to Janus it would be enough.

Cornelia Furia collected her water, reed and inkstone at the end of the lesson, passing back the tablet. Not that she had been allowed to use them. She brought those things each day in hope rather than expectation. Her letters were neat and she loved to form them – it was a shame to see the magister wipe his wax slates with a warm cloth, smearing her work with all the others as if the hours of labour had never existed. She longed to be given white sheets of parchment, but she was fourteen and there was no chance of that. Nor would her mother hear of such a thing. The Furii were an old family, but not as wealthy as some of those who clustered around the emperor . . . She paused in her thoughts. The old emperor. The new one was a young man of great beauty, tall and slim. Cornelia had glimpsed him once at a dance on the Palatine, where wine had flowed and the greatest musicians of the empire had competed for Tiberius to see them. Gaius Caesar had been there that night, his large dark eyes reminding her of a deer. She shook her head ruefully. He would be married to some Silanus girl, or perhaps one of the Valerii. Her mother said those families had fingers in a dozen pies. They played a dangerous game, she thought, just for wealth and power.

For a moment, as the rest of the class clattered out, Cornelia could look into the afternoon sun and dream. She had done so many times and was surprised to find her thoughts returning to the young man she had seen creeping about at the beginning of the class. He usually came in the afternoons, she knew that, tumbling out of a fine carriage with his great block of a companion. Their paths had not crossed until that day, but Cornelia remembered his face. 'Cor . . . mac,' she murmured to herself. She had a name for him then, though such a strange one! His gaze had been dark, almost hostile as he caught her staring. He was closer to her own age, unlike Gaius Caesar.

'Who was that rude young man, magister?' she asked suddenly.

The teacher jumped and she smiled again at the way she could vanish sometimes, as if the world swallowed her up.

'Ah, Domina Cornelia, I did not realise you had stayed behind. Young man? The one who would not leave until I made him?'

She nodded, though she seemed less impressed than he had hoped.

'Cormac, my dear. An uncouth Briton, as I recall. Slave until a few days back, though he claimed to have been made free.'

Cornelia's hopes broke into shards. She would be married to a praetor or a senator, she had no doubt. No freed slave would ever take her hand, no matter how stern and handsome he had been. Families like the Silani or Aemilii already had wealth. The Furii had only three sisters, with a chance to make the best marriages they could. Yet for just a moment, it had seemed as if she and the young man had been the only two in that little schoolroom.

'If you would like . . .' the magister said, 'I could read you one of the senate speeches from yesterday. I had it copied especially.'

She felt her skin crawl, but Cornelia held out her hand for the scroll. He looked disappointed, but the Furii were still not a family to cross. Cornelia smiled to ease his disappointment.

'I will read it myself, magister. Thank you. Until tomorrow.'

It would be a struggle, but if she had to stay up all night, she would labour over it until she understood every word. She sighed as she swept out, feeling the constriction of the heavy stola. It was meant to preserve her modesty, though others her age wore lighter garments. Her mother insisted on it, so Cornelia had to walk like a pavilion.

She crumpled the scroll in one fist as she went, seeing her guards lounging on the street. They had no fine carriage for her, but they would keep her safe from clutching hands and beggars as she made her way back to the house. To the prison her mother called a house, she amended sourly. For all its irritations, her trip to the school each afternoon was one of her only freedoms. She thought again of the one called 'Cormac'. He'd gone off on some errand of his own, free as a bird like all the other boys. She wondered where he was at that moment and envied him.

I I

Three sheets of white vellum, cut square with perfect precision. Three chances at a new life, if he had the skill. The finest trace of veins showed on the surfaces, the only sign that they had ever been part of a living creature. Cormac ran a hand over the first, making a soft hiss. Parchment came from sheep, goat, even rabbit skin. Vellum, though, was made of calf and had a feeling of richness. Each sheet he had stolen would cost a sestertius, even two.

He began to write, shaping letters neatly, returning to the piece of inkstone in a relaxed rhythm. He had to sharpen the reed and spit again, getting a trace of black ink on his lower lip. He didn't notice. On a stone sill in a temple to the god Janus, he plied his craft. This was what he had been trained to do, ever since arriving at the estate. Cormac had a good hand. More importantly, he knew the words he needed. He had learned to read from the documents of a wealthy estate. He knew how such things were meant to sound, the sort of words that sounded official. There was a whole language to it, but he had the keys.

His manumissio formed again under his hands, the words taken from his mind's eye. He found he was even copying the style of letters in the original, so perfect was his recollection. When he was done, he slid the little seal of Silanus from his belt and took a smear of black onto his thumb, wetting it with his tongue. He pressed the ring stone onto the vellum and peeled back carefully, leaving a neat oval, a boar in a laurel wreath with tiny letters: 'Jun. Sil.'

He sat back in awe then, looking on a finished thing.

'Malvo?' He could not resist showing it. Malvo came closer, but of course he could not decipher the letters. The wonder of the achievement was lost on him.

'It is the same as the one you burned,' Cormac said.

Malvo shrugged uncomfortably, sensing he was being blamed. In frustration, Cormac gestured him back to his vigil and returned to work. He felt an ache begin in his shoulders and wondered if it reflected a greater strain. He had owned a manumissio, after all. A case could be made that he had a claim to one, even just a copy.

What he was about to do was an entirely different beast – and he hardly dared think of the third sheet, not then. Plans spun in his thoughts, but he could not quite look at them. Instead, he made himself concentrate on the second. Half a scribe's life lay in such work, he reminded himself.

Those lines were harder as he had only seen one before – and that an old version. The gradus scriptorum could not be sealed with a Silanus mark either . . . His plan fell into pieces as he realised, the taste of ashes in his mouth. He could not even remember the symbol of the treasury, not enough to remake it on fresh vellum. Given time, he could have carved a little stone seal with a knife tip, but he had not thought of that.

Shame burned. He'd had a plan, of making a gradus as perfect as his deed of manumission, good enough to fool the eye of a treasury scribe even. He shook his head angrily as he put it aside and struggled once more for calm. He needed a win. Though his heart pounded and his vision blurred, though he was hungry and weak from lack of sleep, he knew the last one had to be perfect.

The great houses spent fortunes every day. To pay their clients, to maintain their status, to throw banquets and festivals and betrothals all took fortunes. Those fortunes came from rents or war, or were mined from the ground. Half of Rome paid rent to the other half – and the great families owned entire swathes of every city and town across the empire. Their agents collected it all and passed chests of silver to factors for the Silani, or Aemilii. Clever men then checked those figures for discrepancies – but that was a problem for another day. Most importantly of all, moneylenders in the city would take delivery of bulky, dirty coins of copper, silver, even gold. They would offer a note against the heavy specie, a note that could be redeemed in another lender's establishment, or just kept as an asset. Or spent, Cormac assured himself. Antoninus had explained once how those single sheets, stamped and signed by half a dozen owners, could be exchanged for silver from Gaul to Jerusalem.

Cormac found himself hesitating, the reed nib hovering above the page while precious ink dried. If he did this, there was no undoing it. This was the great gamble, the highest reward. He knew he could have lost his life just for using the Silanus name in a bath-house. He could have lost it for pretending he was a client and bluffing a praetor of the court. That would have been a mean and petty ending, he thought.

This was a greater undertaking. If he pulled it off, he would have funds to start out as a scribe – or whatever the future held. He had a vision of himself as a man of authority and high office, like a praetor or the governor of some territory. The girl with the dark eyes would not scorn him then, he thought, sucking one end of his reed. No, she'd melt against him, as her protector . . . It was a very pleasant picture, but he dragged himself back from it, forced himself to concentrate.

Cormac knew better than most how great houses kept their accounts, at least if the Silanus estate was anything to go by. With a little luck, he might redeem a moneylender's scrip for silver or gold, but eventually, that very piece of vellum would find its way to a Silanus accountant. Of course, it might change hands a dozen times before then, if he'd understood old Antoninus properly. As long as they were redeemed in the end, money orders were a sort of currency in themselves. Antoninus had spoken of it all in awe.

Cormac swallowed nervously. The entire system depended on honour, on the note of a noble house being worth something. He was about to stick a knife into that system and hope for the best. His fear was that he had missed some check or balance he had never been told.

Would it work? The truth was he could not be certain. Very few people could read and write. Fewer still understood the basics of the gradus – and of *that* noble breed of scribes, most were employed by great houses or the treasury in Rome. It was one reason there had always been a few young women in the magister's classes. Wives often kept accounts for their husbands, in shops and warehouses across Rome. Just to pay staff and keep a record of profits, usually. It was a useful skill, but in the wider world, still vanishingly rare.

Cormac realised he might in that moment be the only one in Rome with this idea. He could taste metal once again. His hand trembled and he made himself write, breathing through his nose. His last sheet had to be perfect. There was no other.

On the street, Cormac walked at a bustle, as if he was late. That was something he understood without having to be told. Honest men didn't run, or look back as if they feared being caught. No, but they did walk quickly. It made them both pant, but no one frowned or watched two busy young men. He and Malvo became almost invisible. They marched away from the temple of Janus, heading south into a maze.

'I need a leather bag, Malvo,' Cormac said suddenly. 'Something that looks like it has been used a thousand times, something a bonded messenger would carry. I can't just walk into a lender's shop with a sheet of vellum.'

Malvo indicated a bench in a small courtyard. With neatly tended boxes of blooming narcissi and oleander around its edges and ivy up the walls, it looked owned rather than public, but there was no one there. Cormac wondered if he was becoming intoxicated with this new ability. Perhaps it was being set free from the praetor's court that had confirmed it. He could see rules, well enough to avoid them. It felt a little like having a cup of wine in his blood, a slight brightness. With an effort of will, he tried to rein it in, to double-check his idea before sheer recklessness brought the world down on their heads. Yet the square was quiet and he could see a trickle of water in the fountain. He looked around to see who was watching, then muttered a curse. Honest men didn't check, they just went in.

Clenching his jaw, he entered the little space between buildings. This was a wealthy part of the city and no voices went up in challenge. The houses would not be empty though, he knew that. Even in the hours for lunch, there would be mothers and wives and daughters in them, per-haps house slaves working to clean or improve themselves. A slave could be an investment, Cormac knew, if he was willing to learn. After all, when he bought himself free, the money came to the family who owned him, at the market rate for his skill.

Malvo vanished as Cormac sat down, disappearing into the busy streets outside. Cormac saw how pleased the tall young man was to be given an actual task, something Cormac needed and could not get himself. It was part of the reason he had asked for the bag, he realised. Another was that he was simply afraid. Cormac folded and refolded the three sheets of vellum as he sat there, giving them a little more age. He even collected dust from the stone yard and rubbed it along the creases, though delicately. He needed them to look less than brand new, not spoiled. Yet at that moment, they were all potential – and no actual crime had been committed.

If he followed it through and went to a moneylender, he knew he might be hunted for the rest of his life. The treasury took crimes against the structures of Rome more seriously than murder. Death was not uncommon in the city after all, for fools and criminals in particular. Yet coins and moneylenders made the empire work. If he got himself caught, they would be savage . . .

Or they might never find him, he made himself add. Cormac rubbed his eyes, impossibly weary and hungry. The stake was his life either way, just about. He had no money for a meal or a place to sleep that night. So he would gamble. He would *not* be a slave again. That much was certain.

He closed his eyes . . . and was startled awake. The sun had jolted across the sky and Malvo stood before him, panting and looking pleased with himself. He held a messenger's satchel, a flat bag on a long strap that would do very well. Cormac took it from him as he came back to speed.

'Where did you get this?' he said in pleasure.

'Where do you think? You said you wanted a messenger's bag. I took one from a messenger.'

Cormac stood up slowly. He could hear raised voices nearby. Were they coming closer?

'I thought you would fetch coins and buy one! Or borrow one from a friend, maybe! You are perhaps the most recognisable man in this city and you're telling me you just robbed a messenger on the street? How far away? Can you hear those voices? Tell me they're not coming for us.'

Malvo scratched his lopsided chin as he looked back.

'Yeah, we should probably move,' he said.

Cormac made a strangled sound, rising from the bench and marching away from the outrage behind them.

Malvo had the grace to look abashed as Cormac pushed further south and west. The sheets of vellum made a little packet in the bag, alongside a man's personal papers Cormac didn't dare stop to examine. The Tiber was nearby and he had only visited that river once before, having begged Plato to let him fill his phial there the week before the gradus. It wasn't a part of the city he knew and so he almost missed the premises of a moneylender. Cormac felt his heart race – confidence or lack of food, he couldn't be sure.

'Wait here,' he told Malvo firmly. The way he walked was the way he would enter the shop, he told himself. As if he had every right to be there, as if he was late and hurried and weary.

Cormac reached for the door, but it was opened from within. He showed no surprise, just glanced at the massive figure inside who had seen him coming. No doubt the man was a slave employed by the moneylender, a large man used to violence. Cormac ignored him like furniture as he entered, shuffling through his bag for the right papers.

'Salve,' he said distractedly.

The owner came through from a back room, having heard the door. He saw a harried-looking messenger, checking his bag for whichever paper he wished to present. The man adopted a professional smile and stood behind a counter, waiting.

'Cutting it a bit fine today,' Cormac said with a shake of his head. 'Two more stops after this as well. With the emperor's funeral, it's all rush, rush, every moment.'

'The gods bless his soul,' the moneylender said piously.

Cormac heard other voices then, from a back room. He hid his dismay and produced the sheet he wanted. The man's attention was on it, so he didn't see how Cormac's hand trembled, or the way sweat ran down his neck. He was still fairly clean from the baths, in a new tunic and dusty sandals. He looked the part.

'What's this? Silanus?' the moneylender said. 'I don't see too many from Lugdunum.'

'Yes. To be redeemed,' Cormac said idly.

He was just the messenger, he reminded himself. He didn't care where the thing had been handed over for gold the first time. Of course, he'd actually chosen the city of Lugdunum with great care. He'd seen a dozen of those orders in his life, brought to the estate to be honoured from Silanus funds. One that had been made in Rome was too easy to check, he was certain of that. Instead, he'd decided on a date and place to reflect a thousand miles of road, over the Alps. It meant no one could recognise the names he had scrawled on the vellum, names drawn from his own imagination.

He knew it was perfect, right to the second signature, almost across the first. That looked as if it had been signed in haste by some official in Gaul, too busy even to turn the sheet the right way round. There was power in the story of it and the moneylender only nodded as he read.

'I can give you seven right now, with another order for three. That's all I have in the shop. Business has been a little slow recently.'

'I'd hoped to get it all,' Cormac said. 'I don't want to have to come back.'

He was out of his depth in the instant. Should he argue? He wanted to just accept the man's offer, but would that seem suspiciously eager? A real messenger wouldn't want to go back to his employer with another lender's note, would he? Though . . . it would be a real one, that could be redeemed in turn. His mind spun in wonder. His note was real as well in that moment. This was the currency of Rome, money created from ink and air.

The lender shrugged. He really didn't care what some lazy messenger wanted.

'There's another place two streets along. You could try there. Seven is all I have today.'

'Fine then – and a note for the other three,' Cormac said. He made himself sound irritable, but then gave that up. The money was not his. There was a limit to how much he would care about it.

'I expect there's a fair bit of bustle in Silanus circles at the moment,' the man said, making conversation as he unlocked a chest beneath the counter.

Cormac nodded, unsure what he meant. His heart was beating so hard it actually hurt.

'There always is,' Cormac said, when the man looked up.

'Yes, but with the wedding coming, I mean. I heard about that and I thought, "Silanus is rising," you know?'

Cormac nodded, though he still had no idea what the man was talking about.

'It will be a great day . . .' he murmured. That seemed safe enough.

'I'd say so!' the moneylender replied, coming back to the counter. He was chuckling to himself, quite relaxed, just chatting with a customer. Cormac made himself smile in return, though he thought it was probably more a rictus than anything pleasant.

'I saw her once, you know,' the lender went on, 'Junia Claudilla – lovely young lady. I was just telling my wife – that Silanus family is rising, I said.'

'Yes, you said,' Cormac echoed.

He saw the man frown and pause as he opened a pouch and began to count coins. Fine, it seemed he could not be too impatient. Cormac knew the name Junia Claudilla, though he'd never met her. She was a sister to Senator Decimus Silanus, sister too to the master he'd lost out at the estate. It seemed they had made a good marriage for her. He would be expected to know every detail of course, as a messenger for the Silanus family. He dared not ask a single question, though the news had passed him by.

He made himself look around the little shop, seeing items others had brought in to sell or borrow against. There was a fair selection, but when the moneylender began to count coins, Cormac could not have looked away even if he'd wanted to. He was sure a messenger would watch for counterfeit or a miscount, but the truth was, Cormac forgot to breathe.

The moneylender too was watching the coins as he laid them out, like golden buttons on the counter top.

'That's seven . . .' He added a little pouch of leather from under the counter, counting them in again as Cormac watched. 'And . . . there is the note for three aurei.'

He handed over a folded sheet that was older and far grubbier than the one Cormac had created. It had been held by dozens of different hands. He wondered how many things it had bought, how many times it had been redeemed. That was the strangeness of the system. No matter how often they were handed in and exchanged, they were never destroyed. With just a little luck, his order for ten gold coins would still be somewhere in Rome a dozen years from that point, handled over and over again without a breath of suspicion.

Cormac cast an eye over the smaller order. It carried four signatures and was marked with a crest of the Furii house – dated two years before. He made himself shrug, though he wanted to stare at it in awe, then folded it away in his satchel and nodded thanks to the moneylender. The man made his living from loans, Cormac reminded himself. This was merely the life's blood of the city – a river larger and more powerful than the Tiber itself. Somehow, Cormac had dipped an arm into it and not been swept away.

'You have a man with you, I hope?' the moneylender said. 'The street gangs watch for messengers leaving places like mine, just so you know. Not my responsibility, all right? Once you leave the shop, it's on you. Understand?'

Cormac felt a little better about robbing him in that moment. He made himself look haughty and offended.

'I'm too quick for them – and yes, of course I have a lad with me! Don't worry, I can look after myself.'

He bustled back to the street door and waited for the looming fellow to open it. He didn't nod his thanks. Free men hardly noticed slaves, after all. Rich free men espccially.

'How did it go?' Malvo whispered as they strode away.

Cormac waited for a shout to go up behind. If it did, he would run, he decided. He would run till his heart burst.

'Did it work or not?' Malvo persisted.

Cormac kept his silence until they were two streets away, as if he might break a spell if he spoke too soon.

'Keep an eye out for street gangs, Malvo. They might be watching for a nice fat bird like me to come along. Yes, it worked. By the gods, it worked!'

He stopped, panting, leaning against a wall though he

knew it was wrong. Messengers didn't waste time in side streets. It made him a target.

With a wrench, he pulled himself upright. The world swam, but they had funds.

He squinted at Malvo, seeing again the missing nostril and the hole in his cheek.

'Malvo, we need to buy some things. But not here. Before we spend a single copper, we should put half the city behind us. If we head back to where we met, will you be safer?'

Malvo snorted.

'Of course. Those are my streets. I can get anything there.'

'Good. I need wax . . . and a bit of tin, leather . . . a dozen other things.'

Malvo beamed, which was a disconcerting expression. When Cormac moved on, he didn't see the calculating look Malvo gave him. Ten gold pieces was a fortune, more than the gang leader had ever seen in his life. His gaze dropped to the satchel he had already stolen once, leaving its owner unconscious in an alleyway. He liked Cormac, he really did. He was an innocent in the city, but he seemed able to move through it – to *think* his way through it with skills Malvo could hardly understand. He had enjoyed the mad rush from bath-house to temple to moneylender – and now, to the gods only knew where. Cormac was becoming a friend, he sensed that much. Yet he had friends. Ten gold pieces was worth losing one.

12

Cormac made Malvo walk until they were both limping. He didn't even begin to relax until they'd crossed the Via Aurelia. That great artery crossed the Tiber from the west, cutting part of the city in two. Once he and Malvo had negotiated the carts and crowds there, it felt like they were leaving behind all they had done.

Cormac had seen two shops for rent that might have suited him, if they hadn't still been north of the Aurelia and too close to the moneylender. He knew he had to lose himself, to make it almost impossible to stumble across the man again. Not if he was to put down roots – and the gold coins meant he could. He and his weary companion trudged on.

Malvo became more alert, visibly warier as they moved south. Cormac had thought he might relax in his old haunts, but the lopsided young man seemed nervous, casting glances about like a thief until Cormac wanted to shake him. This was part of the city Cormac didn't know, but there were still wealthy districts there. In the same way he disguised himself instinctively, he sensed he should remain in areas where no one *expected* to be robbed. All Cormac could do was judge by the length of garden walls. Too long and he ran the risk of a property being owned by one of the great families; too short or too many floors and there might be a dozen families crammed in, all knowing one another's business.

He ignored a number of signs advertising rooms or workshops, until he came to one that opened on a little courtyard, set back from the road. The day had grown late and they both needed to rest. Like the spot where Cormac had fallen asleep before, this was well tended and quiet. Cormac read the words on the sign rather than the crude drawing of coins – in being able to do that, he was already proof of serious intent.

The man who came out to greet them was elderly, hook-nosed and stooped as if the evening sun was a great weight. He smiled even so at a potential customer, nodding as Cormac pointed to the plaque.

'Come in, come in,' the old man said, gesturing. 'I am the owner, Lanatus. The rent is very reasonable. You are the third to view in the last hour. Did you see the others leave? No? You must have just missed them. I tell you, this shop won't stay empty for long.'

'It includes this little courtyard?' Cormac asked.

The man nodded, beaming toothlessly.

'All built by my own hands forty years ago – and solid. One of the first shops on this street.'

They followed him into an empty place that smelled of sawdust and camphor oil. It had been stripped of its wares, made ready for new owners. Rome didn't stand still, Cormac realised. He inspected a few joists and the counter top as if he knew what he was doing. He had an idea to look for tiny holes of woodworm as well as to sniff for damp, but it all seemed sound enough.

'It is set back from the road,' he said doubtfully. 'There'll be no passing trade, so I'll have to put up a sign.'

'What is your business, if I may ask?' said the old man.

'Scribe,' Cormac said with pride. 'Wills, divorces, marriages and births, contracts, law cases, disputes of all kinds. I'll need a storeroom at the back, with a good lock and just one key.'

'I had one made to keep my tools safe,' Lanatus said with a smile. 'A good cobbler makes his own. There is an artificer at the end of this street,' the old man said. 'Varus could fit a new lock for you, I'm sure. Or you could just use my key. There is only one. The rent is by the half year though, I'm afraid. Paid in advance.'

'How much are you asking?' Cormac said as lightly as possible. He could feel the weight of gold in his satchel and it made him giddy.

'This is a good area . . .' the man said. He was making a calculation, Cormac saw, guessing how much he could ask. He frowned.

'I can't pay much until I start work. I have a little from my . . . father, but I'm newly qualified – just last week.'

'Still, I've never met a poor scribe,' the old man said. He rubbed his jaw with one hand, making a rasping sound over white bristles. 'I can't ask less than sixty denarii.'

He saw Cormac's face fall in shock and went straight on.

'Look, I can let you have the shop for fifty, if we close the deal today. With a room upstairs as well, so you save on rent. I made the bed up there and it won't come down anyway.'

Cormac swallowed. A single aureus coin was worth twenty-five denarii – a hundred sestertii or four *hundred* copper asses. To give up two of his little cache was to spend more money in a single transaction than he had ever witnessed. Yet he had it. He realised the old man had dropped his price once and that would have to do. The shop was warm and dry and he was about to fall down.

'Two aurei for half a year,' he repeated in a breath.

The old man shifted uncomfortably.

'Round here, that is a great price. You'll make it back in a month or two, I don't doubt. There's no other scribe for a mile, so they'll all come to you. If you price your work at the right level. Now, there's a food shop three doors down that always has a hot bowl of something, or a little fowl and fish. The bath-house at the end of the street . . . well, it's not great, if I'm honest. You can pop in there in the mornings, but only the smell lingers, if you know what I mean. Otherwise, there's the Circus, not half a mile off, the theatres. Lot of race-team people live around this place. They all need contracts! You'll be up to your eyes in silver in six months, I don't doubt it.'

He reached out and patted the wall, affection in his eyes.

'This is a good place, well made. I should know as I cut the joints myself. I wax and seal the wood every six months, but I'm retiring to the coast. I might send my son instead, if I don't want to! There comes a time when all a man needs is the sea and a flask of wine, perhaps something to read and a bit of bread and meat – and an old woman to keep him warm. If he can't find a younger one, obviously.'

The man started to wheeze and Cormac realised he was laughing. He chuckled in response, holding out his hand.

'Very well. Two aurei.'

The old man took his hand in a grip that was all knuckles and papery skin. For him, it was an ending, Cormac thought suddenly, a life well lived, with few regrets, from the looks of it.

For Cormac, it was a beginning. He fished two of the precious gold coins from his satchel, handing them across. The old man completely failed to be casual at the sight of those. He'd obviously expected a bag of silver and the sight of actual gold had his eyes bulging. Cormac wondered if he had overpaid, or whether he should have changed the aurei to silver first. He didn't want to be memorable.

He cursed himself for not checking with the other shops on that street. The gold coins were a fortune, but they were all he had. He needed to spend each one carefully, until he could find paid work. He thought again of the unfinished gradus in the satchel. Without it, there was no guarantee of his quality. He would be able to charge only a copper or so, while gradus-certified work could earn silver. Still, he was out of the wind and sun. He had a roof over his head. He looked around at the place he had rented. It felt like a home.

The room above was reached by a flight of stairs more like a ladder fixed to the wall, a tiny, narrow attic with a slit window facing the street. A bed filled most of the space, along with a dresser wedged into the far corner. Cormac looked at it and smiled. He had never owned a place of his own. Of course, he didn't own the shop either, but he could bar the door and shut out the world. He wouldn't find Nartius standing over him as the sun rose, ready to kick him from slumber and set him to whatever needed doing.

The old man left with visible reluctance, still touching walls like favourite old hounds. Cormac brought Malvo in then, ready to lay out the supplies they had purchased on their way through the city. The young man seemed ill at ease, jumpy on his feet as if he wanted to bolt.

'Don't you like it?' Cormac asked him, waving at the shop.

'I can hardly believe it,' Malvo said. 'You're not afraid they'll find out what you've done?'

Cormac shook his head.

'Give me a month and I'll have this place running day and night. Real work as well, Malvo. This city runs on ink – and I can provide. In fact, I'll need my own store of vellum. I could send you to the markets for that tomorrow, maybe. I had an idea of teaching you to read and write. That would mean . . .'

'No,' Malvo said suddenly. He took a step away as if he might flee from the very idea, glancing at the door to the street that stood closed in that moment. He looked trapped and almost afraid. 'I can't read or write. It's not my . . . skill.'

'I think you might be surprised,' Cormac said, 'but I'll find you a place here doing something else if you want. I have some ideas about making inkstones and papyrus sheets in the shop, for example. We can't tan skins here for vellum, not so close to houses nearby. They'd force us out before the first week for the smell alone, never mind the noise.'

'I should go,' Malvo said, speaking over Cormac's plans. 'I've seen some of the old lads around. They've seen me as well. I should go and meet them.'

There was an awkwardness between them and Cormac wasn't quite sure what to say.

'I need . . . I . . . there's a place for you, Malvo, if you want it. I need help, someone who knows this part of the city. Honestly, I can't do it on my own. We'll be making good money too, if I can make a gradus. In six months, I might even pay to sit the real one. You've shown you can be useful. How about starting here with me?'

He was hurt when Malvo shook his head.

'I said I'd drop in, to see the lads. They still think I was taken up by the vigiles. They didn't expect to see me again, not for a few years anyway. Some of them will be saying I must have told the vigiles about the others to be back here so soon. Understand? They'll be thinking the worst, that I'm an informer. I need to settle them down or they'll come looking. He glanced at the satchel, eyes suddenly hard. He didn't want to leave with nothing.

'There's a few older men who will need to be persuaded,' Malvo said. He spoke to the wall, as if refusing to look Cormac in the eye. 'If I could take a couple of those little gold coins with me, I could buy them off, keep them sweet. That's all they care about, understand?'

'I thought you were the leader,' Cormac muttered. He could feel the weight of those coins as if he held them in his hand. He'd given two to the landlord and about half of one more in silver for bits and pieces in a dozen shops. Only four and a handful of silver remained in his bag. He did not want to give more away.

Malvo shook his head impatiently. 'I told you about the older firm. There's always some above and some below. My lads bring whatever they get and I pass it on to men above. They're not good people, Cormac. You don't want to cross them.'

He touched the hole in his cheek and Cormac wondered

again whether it had come from some childhood ailment, or if Malvo too had been tortured.

'You don't have to go back,' Cormac said. 'Not if you work here.'

'You don't understand,' Malvo said in frustration. 'They're . . . like a family. Look, it just works. As long as I don't get taken up and sent to the mines, or branded.'

'They'd hardly need to brand you,' Cormac said lightly. He saw Malvo flinch and felt embarrassed. 'Fine. You can have a couple of the coins. Maybe I can get more.'

'You shouldn't,' Malvo said, spitting words as if he didn't want to. 'Once was clever, but not again, right?'

'What do you mean?' Cormac asked.

Malvo reached out his hand in reply and with the utmost reluctance, Cormac handed over two of the coins. For the freedom they represented, he could not look away, not until Malvo made them vanish.

'There was a man around here, a couple of years back,' Malvo said. His eyes had a faraway look as he remembered. 'He took a young woman on her way home and tried to force her. She fought him, so he cut her throat. Me and the lads found her body the next morning. Thing is, we'd never have found *him*. If he'd left it at that, I mean. We had no description, nothing. He got away with it and though her family was torn apart, he could have lived the rest of his life without anyone ever knowing.'

'What happened?' Cormac asked softly.

'Once wasn't enough, was it? He kept going. The vigiles put the word out – and so did the gangs. You understand? We caught him after the third one and he never made it to a cell. The vigiles probably think he moved away or something, but I can show you where his bones are buried.

Broken bones, for the most part. We put him down like a dog, but my point is that he was free after the first time. If you want my advice, or whether you do or not, it will be to make this shop work now. To never go near a money-lender again, no matter how tempted you are. Or you'll be like that man and buried in some alley, all unknown.'

'I understand,' Cormac said. Deep down, he knew it was advice he was not going to take. The moment of being handed gold coins, of winning them from the world with just his own wits, had felt more real than any other he could remember. He scratched the burns on his chest, wincing. They still owed him – and the debt wasn't nearly paid.

Malvo saw something of that in his expression and looked sad for a moment. He might have turned away, but Cormac gestured to the only chair.

'Sit down before you go, would you? I bought all these things on the way here. Let me at least try.'

Malvo looked at the light, judging the hour. In truth, he was curious. He sat down and watched as Cormac laid a dozen items on the counter top. He had purchased them in different places, from a sheet of tin the size of his hand, to paints and tools, even a strip of tanned calf leather and a sewing needle. Malvo watched as Cormac began to knead a ball of golden beeswax in his hand.

'What's that for?' he said suspiciously.

'You are too recognisable,' Cormac murmured, leaning in to look at him.

Malvo began to rise from his seat.

'You've been saying that all day. You think I don't know?'

'Sit down, then. I want to see if I can do something about it.'

*

It was dark outside by the time Cormac turned to the paints he'd bought. He'd had to go out again to purchase an oil lamp, a pale glass bowl. Suspended on chains from a bronze stand, the light on the flickering surface was a gentle gold in the shop, enabling Cormac to keep working. He was pleased Malvo hadn't taken the opportunity to bolt the moment he wasn't observed.

He'd used the wax to make a mould of the hole in Malvo's cheek, along with a rough copy of the missing nostril. Cormac had used iron shears then to form a shape in tin, hammering edges over so they wouldn't cut like a razor. The skills were all simple ones, but Malvo watched in astonishment. He sat frozen as Cormac touched the thing to his face, making adjustments.

That cheek-piece was joined to a new nostril by a thread of tin, reinforced with leather. The piece of dull metal looked strange whenever he laid it down. Cormac breathed through his nose as he worked and once Malvo understood what he was about, he stopped saying he should leave and sat still, patient as a stone.

'I'm just not sure how to stop it falling out . . .' Cormac muttered. He was mixing paint on the little worktop, using a tiny brush to dab the tin, then matching the result to Malvo's cheek. 'A piece of wax will do for a while, but it will need to be stronger.'

After a time, he pressed the plate into place, letting a sticky ball of beeswax fill the hole in Malvo's cheek. Cormac had no mirror, but he had purchased a brass bowl and he held that to the light, revealing Malvo's features in the polished edge.

'There. That will do, I think,' Cormac said, judging his own work. 'The next one will be better – and I have an idea about fixing a strap of leather between your teeth. You could bite down on it, maybe. It would stop you talking clearly. That might be . . .'

He broke off as Malvo's eyes filled with tears. The young man raised a trembling hand to touch his cheek and nose, painted to look as close to skin as Cormac could manage. To his surprise, Malvo continued to weep, turning the bowl back and forth as he gazed on his reflection.

'Don't you like it?' Cormac said.

Malvo wiped his eyes as he stood up. It was strange to look at him without the hole and missing nostril being all he could see. He looked different with the plate, almost handsome. In the lamplight, he was a different man. Cormac saw him sob once, in a spasm, then turn for the door.

'I'll do a better one . . .' Cormac called.

Malvo went out into the night, stumbling and making noises Cormac had not heard from him before.

He yawned as he turned then. The counter top was strewn with pieces of wax and tin clippings, but he was exhausted. He had gone without sleep before, but not as long. His stomach growled and he raised his eyes to the wooden ceiling. Food would have to wait yet again for the morning. He closed the door and put the bar across, shutting out the city. His place. His home.

Yawning hugely, he climbed the ladder to the tiny bedroom and fell on the mattress. He was asleep in moments, snoring as the stars turned overhead.

13

He slept until the sun was showing. It seemed the window of the attic faced east, which brought a golden bar onto his face and disturbed his slumber. Unsticking one eye where sleep had gummed it shut, he reached under the bed. His questing hand found no pot. Old man Lanatus had taken it with him, of course. Cormac's bladder was painful and he wondered if he'd even reach the bath-house.

His first moments out of the shop became a hobbling run as he looked for it. Half the people up and about at that hour were after the same thing, so he followed them, passing over a copper coin at the door and sighing on a wooden bench with a dozen others. There was a slave there to keep them moving along, but Cormac could relax for a moment, emptying bladder and bowels into what sounded like a stream running beneath. He'd eaten so little over the previous day, he barely needed the old sponge. One poor fellow groaned as a great flood poured out, more than seemed possible. Cormac recoiled from a miasma of illness as it spread, heading quickly into a second room.

He should not have compared it with the Balneae, he knew that. A bath-house for working men – or the one next door for women – was never going to be a palace of fluted ceilings and polished marble. Even so, he was disappointed. The pool was neither hot nor clean as far as he could tell. He grimaced as he hung loincloth, belt and tunic on a peg he could keep an eye on and dipped into it, though he could not see his own feet through the grey water. There were two slaves to oil and clean, but no one seemed to be using them. For the men in the pool, a quick scrub with a pumice stone was enough. Cormac saw one had brought a phial of his own oil, adding to the odd flakes that floated on the water's surface.

The smell of the place was some combination of the toilets outside, bitter sweat, olive oil and perhaps lavender, he wasn't sure. Cormac stared at his belongings as he used his hands to clean himself and then dressed as quickly as he could. He would need to find a laundry, as well as new clothes. He had only two aurei left, along with a handful of silver. It had seemed a fortune yesterday, but he was burning through it at an alarming rate. Of course, there was still the note for three more. That could be redeemed at any moneylender in Rome, but Malvo's words had stayed with him. He'd been lucky once. To be lucky again was to take a much greater risk. He told himself he should consider that note only for emergencies. No one gets caught the first time, he reminded himself.

He nodded thanks to the one taking coins at the door, though in truth he felt almost as grimy as when he had entered. Still, the sun was up and he was on the streets of Rome. He had to buy papyrus in a dozen different grades. Not every customer would pay for parchment, he knew that. He needed a new inkstone too, now his fragment had gone to nothing. He had to have a couple more loincloths, tunics, reeds and wax slates, a tin sign for the shop . . . a hundred things. From that moment, every coin had to be spent like it was his last.

As he walked back, he stopped at a food-seller and slurped his way through a bowl of bean stew. There was no meat in it, but it was so delicious he had a second. Another copper went on that but when he handed back the bowl, he found his thoughts clearer than they had been.

His spirits rose with a full belly. What was he even worried about? He was clean enough! His tunic was still better quality than any he had owned before. He just had to solve the problem of the gradus. He had an idea he might be able to copy the treasury seal if he could just get a glimpse. Jewellers carved the stones men wore in their rings. How hard could it be, with the right tools?

Cormac turned slowly on the spot, as if he could see through the houses to the great forum of Augustus. The aerarium was over there – literally, the place of copper coins, or the house of money: part of the vast temple to Saturn that held the wealth of Rome. Every day, that treasury building took in and paid out fortunes, keeping meticulous records. Cormac stood as if frozen, thinking hard. The building next door was actually the one he wanted – the tabularium, or record office. When he had dreamed of buying himself free, that was the place he had imagined, a haven of order, sitting in the presence of quaestors and handling the accounts and laws and records of senate speeches. It had been a joyous reverie and yet he had never entered those hallowed halls.

He *had* seen it, however, just once, on the morning he

had been taken from the tullianum prison and across the forum to the courthouse. So concerned had he been then with winning his freedom, he'd barely glanced up. He had a memory of towering white columns, but that was all.

Cormac swallowed nervously. It seemed he would be going back, the very thing Malvo had warned against. The praetor too had told him not to be seen again. What authority that man had, to order another to vanish and expect to be obeyed! That part of the forum was one of the few places in Rome Cormac might be recognised, even linked to his past. He'd been filthy before, admittedly. With a messenger's satchel and a clean tunic, with his head down, he might get in and out without a hand dropping on his shoulder. Perhaps they weren't even looking for him! Yet it felt like tempting fate. He knew he was right to fear them all: the army of clients and watchers employed by the Silanus family, the vigiles, the praetor and his scribes, the prison guards, the thousands of praetorians with their plumes. It felt as if he had escaped from the cave of a savage beast and yet was intent on going back for his sandals. The gods laughed at pride, everyone knew that.

As he walked on, a plan came together slowly, drawn from wisps. The tabularium was where the records of Rome were stored. If he had won his gradus fairly, it would have been copied there ... Realisation stopped his thoughts like a punch. Slowly, Cormac leaned against a wall. His new instinct for danger warned him to keep moving, but he could not.

Without a gradus, he could not work as a scribe, not by law. He'd thought he could forge one, but that would leave him at the mercy of every single customer and vigile. If just one nosy bastard decided to check the record in the tabularium, he was done. He'd find himself back in front of a magistrate with slavery as his reward.

The world swam as he reached the shop. The old man had given him a key on a hoop of iron. Cormac fumbled it almost blindly into the lock. In his worried daze, he did not see the ones watching him, waiting for the key to turn.

When the door opened, they crossed the little street and courtyard, pushing him through his own entrance with such force Cormac went sprawling. He reached for a hammer he had left on his counter top, spinning round and waving it aggressively.

'Get out!' he shouted. 'There's no money . . .' His voice trailed off as he recognised two of the three men.

Malvo had been badly beaten, Cormac could see that much. The tin plate he'd made had been lost. Instead, he sported a swollen, purple eye, half closed, as well as a scuffed look as if he'd been subject to a kicking.

'I'm sorry,' Malvo said quickly, 'I . . .' Whatever he might have added was cut off as the largest of them whipped a hand against the back of his head. Malvo's oddly overlapping teeth shut with a snap that made Cormac wince.

'Enough of that, lad,' the man growled. 'Is he the one?'

It was the third man who answered. He too had a swollen mouth and blackened eye, though Cormac could not feel sorry for him. He had not seen Nartius since leaving him on the road outside the Silanus estate. The man's hair was in disarray, as if he had slept on dusty ground. The days of slick dark wings and fine bone combs had apparently passed.

'That's him,' Nartius said.

He looked away from Cormac's furious glare. The one who had struck Malvo chuckled then, a sound both warm and frightening. The man's shoulders were so wide he looked like furniture, easily big enough on his own to block the street door.

Cormac had the feeling Nartius would lunge for him if he tried to reach the ladder. He hadn't even tested the window above to see if he could fit through. That was a mistake, he realised. A shop with a single entrance was a big mistake.

Malvo didn't try to speak again, just stood head down, his gaze on the floor. The obvious leader of the little group looked around in interest. His teeth were always showing, Cormac noticed. He was reminded of an animal skull one of the thresher boys had found once and brought back to the house.

'Cormac,' the man said. 'We've heard all about your good fortune – freed by fate, no less. An old man is poisoned or smothered and there you are, on the road with all the world before you! Your life ahead. I almost envy you in your youth, son!'

Cormac wanted to say the old man had not been murdered, but he thought back to a dozen things he'd let pass at the time. The way Sophia had wailed before all the rest, a cracked note that had bothered him even then. She would have known one herb from another. The strange apology from Marcus at the gate . . . Cormac felt anger rise again. They'd killed the old man? He was suddenly sure. For what? His wealth? How much did one family need?

'Ah, so you didn't know,' the man said softly. He had been watching Cormac's reaction, reading his face. Cormac clenched his jaw, determined to give nothing else away.

'Nartius guessed,' the man went on. 'That's why he

chose to take his freedom. I thought maybe you were of the same mind, but you really didn't know?'

Cormac shook his head, answering despite himself. The man tutted under his breath.

'That changes things, maybe. I thought you were sharper than you seem, a lad who saw the wind change and got out before the rain came down. Looks like I was wrong about that.' He brightened suddenly, the smile returning to his craggy features.

'Still, you've done all right since, haven't you? Look at this place, snatched from the air! Warm and dry, too. Malvo here has told us most of it. I might think he was making it up if he hadn't handed over a gold coin as proof. I don't see many of those, believe me. It gave me a lovely warm feeling, that did.'

Cormac exchanged a flicker of a glance with Malvo. The young man had apparently kept one aureus back – Cormac couldn't blame him for that. All he could do with that knowledge was get Malvo into more trouble. The beating Malvo had already taken stopped him from saying anything. Though Malvo had betrayed him, he'd clearly been made to. Perhaps he wasn't lost, not completely.

'It's my feeling . . .' the big man went on, 'and perhaps you'll agree with me when you hear, that I could use someone with your skills. Someone who can get himself out of a praetor's court and the tullianum, even! Just walks right out with Malvo here, like the gods themselves have blessed their steps!'

Cormac's stomach sank.

'It won't work again, not twice,' he said desperately. 'The praetor said not to come back. As for the tullianum, that was once and once only, I swear it.'

'Oaths are strange things,' the man replied, chuckling. 'It's the same little noise as a curse or a cry for help, but very different, no? Somehow, the gods listen for those oaths, don't they? They listen ... and they come down hard on anyone who breaks one. They bring dark fate and trouble then, don't they? That's my belief, son. Is it yours? Will you swear to Jupiter and Hera and all the ones listening that you speak the truth? Careful now.'

'On Jupiter, that's true,' Cormac said firmly. 'On Apollo, on the older gods. On them all.'

The man looked sour.

'Well, that's all very well,' he said. 'There is another matter. Of you getting real gold from a moneylender. Of walking in, bold as you like – and being given a fortune just for a few words on a sheet of vellum! Now that's a trick worth knowing. If you want to have value to me, son, if you want to keep your life and your bones unbroken, you will not tell me you can't do *that* again. No, you'll tell me you can do it a dozen times, until we are sitting on enough gold to buy a palace.'

He laughed at the vision and Cormac could see an odd light in his eyes. Greed, he supposed, or wonder. Malvo too was watching, nodding, pleading with Cormac to say yes.

'I can,' Cormac said. 'Though I need good vellum.'

'There you go! *That's* what I wanted to hear!' the man said. 'Which means we can be friends and not enemies. You see, Malvo? Your mate is one who knows when the wind changes. It doesn't have to be beaten out of him, not like some I could mention.'

The man came closer then, a figure of such massive strength that Cormac realised two things. One, he still held the hammer, forgotten in his hand – and two, he could not imagine hitting this man hard enough to put him down. He had the awful idea that if he tried, Malvo's master would just take the hammer and beat him to death with it. There was violence in the bitter smell of him, in the odour of damp wool and perspiration.

The man leaned closer still, until their noses almost touched.

'My name is Pugio, son. You know the word? A Roman soldier's knife, as I served for a while when I was young – twenty years back. It's not my real name, but it's what I'm called when men gather and talk of how dangerous it is to cross me. Do you understand? Or do I need to beat it into you?'

'I understand . . .' Cormac began. Pugio hit him with no warning, knocking him sideways. Cormac clutched the counter for a moment of shock and pain, then slipped, crashing down. The hammer fell from his outstretched hand and of course Pugio picked it up, weighing it thoughtfully.

'Look at that iron. Cheap work,' he said. 'Still, I've found it helps if clever young lads don't think they can run rings around me, do you see? It helps to remind them right from the start, that I see *everything* they do – and that I am not to be crossed. Which hand do you use to write, son? The right?'

'What? Don't . . . please,' Cormac said.

He looked for Malvo, but saw he had turned away, his face tight. Pugio turned to Nartius.

'Would you put his left hand on the counter?' he asked.

Cormac would have bolted then if there had been a way out. Nartius was the one who had held him while Senator

165

Silanus burned him with irons, whispering question after question. All that came back and he could not remain still as Nartius took his left arm and dragged it across the counter.

'I need both hands for my work!' Cormac screeched. He could hear the terror in his voice and shame flooded him. Yet in that moment he was not planning, not even thinking. All he could see were flashes, of fear and sickness, of rage.

Nartius unfolded his fingers, though Cormac tried to curl them into a fist. The man had been a figure of calm authority on the estate! Yet there he was, fallen in with thieves and violent men. Perhaps Nartius had always been a follower, Cormac thought, looking into his eyes.

He realised fear had somehow fled. He had formed a thought about Nartius and it had brought him back from the edge of a chasm. He looked into the blocky face of Pugio and did not flinch as the man frowned.

'You don't seem afraid, son,' Pugio said.

'I need both hands,' Cormac repeated, his voice very calm.

Pugio shrugged.

'Clever lad like you? You'll manage. Teach a lesson well and you'll never teach it again, my old dad used to say. Understand?'

Cormac let a moment of silence pass, then nodded, his jaw clenched. The man brought the hammer down on two of his outstretched fingers. Cormac did not cry out. There was a moment of numbness before pain soared, rising like heat. By then, Nartius had let him go and he curled the hand into his chest.

'Remember this,' Pugio said. He seemed dissatisfied

somehow. The way Cormac glared hot-eyed was not the response he had intended to bring about. He had lost his impetus and could not think how to get it back.

'We'll do our bit of business while the Silanus family are at their parties and wedding feasts, all right?' Pugio went on. 'They'll be distracted, and if one of their servants comes asking for a sack of gold, the moneylenders won't question it. Not during a wedding. That's how it works?'

'That's how it works,' Cormac repeated. His hand was throbbing and he could not resist pushing back. 'Though it will take me another day now, maybe two. I told you I needed both hands.'

'No, you'll be fine. I'll leave Malvo to keep an eye on you. Or Nartius, maybe? As you two are such good friends? You should have a doctor take a look at that hand, son. It will have to be splinted.'

'You can keep Malvo,' Cormac said, bitterly. 'Nartius can stay. At least he can read.'

Pugio closed one eye as he judged the young lad before him. He understood how to handle frightened men. One who stared back calmly after having fingers broken was new to his experience. He reached out on instinct, intending to grab those fingers and give them a good twist. That would make the boy more respectful. Pain was the great leveller.

He saw Cormac did not edge back and at the last moment, Pugio hesitated. The lad could bring in gold, perhaps enough to retire on. The thief's dream, that always ended in a gutter. If there was any truth in him needing both hands, Pugio risked his own future. This was the deal that might get him out to some little village a hundred miles away, to take a young wife and bring a couple of squalling brats into the world. If he ever saw

Rome again, it would be with a few colt mares to sell, or amphorae of wine. Pugio could almost taste it, for the first time in years. Hope was a bitter thing and he had forgotten what it felt like.

He let his hand fall.

'I'll leave Malvo, then,' he said. 'Him and you will be great friends, I'm sure. You get that splinted and I'll be back tomorrow morning to check on the plans. Stay up all night if you have to, all right? You don't want to disappoint me. I won't have no use for you then.'

Cormac nodded slowly. A thought came to him and he found himself speaking before he could decide whether it was wise or not.

'Who is getting married?' he asked.

'What?' Pugio replied.

'You said there is to be a Silanus wedding. It's the second time I've heard of it. Who is getting married?'

It was Nartius who spoke, making Pugio turn to watch him from under heavy brows.

'Junia Claudilla,' Nartius said. This was the world he knew and he had spoken out of turn because of it. Cormac hoped he'd earned himself a beating. He hated the one who had been a seneschal at the estate more than anyone else he could remember. No, Cormac realised. He *despised* him. No man should hold another down for punishment. No free man anyway. His hand throbbed at the thought and he felt light-headed.

'No. Who is she marrying?' Cormac said. The room was swaying and he wondered if he would fall down again.

'She is marrying Gaius Caesar,' Pugio replied before Nartius could speak. 'The new emperor. The one they call Caligula. Your old Silanus masters have risen high, boy – which is why they won't notice a fortune slipping out the door, not in the next few days.'

Pugio was wrong, Cormac knew that much. The Silanus family might be distracted at the highest levels. The senator and his father, his brothers, his sister – his sons even! They would all be caught up in the celebration and the rituals of marriage feasts . . . but Silanus *scribes* would still be checking and counting and scribbling away. They might miss a few aurei, or not catch up for a month or two. More than that would be questioned, perhaps taken to one of the Silanus men for confirmation.

Cormac nodded. The one who called himself Pugio would bring the world down on them with his greed. Perhaps he hoped to let it fall on Cormac and Malvo while he vanished. Cormac looked into the man's black stare. Yes, he was sharp enough for that. It meant Cormac had to be sharper still.

He had no allies, no authority, not even his damned gradus. He did have his wits and his will – and he made an oath then and there to destroy this man who had come unwanted into his life.

'I'll have to disappear afterwards,' Cormac said suddenly. 'I'll need a share of the gold.' It had to seem as if he agreed.

'You are bargaining with me?' Pugio said. He smiled even wider and shook his head. 'With two broken fingers? Here's my deal for you. You keep the rest unbroken – and deliver a hundred aurei to me in two days. Or I cut your throat, understand? Careful now. Don't disappoint me.'

'A hundred is too much,' Cormac said in genuine shock. 'I could get twenty, *maybe*. They'll be suspicious for more than that.'

'You might have to visit five places then, won't you? Or ten, I don't care, do I? Just do it all in one day, so they don't work it out before you're finished. One hundred, or I cut your throat. Understand?'

'I understand,' Cormac said grimly. 'Very well.'

'Very well,' Pugio echoed. He was still not quite getting the reaction he wanted and it bothered him. Most men he'd hurt didn't look so calm. He thought of that much gold and nodded. It was worth the trouble.

'Keep an eye on him *at all times*, Malvo. Watch him while he sleeps even. Your life for his, if he disappears. Don't disappoint me.'

He left then, taking Nartius with him and leaving the two alone.

'I'm sorry,' Malvo said immediately.

Cormac saw the hole in his cheek looked sore around the edges, as if the wax and tin plate had been ripped free. He gestured at it and Malvo turned away rather than endure his scrutiny.

'He took it,' Malvo muttered. 'Said he liked me the old way, to frighten the young ones.'

'I can make another,' Cormac said.

'No. Leave it now. Get him his fortune and he'll go.'

'No chance. He'll kill us both,' Cormac said.

Malvo shrugged.

'Maybe. He will if we don't! That much is sure. I don't have a choice, see? Nor do you. Don't try *anything*, Cormac. All right? Pugio is a . . . he's vengeful, all right? Just . . . do your work and get him the gold he wants. That might save your neck – and mine.'

'They'll search for us after, Malvo. You realise that, right? If I do it again – the thing you said I *should never* do again – they will turn this city right over looking for us.'

Malvo had the grace to look awkward as his own advice was repeated back to him. He stood on one leg, head down, twisting a sandal on the wooden floor like a boy caught stealing apples.

'They won't know it was us,' he said at last.

'They'll know it was you, with that face,' Cormac snapped. 'So either you're out right now, or you let me make another piece. I had an idea I could use marble dust and glue to shape it – and I wanted to try that bit of leather held between your teeth. As long as you don't speak, it should let you pass . . .'

'All *right*!' Malvo said, too loud. They faced one another and he saw again how Cormac kept his hand close to his chest. Malvo's face grew flushed.

'I can splint those fingers. What then?'

Cormac considered. He wanted to trust Malvo, but he would not be burned twice. He would not be hurt twice, not when he could avoid it. No, the young man he'd thought was a friend . . . wasn't. When the time came, he'd throw Malvo to the wolves.

'I need vellum,' Cormac said. 'Five or six sheets of the best quality.'

'So we buy some.'

'And when the vigiles come asking? "Oh yes, a lad came in two days back and bought half a dozen sheets of the good stock."'

'We could buy one in each shop maybe . . .' Malvo said.

Cormac looked at him with grudging approval.

'That will give six of them my face though, won't it? The vigiles will have six merchants to question, not just one. No, I have a better idea.'

He thought briefly of the woman wrapped in robes on

the rear bench of the little school. Cormac felt an odd warmth at the thought of seeing her again. It was madness, but he thought he even remembered the scent she had worn.

'We can take more from the school,' Cormac said firmly. 'I'll even leave coins in exchange so that old drunk doesn't go to the vigiles.'

He patted Malvo on the shoulder with his good hand. He didn't notice how much the young man needed to be forgiven, how much the gesture meant to him.

'Don't worry,' Cormac muttered, lost in thought. 'We'll find a way through. On my oath, we will.'

14

Cormac jiggled the bar until the peg fell and the door creaked open. He had spent the morning making a better cheek-piece for Malvo. Something about that quiet labour in the workshop had settled them both. What once had been spinning thoughts became a great still pool. He could find a way through the problems that faced them. On a single day, he *could* take the moneylenders of Rome for a fortune. If everything worked, he might even leave Pugio holding a bag of lead while he and Malvo started new lives somewhere far from Rome.

Gaul would be pleasant in the spring, Cormac thought idly as he crossed to the door of the schoolroom. If he came away with sixty or seventy aurei – after Malvo's share – he might even hire a boat and cross that little sea to go home. Beyond slave raids and a few reckless traders, the Romans hadn't returned to Britannia, not since Julius Caesar. Cormac might actually see the white cliffs of his dreams again, with all his adventures behind him. It was a strange thought. Britannia was a world he no longer knew, after all. It could not be home. He would be a stranger there, one who spoke a strange tongue.

The magister had his feet up on the desk once more. Cormac grinned, but the expression froze as the man opened his eyes and looked blearily up at the ceiling. Another wineskin lay on the table, but it was a plump thing, a plucked hen waiting for the pot. Cormac held his breath as he edged back. Malvo was still by the outer door, watching for a class arriving. He looked across in silence and Cormac hesitated rather than signal to get out. He *needed* those vellum sheets – and they were close by in the little storeroom, piles of the things. The gods were not smiling on him that day, however. Without the key, he would have to break the lock. He winced at the thought. The sort of thieves who broke things were quickly caught. He saw himself more as a mouse, or perhaps a cat. Cats did not kick in doors.

He held up a palm for Malvo to wait, then tiptoed across the tiny yard, ducking under a row of washing that still dripped. Perhaps the magister had not slept well and spent the morning laundering his clothes. Cormac found himself before the lock and closed his eyes as he pictured how it had worked. He remembered pushing in the bronze key, then rotating it, freeing some simple bar within. That bar slid along a slot . . . moving aside a bolt.

The magister had spent money to protect his most valuable stock. Cormac could remember the shape of the key he'd used. The head had been the figure of a woman with the key cut as if to resemble her kneeling legs, a shape bent at the knee and ankle.

He fumbled in his belt, looking for one of the pieces of tin he'd cut away while making Malvo's cheek-piece. His fingers found only a fresh reed, his tiny knife and another fragment of inkstone. He had replaced his most precious supplies, but if there'd been a strip of tin, he had left it on the workbench.

Malvo cleared his throat, somewhere on the other side of dripping clothes. Cormac grimaced, imagining the bolt the key would move. It entered the door frame . . . there. When all else failed, he was sixteen and strong. He took hold of the door handle and heaved in the opposite direction to the bolt, compressing the hinges. The door protested, but it shifted even so. Cormac saw white lights and pulled back as well as up. With a release of breath, the door came free, sagging in his hands.

He looked in dismay at the protruding bolt, now a bent bronze tongue. Malvo cleared his throat again, more urgently. There was no more time. Cormac grabbed a handful of vellum, a great sheaf of the stuff. He had brought a pouch of silver and he was fumbling for that when Malvo gave a shriek. The sound so startled Cormac he half-dropped the sheets. They slid from his grasp and he had to crouch to keep them from spilling across the ground.

The man who had been creeping up on him missed his first grab as a result. Cormac scrambled back when he sensed he was under attack, but he could not stop hands gripping his tunic, taking both his arms. The papers dropped with a hiss, sliding across the ground.

Cormac watched in horror as one of his captors lost his temper with the row of washing and swept the whole lot away. He heard the magister yelp in protest, but Cormac could only stare at vigiles holding Malvo like a trussed bird.

'It *is* him! I knew it!' the magister said triumphantly. He was collecting up his wet clothes rather than leaving them to be trampled. Yet his expression was malicious as he came to stand before Cormac, arms full of damp cloth.

'You thought I wouldn't notice? Three sheets of the finest vellum from my own store? It will cost you more than whatever you got by selling them, be sure of that. A slave stealing from his old teacher! You disgust me.'

'A freedman,' Cormac muttered. The magister was like a yapping dog, hurting his ears. He couldn't think while the man stood there, swollen with triumph. Cormac still hadn't got over recognising the vigiles. One of them was binding Malvo with a bit of rope, but it was the leader who smiled like a favourite uncle, making Cormac's stomach fall.

'The magister here reported a theft from his storeroom,' Terentius said cheerfully. 'It's almost always one of the pupils, did you know that? You'd be surprised how often it happens. I said we'd leave a couple of lads to watch his door. Honestly, if you'd left it till tomorrow, we might have moved on! You do have some nerve, son! I thought that in the praetor's office.'

Hope kindled in Cormac's breast as Terentius spoke.

'You remember my patron,' Cormac said, fixing his gaze on the man. 'You'll see too that there is a pouch of silver coins there – on the ground by the door.'

It was the magister who snatched that, opening it and exclaiming. Cormac's thoughts whirred faster.

'There's no theft, not if we paid for those sheets. Which we did, as you can see. I needed those sheets for my work – and you know my work is not always something I want to describe, not while every ear is listening.'

'Interesting,' Terentius said, rubbing his chin. 'Though, of course, you might just have dropped that pouch when my man grabbed you. Still, you've come up with a fine explanation in no time at all. What an imagination you have!'

'Every word is true,' Cormac snapped.

Terentius' smile faded, his scowl an ugly thing.

'You are a liar and a scoundrel, son. A wondrous good one, but still. Bring his mate here, would you?' He addressed his own men and Malvo was dragged across the yard to stand alongside Cormac.

Terentius whistled softly as he examined the new cheek-piece. This one had been formed from marble dust combined with glue, painted as it set. Malvo flinched away as Terentius ran a fingernail around the edge. One of the vigiles grabbed the young man by the jaw to hold him still.

'Beautiful work,' Terentius said. He frowned as he glanced at Cormac, as if it didn't fit with what he thought he knew. 'Your doing, is it?'

'Yes,' Cormac muttered.

'From a distance, even I wouldn't have known Malvo here. It's not perfect when you stand this close, but still . . . a strange thing to do.' Terentius nodded in what looked like true appreciation.

'You know my patron,' Cormac said again. 'He will not be pleased when he hears of this.'

Terentius chuckled.

'Good for you, lad, honestly. Others would have given up by now, but not you. You just keep looking for what-ever might work.'

He stared at Cormac in a sort of wonder, walking around him as if he had never seen such a strange creature.

'Your difficulty, Cormac Cantii, is that I took my only rest-day morning and spent it with one of the seneschals of the Silanus household, up on the Quirinal. That house you claimed to know when we spoke last, do you remember? Fine, pompous fellow he was. I might have been thrown out on my ear if not for what I told him. He was all attention then, let me tell you! The Silanus name used without permission? Oh, it was all rosewater and little cakes then, with a cup of Falernian wine while I talked! I even met the senator when he came out. Fine figure of a man, by the way, just as you described him.'

There was no point continuing to deny it. Cormac's stomach had begun to ache and he sagged slightly in the arms of those who held him. Terentius' smile broadened as he saw. Cormac imagined the man had seen the collapse of hope many times. He enjoyed it, that was obvious. For all his apparent goodwill and chuckling nature, there was a cruel core to him. Cormac almost preferred men like Nartius and Pugio. At least they were honest.

'He said to me . . . Senator Silanus this was,' Terentius went on genially, 'the one you met at the estate of your old master, not his father . . . where was I?' It was all a performance, for the benefit of his vigile cronies as much as the two prisoners. Cormac glared back, but he was done. He tried to tell himself he had known freedom for a while – true freedom, owing no man and living by wits alone. Despair threatened, not just the semblance of it. His thoughts stilled, little wings visible where once they had been a blur.

'He said if I was ever lucky enough to cross paths with you again, I was to bring you to him. Day or night, he said. He mentioned a reward – I blush to tell you how much it was, but it will keep the lads and me in wine and bets at the Circus for a year, I'll say that much.'

He leaned close to Cormac as he had once before. The

man enjoyed his power, Cormac saw. Perhaps the job was made for one like him.

'I've been looking for you all over Rome, my lad. When I heard some sheets of vellum had gone missing from the very school you mentioned on our first meeting, well . . . I thought it might be worth watching the door. Pigeons do come back to their old nests, do you see? I wasn't expecting you just to drop into my lap, but the gods smile on honourable men. I'd have caught you sooner or later, either way. Because this is my city. Not yours. Not Malvo's here. *Mine.*'

The last word was a growl and Cormac thought the vigile was thinking of punching him. He tensed his stomach muscles rather than be surprised, but the street door opened. Terentius spoke over his shoulder without looking.

'Vigile business,' he said. 'Come back later.'

'Well, we're not thieves and we're not a fire to put out, so try that again,' a voice came from the street.

Terentius looked up in astonishment. When he saw the plumes of a praetorian holding the little door open, his mouth set hard. Terentius gestured to his companions and both Cormac and Malvo were dragged over to the street door.

'What about my broken lock?' the magister called behind them.

'Buy a new one with that purse of coin,' Terentius snapped. He went first onto the street and the bright day made them all squint as they followed.

Two praetorians stood there, calm as statues though six men came out. It was as if the soldiers saw no threat in them at all. Cormac noted how the vigiles lost a great deal of their aggression as they faced real legionaries. Even Terentius stood awkwardly, denied his usual authority.

'What is your business here?' the praetorian demanded.

The man loomed somehow. Cormac could see a white plume on his helmet, formed from horsehair trimmed and waxed. He was already tall, but it lent him even more height. Cormac felt like a boy in the presence of his father – and so did the vigiles from the look of it. The praetorians *gleamed* in the sun, as if every metal stud and edge had been polished. Yet they were professional soldiers, an elite selected from twenty-eight legions of Rome to protect the imperial estate. Cormac wondered if there was something he could use in the way they glared at his captors. There was no respect in them, not for vigiles. He exchanged a glance with Malvo, trying to warn him to be ready.

'I am catching . . . a thief,' Terentius admitted reluctantly. 'My lawful responsibility, as you point out.'

'And you had to do it today, did you? While the emperor is being married?'

The praetorian was suddenly angry and stepped forward as if he might actually draw his sword. The vigiles looked like whipped dogs, Cormac noted with surprise. If he pulled free, would Malvo have the wit to do the same? Cormac waited for the right moment. He had the sour feeling these men would not be easy to outrun.

'This street is *meant* to be nice and quiet,' the praetorian went on. 'Because I am patrolling it. Do you understand? You can chase your thieves and poke around in burning ashes any day of the week. Today, though, the emperor has asked if we wouldn't mind keeping it down while he enjoys his wedding ceremony. He didn't say anything about charging around kicking in doors and talking at the top of our voices, did he?'

Terentius shook his head in answer. The praetorian leaned closer.

'Are you *deaf*? Can you see my plume? The answer to my question is "Yes, optio" or "I'm sorry, optio." Then you and your inbred mates leave my street – quiet as mice. Or I will make an example of you, for the benefit of anyone else who might be trying to spoil the emperor's special day. Is that understood?'

'Yes, optio,' Terentius said. His gaze dropped to the gladius the man carried. 'Is that silver on your scabbard there?'

'Is that *what*?' the praetorian said, narrowing his eyes.

Terentius leaned closer still, though whether it was for his own pride or because his men were watching, Cormac didn't know.

'I just *asked* . . . if that was *actual* silver on your scabbard. Takes a lot of polishing, silver. That's all. I was just wondering how long you had to spend polishing to get it like that.'

The praetorian sensed the resistance in Terentius and regarded him for a long moment. Cormac watched the man realise he could hardly draw his blade for being asked a question. In his own way, his entire manner was about bluffing others to obedience. He would respond with violence if the call came, but he relied on never getting to that point.

'Just move on,' the praetorian said at last.

Terentius nodded and Cormac felt himself almost lifted from his feet as he was borne away. The group of four vigiles and their two prisoners went quickly down the road and turned towards the Palatine. It was the skinny one Cormac thought of as second in command who spoke then, his voice nervous.

'Are we not taking them back to the watch-house?'

Terentius shook his head, still annoyed at being spoken to like a child by praetorians.

'Senator Silanus said if we saw him again, to bring him in.'

'Yes, all right, but perhaps not today though? The emperor is getting married, you heard the praetorian. To that Silanus daughter. We could wait till tomorrow, couldn't we? Put them in cells for the night?'

'He said day or night, any hour,' Terentius replied. He glanced at Cormac, who was listening to every word. 'He said he would reward us well. I might buy a bit of silver for my knife like that fine peacock back there. Double pay! For what? Just to stand on street corners and buy new plumes for their helmets? *We* do the real work in this city, lads. We're the ones who catch thieves and murderers – and yes, put out the fires. I don't see any praetorians helping with that. No, they stand around in shiny uniforms that never saw a battlefield, spending the pay of *two* legions in every whorehouse in the city. While we have to buy our firewood in winter, and argue with the treasury over every coin spent.' He made a disgusted sound. 'Double pay for six thousand men – and the arrogance to think they deserve it. Ah, it just gripes at me, that's all.'

He turned to the skinny one.

'So yes, we are taking these two to Senator Silanus, as he made me promise I would if I found him again. Per-haps we'll see a new roof on the watch-house with the reward, or new sandals for the night watch, something we can actually use. Better than buckets to catch the rain, eh? Anyway, the law goes anywhere, at any time. I'll find a way of doing it quietly, don't you worry.'

Cormac saw the skinny man exchange a nervous glance with his companions. It seemed Terentius was not a patient leader of men. Perhaps he could use that. There had to be something.

The Palatine was not quiet, not like the rest of the city that day. As soon as they began to walk up the hill, the little group of six were swallowed in a bustling crowd. Thousands streamed in every direction and there were more praetorians than Cormac had ever seen. They stood like islands on every junction, but also patrolled in sixes, maintaining order by presence alone. Not that the common people of Rome were much in evidence. On that day, the staff of noble houses were the ones rushing about. Slaves and employed alike were busy with a ceremony that had started on the Capitoline hill that morning, then moved up to the imperial precinct on the Palatine for the wedding feast. Cormac felt he was moving out of the underworld to the home of gods, as if he climbed Mount Olympus.

There were no beggars or street children on the Palatine that day either. The people were clear-faced and well fed, racing to fulfil a thousand errands. He saw cakes being carried on carts and a troop of men in identical red robes leading white bulls on halter ropes to their sacrifice.

The vigiles were uncomfortable in such a crowd, Cormac could see that. Terentius and his companions were jostled and shoved as they made their way up the hill. Cormac's hands had been bound behind his back by then, as firmly as Malvo's. It made the idea of running hard to imagine. Still, he looked for a chance. He could lose himself in a crowd like this, he was certain. Like a fish dropped back into a river, he would not be caught again.

The little group was stopped and challenged by prae-torians as they reached an entrance bedecked in flowers. The air itself was strong with the scent and Cormac could hear music wafting from inside. The skinny one was look-ing nervous again, his eyes pleading with Terentius to give it up. Unfortunately, Terentius was like a bull, push-ing through any obstacle in his way. Cormac wondered if injured pride had something to do with that. It was not a luxury he had allowed himself to develop, but it still inter-ested him.

Invoking the name of Senator Silanus took them through the outer gate and into the imperial grounds. The roads were less crowded there and the little group stood out, as if the reality of the streets had somehow seeped through to a wedding celebration. Men and women frowned at the vigiles as Terentius asked for directions to the senator. He was pointed towards a great hall with bronze doors twice the height of any of them. Yet before he could take more than a single step, another pair of praetorians blocked their way.

Cormac saw an even more ornate helmet on one of them. There were gold horses adorning the polished cheek-guards, a work of art as well as armour. Terentius seethed as he was made to stand, the man's hand touching his chest with fingertips.

'I don't know what you think you're doing,' this praetor-ian said, 'but it will wait.'

'Senator Silanus . . .'

Bells sounded across the Palatine and a great cheer went up. It began somewhere indoors, in thousands of voices, then spread to all those who stood nearby. Further still, Cormac could hear it echoed in the hills below, as all of

Rome responded. The emperor was married. Husband and wife would come down the Palatine that evening. They would show themselves for the people to cheer and throw flowers or green palm leaves. Bread and wine would be handed out in a thousand places and all Rome would eat and drink on the imperial purse.

The praetorians didn't cheer. Instead, ranks of them came marching up the road, lining it with swords bared to the setting sun. Cormac felt his mouth dry as he watched the wedding party leave whatever temple had hosted the ceremony and walk together across the crest of the Palatine to the banquet. He felt his mouth open in awe as he saw a young man in a robe of white and purple, a wreath of gold leaves on his head. Emperor Gaius Caesar. Caligula. The slender youth walked hand in hand with a woman Cormac saw was both beautiful and visibly pregnant. A man who had to be her father walked one step behind the happy couple, and . . . Cormac felt a piece of ice enter his stomach. Senator Decimus Silanus walked alongside his father, talking earnestly to him. The man who had come to the home of his brother and tried to buy free slaves back to their previous state. The man who had stared into Cormac's eyes as he held hot irons to his chest. The spot itched, still far from healed. Cormac longed to rub or scratch it, but his hands were bound.

He knew he should not stare. Terentius was distracted, blocked by praetorians as he tried to be seen. The skinny one was terrified even to be there and the other two were out of their depth. This was his moment, Cormac decided. He tried to catch Malvo's eye again, but of course he was gaping at the emperor. Cormac clenched his jaw. Malvo would have to fend for himself.

Terentius half-turned, as if he could hear the thoughts of his prisoner. Perhaps he'd developed a knack for reading their intentions over the years, from the way they tensed or began to sweat. Whatever it was, Terentius reached back and drew Cormac to the front at the exact moment he might have wrenched free and tried to run.

The praetorian frowned at whatever was happening. He had his back to the marriage party, the better to keep an eye on the miscreants before him.

'Wait till they're all past and then you can cross the road, or do whatever you want,' the man growled at Terentius.

He was taller than the vigile, Cormac noted idly. Perhaps praetorians were chosen in part for their height. Cormac slumped, held like a rabbit in Terentius' grip. All he could do was let his weight be a burden, though the thief-taker didn't seem to tire.

'Senator *Silanus* told me to come to him, day or night,' Terentius growled back, his voice loud even as cheering grew around them.

Cormac saw his life change. The senator and his father were just a couple of paces away when Terentius spoke. Both men heard their name, but it was the younger one who looked up in recognition. His gaze dropped to Cormac and he almost stumbled in surprise. Senator Silanus muttered a few words into his father's ear and the man nodded and went on without him.

From one breath to another, Cormac found himself facing someone he had never thought to see again. Senator Decimus Silanus tapped the praetorian on the shoulder as if relieving him from duty. Perhaps he had that authority, Cormac thought, or just assumed it.

'These men are with me,' Silanus said. He smiled.

15

'Congratulations on your sister's wedding day, senator,' Terentius said. He glanced at the praetorian still partly in his way. The man edged aside, his expression promising retribution. It seemed praetorians were not used to having their authority challenged. Cormac sagged further in the vigile's grip. There was no give in Terentius. His fingers were like iron.

'I believe I know him!' the senator said with visible pleasure. '*This* the one you told me about? The one who used my family name?'

Terentius nodded, bowing his head as if in the presence of priests.

'We caught him stealing from his old school, dominus. He'll get time in the mines.'

'Oh, I think we can do a little better than that,' the senator said.

The expression was the one Cormac remembered from the little room with the smell of burning. He gagged suddenly, his gorge rising.

'Decimus? What calls you from my side on my wedding day?'

The senator spun round to see his sister standing in the road. Her arms were folded and bare, while a white stola and veil of pale orange fluttered in the rising breeze. The rose petals scattered for her were blowing away, Cormac saw. She looked incredibly beautiful as they danced around her feet. Somehow, his gaze still slid past her, snagging on the attention of another. He froze then.

Terentius too suddenly stared at the ground. Everyone else stood as if time itself had stopped. Junia Claudilla was sister to one senator, daughter to another. The fact that it was her wedding day would have earned her a respectful audience just about anywhere. Yet it was the attention of her new husband that made them mute. Even Cormac tried not to slouch, watching from under lowered brows.

Decimus Silanus was torn, Cormac could see that. He held up both hands, palms out in a gesture meant to appease her.

'It is a private matter,' he said to his sister. 'I will be along in just a few moments, I swear.'

'There will be no business on my wedding day,' she replied, sulking. 'You promised me!'

'The family doesn't sleep,' he said quickly, reciting a well-worn phrase.

'*Decimus!*' she snapped.

Her new husband heard that note of anger and slid through the crowd of guests and well-wishers, appearing alongside his bride.

Senator Silanus turned to one side rather than present his back to the emperor. He bowed as well, Cormac noted, as did the praetorian and everyone else near that spot. Voices died away and Cormac wondered if he too should bow, or perhaps kneel if the hand on his tunic would allow it. He was a prisoner, after all. Did the rules of respect and good manners still apply to prisoners? He remembered it was the man's wedding day and dipped as best he could. When he straightened, Cormac saw the emperor was watching him – and his eyes were colder and darker than Cormac could believe. He found himself trembling. Malvo's deformities were ordinary in comparison. There was no ring around the emperor's pupils, as if each eye was a pool of ink.

'This young man invoked our family name, Claudilla,' the senator continued to protest even as he bowed. 'He used the name of Silanus to escape the praetor's court – Gaius Gracchus was sitting, you know him. Dear sister . . . Your Majesty . . . this criminal is a living blasphemy, a freed slave who desecrates and outrages the natural order.'

It was his sister who spoke then. Her face gentled at the sight of Cormac and Malvo, held like broken birds, awaiting their fate.

'They look so miserable though,' she said, pouting. 'Can they not be spared? Your punishments are always so *cruel*.' She shuddered, though it seemed to Cormac more of an act than her bright interest.

Her brother snorted.

'You girls and your mercy! Punishments exist – the law exists! – so that louts like these don't take advantage of families like ours! You can see that, surely, Claudilla? You see why I thought it serious enough to stop? For a low-born slave to use our name . . . it is beyond justice, beyond mercy. Please, my dear, please go on to your feast. Your Majesty.' Once again, he tried awkwardly to include the emperor in a conversation between brother and sister. 'The senate guests will be wondering where you both are,

I'm sure. I will decide the fate of these two and take my place with you in a moment, I promise.'

Cormac watched as the young woman folded her arms across her chest. She did not seem to care for her older brother's authority.

'You promise? Gaius,' she said sweetly to her husband, 'would you remind Decimus he also promised there would be no family business on my wedding day?'

The young emperor tilted his head slightly. There was a coiled look to him, an impatience. His hands rose to join before him, loose-limbed, one finger tapping on the rest.

'I seem to remember,' he said. 'There were so many things said.' His voice was cool but firm, Cormac thought. In all his youth and strength, he was a fine replacement for Tiberius. Yet those eyes . . . they were terrible somehow, black as rage.

The senator grimaced. He stood taller than the young emperor, bronzed and handsome, a fine example of Roman power. Decimus Silanus wore a kilt and tunic that day under a white cloak, but had thrown it over one shoulder so that it revealed his right arm. Cormac could see muscles shifting there as he struggled between his desire to see this through and the obedience expected. Yet it was clear where power lay on that golden evening. Junia Claudilla had risen from a minor Silanus daughter to the wife of the emperor. The senator was still adjusting to her new rank and status.

'Of course I will come,' the senator said to his sister. He bowed again to Caligula, though the young man had barely spoken. Silanus did find the will to look Terentius in the eye, the senator already moving away as if drawn against his will.

'These men are to be taken outside the city walls and

made ready to be crucified. I would like to witness it, as a member of the family they have wronged. I will attend if I am able. Go on without me either way.'

Malvo made a sound of wrenching fear and misery. Cormac didn't dare look at him as his hopes broke to fragments.

'No,' the bride said with absolute firmness. 'No, Decimus, you will not kill these young men on my wedding day! Do you want me to remember that whenever I look back?'

'Claudilla, *please* . . .' Decimus Silanus said.

She stamped her foot, bruising a drift of the rose petals that had gathered like snow around her sandals.

'No! I told you to stand with me, Decimus, for just one day. I told you and father, there was to be no trading and no *politics* at my wedding – yet here you are, talking to common men. No, I forbid it. Shall I ask my husband to pardon them?'

She turned to Caligula. His forefinger tapped away on the back of his other hand. Like a crow pecking at flesh, Cormac thought. The skin was growing pink there. The sound of that tapping could suddenly be heard by everyone except, apparently, his wife.

'Gaius?' she said, without looking back. 'This is in your power, is it not?'

'It is,' he replied, though he too was watching her brother.

Decimus Silanus gave way before authority he dared not question.

'Very well, Claudilla,' he replied, forcing himself to smile. 'Though these brave vigiles did catch them stealing. I would have thought . . .'

'No,' she said again. 'Have Gracchus sentence them to the mines if you must, but let them live. They are young men. No more than . . . ten years, Deci. Is that clear? Let it be another gift to me.' She smiled at Cormac and recoiled slightly when she saw Malvo's odd face. 'I'm sure they will think kindly of Silanus then.'

The young woman seemed to understand instinctively that her brother's last shred of dignity depended on leaving him to it. She took her husband's arm and allowed herself to be steered away. Her father and the other guests began to move once more, having halted with the bride and groom. Junia Claudilla left her brother to grind his teeth in frustration.

Cormac didn't know whether to hope or not. He thought he could taste bitterness and swallowed spit, feeling faint. He had stared a terrifying death in the face, then had it forbidden by a young woman who cared only for memories of her wedding day. He had been snatched back from death on a bride's whim. That stung, though he could not take a moment to consider why, not when Silanus would announce his fate.

The man looked as if he'd dropped an aureus and found a copper as. He reminded Cormac of his son Marcus then, sullen when the world did not play as he'd hoped.

'You heard my sister's wishes,' the senator said grimly to Terentius. Decimus glanced down the road. Just as she passed into the hall beyond, his sister looked over her shoulder at him. She knew her brother. He scowled.

'Fine. Take these two down to the magistrate's court. Be sure Praetor Gracchus understands the sentence will be no less . . . and no more than ten years in the mines. I have known men die before completing such a term. I believe I mentioned a reward for the vigile who found them. Is that right?'

'It is, sir,' Terentius said.

'Good. I will keep it until tomorrow evening. I'll want to hear then how they fell on the way down to the forum, how they were cruelly battered in the process, so my friend Praetor Gracchus could hardly recognise them. Do you understand me? Am I making myself clear to you?'

'It is a very treacherous road, dominus,' Terentius said, nodding. Malvo gave a wail then and began to struggle. The skinny vigile punched him twice in the mouth to make him stop, the sound choking off.

'That's the sort of thing,' the senator said, approvingly. 'I'll want to hear all the details. Make them fall hard. Make them *remember*, as they go far from the sun like rats, that they should never have allowed my family name to cross their lips.'

Cormac didn't struggle as the vigiles dragged them away. He felt beyond it, as if the fight had been drawn from him like poison. There was no way out. The court wasn't far from the bottom of the Palatine hill, he remembered that much. There was certainly no place where he might pull free now, not with his hands bound. No, he accepted it. He walked along with the vigiles and wondered when the beating would begin.

He was actually surprised to reach the forum without being struck. Terentius kept a good grip on his arm, but the man looked red-faced and slightly shiny in his expression, as if he was controlling anger or embarrassment.

The praetor was at the front door with one of his scribes. They were clearly locking up for the day and Cormac could see the man was in his finest toga. He may well have been expected at one of the celebrations that would begin that night and go on for days, all across the city. Rome would cease its labours for a while and there would be sore heads, affairs begun and ended – even unexpected pregnancies for a long while after.

'Come back tomorrow,' the praetor called without looking.

'It's me, Gracchus,' Terentius said. 'Come to you from Senator Silanus. I'm afraid it won't wait.'

The name Silanus was enough to hold the man still. Cormac watched as the praetor glanced at the setting sun and decided whatever it was would have to wait.

'Two prisoners,' Terentius added. He didn't seem happy about it, his tone gruff. 'Cormac here is the one who used the Silanus name . . .'

'Oh, I remember him,' the praetor said. 'Only too well. I take it he was lying? I thought so at the time, you know.'

'Silanus denied him, anyway. He and his companion were caught stealing paper. Malvo here was always a common thief. His mate? Well, I think he's a different sort, but the sentence is the same. I have that from the emperor's new wife, Gracchus. Junia Claudilla told her brother to be merciful and he was of a mind to grant her wish. Ten years in the mines.'

The man looked affronted.

'Not even whipped? I prefer the punishment to reflect the crime. Justice must be seen, you know that! Or we will be overrun. Do you remember the way this one spoke in my court? Their crimes cry out for blood, Terentius. Impalement! Or nailed. Ten years is not much for dishonour. Not on my behalf, you understand. The court is above such concerns. No, for the . . . offence they caused Decimus. He was like a pacing lion when he heard about his name being used, I tell you! Up all night raving about gangs in Rome. Well, perhaps his sister can bring the praetorians down on those common men now. By the gods, I would nail them all for the crows! I am weary of seeing them come before me. When this year ends, I will be exhausted by my duty, I swear.'

'Well, I'll still be here, at least,' Terentius said. 'Praetors may serve their term, but vigiles remain as long as we can patrol. It'll be my city for a while yet.'

'Oh, I know, I know! You've seen half a dozen stout fellows like me, all trying to hold back a tide threatening the city, the filth and crime that would wash over us all if we didn't stand in its path. No, it has been my honour to see your men working themselves to exhaustion while others sleep. If we weren't here, street scum like these . . .' He indicated Cormac and Malvo with a disdainful expression. 'Well . . . the city would be a sewer, worse than it is.'

'Agreed, Gaius,' Terentius said grimly. 'Still, what do I do with them today?'

'There is a ship at Ostia, setting out for mines in Gaul . . .' the praetor said, looking away as he thought. 'Another for silver mines in Egypt, waiting for cargo. You could add your pair to either one – just chain them to the rest of those I sentenced this week. You know we always need more. They are brave and strong enough when it comes to threatening good men and women in the city, but not when there is work to be done, eh? No, they shrink and wither then! We must always have a new crop.'

He and Terentius were relaxed with one another, Cormac saw again. Old friends, with no awareness of the ones waiting to hear their fate. Perhaps they were too used to slaves to care what prisoners thought. Yet he was free. He cleared his throat, interrupting them.

'Will there be no hearing then, Praetor Gracchus? No jury, or speaker in defence?'

Terentius struck him, knocking him down. It wasn't as hard as Pugio had hit him, but he fell anyway, yelping as he knocked his poor fingers.

'You'd better learn to keep that tongue still,' Terentius said. 'I caught you myself, remember, with those sheets of vellum.'

'Vellum I paid for,' Cormac muttered, standing up.

Terentius hit him again, harder than before. His nose was pouring blood and Cormac choked on the iron taste, swallowing some and gagging. Still, he stood up. Malvo was watching in horror, but he was sick of these men discussing his fate as if he had no say at all.

'I have you for stealing the sheets,' Terentius growled, 'and whatever you were doing with Malvo's little gang of mates when I caught you before. I have you for using a name you have no right to. For lying to a praetor, even. The mercy of a young woman is the one thing that means you might live, understand? But if you answer me back again, I will knock your teeth into your throat. Understand me?'

Cormac nodded, spitting blood. He could see the praetor wanted him to speak, the man grinning as he watched another humiliated into silence. Cormac said nothing until his enjoyment faded to frustration.

'So,' Terentius said at last. 'I'll take them to Ostia tomorrow morning and speak to the ship's overseers. Egypt or Gaul. Hot or cold, lads?'

Neither of them dared answer, so Terentius shrugged.

'Cold then. I hate the cold. Gaul. Mark it in the record of the day, if you would, Praetor Gracchus. Two more for the mines. Ten years. Most don't survive that long, but still.'

The praetor nodded to his scribe and the man fished a thick sheaf from a leather bag much like the one Malvo had stolen. There was a long list there of crimes recorded and sentences given. Rome was a city of records and ink, Cormac thought. It was the only home he knew and he was being taken from it. He wanted to say something, but despair hit him as blood trickled down his chin and dripped onto his tunic. Malvo was looking at him, he realised, in hope of some idea or plan. He shook his head. No. There was no way out.

Prisoners were fed, Cormac discovered, when he and Malvo were kicked awake. A night back in the tullianum prison had been fitful, with broken sleep. The cells had been full and there had been the sound of weeping and sudden shouts to startle him awake at all hours. He devoured a bowl of fish broth the following morning, finding it surprisingly good. There was no spoon given, but he and Malvo slurped it up and even licked the bowls before handing them back. They were not sure when they would eat again, after all.

From there, they were taken to a cart waiting for them. The crowd was gathering as before, but the rotten fruit and stones were not thrown well that morning. Cormac felt something wet land on his neck, but it wasn't too bad. He and Malvo were chained at the ankles and so had to be lifted onto the cart bed, dropped like cordwood. They both scrambled to sit upright then, while guards from the tullianum secured bolts across, running chains through the manacles with the ease of long practice. They chatted among themselves as they worked, about women and some new winner at the chariot races.

Terentius appeared at the driver's seat, looking down on

half a dozen captives. He sighed then, stepping into the cart and making it creak as he checked the chains. Cormac glared at him, knowing his nose was still swollen and red. He tried not to flinch when Terentius looked back, but at least he looked. It mattered somehow to be seen, not just ignored like a bullock on its way to slaughter.

The cart rattled across the stones of the forum, heading out of the city – onto the road that led to the port of Ostia. Cormac found tears coming to his eyes and turned his head rather than let Malvo see. He was leaving behind everything he had ever known. He had failed, he realised. He was just sixteen years old and his whole life was over. They would take him to some deep hole in Gaul and throw him in, never to be seen again.

As the cart left the city, he began to make a tally of his life, listing victories and disasters one by one. There were many more of the latter. The only moments of kindness he could remember had come from Sophia in the kitchens. It was true Cormac had been freed by the old man's will. That had to count, though he had not known then how hard freedom could be. Beyond that, he supposed he had to add Malvo to the credit side of his ledger. He might need a friend wherever they were going, after all. There was not much else, unless he counted the whim of an emperor's wife. No, that too was on the credit side, he admitted grudgingly.

The result was a list, a litany of those he hated: Marcus Silanus, Decimus Silanus, Nartius from the estate, Praetor Gracchus, Pugio, whatever his real name was . . . and Terentius, the vigile. Between them all, they had pulled him down. They had ruined him. He spent the journey to the port imagining their death and humiliation. It was all he had left and it was cold comfort.

PART TWO

AD 43

16

Cormac knelt on a pad of cloth. Up above, it served as his tunic – the same filthy rag he'd been wearing when he was sent to the mine. While he chipped away below, he wore only loincloth and sandals. Not that he was cold. The tunnel was warm so deep underground, as if they dug close to the underworld. Old Antoninus had described Pluto's realm as a gloomy place, where golden fields waited for obedient slaves, but torture for wicked ones. It still felt like that sometimes, when the lamps failed and Cormac was in darkness so complete he might have been buried.

He'd grown taller, at least in the first couple of years. He'd noticed it in part because Malvo hadn't loomed quite so effectively, but mainly because he'd had to learn not to bash his head against the roof each day. It was just three feet high where Cormac dug – narrowing at the end like the tip of a worm working its way into rock. Further back, there was space to stand, and out by the main shafts, miners before him had left natural columns to prevent the earth snapping shut. They'd cut little alcoves to hold smoking oil lamps as well. Those made the air thick, but light was vital down there. A miner had to see what he was hitting, looking for little flakes of gold.

Cormac grunted, shifting position. His back had already begun to hurt, with a full shift ahead. His shoulders grazed the walls as he jabbed the tip of a heavy iron into stone, making quartz spark. His shoulders were bigger too, the muscles ridged from years of this sort of work. In the beginning, the other miners treated newcomers like soft city boys. He and Malvo had looked out for one another just to survive. It had been hard even so. Cormac grimaced at bad memories, jabbing with the iron. Malvo had killed a man down in the dark in the first year, where no one else could see. He'd broken the fellow's skull with a stone. There'd been a lot less trouble after that.

Cormac saw a gleam, a fleck of the sort that floated through his dreams some nights. It was such a tiny thing to be so important, but he spent entire shifts trying to find one. He had to tap that piece clear and put it in his pouch. He knew he'd endure another inspection before he was allowed to get something to eat. He'd be made to show there was nothing under his tongue, made to bend over so they could part his buttocks. The senior overseer was convinced the miners stole half of everything they dug out. The man seemed obsessed by it. The searches were unpleasant, but so common they became routine in that place, just one more humiliation to endure. A few of the others had laughed at Cormac the first few times, at his outrage perhaps, or his fear. They'd made comments about Malvo too, until he'd killed that one who'd thought he was weak. Cormac had held the man's arms in the dark, while Malvo hit him over and over.

He'd thought they'd be taken out and crucified for that, but it seemed the guards hadn't liked the man much either. They'd just put ropes on his body and dragged it up to the sun. Accidents were common, after all. Men were crushed, or gashed so deeply by some tool they just lay down and died.

Death came quickly so far beneath the surface. Cormac had heard the tunnels creaking once, before a huge slab dropped on a dozen men. They'd been turning at the noise when the ceiling came down like the earth stamped them flat. He didn't even think they'd cried out. He couldn't fear death when it came like that. It would be like snapping his fingers and closing his eyes in the same moment, too quick to worry about.

There were two ways of dying he did fear. Each dawn, the miners were marched from their little camp in the Gaulish forests, out of the main gate and over to the nearest shafts. The guards went with them and they were chained together for that short stretch, until they went down below.

Set twenty paces apart, the drop shafts followed seams and veins of quartz invisible to those who didn't descend – a world those men knew better than the one above. They had cut handholds in each shaft, and Cormac knew he could scramble down like a rat on a rope after years of practice. He'd even told new men how to do it without losing grip and falling. They had to jam their hands right into each slot, clenching a fist though skin scraped raw. That grip could hold a man's weight if his feet slipped, as all the old hands discovered sooner or later. Cormac told himself it was because he might be beneath one of them, swept off the shaft by some falling body. They looked to him, he noticed, as one who knew things. Or just one who had Malvo watching his back. He and Malvo had survived six years, after all. They'd been hardened in that place. Battered, but still there, working like moles underground for a dozen hours a day.

At the start of each shift, one of the overseers lowered a lamp with a little flame on a rope. Cormac didn't understand exactly how it worked, but in six years, he'd seen that flame snuff out three times. When it did, the man would mutter 'bad air' and raise it up, relighting it two or three times until he was sure the flame wouldn't last. After that, no one was allowed to use that shaft. They were marched off to another and quotas were behind for days.

The year before, Cormac had seen two men brought out without a mark on them, but dark around the lips, as if they'd eaten soil. He'd known them as hard men, not much given to talking. They'd looked out for one another and never taken part in the attacks on new ones, not like some of the others. Their bodies had flopped as they were heaved up, as if they were drunk or just asleep. The overseer in charge of that section had closed the shaft for three days and taken his time with lamp and ropes when he tried again. Cormac had heard him cursing into his beard.

Cormac swore as he jammed his fingers, the smooth flow of his thoughts breaking apart. It was how he survived long shifts. He thought back over old conversations, old mistakes, of everyone he wanted to repay for putting him in that place. Then he would jar his left hand and sudden pain would make him gasp. The old breaks had healed badly, giving him two fingers that wouldn't bend.

He'd learned to work around the problem, but when he was all hunched up, when it felt like the world wanted to squeeze shut, he sometimes hit a bad angle.

At least it was his left hand, he thought. He wondered sometimes if he would still be able to write when he came out. A scribe's hands were agile, clever things, or at least they had been. When he looked at them now, they were heavier, wider. His thumbs had thickened and he had scars that had never been properly stitched. The skin was smooth on those old cuts, but didn't stretch like skin should. It split sometimes when he worked, dripping beads like rubies onto pale quartz.

He put another flake of gold into his pouch, a piece about half the size of his smallest fingernail. That was a good one, he thought. He knew some of the lads swallowed flakes like that. They had to avoid the toilet shed after, where everything was checked and sifted. It was one of the punishment jobs in the camp, for those who had answered back, or stolen food. They were always starving, of course. A little less so after sifting through the stools of two hundred men.

Cormac let his thoughts drift again as he jabbed with his iron, then checked the pieces. His hands were always sore. Like his lower back and his knees, something always hurt. Yet he was far stronger than he had been, he knew that. Wider too than many of the men who had been sentenced later in life. At twenty-two years old, his hair had grown to his shoulders and had to be tied back. Even his voice had deepened. Cormac still dreamed of those frantic days in Rome, rushing from one place to another with a mind full of plans and possibilities. It was a different life though. The mines had changed him. He was not sure he would even recognise the young lads he and Malvo had been.

He heard someone swear a little way back. The closest lamp was guttering in its alcove as oil ran low. Cormac cursed as he saw the light fail. The boy Severus was meant to keep them filled, but he was easily distracted. Or hurt, maybe. Cormac had seen a few of the new arrivals watching the kid. One of them was a hard-faced, bony sort, about as tall as Malvo. Cormac didn't know if Nepos was Gaul or Greek, but he was pale as sickness, except for the parts he never washed. Those were grey. Cormac didn't like the way Nepos had fastened on to Severus, but there was only so much he and Malvo could do. They could protect themselves well enough. If they started expanding that protection to others, it would be a challenge. Nepos already had his mates, a little group of them. So Cormac looked the other way. There were just too many ways to die in that place. He dug harder, as if the rock face was Nepos himself.

Cormac saw a trickle of water appear between his knees like a snake. He stared in horror, then smacked his head on the ceiling as he jerked away, shuffling desperately backwards. There was no room to turn and his heart thumped wildly. Water was the way to die he feared most, more than bad air even. The stuff just seeped into mines, slowly if the gods were with them, quickly if they were not.

The original shafts were often sunk within range of rivers. There was something about those ancient courses that seemed to collect gold. The overseers used the rushing water to set up sluices and cleaning gates as well. Yet it meant there was always a threat of water breaking through to the mines themselves. Cormac had seen three shafts abandoned when they hit some underground stream. The drop shafts filled with brown swirling water then, faster than anyone could climb out. They'd lost thirty men in a single day three years before, as well as a seam of gold thick as a man's thumb.

'Malvo! *Water!*' Cormac yelled as he backed up. 'Get out!'

He passed the tunnel where Nepos had been chipping at a good vein. Cormac caught a glimpse of hissing spray coming from a dozen places in the rock face, while Nepos tried to stem the flow with his hands. He was already drenched when he saw Cormac gaping at him.

'What do I do?' Nepos shrieked.

He had been in the mines less than a month, Cormac realised. He may not have seen a shaft lost before.

'Press tighter,' Cormac snapped. 'I'll fetch the overseer.'

Nepos redoubled his efforts to hold the water back. It was impossible, but he didn't know that. Cormac felt a pang of regret for what he'd done, but that was an echo of a previous life. If Nepos drowned down there, he wouldn't be calling Severus to visit him in his bunk again – and the lad wouldn't be weeping in the mornings and flinching from every touch.

Cormac stood taller as he reached the bottom of the main shaft, a few steps ahead of Malvo. Water was already swirling at ankle height, rising to their knees in just moments. He saw one of Nepos' mates wading out of his own gallery tunnel, counting heads and swearing.

'Nepos!' the man bellowed, cupping his hands to make his voice carry. 'Leave it. We're going up.'

To Cormac's disappointment, Nepos gave up trying to hold back the flood and staggered out. The lamps had all been snuffed by rising waters, but there was light enough to see up the main shaft, even as the galleries went dark. Malvo nodded to Cormac and began to climb – sixty handholds in the shaft wall to reach the surface. Cormac had to push past grasping hands, but he was going next. Water rose to their waists below him and the others began to shout in fear. He climbed quickly, though he could have blocked the shaft until Nepos and his mates drowned. That would have been a different beast compared to telling a man to hold back a flood.

There was a great gasping and panting beneath him as he rose. Cormac growled in frustration as he climbed. Those seams had been the best he'd seen that year. He knew the overseer would try to save the mine. He shook his head, concentrating. The flood had already filled the galleries and was rising in the shaft itself. Nepos was lowest and he began to yell for the others to go faster.

Cormac placed each hand and foot with care. If he slipped and fell, they would all drown. Below, Nepos began to swear, pleading with them. When Cormac glanced down, he could see the water had risen to Nepos' neck as he struggled to stay ahead.

Hands reached for him as he came out. Cormac was dragged onto a muddy field, once a stretch of virgin forest. The trees had been cleared and the ground made a swamp by feet tramping back and forth every day, all for what lay far beneath it. Word of the river breach had gone round and other teams were pouring out from their tunnels, fearing the flood would spread until they all drowned.

Cormac's shaft was surrounded by interested men. The mine guards were there as well as the cooks, their lunch stew abandoned. Those men were given extra rations for taking a turn with the massive cauldrons. Cormac knew one of them was a poisoner, but that had been a personal matter, not a hobby. Twelve years in the mines for serving his wife her last meal. No one else had fallen ill since and the fellow had a knack for mushrooms, there was no denying that.

Cormac was still panting as Nepos made it to the surface, followed on his heels by a spill of water that spread in a great brown pool, making all the bystanders retreat. There were rules on the placing of down shafts, so Cormac knew the next one would be exactly twenty paces away. If the water didn't fill that one from below, it might start pouring in from above. The overseer would have a fit.

Not far off, Cormac could hear the sound of the river. There had been a lot of rain over the previous few days. The thing was in flood, much louder than usual. He wondered . . .

He saw something flicker and ducked to one side. He was never quite relaxed, not as he had once been as a boy in Rome. He saw Nepos lunge with a knife in his hand. Cormac took a cut on his forearm, but barely felt the sting as he jerked away. He shoved Nepos hard as he started to stagger, off balance. He'd put his whole weight behind the stab and fell badly, coming up roaring.

'You left me to *drown*,' Nepos raged, facing Cormac with fists bunched.

The knife had vanished in his fall. Cormac saw Malvo put his foot on it, pressing it into the mud before Nepos could find it again. He noted the man had lost his digging iron as well, no doubt abandoning all his tools in the rush to get out. Cormac smiled then. His own iron was hooked through his belt, too precious to leave. That belt was the same one he'd worn in Rome, though he'd had to punch holes to accommodate new muscle. Cormac slid the length of iron out and held it where Nepos could see.

'Come on then,' Cormac said, rolling his shoulders.

Nepos looked at the bar in his hand, as well as the way Cormac stood ready. He sneered, shaking his head.

'Don't go to sleep,' he said, turning away.

Cormac almost hit him then, wanting nothing more than to bring the iron down on his head. It was Malvo who grabbed his arm. Cormac looked up to see the overseer coming, the man's expression stricken at the pool of water.

'What are you all doing just standing there?' Farix demanded. 'Cormac, Malvo. Fetch the screws.'

Cormac eyed the massive wooden tubes he and Malvo had piled outside the sheds. In his first couple of years, Cormac had been surprised what two or three hundred men could do with just billets of wood, a few iron pieces, pulleys, levers and wedges. He'd seen rocks split that looked as if they would stand to the end of time. He'd built a bridge alongside work teams to transport ore over a river, cutting wood and stone and mixing lime mortar with the others.

Some of those who had been sentenced had been carpenters or builders in their old lives. Those skills were valuable anywhere, but especially in those forests. It wasn't just a matter of better rations either, Cormac had seen that. Stonemasons and carpenters were never worked to death, not like some of the slaves. They had an advantage when it came to disputes as well – overseers like Farix would take their side more often than not, just to keep the peace. Cormac had set out to learn from them. He lent his labour and strength, asking questions until they either taught him something new or told him to shut up.

It had been a hard few years, but he and Malvo had learned to make themselves useful. Malvo in particular had a knack for cutting stone, as if he could see the seams inside and put the wedge in the right spot every time. Overseer Farix wasn't a fool, of course. He knew exactly what they were doing, but he did need competent men – and he believed such men were less likely to knife him as he slept. Farix was a Gaul and though he could be surly, a cup or two of wine gentled his nature and soothed his suspicions.

That Gaul had hunted forests much like those when he'd been a boy, as Farix told it, taking boar, deer and hares for the family pot. For all the filth and danger, his love for the land was clear. He was even proud of the gold it produced, as a farmer might be proud of his crops or his children. Farix had been like a dog with two tails when he heard who sat on the imperial throne in Rome.

News of that had seeped down to the mine crews, rumours and whispers that were never more than half-true. Cormac had been shown a coin with a new face the year before, a profile he did not know – and the name of Claudius to replace Gaius Caesar. He'd made the mistake of telling them how he'd met Caligula, or at least stood in the same road on the man's wedding day. Some of the older ones had mocked him then for having airs and graces. Even Malvo said to drop it and he'd been there as well.

It had been Farix who'd told Cormac what had happened to the young man he remembered, the one with the cold, dark eyes. Instead of ruling the empire for fifty years as they'd all thought, Caligula had lasted only four. The wife Cormac recalled, radiant on her wedding day, had gone on to die in a birthing room, the child cut out of her as she screamed.

Cormac shuddered when he thought of it. The young emperor had called her father into the room, so Farix said. The overseer told the tale with awful relish and new details every time. It seemed that Silanus had leaned over his dead daughter – and Caligula had cut the old man's throat, sending him after Junia Claudilla with some whispered message for the newly dead.

That news had brought a more complex response in Cormac than simple satisfaction. The Silanus family had lost their best chance at founding an imperial dynasty, it was true. More, they had lost the head of the family. Cormac supposed it meant the older son was now first amongst the Junii Silani. Senator Decimus Silanus would have inherited everything his father had owned as well. It seemed the one who had burned Cormac at the old estate was still blessed by the gods.

After that day, the emperor had gone quite mad, at least as Farix told it. Cormac thought he had to be exaggerating, but even half of it would have been hard to hear. Gaius Caesar had torn through the senate, ruining families, taking whatever he pleased like an angry child. It had all come to an end when his own praetorians stabbed him to death on the Palatine.

The uncle they'd found to replace Caligula had been born in Lugdunum, in Gaul. That was enough for Farix, anyway. The overseer raised a toast each night to Emperor Claudius and prayed for his soul. In his cups, he would talk of having a Gaul in command of the empire at last, of good men who might now be rewarded for loyal service, instead of being forgotten in a forest at the arse end of nowhere.

Farix had learned he could trust Cormac and Malvo

not to repeat what he said, or take advantage of his indis-cretions. They even shared a skin of Gaulish red when Farix was sent a new one by some distant wife. Unlike the miners themselves, Farix was paid for his labours, with no way to spend it in the forests. He answered to the senior overseer, but that man had a cabin by the river and hardly cared what they did as long as they met the quota of gold.

Cormac knew Farix kept a pouch of his savings in his tent. He'd seen it once when he brought the man home rather than let him sleep drunk under the stars. It was the sort of thing Cormac always noted, but he needed Farix's trust more than a few denarii.

The tubes he and Malvo laid on the muddy ground were based on the workings of Archimedes, Cormac under-stood that much. In all honesty, the actual design was not that complicated. One end of a tube was put under the surface of water and a handle turned. A sort of screw rotated inside and water was drawn up on the blades until it splashed out the other end. With a dozen of them together, with buckets and troughs and slaves working day and night, they could drain a flooded mine back to silt, then drop down shafts on ropes to dig out the rest. Other teams would dam the river further up, turning the flow so the waters stopped coming in. They'd done it before and Cormac knew all the steps. It was brutal work, with the sole benefit of being different to hacking at a rock face.

He and Malvo went back and forth with the largest tubes, carrying two between them. There were a few sizes in the sheds and he supposed they would need them all. He was aware of Nepos watching as he put each pair down. Malvo saw that as well and shook his head.

'He'll try something,' Malvo muttered in warning.

'Good. I want him to,' Cormac said curtly, his face flushed with effort.

Malvo rolled his eyes. It had been Cormac who'd kept him from despairing in the first years, Cormac who'd planned and watched for advantage, choosing to help Farix over a different overseer with a streak of cruelty. They'd learned together and it had been Cormac who shared every knack and scrap of knowledge. Malvo owed him a debt and he wasn't sure his friend even realised. Still, Cormac was many things, but he wasn't a killer. Malvo noted the way muscles writhed in his friend's arms as they shifted the tubes together. He was strong enough, but not vicious, not the way he needed to be.

'If he dies in the mine,' Malvo said on the way back, 'the guards can pretend it was an accident. In the camp though . . . no. You understand that, right? I don't want to be strung up or nailed because you told him to hold back a flooding tunnel.'

Cormac chuckled at the memory, but Malvo frowned.

'It's not funny, Cor. He's a vicious bastard. He'll kill you.'

Cormac saw the boy Severus had waited for them at the shed. He had one of the smaller tubes in his arms, though even that was too much for him.

'Give it here. I have it,' Cormac said gruffly. 'Thanks.'

Severus grinned at him. Cormac met Malvo's eyes then and his friend understood.

'All right,' Malvo said. He rubbed his lopsided jaw as he thought, then raised another of the great tubes on his shoulder, balancing it as they walked back. He sighed. It looked like they were going to kill a man.

17

Death was always close underground. If it didn't come from bad air, flood or a rockfall, it could come in violence. Snuffing lamps and hammering someone to death in the dark had happened a dozen times in the six years Cormac and Malvo had been on the crews. The first one had shocked Cormac to the point of not being able to sleep properly for a month. When it happened again just a month later, it had been the result of some dispute over food, something so trivial it had made him sick with despair. Yet deaths were still less common than deliberate injury – an iron brought down on a stray hand, or a few quick punches in the latrine line to settle a score. The trick lay in seeing it coming and making the cost too high.

One time when Farix had been drunker than they'd ever seen him, he had taken on the air of someone confiding a secret. The overseer had told Malvo he'd been lucky. The guards hadn't liked the man he'd killed – and anything like a formal trial would lose another skilled worker when they were already short. The quota was what mattered most, so they'd chosen to look the other way. The broken skull had been recorded as a mine accident, the body buried deep in the forest. Farix had wagged his head in warning as he'd said they couldn't do it again. The Gaul had been wildly drunk, but also serious, poking Malvo's bony chest to drive the point home.

What he and Cormac planned instead would cause a great deal more damage, but at the end, Cormac thought they wouldn't be left for the crows, or nailed to a tree. If it went well. Malvo preferred simpler plans, like holding Nepos under water until he drowned. That might have worked if the man hadn't kept his mates close. They came and went together and watched Malvo all the time. He was a shield to Cormac, as Malvo understood very well.

When the miners dammed the river, the waters began to recede right away. Only when the tunnels below blocked with silt did the level stop dropping. The screws were brought in then. Men sat on baskets of ropes to be lowered down, taking water out in leather buckets. It was slow work and they all took shifts as the days wore on.

At the bottom of the drop shaft, the silt had settled in a great bank of clay and grit. It had to be dug out, with heavier buckets drawn up, one by one. Another week passed, with the senior overseer roaring at Farix more than once. That man didn't care who died or collapsed. He just wanted the mine to produce.

Malvo and Cormac took shifts with the others, always watching for Nepos or his crew to come sidling up, perhaps with another knife. Even without a feud, there were accidents. Holding a peg for another always meant the chance of broken fingers. An iron dropped down a shaft could leave whoever it struck unable to speak. It was exhausting to be watching each other's backs every waking hour.

At the end of the second week, the galleries between drop shafts were being excavated and space had been cleared for more than one man to go down. Malvo was up top seeing to the ropes. They'd had to pull one half-drowned lad out of collapsing sludge that very morning, but they were making progress. Nepos had gone down with two of his mates, leaving two more to wrestle buckets of clay at the top – and to keep an eye on Malvo.

Malvo frowned, looking into the hole. He raised his arm, with a scrap of cloth in it, waving it back and forth.

'What are you doing?' one of Nepos' crew growled. The man was ready with his iron and Malvo warned him with a glare. He kept waving his hand.

'I thought I heard something down there . . .' Malvo said. 'I'm calling Farix over.'

In fact, the overseer wasn't far off. The Gaul was already coming to see what Malvo wanted.

Malvo heard a sound like distant thunder then. He stood up, wide-eyed as Farix arrived.

'What was that?' the overseer demanded in a panic. Farix too peered into the shaft and they all felt the ground tremble. Farix looked up in horror as he and Malvo turned in the direction of the river.

Malvo knew Cormac had slipped away to the new dam. Judging by the sound, he'd hammered out a couple of key pegs and boards, releasing the river to its old course. In the tunnels below, the men had dug through to the original breach. Nepos would have been peering right into the hole he'd tried to block.

There was a roar from the shaft and a brief cry, choked off in an instant.

'The river!' Farix shouted. 'Pull the men out! The dam has broken!'

He watched in horror as water rose in the shaft, much faster than before. With half the galleries choked, the river came through like a fountain. Nepos and those with him had no chance at all, tumbling in water and darkness. Malvo winced at the thought.

He and Farix watched as water surged up, undoing two weeks' work in moments. Some of the other men heaved on the ropes, but they jammed, caught on snags down below. There was no sign of anyone coming to the surface. Malvo counted beats in his head, until he was sure no one remained alive.

Other teams poured out from nearby shafts, swearing and blowing. Malvo saw Cormac had trotted back to join the crowd, breathing exactly like a man who had run half a mile. Malvo hoped no one else noticed how wet he was. His friend was lucky not to have been swept away and drowned. Still, it meant the boy Severus would sleep better that night and all the nights after . . .

Malvo saw Farix turn from the flooding shaft, even as the brown pool spread. The others looked up one by one and froze. Cormac too was staring at something, Malvo saw, his friend's expression strange. He looked away from the flooded mine at last, to see legionaries standing in the woods all around them.

With all the yelling and the roar of waters, those men had approached unseen. They stood like ghosts between the trees and Malvo saw a number of the miners make signs against evil. Legionaries were to be feared at the best of times . . . Malvo peered at them, feeling his stomach clench. No, not just legionaries. He remembered those uniforms from a different life. These were praetorians.

One of the strangers stepped forward, his plume cut to perfect neatness. Malvo remembered the vigile who had asked about the silver chasing on their scabbards. The same design was on this man's sword, as if it were made for beauty as well as use.

'Who's in charge of this shithole?' the praetorian asked.

Farix looked for his superior. In that moment, the man was on the other side of the river, no doubt in the sheds where gold was cast to be sent to Rome. At any sign of trouble, the man retreated there, convinced they were under attack. With the river cutting him off, Farix was highest in rank.

The overseer considered dropping to one knee, but the ground was thick with mud and the pool was still spreading. He saw the praetorian's sandals were clean. To him, those spattered, filthy men must look like wild animals.

'I oversee this shaft – and a dozen more,' Farix said. 'Name of Farix. I am . . . surprised to see praetorians so far from Rome.' A thought struck him and he paled suddenly. 'Is . . . i-is the emperor coming here . . . ?'

'Not yet,' the praetorian replied gruffly, 'and Emperor Claudius has no interest in your mine either. I'm here for workers.'

He held up a tightly bound scroll to show he had orders, but didn't bother to unroll it. Cormac already knew Farix couldn't read, but he still watched with interest. He had strolled over to stand by Malvo as soon as he recognised the praetorian uniforms. Those men were peacocks in that place of mud, sweat and bruised flesh. He assumed they had marched for miles to reach the mine, but no sign of that showed. They gleamed in rich colours, their kit polished. Cormac had to remind himself they were chosen from lesser legions, the best of the best to protect the emperor and patrol the heart of empire. Like Farix, he wondered what they could be doing in a Gaulish forest.

'Workers?' Farix said. 'These men are serving terms in the gold mine here, officer . . .'

'*Centurion* Titus Livius,' the praetorian said. 'And I don't care if they are running a brothel. My orders are to collect every farmhand, smith and stable lad I find. Mine workers will do very well. You too, "Farix". I need about a thousand or so. How many do you have?'

Farix mumbled the man's title and name, then tried again.

'Centurion, these men are bound for terms of service, agreed by the courts. I am appointed overseer for these teams, with twelve years seniority. Some are free, some slaves, but I don't understand your request. I cannot allow them to be taken . . .'

The centurion looked at him then. Cormac wanted to call a warning, but it would have meant his own skin. He knew the reputation of praetorians, better it seemed than Farix did. They were a law unto themselves and he wanted Farix to stop trying to argue.

The praetorian jerked his head and two of his men stepped forward and grabbed Farix by the arms. The overseer protested, his voice growing louder and higher as they tied him to a tree and stripped his back. He fell silent then, while all the crews watched.

The praetorian addressed the crowd while one of his men uncoiled a great length of some black oiled thing. It shone like a snake and the end twitched, making Cormac wince.

'Despite the objection of your overseer, you will accompany my cohort as we march north. My men cannot be expected to dig latrine pits and help grease galleys into the sea. That sort of work is beneath the emperor's personal guard, as you can imagine. You will complete those tasks and any others asked of you. Until such time as you are left on the shore, waving us all goodbye like our favourite whores. At that point, you can come back here, or settle down with a farmer's pigs for all I care.'

As the centurion paused for breath, the whip was laid on. Farix gave a great shriek, going very red. The pain knocked the air from him with every strike, so that he could hardly draw breath between and then only to howl. Yet it went on and on. Cormac knew a man could die from forty strokes of the long whip. He counted forty, then after a pause, forty more.

The mine teams watched as Farix was murdered in front of them. The whip cut skin as it landed, slicing flaps of muscle and spraying blood. They saw ribs exposed, then cracked under the strokes, each one like a blow from an iron. The overseer had not been much hated in their camp, not like some of the others. The teams watched in fury as the praetorians showed their power over them all.

Farix coughed with each blow for the last few, leaking blood from his mouth. He slumped on the ropes as his legs buckled and when they cut him down at last, there was no life left in him.

'Well? What are you waiting for?' the centurion bellowed. 'Form *a line* . . .'

They moved rather than risk that cold attention settling on anyone else. Cormac and Malvo shuffled with the others.

'Are there any more back in camp?' the praetorian asked.

Cormac shook his head with the rest. He almost groaned when he heard a higher voice asking what was happening. The boy Severus had come running from the sheds. The praetorian gestured and one of his men shoved the boy into line. Cormac silenced his questions with a look and a shake of his head, fearing another example.

'Have we joined the army?' the boy asked in astonishment.

The praetorian made a disgusted sound.

'This is not so great an honour. You are auxiliaries, lad: camp followers for a campaign. Not legionaries, certainly not praetorians. You will cook and repair and polish. I will rest my boots on you to tie my sandals if I feel like it. Is that understood?'

The mine teams all nodded again, their gaze drifting to where Farix stared at nothing. The centurion seemed satisfied.

Cormac looked at Farix, then the cook who had poisoned his own wife. The man did know his mushrooms. Cormac remembered a few more things about the praetorians as well, such as the fact that they were paid twice as much as any other legion. It didn't make them popular, he'd heard. He supposed they didn't need campaign followers either, not in a normal year. Yet if they were on the march, it *had* to mean the emperor was as well. What was Emperor Claudius doing in Gaul? It all meant something. Cormac couldn't help wondering what double pay would look like, weighed out in coins.

'He said it was a gold mine, Quint,' the centurion muttered to one of his subordinates. 'Someone should check the camp. Make sure there's nothing . . . valuable – or more men skulking about, waiting for us to move on.'

That man nodded and on impulse Cormac raised his

hand. He heard Malvo make a choking sound next to him, but kept it up.

'I can show your man the way, centurion,' Cormac said. He heard one of Nepos' mates mutter a filthy curse at his back, but they were missing their leader and he did not fear them, not with Malvo glaring. Those odds had changed and he had to think ahead.

The other soldier waved him out of line and Cormac trotted along the path back to the camp. He knew there was no one else there, but he'd guessed the praetorian was only interested in the slugs of gold they cast, each the product of a dozen shifts. Those were on the other side of a raging river, but the praetorians didn't know that.

Cormac rolled the most valuable tools into a leather wrap, making himself helpful. The optio wasn't interested in those, though they were hard to forge and worth more than he understood. Instead, the praetorian peered into grubby tents and outhouses, even the latrine shed and the storerooms. He scowled at piles of turnips, though Cormac saw him bite one. He watched while the man kicked in the door to the shed where Farix had slept, vanishing inside. Cormac dashed across a muddy path then, entering the little office where the overseers kept count of shifts and sentences.

Cormac snatched a handful of sheets. They weren't fine vellum like he'd known before, more like cheap rabbit skin and a couple of better quality that were grey with age and use. He pressed the sheaf to his chest under the tunic, stepping back on the path as the praetorian reappeared. The man threw a cooking pot through the air and Cormac caught it awkwardly with one hand, trying not to drop the sheets he gripped close with an elbow. He was not too distracted to see the man tucking a pouch of silver coins away. It had been a year of savings to Farix, but in fairness the overseer didn't have much use for it, not then. The praetorian seemed pleased, but he still made Cormac undo the leather roll. There were no coins or gold nuggets hidden amongst the old drills and chisels, however.

'These will be useful,' Cormac said. He didn't want to leave pieces of forged iron to rust forgotten in the forest. The praetorian shrugged as Cormac tied it all into a neat roll.

'Just get back in line,' the praetorian said gruffly. 'Understand? You'll march till your feet bleed.'

Cormac nodded, though he didn't think the man knew miners, not at all. In that moment, he thought he could march until he saw the sea and not complain. For Farix, he would.

In some ways, life had stood still for Cormac and Malvo in the mining camp. Six years before, they'd been taken by sea from Ostia with around eighty men, chained at the ankles to stop anyone trying to run. Raw skin had thickened under those shackles by the time they'd reached northern Gaul. In the years since, Cormac knew they'd both grown stronger, but the world had gone on without them. Even the news of Caligula's death had come long after the event, from a trader bringing grain and black bread.

With praetorians before and behind, two hundred miners were marched from the camp, through forest as deep and thick as Cormac remembered. When they broke out onto a wide road, it was almost like being reborn. The sun was on the stones there, a road that might have been Rome itself for all it promised.

Cormac stared like a boy. He and the mine crews had come out on the crest of a long rise. When he glanced back, he stopped in astonishment, making the man behind him curse. The road was *filled* with marching soldiers and lowing oxen, mile upon mile of them. Cormac and Malvo joined the flow, while praetorians lined up on either side of their little column. In the first few hours, Cormac saw three different legion banners as well as a hundred carts waiting on the verges. The praetorians came through without stopping, their reputation clearing the road ahead.

There were just five hundred under the centurion who had killed Farix. Cormac assumed that was a single cohort, but he could not be sure. It was a whole new world and he listened to everything he could, quietly learning. He and Malvo had expected to be put onto that road four years later than this, ready to walk a thousand miles south to Rome, taking work along the way to keep spirit and flesh together. It grieved Cormac to be walking the wrong way, north instead of south. Yet the image of Farix remained clearly in his mind and he said not a word.

When they camped the first night, the poisoner volunteered to help prepare vast pots of some dark sludge that actually smelled quite appetising. The legion already had one cook, who added lumps of dried fish and ancient vegetables. Cormac ate every scrap, as he always did. He knew the man from camp wouldn't poison his own, though he wasn't sure about the praetorians. For an elite force, they seemed oddly underprepared for the wilderness. They did have carts and tents, though it was Cormac and the others who had to pitch and strike them. Each day's march ended with hard physical labour, a bowl of reheated sludge and the happy chance of exhausted sleep.

Malvo looked to Cormac in clear question the first night. There was a surprising amount of confusion in the ranks of a moving army, especially one as vast as this. Cormac thought he and Malvo might slip away in the dark, but the praetorians would be watching for exactly that, at least for a while. They kept men on guard as a matter of course, whenever they made camp. They marked off clearings, with no one allowed across the boundary. Cormac watched in fascination as they stood shifts and muttered passwords of the day. He and Malvo would have had to creep past alert men, standing ready to challenge and blast a warning note from horns. In the end, Cormac shook his head and let Malvo sleep.

He counted thirty milestones the next morning, until he had cause to remember his private oath not to complain even if his feet bled. He'd formed a poor opinion of the praetorians to that point, but they marched as if distance meant nothing. They expected other legions to move aside like carters or heralds, or anyone else in their way. They were the emperor's personal guard, after all. Cormac supposed it explained their vanity. Other legions stepped off the road to let them pass, which showed something about their status. The more interesting question was the location of the emperor.

It wasn't until the eighth day that they crested a hill and looked down on a sea of glittering blue. Golden sand stretched in the distance, but before the shore a maze of walls and buildings had sprung up for miles, from animals penned by stone enclosures to the sort of wooden dormitories Cormac knew from camp. He saw palisade walls of sharpened logs as well as watchtowers and lines of men patiently waiting to be fed. It was a city, built to house legions as they gathered. He blinked into the distance as he took note of a vast tower on the rocks by the shore, a line of smoke issuing from some fire at the top.

Cormac realised he could smell the camp when the wind changed, making him cough. He thought he'd grown used to the latrine shed when he'd been set cleaning duty there. It seemed thirty or forty thousand men and as many animals somehow refined the odours and strengthened them.

The praetorians drew to a halt. Cormac watched as Centurion Titus marched to the front. His expression was of one who had trodden in dog muck, yet he snapped orders and began to inspect his men, preparing to return to civilisation. Cormac watched everything, seeing how the officers took pains to restore the lower ranks to shining perfection. He couldn't tell if it was the chance of coming before the emperor or rejoining the rest of the legion that meant so much to them. Centurion Titus made them check and polish every piece of kit, with knots tied just so and horses brushed to gleaming.

When the centurion was satisfied, the cohort looked a lot neater and less road-stained, Cormac had to admit. Some drummer boy had even offered the mine crews a chance to wipe a cloth over their own faces, dunking it in a bucket. They moved on only when another legion came up the road behind. It seemed Centurion Titus wasn't willing to follow Legio II Augusta down to the coast.

Cormac could only stride along with the rest, approaching the vast enterprise that had taken over that part of Gaul. Back in the forests, it had felt like he marched with an army. On that shore, they were simply swallowed in a greater host. Cormac passed men working horses on long reins. He

227

saw cloth being woven and half a dozen tanneries with their usual foul reek. Legionaries on exercise runs loped past in chanting groups, revealed by their tattoos.

Malvo nudged him and Cormac blinked as they passed a massive creature he had never seen before. Huge tusks arced out in lengths and Cormac's mouth dropped open. Hannibal had ridden such a beast across the Alps, he recalled. It was a part of his memory he had kept bright in the mines. He'd told Malvo a thousand stories he'd read in the histories. Hannibal's war elephant had been named . . . Surus, he recalled. The Syrian.

Cormac wanted to dart over, to get close to such a wondrous creature. Yet he remained in line with the mine crews as the praetorians sent horsemen on ahead. They were always rushing, always working, Cormac realised, never still.

Centurion Titus had collected dozens more recruits from farms and villages along the way. Those Gauls still seemed stunned by the change in their fortunes. One had tried to run and suffered the same fate as Farix a few nights before. It seemed the centurion had a limited imagination, though the example was certainly effective.

With the sea just a mile or so away, they all marched into the belly of the legion beast. Another cohort of praetorians joined the one Cormac thought of as his own, forming a group of at least a thousand, along with the few hundred camp followers. They stopped only for Centurion Titus to get directions from some functionary. They trudged closer to the shore then, to where huge wooden towers stood. Gulls wheeled and cried in the salt air, while guards kept watch above the great host. Cormac saw the towers had wheels and wondered if the elephants were there to pull them.

Massive gates opened onto a sandy yard close to the dunes, surrounded by walls of mortared stone and sandbags. It had the air of a temporary place, but the mine crews were marched to the centre and roared at until they stood roughly to attention.

Cormac and Malvo were inspected by what seemed to be more experienced auxiliaries. The leader was a bald man who announced himself only as Paullus. He reminded Cormac of Pugio back in Rome, at least for his slab-like build and bow-legged stance.

All the mine men stared into the distance as they were peered at and prodded. Malvo's face was turned this way and that, the hole in his cheek and missing nostril examined with a noise like a clucking hen. Still, he could lift the ball of stone Paullus rolled to his feet. When Malvo threw it on command, the bald man made a note on a wax slate and looked impressed.

Each of the newcomers was asked what skills they had. Cormac admitted to knowing joints and stone-cutting like the others. He held back that he could read and write. Caution had been hammered into him over six years and he volunteered nothing. Like Malvo, he endured fingers opening his jaw and men peering into his throat for marks of disease. Despite his stiff fingers, he too lifted the stone ball easily, surprising himself when he threw it further than Malvo had.

'Well, lads, you're fit enough,' Paullus announced, rubbing his bald head with the flat of one hand.

Cormac looked along the line and saw not one of those he knew had been turned away. He felt an odd pride in that.

'You can sleep in the yard tonight,' Paullus said. 'There'll be guards on the walls, so don't get any ideas about wandering off. There's more men in this camp than a city – and any one of them will cut your liver out if you answer back or step out of line. Remember this. You may be fit, but you ain't *trained*, not like legion men. So don't speak out of turn. Don't draw a knife unless you want to be made to eat it. Don't even talk loudly, not when free men are talking. Do the work you're given without complaint. Say "Yes, master" to any order of any kind and you might live. You're not worth much to us, but you can work yourself to death in the knowledge that it is for the praetorians – and Emperor Claudius.' Paullus smiled unpleasantly, showing missing teeth. 'Let that name be your watchword and your comforter.'

Cormac found himself clenching a fist. Perhaps he had grown used to being treated as a man and not a boy. He had grown in the years since leaving Rome and yet this bald whoreson wanted him to keep his head down like any slave. It brought a bitter taste.

Horns sounded nearby, a great cacophony that rose and was joined by more, like a message carried over distance. Paullus and the other auxiliaries looked suddenly worried, the relaxed style vanishing. In the road outside, Cormac could hear shouts and warnings, growing louder all the time. He looked to the gateway, still open.

'He's here,' Paullus shouted to them. 'Kneel if you see him. In fact, fuck it, kneel now, all of you.'

They dropped obediently to the dusty yard. Cormac bowed his head and still tried to watch as a massive column thundered past outside. He recognised praetorian uniforms as they tramped in lines that never seemed to end. These ones were marked by road dust and Cormac began to count. Six to a line – a row? He'd seen forty or so rows march past, though there had been some carrying banners and great curved horns as well. He made a guess at three hundred men already seen, then began to count in earnest. Malvo heard him muttering numbers and jabbed him with an elbow. Cormac warned him off with a sharp gesture.

When eight hundred had crossed the gateway, Cormac saw white horses, then a dozen carriages with men inside. He had to guess at numbers there . . .

The world seemed to slow as he saw a man on horseback, wearing a robe of purple and white. Emperor Claudius was not young as Caligula had been, nor unusual in his looks. If anything he was a little thin, as if he'd been ill. He squirmed as he rode, perhaps bothered by itching piles.

The kneeling men watched in awe as the emperor passed close enough to shout to, not that any of them would have dared. They saw an open carriage trundling behind the emperor, where a woman of arresting beauty sat with what must have been her young son. Cormac watched a thickset boy glaring around, his delighted gaze fastening on the kneeling miners. The lad laughed and pointed at them, but they were past before his mother could turn.

Cormac felt a sting of humiliation, one he could not afford. He had kept his head down for years in the mines, just serving time and counting the days to being released. Why did the sight of an emperor cause him to breathe harder, like some bull with the scent of a cow in the next field? It made no sense and yet he was troubled. The praetorians had come into his life unasked, into his forest. They had taken him from service in the mines and marched him away with all the others. They had killed harmless old Farix, just to make a point. It had woken something in Cormac, something that had been asleep for a long time. It was not rage, or resentment. He'd known those dark emotions and learned to be patient. No, it was the sense of being treated as a slave again, of being helpless.

Perhaps it was in part because he had seen the sea, a stretch of waters he had been made to cross when he was just a child. Over there was the place all these soldiers had come to invade. Anyone could see that was why they gathered in such numbers. That was why so many ships waited on the shingle, ready to launch. They had come for war – and land.

More praetorians marched behind the emperor, at least another thousand before Cormac gave up counting. His knees were aching and he wondered how bad it might be to rise up without being told. Though anger surged, he made himself remember Farix. Pain didn't matter much, not really.

A cart passed the open gate then, one that caught his eye. Praetorians clung to it like flies. Two sat up with the driver, with two more on each side, standing on stubs of polished wood. Cormac saw a massive chest on the open bed, about as long as a man and bound in black iron straps. Two more like it followed and he watched all three pass with a thoughtful expression. There were six thousand praetorians, he recalled Malvo saying. Even if the emperor had left a third of that number in Rome to keep the peace, he must have four thousand with him. They were paid twice as much as any other legion for their service to the emperor. Cormac didn't actually know how much that was, but he began to add figures to a rough guess. The numbers made him raise his eyebrows. If the officers earned more, it could be half a million denarii on each cart, an amount of silver and gold he could hardly imagine. He began to imagine it, and what he might do if such a fortune fell into his hands.

The emperor's procession came to an end at last. Cormac let himself be swept up in a thousand tasks as Auxiliary Paullus bellowed at them to stop mooning around like lovers and fetch everything from iron nails and spades to sacks of leeks for the evening soup. Cormac took a spade and trooped out with a hundred others to dig what appeared to be a massive trench around a new camp on the sandy coast.

He and Malvo grinned when they understood the task. This was work they knew better than most, but in sunlight and fresh sea air rather than underground. Within the hour, Cormac had the farm boys and villagers working alongside miners like they were born to it. Fit, but not trained, Paullus had said. It was a fair comment.

Logs were brought down and piled by the thousand, well used from the look of them. With Paullus overseeing the work, Cormac and the others raised a massive palisade that stretched a thousand paces a side. More men raised tents, to some plan known only to the auxiliaries. Yet by the time night fell, the praetorians had a formal camp, complete with walkways, gates and cooking fires. Cormac and the others were streaked with muck and exhausted as they trudged back up the hill to the yard. The poisoner was there to greet them, with some sort of stew with actual hare and red wine in it. Cormac cheered with all the others, but he kept watching as well. They may have treated him like a slave, but he was free where it mattered, deep down, where they could not see.

18

'If you are unlucky enough to face a raid on our camp, you will encounter blue-painted savages,' Paullus announced to the standing ranks. 'Those bastards love to steal even more than they like carving up our lads. If they see you milkmaids milling around behind the fighting legions, they will try their best to creep up and slaughter you! If that happens, we will have lost cooks and grooms and metal-workers as well as you latrine-diggers – men who actually serve a purpose!'

Malvo and Cormac exchanged a quick and slightly nervous grin. They had not expected to be trained. The praetorians in the woods had made no mention of it. Perhaps it was the physical strength of the miners that had prompted the drills, or just that they would be crossing the sea and following praetorians to a field of battle. It made sense for them to receive some sort of basic training in weapons and staying alive.

With his bald head and wide frame, Paullus seemed comfortable with the gladius he hefted to show them. He'd brought a few dozen of the blades from some storehouse, short, workmanlike things with no silver chasing or any other ornament. Yet they were new and viciously sharp.

Paullus rapped one gladius on another, making a bell-note ring across the yard.

'*If* you are attacked, you will probably stand still and piss yourself. That is the most common reaction to seeing a horde of filthy tribesmen coming at you. It is the *wrong* response! Instead, you will take up whatever weapon is to hand – a cleaver, an axe, a bit of wood, whatever you can grab. You will watch your lice-infested maniac begin his great swing, trying to take your head off in one blow – and you will stab him in the gut. Is it funny, Cormac?'

'No, dominus,' Cormac replied.

The bald man was not appeased and gestured for him to come closer.

'You'll do, then,' Paullus growled at him. 'Stand still while I show these lads. And don't move, or I'll cut you.'

Cormac nodded grimly. With swords in short supply, he had been given a cleaver more suited to chopping beef ribs. It was a good weight, but he felt clumsy and slow compared to Paullus. Fit, but not trained, he reminded himself. This was a skill like any other.

'It *might* save your life to know savages tend to favour big sweeping blows. They want to cut you into two pieces and rape you afterwards. Except for you, Malvo. You're safe, I should think. They *will* roar and yell to make you panic. The correct response is to be calm, to wait for them to show their open chest like so, then . . . *in.*'

He punched with the gladius, like a boxing jab. Cormac tensed as the tip touched his chest. Paullus grinned at his expression.

'Do you see? A big swing takes more time than a little poke like that. You can stab him before he brings the blessed sword of his fathers down on your thick head. Even a small knife will take the wind out of his sails, if you stab him in the right place. Not *once* though! Stab a man once and he might just get annoyed and *kill* you! No, you stab him half a dozen times to ruin his day, then give him a great shove, see? So he falls over. And on to the *next*. If you are lucky enough to have a gladius, you might try chopping blows – fingers, knees. Stabbing the bastard is *quicker*. Let's have you in pairs now, practising your first moves like I showed you. Remember? One, two . . . *three.*'

He stabbed again, like a snake striking. Paullus looked up at Cormac, disliking the way he was being observed.

'All this to make legionaries of us?' Cormac murmured.

The man snorted.

'I am not a magician, son. If I had ten years, maybe. Not praetorians though, you understand that, right? Praetorians are hand-picked, the best. Born killers, they are.'

The trainer brought his gladius back to first position. Cormac dropped his right foot slightly rearward as he'd been taught, widening his stance so that he was steady on the sandy ground. He loosened his shoulders and raised his cleaver.

'Very well then, pup,' Paullus grunted. He smiled unpleasantly. 'Let's see if you've learned anything.'

By the time they were allowed a break at noon, Cormac was panting so hard it hurt. Paullus had battered him like a rug in spring and everything was either bruised or cut. He thought he would see pink in his urine again, without doubt.

Even long shifts in the mine hadn't prepared him for the exhaustion of sword drills, over and over and over, until his arms were criss-crossed with weeping red scratches and so heavy he could barely raise them. Malvo seemed to be thriving on it, which was more annoying. The wiry Roman earned nods of approval from Paullus and a few of the other trainers. They'd started to teach his friend more complicated techniques. When Cormac tried to copy those, they'd bawled at him, telling him to get back to basics. Malvo had enjoyed that and been clapped on the shoulder by another trainer as the swords were collected.

That was what mattered, Cormac decided. Paullus and the others might say they wanted auxiliaries who could fight off a raid, but they didn't trust them, not with a proper weapon. It wasn't *just* a way of keeping them busy until the fleet launch, but perhaps that played a part. As Paullus said, they didn't need more soldiers. Not with twenty thousand massing in one place.

Cormac no longer found it strange to see so many armed men. The surprise lay in how many they needed alongside to stay on campaign. As far as he could tell, there were at least as many in the auxiliary camps as the legions themselves – before he even counted galley crews. From smiths and leatherworkers to an army of tent- and rope-makers, they were all loyal to their own legions. He supposed it was why the praetorians had come searching for men on their march north. Of all imperial forces, they wouldn't have had proper auxiliaries, not with quarters in Rome. Praetorians didn't need tent-makers or weavers, or even cooks. Still, it meant a host of new faces and that suited him well enough.

After a lunch of fish stew and hard bread, Cormac and

the rest were marched down to the shore. It was hard for Cormac not to stare across the waters then. The summer was wearing on and when the sea glittered and the air was clear, he could see white cliffs in the distance, a pale thread above the waves. It brought a mist to his gaze, one he hid even from Malvo.

Paullus was there as always to harangue them, a blue-bottle in the guise of a bald man. Cormac groaned when he saw Paullus gesturing to the galleys beached all along the shore. From filling in latrines to repairing stone walls, his group seemed to get the hardest tasks, at least while Paullus was present. The worst by far were launch drills, to get galleys into the sea. It seemed this new emperor liked to plan his invasions down to the last detail. Every single aspect would be practised and prepared before the day.

The first time Cormac had approached a row of stranded galleys had been with a sort of quiet wonder. He remembered placing a hand against grey wood that was warm under his touch, as if it had soaked up the sun. Some of the ships were golden, with new timbers cut and shaped for this campaign. Others had been rowed and sailed over decades. They all had to be oiled, made proof against sea spray and the rain that was so common on that coast. Cormac had been up on a dozen galley decks, wiping olive oil into cracks and weathered planking. He didn't mind that. No, the task he hated was the one that might cost an arm or a leg, or his life.

Coming in, the galleys rowed at speed onto that beach. The sea was often rough between Gaul and Britannia – too rough to remain at anchor in a storm. Yet when they were beached, the keels sank into trenches, easing deeper the longer they remained. The damp sand took a grip on them, one that was difficult to break. Even with ropes stretching out to galleys on the water, it was hard to start them.

The job of the auxiliaries was to take hold of bronze rings set into the keels – and to heave in unison. They rocked back and forth, answering a chant with grunts while their feet sank in crumbling sand, until they stood in pits.

Cormac took hold, with Malvo just behind. He could see men's heads moving on the shadows that fell across the beach – there was no point launching galleys without crews. All that morning, hundreds of legionaries had climbed up long gangways. They waited then on slanting decks to be towed off. Cormac smiled unpleasantly at the thought of their nerves. He'd seen a galley go bottom up, turning right over in the shallows two days before, when a different legion was practising exactly this. It was a frightening manoeuvre, no matter where you stood. Still, they were up in the sun, while he and Malvo waited with two hundred others, hands on a bronze ring and with a massive weight looming too close.

Cormac braced himself, waiting for the order. Two ropes had been rowed out to a waiting galley, then drawn taut, seawater falling in glittering drops as they sagged and sprang with the movement of the sea. He muttered a prayer then, to Janus, asking for Malvo and him to be kept safe.

Paullus was watching, of course, though not taking a loop himself. Cormac had seen how the man acted as an overseer, always out of danger. The ones gripping the keel like a woman were not so lucky. If the galley shifted under its own weight . . . Cormac shuddered. On the first day, he'd seen a man go under as the keel moved, unable to step clear and dragged beneath the sand. It had been one of Nepos' old crew, so Cormac hadn't minded that, but it had been an ugly way to go, at least until the screaming cut off. They'd dug him out after, but he was gone. His leg had been cut cleanly, blood staining sand darker. Another man had been caught up at the front the same day – the pointed end, whatever the crews called it. He'd slipped under as if it mounted him, cut in half. The men had joked about that, though it had shaken them so soon after the first. Cormac reminded Janus to keep an eye on him. A god with two faces could do that, maybe.

The worst day had been a full week after those deaths, when the men had almost accepted them as brutal flukes or bad luck. Then a galley had suddenly leaned, crushing half a dozen heaving on that side. They'd all been pale and still by the time their mates dug them out.

Cormac was grim as he took hold of his loop. Every time he'd seen men die, the galley had launched, been put through its trials, then raced right back to the same berthing spot on shore, ready to begin again. He had understood then, really understood, his value to the legion. Praetorians would never do such work, not when it left so many dead or crippled. If he'd been tempted to feel some kinship with them, the work on the beach made that impulse disappear like frost in summer. Instead, Cormac watched and learned everything he could.

'Ready! One, two . . . and *three*!' Paullus roared.

Cormac and Malvo heaved along with the rest, keeping an eye on the broken sand underfoot, trying to make sure they would not be dragged under when the keel moved. Cormac held his loop in both hands, always ready to jump back. Sweat poured into his eyes, stinging him. He could not wipe his face, not then. He felt a tremor in the wood as he brought all his strength to bear.

'One, two and *three!*' Paullus shouted, over and over. 'Put your backs into it, you whoresons, or we'll be here till dark.'

Cormac growled as he heaved, but the tremor came again as the ropes creaked over the sea, hard as irons. With a grinding sound, the galley began to move. The trick was making sure it kept going, drawn into the sea by the glittering ropes. If Cormac and the others let go too soon, the boat would stop – and that was when it was deadly to be under its keel. Yet if they held on too long, the ship's wake could send them tumbling, or drag them with it. Just being close to that massive thing was frightening. It felt too huge to move. Even the sound was a vast roar as the galley slid at last, spraying pebbles so that men ducked away in fear. Sand churned like water around their feet, rising and falling, swirling in odd patterns. Cormac waited for the cry of pain that would signal someone had been caught.

It did not come and he breathed again. Paullus nodded, then pointed to a different galley where ropes already shone like jewels out to another. It had to be half a mile across the sand, with entire crews working to repair a smaller boat in between. Cormac wondered if those men saw as many injuries. He didn't know woodwork beyond the basics, but he recognised the tools and it didn't look too hard.

'That one next,' Paullus shouted, confirming the bad news. 'Come on, move, you old women. They can't practise landing drills without being on the water. We have three more to launch before we can go back.'

Cormac trotted along the shore with the others. Huge

storehouses faced the sea there, with sacks of food and supplies piled high. On previous visits, the doors had been barred, but they were open now, the whole seafront buzzing with a new urgency. These weren't just drills any more, he could feel it. It wasn't something the officers would ever share with lowly auxiliaries, but it was happening. The warehouses were empty, most of them, with galleys gathering out at sea in vast numbers. In just a few days, they'd all be on the storm-tossed waters, heading for a foreign shore. He was suddenly certain, with all the bustle explained.

Cormac glanced into each warehouse as he came abreast, blinking slightly as he found one that would do. He let himself ease back so that he walked next to Malvo.

'I might have an idea,' he said.

Malvo looked up in wild surmise.

'You're sure?'

'Maybe . . .'

He didn't have it all, not then. There were too many ears around to discuss it, and Cormac didn't trust anyone but Malvo. His friend had earned that much in six years. Yet even that weak assent was enough to make Malvo clap him on the shoulder and clench one fist. Cormac looked to the next galley they would launch and saw uniforms he knew up on deck. Praetorians stood up there, gathered on the high rail against the slope.

They were not coming back, Cormac realised. The emperor was sending his advance guard to slaughter natives . . . and they would want the auxiliaries to lay out a camp. How many were there on a single galley? A cohort? He felt a sudden pang of dismay at the thought of being marched onto another of the ships, right then and there.

He had a plan! He could feel it slipping away and cursed the army. Paullus had been a little odd that day, Cormac thought. He knew something was up, that was clear.

Cormac made a silent prayer to Janus once again. He and Malvo were not soldiers. The legions had no idea what they would be facing as they landed on the wild coast. *They* were the hammer, the first landers – and when they had finished butchering the enemy, only then would they want to rest and eat and sleep in a dry camp. Cormac looked at the sun and saw with relief that it was low, the wind catching banners on shore. The galleys would surely anchor for one last night, readying themselves to cross in the morning. They'd have the whole day then. It meant he and Paullus and all the rest could be leaving as soon as the sun rose.

Cormac swallowed, though his throat was dry as bone. Armies were slow things, he'd seen that. They were not unlike galleys that slid into the sea, the movement barely perceptible at first, then faster and faster, rushing to action. His chance had come and he prayed he would not lose it. How pious he had become in his years away from Rome! If he ever saw the temple of Janus again, he knew he would have to leave a good offering.

First, though, he had to survive another launch without being injured or killed by the work. A plan was forming, but it wasn't ready, not then. He needed wine, for a start. Perhaps he should pray to Bacchus for that. Yet Janus was his patron and he could not desert him. If the god of gateways and beginnings could grant them just that much, he thought he really might have a plan.

Cormac loped along a street, for want of a better description. It was part of the camp that stretched to the horizon east and west, but he supposed this army was at least the size of a city. They certainly seemed to need latrines dug often enough, or filled in ... He shook his head, concentrating on the task. The yard he'd left behind wasn't a prison and men like Paullus usually slept soundly when they'd eaten. He and Malvo had seen a place where they could climb over the sandbags. Some of the others had crept out over the previous month, returning by dawn with drunken stories. One or two hadn't come back, but been found cold where someone had left them. No one seemed to mind, not really. There was just no way to tell whether their absence would be noted. Cormac thought he'd be all right. Yet for all he knew, there was already an alarm going up, with the rest of the auxiliaries roused from bed to begin a search of the camp.

The guards and passwords had been getting a lot less slack over the previous few days. He knew now it was because they were leaving, actually crossing at last. What had been ignored a few weeks before was suddenly a matter of life and death – like sneaking out after dark.

He trotted on, looking into every alley and side road, expecting to be challenged. He pressed his hand into the wineskin he carried. That had cost him all his pay, though being paid at all had been a surprise. They never had been in the mines. Yet it seemed auxiliaries earned a wage like anyone else. Paullus had noted their names and pressed actual silver sestertii into their palms. Granted it had been just three coins for a month of brutal work, but it had saved Malvo his best knife in trade. Cormac cradled the skin in his arms, hearing it gurgle.

He saw two men step out into the road when they heard him coming. His stomach clenched tight, bringing back memories of vigiles. No, he was no longer a boy. The bigger worry was if Malvo saw him being stopped. His friend was shadowing him in a side street and Cormac began to sweat at the thought of him rushing to the rescue. Two men were always an object of suspicion, that was just common sense. One man was a messenger, two were thieves.

'Who goes there?' one of the legionaries said. The voice wasn't wary, not in a camp surrounded by his own. Cormac relied on that and kept his reply light and cheerful.

'Taking wine to Prefect Rufrius,' he said. 'My back will be striped if I'm late, so . . .'

'Give it here,' one of them said. 'I should taste it.'

'I'll need your name to tell him then, if you're going to break the seal,' Cormac retorted.

The legionary aimed a kick at him and he dodged away.

'I'm already late,' Cormac said, moving out of range. 'You can follow me if you like though . . .'

He chuckled and one of the men called him a name. He scowled as he was expected to, giving them what they wanted so that they felt they had the win. They did not see him smile as he trotted on. At the crossroads, he caught a glimpse of Malvo running along with him. They nodded to one another, heading to the most dangerous part of the camp.

The emperor was still present on that shore, Cormac had learned that much. It seemed this Claudius would not go with the first wave of galleys, at least until they had established a secure camp in Britannia. One of his legion legates would take those first risks, which made sense. Aulus Plautius was an experienced commander, after all. As Cormac understood it, the new emperor was more of a scholar.

He was challenged twice more before he reached the barracks where the emperor had his quarters. Each time, having a fat wineskin under his arm was enough. The officers were always calling for more wine and Cormac had the word of the day when they demanded it. He'd given it to return to his own yard that evening, after all.

The worst moment was when he caught a glimpse of two legionaries in shadow. Malvo had seen them almost too late and barely ducked into an alley. Cormac had held his breath until his friend appeared once more on a roof above, shinning down unseen. He had blackened his face with soot, Cormac realised, made almost invisible in the dark. He nodded nervously. If any of this went wrong, they'd be killed. He'd weighed all that up already. The truth was, some risks were worth taking. In that moment, Cormac thought he could shrug and throw his life away. He could fling it from him and not care. It made him braver, in a sense. It made him strong.

Cormac walked up to a pair of praetorians standing guard on a door tall enough to allow carts and horses to pass through. He tried not to tremble at the thought of an actual emperor sleeping within earshot, or even that beauty he kept with him. The praetorians protected the emperor, unless they were killing him. Cormac shook tumbling thoughts to stillness – and smiled.

'Message from Prefect Rufrius,' he said. 'First pay cart to come down to the loading sheds.'

One of the praetorians held out his hand and Cormac handed over a piece of folded parchment, doing his best to look bored. The order was his cleanest piece, but it had been used at least once before and then sanded back. It was thin in places, but it had a seal mark in ink and a scrawled name. Cormac tried not to wince as the praetorian clearly read the words. He'd had to guess at the prefect's signature, writing in a diagonal as if the man was too busy to sit down.

'Signed it on my back,' Cormac said with a shrug. He told himself to shut up as the praetorian looked at him without a word. The man seemed interested in the wine-skin he held. Cormac shrugged.

'Can't let you break the seal, sorry. It's Falernian. Legate's private supply.'

The praetorian grunted, rubbing his jaw with one hand as if he could taste it. Falernian was the best, a single cupful costing a week's pay for a legionary. Not that it was Falernian, of course. This was just a rough local wine, all Cormac could afford.

'Prefect Rufrius has already left,' the praetorian said.

Cormac nodded.

'He gave me the order as he went on board,' he said. 'Not up to me. Said he wanted to keep the legion pay with him.'

The praetorian looked irritated, exchanging a glance with his companion.

'I think we should fetch Titus out of his bed.'

The other man groaned.

'Are you sure? Last night of proper sleep. The centurion will be furious.'

Cormac tried not to show the fear that fell on him like a wave. He remembered Centurion Titus Livius from the woods.

'Go on,' the first praetorian said grimly. 'Fetch him. I'm not making the decision. Go. I'll wait.'

19

Malvo fretted as he trotted dark roads, heading down to the sea. Cormac was right, he knew that. The camp was tucked up in bed, mile upon mile of snoring men. The only ones awake before the invasion were shift guards – and they were twitchy with nerves and far from relaxed. Cormac had said two of them walking together would raise hackles the whole way. One man alone might be a messenger, a servant – someone sent for more wine maybe, with all the proof he needed under one arm.

It had worked. Malvo had watched Cormac talk his way past more than one patrol, peering at them from a side street. Those men had probably held Cormac up just to break the boredom, he knew that. Malvo had come close to rushing the second pair when they didn't look like they would let him go. The name of Prefect Rufrius cleared the path, or perhaps that of Legate Aulus Plautius. Those were names no one wanted to cross, not the night before they went into battle.

The hardest part was leaving Cormac alone as he

approached the praetorian barracks. The emperor himself was somewhere inside, lying on cushions and protected by the most ruthless, violent men in all the legions of Rome. Malvo could still remember the way Farix had stared in death, torn and broken just to make a point. He could have watched that barracks burn to the ground and not considered lending a hand.

He tightened his grip on the leather roll of tools, took a deep breath and left Cormac to it. The trouble was, he wanted to protect his friend, as Cormac had protected him so many times. One man was a messenger; two were thieves. Malvo found himself muttering the phrase like a prayer as he went on.

Alley by alley, corner by corner, he wound his way down to the shore. It was hard to find a straight path in the dark. A face marked in lampblack made him hard to see, but he could not bluff his way past anyone either. Whenever Malvo saw guards, he went around them, or over if there was a way to reach an upper floor. That brought its own dangers, especially if he lost his footing and broke his neck. More than once, he crept over tiles that cracked underfoot, half-waking those who slept inside. Each time, Malvo stood like stone until it was quiet again, then moved on.

Back on the road, the moonlight was no friend as he approached a crossroads. He could see the shore ahead, just forty paces or so, the sea silver and still as a pond. The rest of the galleys would cross as soon as the sun rose, he was certain . . .

He reached the corner and someone grabbed him. Malvo had a glimpse of two big men in legion uniforms. They'd been leaning against the wall in companionable silence. His footsteps had given him away.

He wrenched clear as they recoiled from what seemed a moving shadow. One of them made a sign against the evil eye. It helped Malvo to break free and his instincts had been honed on much older streets than those. Without looking back, without hesitation, he broke into a sprint across the open road, legs pumping. The two guards exchanged a glance and went after him.

He could run all day, Malvo told himself, skidding as he rounded a corner. Corners were vital and he strained his eyes in the moonlight, looking for some shadowed roof he could scramble up, anything that would break their view of him. If he could just get two corners ahead, all he would have to do then was remain still. They'd never find him, not unless they roused the whole camp.

He groaned as he ran. It wasn't vigiles after him. Legionaries were fit as hares and they actually could decide to wake the camp at any moment. His only hope was that they were the sort of men who leaned on a wall rather than patrol.

The moon seemed to follow as he ran, lighting him up. He knew if he went out onto the sandy shore, there would be more guards patrolling by the galleys. He realised he was close to the shed where Cormac had said to hide and wait, but he didn't dare head for it, not then. The guards were too close and if he went to ground there, they would search the warehouses, one by one. He swallowed hot spit. He had to lead them away, even if it meant Cormac was on his own.

The flashes of moonlight and darkness were confusing, with echoes and glimpses and panting breaths. Malvo saw one low porch and tossed the roll of tools onto it, then launched himself up. He didn't stop there, but grabbed the roll and scrambled onto a slope of tiles. He could hide up there, he thought. They'd never see him.

Something snapped underfoot and he flung his arms wide, barely saving himself from going over the edge. The tool roll came undone and he could hear iron things rattling and knocking together, then somewhere nearby, a man's voice yelling. They'd heard, of course they'd heard. He'd probably roused the whole street.

Swearing to himself, Malvo closed his hand on something iron and dropped back to the road on a different side. He was panting and cursing, but he could hear running steps and wasn't sure which way to run. They'd lost sight of him for a moment, at least. Go. He had to move.

He turned quickly to take a new direction when both men suddenly appeared, breathing hard. Their faces lit up to see him staring at them, just standing in the open. Malvo blew air and set off once more. A thought came, a memory he had not brought to mind in years. He remembered when he'd run streets in Rome, hiding and chasing other boys. There was a trick he'd used then. It had worked on vigiles. It might work on legion men as well.

He found his way back to the crossroads where they'd tried to grab him in the first place. There was a low wall there and instead of racing past, he jumped over it and lay down, vanishing as they came round the corner behind. Malvo shuffled right up into the base of the wall, hidden by shadows. This was the trick he'd used a dozen years or so before. Hunters did not expect their prey to crawl near their feet. The key was to come so close either man could have reached out and touched him – and not be seen.

Malvo heard both panting legionaries lean on the wall.

They'd recognised the spot, of course, taking a moment to consider what to do.

'Where do you think he went?' one of them muttered. 'He led us in a circle, so he doesn't have a plan.'

The legionary had his back to the wall as he sat down on it, still breathing hard from the run. Malvo was looking up at him from the dark. His heart was a drum. They would surely hear it thumping. He tried to breathe as if through a reed, without making a sound. Even his lampblack had smeared with all the sweat that poured off him. He could taste the stuff as it dribbled in through the hole in his cheek. He blinked as it stung his eyes, not daring to move. He had a knife. If they saw him there, he would spring up and wreak havoc.

'I would say . . . that maybe we're back where we started and don't need to mention someone out to meet a whore or to settle some private score before we sail, or whatever that was. What do you think?'

Malvo watched as the other one nodded slowly.

'If we call out the optio, he'll have us searching the whole area until the sun comes up. While he goes back to sleep. Not much point wasting time like that on the night before we go across, is it? That's just my opinion, you understand.'

They were only soldiers, Malvo realised. Not heroes of legend, just ordinary men who would prefer a simpler life. His grin faded when they settled. He was stuck there as long as they remained, unable to get to Cormac and play his part. He considered stabbing one, but he'd never get them both and that really would rouse the whole camp. Instead, he lay very still in the shadow of the wall, trembling with frustration.

*

Whatever else Centurion Titus Livius was, he was a praetorian first. Cormac had expected to be made to wait for an age, with his heart racing and lines of sweat creeping down his neck to betray his fear. The sentries were as suspicious as guard dogs, ready to attack anything they saw as a threat. Cormac plastered the meekest expression he could manage onto his face, almost one of idiocy as he stood there in silence.

In the end, the centurion had either been awake or slept lightly. Titus came out of some inner room as neat and brushed as if he'd been waiting for the call. His uniform lacked only the metal breastplate and helmet Cormac remembered. Instead, the centurion wore a linen tunic and a leather liner that left his arms bare. Cormac could see the praetorian scorpion inked on his shoulder, with some figures that had to be his cohort and century in the legion.

Cormac tried not to edge back when the man stood too close, peering at him in suspicion.

'Message from Legate Rufrius, centurion,' one of the guards said. 'Thought you should see it.'

'Show me,' Titus growled, glaring at Cormac. The man's eyes were bloodshot. To hold high rank on the eve of an invasion was to be driven to exhaustion.

Cormac looked into hard, brown eyes without blinking. He handed over the folded sheet of parchment, then relaxed, as if he had no personal stake or interest. His hands were trembling, so he gripped the wineskin behind his back, almost as if he stood to attention.

The centurion read the words, a scowl drawing his brows together.

'Prefect Rufrius went on board earlier this evening,' he said neutrally.

Cormac shrugged. A messenger did not have to explain the actions of senior men, just carry their orders.

The centurion frowned further. He did not like insolence, as Cormac knew very well. At any moment, he expected the praetorian to remember him from the forest. He told himself he'd been just one of a host of faces, all cowed by the violence they'd witnessed. Yet he had felt this man's gaze crawling over him then, challenging him. Had it really meant so little to Titus Livius?

There was no flicker of recognition in the man's eyes.

'Just one of the pay carts?' Titus grumbled. 'There are three.'

Cormac swallowed nervously. The last thing he wanted was for all three to come down to the docks. It would mean opening other sheds and many more guards. He cleared his throat.

'There's a shed and a galley ready for the first, dominus,' he said. He could see the irritation in the man – a soldier given orders he didn't like, by some senior officer who cared nothing for his troubles.

Cormac didn't want to speak again, but the praetorian was shaking his head, a hair's breadth from refusing and just sorting it all out in the morning. He made himself go on.

'I heard the prefect say it was to pay a bonus on landing, dominus.'

All three praetorians brightened at that, the centurion most of all.

'Ah! That makes sense, though I dare say it comes from higher than old Rufrius. That miser has us sign for every coin. A bonus! Good, though we'll earn it against those blue bastards on the other side, I have no doubt.'

Cormac made himself nod and smile. He supposed he was one of those blue bastards, just without the dye staining his skin.

'Very well then,' Titus said, his mood visibly more cheerful as he addressed the guards. 'Fetch . . . four men to keep guard. I'll go along myself for the dawn watch.'

Cormac could say nothing more, though his heart sank. He'd known they would not let a third of the legion pay go off without some sort of guard. Five men though . . . He hoped Malvo was in position, or they would be lost. A thought struck, chilling him. Prefect Rufrius of the praetorians *was* out with the fleet, ready to row and sail across. It meant there was no way to countermand the orders he'd apparently given, not then. If Cormac and Malvo couldn't escape, they'd be accompanying that chest to Britannia in the morning, as part of the invasion.

Praetorians moved quickly when they had orders, Cormac discovered. He tried not to widen his eyes when they brought out one of the carts he had seen before, hitching a four-horse team to it. Perhaps they'd already eaten the oxen, he thought nervously.

In the darkness, that team whinnied and stamped their hooves on the stone yard. Half the legion would be woken, Cormac was sure. He stood alone in the midst of them, forgotten as four praetorians came out yawning. They moved faster when they saw Titus was present.

The centurion snapped out a string of terse orders. In moments, the four men were holding on to the raised sides of the cart, standing with slightly bent legs on wooden bars made for the purpose. Titus climbed up then to the driver's seat, higher than the rest. He looked uncomfortable up there and Cormac wondered if the man had ever driven a team. A centurion might come from noble stock or money, or he might have risen through the ranks. For all Cormac knew, this man was the product of the same alleys and streets as Malvo, but with twenty years of hard service behind him.

The centurion looked down as Cormac came to stand by his sandal. The man watched the barrack yard gates opening and fiddled uncomfortably with reins and a long whip. Cormac met his gaze hopefully. He could run along well enough behind, but in that moment he was reckless. He *wanted* to sit up there and snap that whip himself.

'Do you know . . . about horses?' Titus growled down.

Cormac took it as an invitation and climbed onto the seat. It was like sitting in a bath with a snake, he thought. Coils slipped through milky water and he couldn't know if he would feel a sudden bite or not. Yet he was twenty-two. If the god Janus was watching, he might smile at the madness of his follower. Cormac was surprised to find he was enjoying himself. He could not explain it, but there it was.

'I've seen it done many times, dominus,' he said. 'I don't mind driving the team.'

The centurion handed him the reins and sat back. The gates had been drawn open by the first guards and the horses were ready to go. Cormac had seen how heavy this cart was, built for its purpose in iron straps and oak. He knew better than to snap the whip and hurt the team with a sudden lunge. Instead, he tapped their backs with the reins, clicking in his throat to urge them on until they took the weight and made it move. He had to yank hard to get them to make the first turn – and there was the road before him, pale under moonlight.

Cormac whirled the whip, flicking it back and forth until

it made a cracking sound that echoed from roofs around. The cart rumbled on the road, a deep note that rose as they went faster. The wind built to a breeze and then a gale. Cormac was alive and free and he had a cartful of legion pay at his back. He could feel the centurion staring at him in consternation and perhaps it was the constant strain and danger that made him feel drunk.

'Slow down, you fool!' Titus shouted over the noise. 'You'll have us over. Slow down, or I'll . . .'

Cormac felt his face burn as he did as he was told, standing up slightly to heave on the reins. The horses responded well enough, ceasing their mad dash through the makeshift town, slowing until they were walking again. He'd covered the whole distance to the shore in what felt like moments. A glance back showed him the four praetorians on the sides promising murder with their eyes. No doubt they'd been jostled and terrified on their unsteady perches. He could not regret it, but he realised he had to pretend to, or risk the centurion's wrath.

'I'm sorry, the horses got away from me a bit there,' Cormac said sheepishly. To his surprise, the centurion chuckled.

'Because you snapped the whip over their heads, I should think. Made me fear for my life then!'

Titus laughed in relief as Cormac dared to glance at him. He had expected anger. In that moment of glorious rebellion, for the memory of Farix, he had chosen not to care. He had *not* expected the centurion to clap him on the back. It felt somehow obscene. Monsters should stay monsters, he thought.

'Where is this storage shed?' the centurion said, peering into the dark.

Cormac kept the reins snapping lightly as he turned the team along the front, heading for the line of rough buildings he'd seen earlier that day. He noted two legionaries standing at attention by a stone wall as the cart passed by. They looked the very image of disciplined attention and Cormac assumed they'd heard the cart coming. When they stepped into the road, he slowed instinctively to answer to them.

He felt the reins taken from him before he could do more than blink.

'Second Augusta,' Titus said, his lip curling. 'Goat fuckers, every one.' He raised his voice to make sure they heard that last, while snapping the reins and moving the team to a trot. Cormac's example had shown him how to do it, it seemed.

'Praetorian business,' Titus called back over his shoulder.

The patrolling legionaries scowled at that. They even followed the cart to the next crossroads before giving up and coming to a halt. One of the praetorians on board called a phrase then, one even worse than Titus had used. It seemed legions reserved their worst insults for each other.

With Cormac giving directions, the centurion guided the team through a gap in a stone wall and onto a shingle track where the row of storage sheds waited at the end. Most were barred and closed for the night, but Cormac counted along the line and picked the one that had been empty that afternoon. He dared not look at the galleys out at anchor on a silver sea. Half the night had gone and he had a terror of the sun rising.

The praetorians all jumped down when Cormac pointed to the one he wanted. They made themselves useful then, heaving open doors and guiding the horses inside. Once they took hold of the reins, Cormac realised the journey was at an end. They closed the doors on the wind and sound of the sea. One of them sought out a lamp on a wooden shelf, sparking a tiny flame to life. In that echoing shed, it was more for comfort than actual light, but it was still better than sitting in total darkness.

Cormac climbed from the high seat. He kept his wineskin close at his side, though it made sounds like a stomach denied food.

'You four lads take the first watch,' Titus ordered. 'I'll sleep on the cart.' He eyed Cormac, not quite sure what to do with him. '*You* can sleep on those old sacks, or stay up, I don't care. We'll wait here for dawn – and don't wake me up.'

Cormac gripped the wineskin almost for comfort, like a child's doll. He felt the centurion's attention fasten on the thing. Slowly, Cormac tried to turn away from that gaze, hiding the skin behind his back.

'What's the wine for again?' Titus asked. He licked his lips as he looked at it. Cormac did his best to hide the thing that had cost him all his pay.

'It's Falernian. I bought it for Legate Rufrius,' he said.

'Give it here then,' the centurion said. 'He won't mind if I have a taste. It looks full, anyway.'

There was an unpleasant light in his eyes and Cormac tried to look stubborn.

'I can't, dominus, I'm sorry.'

The centurion was not a man used to being baulked in any way. He made a gesture with one outstretched hand, as if calling Cormac closer.

'Give it to me. It's a cold night and the thing is full.'

Cormac took a deep breath, knowing what was going to happen. He had to refuse, because a man who carried it for Rufrius would refuse.

'I told you, I can't . . .' he began.

The centurion stepped forward and punched him in the face. It was a quick jab at his nose and Cormac tasted blood and stars as he fell backwards. He was no longer holding the wineskin, he realised. Titus had snatched it from him in the same moment, like a trick. The man was fast when it came to his trade.

Cormac scrambled up as the centurion broke the seal and gulped the wine. The man was watching him in case he lost his temper, which was interesting. Titus held up one finger like Cormac's old magister used to do, a signal to wait, or not to interrupt.

Cormac glowered, feeling his nose swell and blood come leaking from it. He spat some of it on the sandy ground, saying nothing as Titus lowered the wineskin, though he held out his hands.

'Give it back now,' Cormac said thickly. That was a challenge and the man just laughed, then tossed it through the air to the others. One by one, they all drank.

By the time they returned it to its owner, it was a much shrunken thing. Cormac glared at them all in furious dismay as he held it once again.

The centurion belched into his fist.

'Not Falernian, by the way,' Titus said. 'You were robbed if they told you that. Not even close. More like piss and vinegar. But good enough on a cold night. Cheer up, son. You'll see a new land tomorrow.'

20

With Titus snoring on the cart bed, the four praetorians settled down to a night's watch. Cormac made himself a seat on a pile of old sacks as they talked and chuckled. The wine they'd drunk lightened their mood for a while, but the sound of waves on the shore was soothing and the night was very still. Silence drifted in and, once established, sat like a weight. Cormac could not see the night sky with the roof overhead. He felt time stood still, as if he had found his spot in the underworld, but not in fields of Elysium, where men might feel the sun. No, he had been cast into the pit of Tartarus, to endure an eternity of gloom . . .

He sat up with a start when one of the guards slid down the wall, dropping first to a crouch, then slumping to the side. One of the others hissed a worried question, then kicked his mate in the back to get him up. Cormac had an idea falling asleep on watch earned some brutal punishment, but the man did not stir.

The wine *was* cheap stuff, Titus had been right about that. What had cost both Cormac and Malvo a month's pay in coins had been persuading the poisoner to add his store of dried mushrooms to it. The man had seen their need and held out for everything they had, but Cormac thought he'd been a bit too happy about it even so, his grin a little too wide. It had made Cormac wonder whether they actually had been safe with him preparing food in camp. From the way the fellow had hummed as he worked, it looked like it was a hobby after all.

The result had been a wineskin that would knock a man out, Cormac had been assured. His role had been to play the reluctant servant, the shy bride. Men like Titus loved to take what they were not freely given, Cormac understood that. If he'd offered the wineskin as a gift, they might have refused. Holding it back had been the lure to catch them. He'd tasted blood on his lips as the price, but they'd drunk almost the whole thing just to make a point. It was an instinctive understanding they shared, those men. Cormac grinned in the darkness as another one fell.

The third staggered where he stood, legs bending while rags of will remained. The praetorian made a confused sound as he understood something was seriously wrong. He staggered further, fighting the effects. In his confusion, he knocked against a great pile of wood stacked along one side of the storage shed. The whole thing toppled, spilling spars and old planking with a crash that was very loud in the night. One of the horses whinnied and Cormac froze as he heard a startled voice exclaim on the cart.

The whole thing creaked as Titus made a growling sound, sitting up. In that dim blackness, Cormac saw him swing a leg over the side, feeling for the bar to take his weight.

The fourth man dropped hard. The third had fallen

across the spilled wood and still moved for a time, limbs skidding on a slowly shifting mass. As he too grew still, Titus climbed down, breathing hard and making a great labour of it. The centurion paused on solid ground, holding the side of the cart and leaning over. Cormac blanched as he heard him vomiting in great heaves.

'What was in that wine, eh?' Titus said to no one in particular.

In horror, Cormac watched him step away from the cart, the smell of stomach juices thick as the man wiped his mouth. Titus straightened up and regarded the fallen figures in silence for a long moment. Cormac thought furiously, helplessly. He sensed more than saw when the centurion turned towards him.

Titus drew his gladius, the sound like a hand across parchment. Cormac edged away on his buttocks, feet pushing desperately into the sandy earth. The centurion had emptied his stomach of the drugged wine. A patch of ground still steamed with it. Cormac felt the wall of the shed and tried to push himself up as Titus advanced, more alert with every passing moment. The centurion pressed him closely, holding out a blade that could take his life in a beat.

'What have you *done*?' Titus snarled. The words were blurred and Cormac saw he swayed as he stood there, fighting the effects. 'Are they dead? *What have you done?*'

'It must have been bad wine!' Cormac said. His eyes were perfectly adjusted then and he thought he could read the intent of the man who pressed an iron point against his chest. Cormac knew he could not move fast enough to live.

Another of the horses made a snorting, whinnying

sound, stamping the earth. The little oil lamp was burning low, but Cormac could just see the centurion's face, enough to spot the moment when Titus decided to kill him. It was a typically praetorian response to a problem, as Cormac had learned all too well. He felt the night on his skin as a shadow moved behind the man. It rushed, like a cloud across stars.

There was a crack, like wood breaking. The praetorian spoke a few words, but indistinct, without sense. Cormac saw Malvo behind him, a spirit of vengeance. His friend had hammered a piece of wood across the back of the praetorian's head.

Titus Livius fell sideways, following the path of the blow. Cormac gasped as he felt a bright stripe across his chest. The gladius had been resting against him and the thing was wickedly sharp. He pressed his hand to the cut, feeling the sting. Cormac watched stunned as Malvo raised the billet of wood and brought it down once more. Then again, to be sure.

'I thought you'd got lost,' Cormac hissed at his friend. He could not look away from the praetorian lying at their feet, eyes staring, skull broken in. The awful wrongness of the wounds held the gaze, or perhaps it was just that Cormac needed time to catch up.

'I got in here, didn't I?' Malvo muttered. 'Just ahead of you. In fact, you drew away the two who had me pinned. They were chasing me for a while. Could still be looking . . .'

Malvo threw down the wood and went to peer through a crack in the shed wall. Cormac could see moonlight lending a silver sheen to him. He wanted to sit down and just breathe for a while.

'No one out there,' Malvo said, coming back. 'Come on. Wake up! I need you sharp now.'

'You *killed* him,' Cormac whispered. 'They'll never stop hunting us now. Never.'

Malvo stood very still, weighing his friend. He knew Cormac wasn't ruthless, not as he needed to be. The mines would have broken him on his own – without Malvo there to watch his back. It was one thing to knock a few pegs out of a river dam, another to break a man's skull and smash the bones of his neck with a bit of wood.

'He was going to kill you,' Malvo reminded him. He wasn't pleased at the note in his own voice. He didn't need to explain!

'I know . . . I know. I'm sorry.' Cormac shook himself, casting off his doubts. He knew he'd spend months or years going over this night, but he could press it aside for a while. 'Should we tie up the others?'

Malvo lifted the little lamp from where it sat, bringing that single point to look at the faces of the fallen men. He kept it away from the murdered centurion, so as not to lose Cormac to a reverie again.

Cormac watched as his friend reached out and gripped the nose of one of the praetorians. He hissed a warning, but the guard didn't groan or splutter. He didn't move at all.

'He's dead . . .' Malvo said, standing up. 'And . . . this one too. They're all dead.'

Cormac swore. That damned poisoner had said they would be out for hours, but he'd been grinning to himself as he stirred and crumbled, making jokes about not licking the spoon. The vicious little bastard had either added more than he'd realised or mixed a fatal dose deliberately.

If he'd been present, Cormac might have throttled him, though he supposed it didn't matter then. Not with a centurion already dead on the floor.

He and Malvo looked at one another. They were alone in a silent shed with four horses and five dead men – and a chest full of legion pay. Slowly, they turned to look at that massive thing, bound in iron.

'Did you bring the tools?' Cormac asked, a sense of awe on him.

Malvo was silent and he turned to see what the matter was.

'Ah. Well, I *did*, but I was chased . . . I lost a few bits.'

Cormac felt his heart sink.

'What do we have?'

Malvo went to the back of the shed, where he'd hidden himself before. He returned with a drill, a simple auger in iron and wood. It was all he'd been able to grab when the tool roll went flying.

'Where's the rest?' Cormac said. He almost grabbed Malvo by the tunic and shook him in frustration. 'We need a hammer, Mal – and chisels. How can I break locks with just a drill? Tell me, how can I do that?'

'I'm sorry,' Malvo said. 'I went over a roof and they all spilled and came loose.'

Cormac nodded. His friend had come through in a pinch, he reminded himself. Malvo had saved his life. He clapped him on the shoulder and climbed up onto the cart bed, making sure not to look at the corpse of the centurion as he stepped over him. At least there was no blood, Cormac realised. The sandy earth drank it in as fast as it spilled.

He held out his hand for the lamp and Malvo passed it

up. It was the work of a moment to check the locks and bands were just as massive as he'd feared. A club hammer and a chisel might have broken them, but maybe not. Three big locks secured the lid to the rest of the chest, with no sign of any keys. Cormac supposed the legion treasurer would have those, or perhaps the legate himself. He sat back then in a sort of weary acceptance, while Malvo peered out, checking the shore for patrols.

'Anything?' Malvo hissed.

Cormac shook his head.

'Locks I can't break. Hinges I don't have the tools to wrench apart. Iron bands holding the chest to the cart bed. More iron on the corners. I can't do it, Malvo. Either we take the whole thing, the whole team out . . . or we give up.'

'I'm *not* giving up,' Malvo spat. 'What, go back to Paullus? Join the invasion fleet? Not a chance. Fine then, we'll take the whole thing.'

'They'll never let us walk four horses and a cart out,' Cormac said. He still had paper, he reminded himself. Could he create a reason to take a legion pay cart through an armed legion camp? He rapped his knuckles on the chest in irritation.

The sound interrupted his thoughts. *Some* parts of that chest were wood – and he had a drill. He blinked, his heart beating faster.

'Underneath,' he said.

He climbed down as Malvo stared in confusion, ducking underneath and using the dim light to reveal the wooden cart bed. Not all the chest was iron. If he drilled from below, he could reach the chest. Visions of silver coins spilling down filled his imagination as he began to turn the auger, setting the lamp down. Malvo guessed what he was doing and took up the light.

In the cramped space under the cart, miner's muscles were perfect for such a task. Cormac had used screws to drain water a dozen times, after all. This was the same, but without the wooden tube to prevent a flood from spilling. Instead, shavings of oak came spiralling down, the smell almost sweet. Cormac chuckled when the drill plunged from the cart bed into a different wood above. This one smelled different, perhaps beech or cedar, he didn't know.

Cormac grinned in anticipation. He heard the point squeak as it reached some obstruction, so put all his strength into it, grunting and gasping. It wouldn't go any further!

'Bring the light close,' he said to Malvo.

The tiny lamp showed enough to make them both despair.

The drill had cut a circle of wood through the cart bed and the bottom of the chest. Yet what lay beyond was a layer of rusty iron. Only the sharpest part of the drill had pierced that sheet. Cormac could see a hole there, no larger than a fingertip. He tried again, pressing up with all his strength. The big drill squeaked, but beyond that piercing point, the next part of the auger was just too wide and shallow. It made quick work of wood, but iron was its master.

Malvo insisted on taking a turn, of course. Cormac handed over the auger and held the lamp while the other man sweated and swore.

'It's so *close*,' Malvo said in frustration. 'I think I can see silver in there.'

Cormac didn't want to remind him of the missing tools.

If he'd been able to break the locks, they could have had the lot. As it was, the pay chest might as well have been back in Rome for all the good it was. He peered up inside at Malvo's request, but it was fruitless. They would have to go back to the auxiliaries, or find somewhere to hide until the invasion army had gone across. That came with a risk of being captured as deserters though. The punishments for that were truly horrific, designed to deter others.

Cormac shivered, feeling the cold of pre-dawn. There couldn't be much longer to go before the sun rose . . . He stopped breathing, then took the drill from Malvo, picking another spot on the underside of the cart bed and turning the wooden grip at furious speed.

'There won't be any gaps,' Malvo said miserably. He too felt the crushing weight of failure. To have come so close hurt worse than not trying at all.

'Don't need gaps,' Cormac grunted, already panting. He made another hole and just as before, the point of the auger pierced through while the rest just scraped against the plate, grinding a bright and shallow circle.

Cormac pulled the drill out and began a third. Malvo looked at him as if he'd lost his mind.

'What do you mean you don't need gaps?'

'Keep that lamp going,' Cormac said. 'We're going to need it.' He grinned as he worked. 'We need holes, Malvo. We need to make as many holes as we can.'

They took turns with the drill, sweat pouring from them both and stinging their eyes. While Cormac laboured beneath the cart, Malvo took one of the spars and began to scrape out shallow graves. The storage shed had a large floor and the earth was mostly sand. Panting, they rolled dead praetorians into each one, smoothing sand over them.

By the time Cormac looked up at forty-eight holes in the underside of the cart, he reeked like he'd finished a long shift in the mine. He stood up and tossed the drill down. It was blunt by then anyway.

He peered out of the shed and scowled. There was no sign of the moon, which meant the night was far advanced. He tried not to think about dawn then. If the sun rose, all their labours would be for nothing.

'Go on,' he said to Malvo. 'There's no one out there.'

Malvo brought the little lamp to a pile of shavings and kindling under the cart. He and Cormac had decided it would work best as a ring of fire, with wood piled around to block most of the light. There was more than a chance it would spread, but there were no other choices, not then. With just a blunt drill and a lamp, this was all they could do.

Cormac winced as the light grew, despite the wood they had placed to surround it. He had a vision of the storage shed gleaming through the planking, easily visible to ships at anchor. What would it take for some officer to send a boat to investigate? There would be men on watch, he imagined. Men with sharp eyes. He swallowed, hands trembling with fatigue. He had done everything he could – and he could not be sure it wasn't a waste of their last hours. He and Malvo could surely have made their way back to the auxiliaries, perhaps to administer a beating to the poisoner as he slept. Instead, they had used the last of the darkness to take a risk.

He heard the cart creaking and scratched the back of his neck where sweat crept and itched. The wood was dry enough. The heat was building and he had visions of that iron sheet glowing cherry red. Some praetorian craftsman had placed it there to foil exactly what he and Malvo had been attempting, but he hadn't planned for fire, or at least Cormac prayed to Janus that he hadn't.

Malvo bent over to peer under the cart. After a while, he fed in more wood, but always to the ring around the edges. Red embers gleamed there by then, while the cart creaked and complained, its timbers charring.

'No sign . . .' Malvo muttered, over and over.

Cormac heard the horses snorting and looked up in worry. They seemed to be watching the fire, turning their heads and eyeing it. Where before they had stood almost asleep in the dark, now they were stamping and making noise. He cursed under his breath.

'We should get the horses out before they kick down a wall.'

'Is it the fire?' Malvo asked.

He knew nothing about horses, of course. Cormac had a memory of being told about a stable fire, but he wasn't an expert either. Yet one of the horses made a shrieking sound. Someone would come to investigate if that went on.

'I think so. We can lead them out along the shore. They'll find their own way back. Have another look. Anything?'

Malvo bent down, to where the flames licked right to the cart bed, charring it. He hesitated, then an expression of awe and delight spread across his face.

'Come and see,' Malvo breathed.

Cormac crouched down and watched a silver rain begin. Droplets of molten metal came from the pierced sheet, falling into the hole they had dug in the sand. Cormac wanted to reach in and scoop up a handful of them, but it was too hot. The fire was a furnace then, so that he felt the sting of it on his skin.

Another of the horses kicked out at the wall and he swore. Someone really would hear that.

'Let's take them out. We can let them loose on the sands or tie up the reins. Come on.'

He and Malvo took two each, rushing them out into the night. No, the dawn, Cormac realised. The sun wasn't yet visible, but the legions of Emperor Claudius were not the sort to lie abed, not on the morning of the invasion. The moment he could see Malvo's dark expression, he feared a shout going up or some challenge.

They ran together along a dry stone wall, looking for a breach where they could let the animals go free.

'We'll hide up for the day,' Cormac said. He was so weary he could barely form the words, but he knew Malvo looked to him. 'We'll cover ourselves in scrap wood or dig into the sand at the back of the shed, somewhere no one will think to search. We'll let them all go over – and then we'll fetch out the silver. I'll find another cart, maybe. There must be farms somewhere.'

He and Malvo turned the horses into some sort of marshalling yard. Cormac saw a group of lads carrying sacks at the far end. He tensed as one of them raised an arm, clearly calling a question.

'That's it, leave them,' Cormac muttered.

Some young cockerel was coming over, gesturing and shouting. Malvo waved at him and Cormac laughed, ushering his friend back onto the shore path. They'd come barely a mile, but it would be enough to lose themselves . . .

He stopped, staring into the distance. The sky was grey

over the sea horizon. The day would be clear, with no more delays. It meant he could see a line of black smoke where he had set the fire to melt a legion's pay. Cormac spat a curse and ran, Malvo on his heels.

He made his way back in a daze almost, a sinking state as if the world had grown still. A line of gold had appeared in the east and the whole shore seemed to be waking up. What had been silence became noise and clatter with every step. All the while, smoke grew and thickened, rising to the dawn.

Cormac and Malvo stopped on the beach. They had worked all night and they were filthy and exhausted. There were legionaries standing on the shore there, watching the shed burn. Their camp followers were busy clearing stores away from the fire.

Cormac swallowed as the roof collapsed. He could see where the cart stood. It had burned too well, taking the whole shed with it. He stared at iron spars in a great tangle, with a cartwheel charred to ebony. Even as he spotted that shape, it broke under its own weight, joining the heap of twisted metal. The pay chest of the praetorians was gone. It would be just a mass of iron ribs when the ashes were cold. He and Malvo could come back in the dark. They knew where to dig, after all. As long as no one found the bodies, they had a chance . . .

He felt a hand on his shoulder and twisted away. Cormac turned to see Paullus there, the bald man watching the fire.

'I see you've been trying to put that out. Some fool knocked over a lamp, I should think. Good lads though. Come on now! Empty-handed? What did I say about that? Everyone carries something. Here, you can take one of those pots. No easing ships into the water today, lads.

Nice, easy work. Come on, don't stand and stare. Go down to the boats with the others. The sea is calm and there's barely a breeze. By this evening, gods protect us, we'll be in Britannia.'

The big man clapped Cormac on the arm and the line of auxiliaries trooped past, heading down to the boats. Cormac saw the poisoner watching with raised eyebrows, looking for the wineskin. He scowled at him.

'We'll come back,' Cormac muttered to Malvo, struggling with despair. 'I swear it.'

The two of them slipped in with the others, a vast crowd coming out of a makeshift town. More than forty thousand were on the move that day. Three of them would drown in the surf, Cormac learned later. Two more would break bones and one of the camp followers had an arm crushed and died as it was cut free. There was also one small fire in the dock sheds.

Cormac went from a boat to a rolling galley filled with men and supplies. The praetorians had noticed the absence by then of a centurion, if not the four others who lay buried under damp sand. Cormac kept his head down as names were called, but in the confusion, everyone assumed they had gone with another ship. Armies moved in chaos, he and Malvo had learned. When they did move, it was like a wave breaking.

Cormac watched the smoke dwindle to a thread as the sail rose and snapped taut. For all he knew, some servant was digging around in the sand and discovering the melted silver drops at that very moment. He stared at that shore for a long time. He was going home – and there was nothing he could do about it.

2 1

The god of war crossed to Britannia that day, Cormac was certain. For the first few hours after leaving the Gaulish coast, he'd been looking back – in reality as well as his thoughts. He'd been struck by a fear that he wouldn't be able to find that single shed again, never mind the spot where the cart had collapsed under falling beams. What would happen when the praetorians missed their men? When they missed the pay chest? What if they found it and cleared away all the ash and iron? Or worse, built another shed in that spot, or something more permanent? He clenched his jaw, fixing every memory of the night before until he was sure he would not forget.

Slowly, he made himself turn from that inner concentration. The sail strained in a strong wind. With four hundred men on deck and a hundred ready on the oars, the sea hissed fast under the keel. Cormac had imagined that crossing a thousand times. He'd pictured a little old mother in a turf house against a hill, throwing up her arms when she recognised her boy. Or his father, some dark-bearded warrior, out stalking deer when the news came. He would surely rush home then, to see his lost son returned. Sometimes, they lived in a stone house, or a simple village hut. On sunny afternoons at the estate, Cormac had daydreamed a dozen different paths.

He had *not* imagined sweeping across the sea in a fleet of galleys, spreading sails and oars on either side, filling the seascape like studs on armour. Those ships lunged at the land where he'd been born, threat in every plume and rope and oar. Cormac stared at the coast ahead until even Paullus noticed and strolled back.

'Nerves, is it? You don't need to worry, son. The legions are the hammer going in, not us. Did you see those lads reading Caesar's commentaries aloud yesterday?' The man chuckled. He didn't seem to know Cormac and Malvo had been absent, which was fine with both of them. Cormac nodded and smiled, though he felt ill.

'Old Julius had a hard time of it, right enough,' Paullus went on. 'The lads read all his descriptions of war dogs and fighting in the shallows. They've gone in hard, I should think. We're in the last third, anyway. All the really bloody work has been done.'

'The last third?' Cormac repeated.

Paullus looked to see who was listening and lowered his voice.

'The emperor's personal guard doesn't like to get its hands dirty, if you know what I mean. These lads will keep Emperor Claudius safe by not going near the fighting. That's for Aulus Plautius and his commanders. See the ship there, the one with purple banners? That's the imperial galley. The praetorians on board that won't be chasing hares over green hills, not unless things go very wrong.'

'What do *we* do, then?' Cormac asked. He felt his thoughts quicken as he accepted this was happening. He would land in Britannia, the land of his birth. At some point, the emperor would want to return home. Cormac would just have to be useful, too useful to leave behind when the time came.

'We do what we always do. We feed them! We replace their kit, build walls, tend horses, lay roads – anything and everything that doesn't involve cutting someone's throat. Which we will also do, if those blue-skinned savages try to attack any camp of mine. Unless I was wasting my time teaching you the basics, sunshine? I hope not.'

Cormac nodded and tried to smile. The sail was brought down as they drew closer to the opposite shore. It flapped like a mad gull as it was folded on deck and massive oars rumbled out. He could see ships by the hundred on either flank, working hard not to crash into one another, with as many already on the shingle. It looked . . . He waited for some pang that would mean home. The truth was, it reminded him of Gaul.

'It looks like where we've just been,' he muttered, shading his eyes.

Paullus shrugged.

'One of the mapmakers told me this used to be a river, this sea. Thousands of years ago, he said. It grew and grew as waves came in. So I suppose it was one land once. Still, it's a hard coast now. It's been a hundred years since we came over, anyway.'

It had been more recent than that, Cormac thought. Slavers raided those shores every summer, burning villages, taking children and young women to be sold in Gaul. It was a very profitable business, he knew that much.

The thought was a strange one. He was not sure in that moment whether he saw himself as Roman or one of the people they raided. Rome was in the words he spoke, the manners and laws, the culture he had been taught. As he faced that shore, it felt almost like a mask he could throw down, revealing something else underneath. Even that was an image from a play, he realised sourly. The old master had staged a festival of drama once, years before. Cormac had watched spellbound as actors performed the classics. They all wore masks, and put them on or took them off as easily as breathing.

The fleet had rowed and sailed further east in the crossing, leaving the white cliffs behind. What awaited them then were plains of shining shingle, hissing with the strike of waves.

One by one, each galley picked its spot and then surged for land at best ramming speed. Cormac could see an elephant already on shore, the huge beast being led down a gangplank from a galley that leaned at a dangerous angle. He swallowed, preparing himself.

'Here we go,' Paullus said.

Praetorian officers were roaring orders to the men labouring below, exhorting them to give their all. A space lay ahead on the shore, but the current was tugging them past, to where they would foul another galley on its run. That ship's master was already bellowing, waving for them to stand clear.

The oarsmen heaved below deck. The galley jerked forward, sending some of the auxiliaries tumbling. One went overboard, shouting in panic as he tried and failed to find a grip.

Paullus chuckled.

'I hope that tart can swim,' he said.

Malvo looked at Cormac with wide-eyed fear. He had only once had his head underwater in his entire life – when he and Cormac had bluffed their way into a bath-house. The idea of being able to paddle about like a duck on the sea was a mystery to them both. Cormac saw the men at the rail look for the one who had gone over. They shook their heads and someone made a mark on a wax slate. They would record the number of drowned men, but nothing more. Cormac thought of the bodies he and Malvo had buried in the damp sand. He had not always been so careless of life. Perhaps they had made him so.

No, he thought with surprising force, clenching a fist. He was *not* the result of how he had been treated! He had more pride, more wit than that! His choices were his own, his masks his own, his sins his own, no one else's! He would live with the results, good or ill, or be no man at all.

The galley crashed onto the shingle, cutting a great blade as it rose and rose, then came to a halt, hanging in air for an awful moment, then settling. All the men breathed again. Paullus put out a hand to steady Cormac as the ship leaned left, creaking and protesting. At sea, it had been a fast, proud thing, a fish that darted where it wanted. Beached, it was dead, made helpless.

Cormac found himself panting. In moments, long corvus planks were being attached to the lowest side. Praetorians and legion men went off first, forming squares on higher ground as they sought out their companions and began to impose order.

It was at least another hour before Cormac was bouncing down the wood with Malvo at his back. He hesitated at the last step, but there was a line of auxiliaries coming after and he had no time to stand and think how strange it all was. He stepped onto shifting stones – and there he was, standing on land that had birthed him, where he had been nursed and rocked by a winter fire to keep warm.

He blinked at a memory he hadn't known was there. Perhaps this place would speak while he stood on it. It was an odd thought. In that moment, he was Roman. What else was there? It was true he'd grown pale in the mines – working underground for the hours of daylight will do that to a man. When he and Malvo had run the streets years before, Cormac had been tanned, his hair and skin touched by the sun. Yet he was from this shore.

He pretended to tie a sandal thong, dropping to one knee. Hidden from all the others, he plunged his hand into the shingle, taking a handful of small wet stones. He felt no thrill of recognition. In confusion, he let them fall.

The imperial galley had landed safely. As Cormac watched, the emperor himself descended to the shore, where horses had been brought to carry him. The woman Cormac remembered from the camp came behind, looking around with what might have been an expression of grim endurance. The fat little boy leaped the last part, stumbling and laughing as he touched the shingle. Cormac smiled to see that, then watched in wonder as the emperor dipped down and kissed the stones.

Horns blew and Paullus was suddenly there, roaring orders to get into line and stop talking like washerwomen on a day out. The praetorian auxiliaries stood in silence as he inspected them, shaking his head at their posture, filth and general slovenliness.

'You sorry bastards are a disgrace to the legion,' Paullus bellowed, 'though in the absence of better men, you may redeem yourselves with unceasing labour. Take shovels from that pile and follow me. You will observe a boundary marked with rope and flags in the meadow yonder. That will be the first camp and it will be finished tonight. You will make of it a fortress fit for the emperor to visit if he so chooses! You will dig a rampart of standard height and length, with gabion baskets at the core. I need a dozen volunteers to collect the empty ones from the hold of the ship, a dozen more to fill them with shingle, then carts and drivers to bring them up to the camp.'

Cormac found he and Malvo had been volunteered to fill baskets. When the rest of the auxiliaries marched a mile inland, he remained on the beach, using a spade of iron and pine to shovel stones into open wicker baskets someone else brought over and laid out. With loose shingle stretching as far as the eye could see, the work went quickly. Each full gabion had to be lifted onto a cart bed and then dragged clear, but the task was simple enough and Cormac and the others settled to it.

The equipment of legions vomited out onto that shore. Cormac saw carts assembled from spars and wheels, oxen set down in great slings. More baskets were brought to be filled, in sixes that fitted inside one another. Cormac hadn't seen shingle used before, but he could imagine the wall they would make when full ones were stacked and covered over in loose earth, well stamped down. That massive wall would be set with sharpened stakes and have armed legionaries patrolling walkways along the crest. It would be a fortress on that coast. The legions could rest there without fear of attack, or just set their auxiliaries to building another a few miles further on.

A horseman caught Cormac's attention as the man

approached the work team. He seemed red-faced about something. Cormac kept his head well down with the others, preferring not to be noticed. Messengers could be all right, though he'd found most of them more concerned with their own status than being pleasant. This man wore a helmet and fine mail with strap boots that looked new. A red cloth fluttered at his throat and he wore a tunic of the same material under the mail. It looked a good weave, Cormac thought. The rider's lower legs were wiry, without the sort of heavy muscle Cormac had seen on legion riders.

The stranger looked on the sweating team with a disdainful expression. When no one asked him what he wanted, he frowned, startling as if he'd heard a fly. Cormac glanced at him from under lowered brows and of course the man saw.

'You,' he said curtly, singling Cormac out. 'I am Tribune Gaius Perca, Legio II Augusta. Who is in charge here?'

Cormac looked again at the man's unmarked equipment. Tribunes were some sort of noble class, though he wasn't sure of their place in the chain of command. This could be some favoured son, perhaps one who had not seen battle before.

'We do have a senior man, dominus,' Cormac replied. 'Paullus is at the camp, over the hill there. This is just a work team, filling gabions, as you can see.'

'Yes! Gabions that belong to the Second Augusta!' the man retorted. 'Who gave the order for you to take them? I will have the skin from his back.'

Cormac winced.

'I don't know about that, dominus. Someone stacked them here for us. We just fill them.'

'Well, empty them again and put the empty ones on your backs! I have orders to return our property. You will be my mules. Well? Are you deaf? Did you not hear my order?'

Cormac regretted ever looking up, but he took a deep breath.

'These are for the praetorian camp, dominus. If you ask there for one named Paullus, I believe . . .'

He saw the man's eyes widen as he looked past the work team. Malvo spat a curse and Cormac shook his head in warning. This was not a man to insult, he was sure of that much. Tribune Gaius Perca looked a spiteful sort, and Paullus could not protect them from the wrath of a noble son, not one attached to another legion. That was the kind of conflict that led to senior officers taking it out on subordinates. One wrong word would mean stripes or lost rations, or both.

Cormac glanced over his shoulder and saw what Malvo and the stranger had both seen. He made a strangled yelp. Where the trees came close to the shore, a group of men were running towards them. They were not completely blue, not as Paullus had described them before. Yet they had stained their faces, hands and shins. He could see yellow teeth and eyes against that dye. Cormac gripped his spade and wished for the swords Paullus had made them use in the marshalling yard. Still, a spade was better than nothing. He growled to the men around him.

'Stand close, you bastards. If you run, they'll kill us all. Stay with me, or answer to me after.'

He felt Malvo's hand on his shoulder and the two of them moved to the front, spades held ready. Cormac felt the skin crawl over his stomach. What he wouldn't have given for armour, even one of the leather liners the praetorians wore under plate! Anything but this feeling of being as vulnerable as a child.

He felt the men around him shift. Some of them turned to look for anyone coming to help, but they stayed where they were, rooted in the shingle. Perhaps they'd heard and understood what had to be done, or were just too afraid to run on that shifting surface. Cormac blinked at the heavy baskets.

'Two of you stack the gabions!' he snapped. 'Make us a wall.'

He could see twenty or thirty of them coming in fast. They were running in silence, armed with swords or axes, some with a sort of buckler held like a shield. The ones in front had only an iron blade and whirled it around their heads. Cormac saw a few of those were naked as babes, their skin marked in blue and red. He felt fear sap his strength.

Of the dozen men around the gabions, two big lads sprang up and tried to stack a few. The rest clustered behind that poor shelter, while the savages closed at frightening speed. Cormac looked over his shoulder to where the young tribune was still sitting his horse, mouth open. Gaius Perca had not given an order, not said a word since sighting the raid, though he had seen it first.

No one else was close, Cormac realised. In the distance, he could see men by the galleys, pointing towards where he stood. Word would spread and the response would be brutal, he had no doubt about that. Yet it would not come in time. The tribesmen had seen an isolated little group out on the edge of the Roman landing and taken the chance to shed blood.

Cormac watched in silence as they came loping in, the

284

blue men suddenly howling like wolves. No one around the gabions ran. He didn't know if it was courage. Perhaps it was the anger of working men interrupted in their labours – or some sense that they were praetorian auxiliaries. Whatever it was, they did not move.

'Steady, lads,' Malvo said. His deep voice settled nerves, reminding them all they were not alone. Cormac narrowed his eyes, picking the one who would reach him first, readying his spade to smash the shrieking bastard into the next world.

Cormac blocked the first blow, then jabbed his spade tip into the man's throat. Paullus had taught them all that much. Throat and groin and armpit were the three targets when a man was trying to kill you. There were big veins in those places and blood came pouring from just a small gash. Yet the spades were rounded at the tip and blunt from shovelling stones. Cormac saw his prod batted away and switched to using the spade as a club. He could swing that well enough, but men around him were being butchered. He and Malvo watched each other's backs and so survived the first onslaught, though they were forced to retreat from the wall of gabions.

To Cormac's surprise, the young tribune gave a great war cry then, digging in his heels and drawing a gladius. He had been like a statue before, but when he came to life, it was with rage and skill. Gaius Perca was not a coward, Cormac realised. He could have ridden away easily enough. Instead, the young Roman made good use of his mount's height and presumably better training than Cormac or Malvo had known. As Cormac took a chance to duck back behind the baskets, he saw Perca kill two savages with neat blows. His gladius was not a blunt weapon. They clustered on him, but as they tried to drag him from the saddle, he despatched them coolly.

As they fell, the young man bellowed his own challenge. In reply, one of the tribesmen threw a stone the size of a hen's egg with great accuracy. It cracked against Perca's helmet, stunning him. Even then he might have recovered, but another of the blue-stained maniacs jumped and snagged his mail, dragging him over his mount's haunches. He hit very hard. Gaius Perca lived and moved still, though there was blood on his face. Cormac reached for him, trying to drag him behind the wall of filled gabions. He was knocked away when a tribesman threw himself on the fallen tribune, straddling him. Though Gaius Perca tried to fend him off, the savage hacked an axe down on his head and face in a frenzy, screeching all the while in obscene triumph.

Cormac found himself grappling another, falling and rolling together. The attacker did not expect his strength to be matched and overborne. Grunting, Cormac gripped the hand on his throat, bending it until something snapped and the man shrieked. His blue-stained berserker gnashed teeth at him. The man snapped like a dog, nuzzling Cormac's neck as he tried to get a grip. Cormac recoiled, trying to kick him away. The smell of unwashed flesh was in his nose and he wanted to vomit as he rubbed a curd of wet spit from his throat.

Something swung for his head – and it was Malvo who stopped a killing blow, taking a blade through part of his forearm. It ripped free and Malvo yelled in shock and pain. His spade handle had snapped and he jammed the broken end into his attacker's mouth, breaking teeth and ripping off part of a lip.

Cormac fell backwards and in that moment he understood only he and Malvo still lived. Roman horns sounded in the distance, but he looked into snarling masks of hate and victorious glee.

From the depths of his mind, words came, words he had not heard for a dozen years or more, ones he did not know he knew.

'I am Cantii,' he shouted in their strange tongue. 'Home! My land!'

The man standing over him raised a sword still red with the blood of Gaius Perca. He blinked in confusion at the sounds Cormac dredged up. It broke whatever violent fever had gripped the man. The Briton looked across the shore, to whoever was coming to repel the raid. The man snarled defiance at their approach, like a trapped dog.

Cormac just breathed. His spade was gone and he lay on his back, helpless. He could not resist, not any longer. He saw the man look to Malvo, his friend holding his wounded arm and glaring. There was no threat there.

The blue-skinned man spat blood and phlegm on the ground and glanced at the fallen tribune. He stalked to him, tearing a golden locket from Gaius Perca's neck. A band of gold was wrenched off a finger and a good Roman dagger went into his belt. The savage looked up as he secured his prizes. The ones coming were getting close.

Cormac felt the man's attention return.

'Cantii,' Cormac said again.

The man shrugged and trotted away with his brothers and their treasures, leaving more than a dozen men spilling blood into the greedy shore.

Left alone, Cormac and Malvo stood slowly. Malvo's arm was dripping, the cut making it useless as it hung by his side.

'You should get that wrapped and cleaned with wine,' Cormac said. 'Get a legion doctor to have a look at it.'

It was not what he meant to say, but he didn't have the words. Malvo nodded anyway. They'd thought they'd known death in the mines, down in the dark. It seemed he walked this shore as well.

They were surrounded by corpses. The horse had gone trotting off when its master fell, but now it returned, nuzzling at his body. The rest of them had been auxiliaries – miners – men Malvo and Cormac had known. They'd worked together, deep underground. They'd sparred too in a yard in Gaul, with Paullus expressing cheerful disbelief at their lack of skill. They hadn't been friends, not exactly, but Cormac and Malvo had known them even so.

Cormac found he was weeping as he stood there. Malvo saw and stepped in front of him when legionaries approached. They came in a group, but they'd already seen it was too late. There was not much urgency in them.

The last of the blue-skinned tribesmen vanished into the distance, reaching the trees. No one seemed to want to go haring after, Cormac noticed.

'I'll report it,' a legionary said. 'My cohort will sweep those trees. If they're still there, we'll string them up.'

Cormac looked at him, seeing a different uniform to the praetorians.

'They won't be there,' he said, glancing across the open shore. He wouldn't be, he realised. He'd still be trotting away from the beach, or planning an ambush for anyone daring to come in off the coast. He wished the legionary luck.

'Were you with these lads?' the man said.

Cormac hesitated and took a deep breath. The salt air cut his lungs, sharpening him. He looked at Malvo in silent warning.

'No. We are . . . we *were* servants to Master Gaius Perca here. His father is going to get the worst news tonight.'

'Right. You'll tell him?'

Cormac shrugged. He was too filthy to be a manservant to a noble son, though the legionary didn't seem to have noticed. He needed to wash and find clothes unstained by soot and blood, assuming that was even possible.

'It's my duty,' he said. 'More's the pity. I'll need to take my master's body to a doctor – to be wrapped. We'll carry him home after that. He's an only son, you know. This will break his mother's heart.'

Malvo dipped his head to hide his surprise, holding his wound in his other hand to slow the blood. The gesture made the others do the same, so that they stood as if in solemn prayer, surrounded by dead men.

The tide was coming in, approaching that part of the shore and reaching the feet of the fallen. Cormac glowered at it, seeing how some of the beached galleys rocked slightly as waves came under their keels. This was a strange place, a place where rules didn't matter.

'You lads could help by dragging these men clear,' he said. 'Send a runner to Paullus in the praetorian camp, would you? Tell him his basket party were killed or captured.'

'Captured?' the legionary said in horror.

Cormac nodded, rubbing his eyes.

'A couple of lads were dragged away by those bastards. I couldn't save them.'

He sighed, then gestured to Malvo to help him with the body of Gaius Perca.

'I don't envy them now, I tell you that. Could you take the reins of my master's horse, dominus? If you're heading back to your own camp?'

'Of course,' the legionary said. He sent others scurrying away to inform the praetorian auxiliaries, then trudged with Cormac and Malvo along the shore, lost in solemn tragedy.

22

Cormac was standing on the shore not a full mile from the scene of the violence when Paullus came out. He was fairly sure he recognised the man's bald head and wide frame at less than a thousand paces, but he kept his own face turned away, watching from under lowered brows as he prayed to Janus. If the auxiliary came marching over to speak to the servants of Gaius Perca, it would lead to some difficult conversations. Or they'd see him coming and go to meet him halfway. Cormac felt his stomach twist. He remembered the man's skill with weapons from the yard in Gaul. He did not think he and Malvo could overcome Paullus, not in a fair fight.

'You've done it now,' Malvo said, appearing at his shoulder. 'He'll want to hear what happened. Paullus, I mean.'

Cormac jumped.

'Stop sneaking up on me like that!' he snapped. His friend could move like a ghost sometimes. It was disconcerting in such a tall man.

'He'll count the dead and be told two of them were dragged off,' Cormac said.

Was the bald man looking in their direction? It was hard to tell, but he thought so. The soldier from Second Augusta had brought the riderless horse back to his own camp, leaving it in the hands of stable lads. A legion doctor had washed and stitched Malvo's arm there, wrapping it in cloth to protect the wound from foul air that sometimes rose at night. All that had taken time and the sun was setting as Cormac saw Paullus trudge down to stare at a butcher's field. Yes, someone was jabbing the air in Cormac's direction, he saw in dismay. Paullus was pointing in turn, nodding, clearly discussing the only surviving witnesses.

Cormac watched the body of Gaius Perca brought out and given into his care. The men of Second Augusta had been respectful with their youngest tribune. The corpse had been wrapped against the view of common men, the terrible wounds hidden. Cormac wondered if the father would recognise his son when the body was returned. He wrenched his gaze from it. In the distance, he saw Paullus set off towards them, striding across the shingle. He heard Malvo curse under his breath.

'We should take our master on board,' Cormac said to the bearers.

They didn't mind someone else doing their work and stepped back as he and Malvo grabbed an end and made their way quickly up the gangway. With the galley leaning, it was steep enough to make it hard going. Cormac didn't dare look to see how close Paullus was until he reached the deck. When he risked a glance then, his stomach sank. The man had covered half the distance. He marched like a soldier, as if he would not tire.

Cormac and Malvo exchanged a look of wide-eyed panic. If Paullus came close enough to recognise them, they would be taken as deserters. The punishment was worse in time of war, as Cormac had heard. Some of the miners had talked through the details with a sort of sick relish. Impalement was the end of it, though men did linger even then.

Cormac watched as ropes grew taut, the long cables rowed to a galley already at sea. The waves were calm enough and he assumed there were men like him below, digging out the keel and getting the galley ready to sweep into the shallows. He peered past a legion officer to see where Paullus was.

The deck held over a hundred dead, with more stacked like amphorae below. It seemed there had been some sort of battle over a river further inland. Those who had been killed had been wrapped and marked in the records of their legion for return home. Gaius Perca had become one of many, but the deck was full. They would be ferried back to Gaul and two servants of a tribune might borrow a cart there to take a fallen son home. They might even tip a body out in the woods and disappear, if those two were not servants at all.

Cormac could not see the bald auxiliary. He wanted to go to the rail and peer over, but the gangway was still down and he feared catching the man's eye. He made himself pray, which was not so strange on that boat of the dead. Most of the men given that grisly duty would have prayed to Pluto of the underworld. Cormac whispered to Janus on the general principle that an unpopular god would be more inclined to notice the entreaties of a desperate follower.

Horns blew, warning those down by the keel that the galley would move. Cormac began to breathe more easily when he saw legionaries go to the gangplank and secure the chains that would prevent it falling while they heaved it up, hand over hand.

He froze when he heard Paullus speak gruffly, so close he seemed to be on board. No, he was on that gangway.

'I need to speak to the servants of Gaius Perca,' Paullus called out.

Whoever blocked him from coming further up would not survive the man's force of will, Cormac knew.

'If you come any further, you'll be heading to Gaul with the rest of us,' a legionary replied.

Cormac looked out to sea and realised the galley there would be waiting for some sort of signal. It might have been a flag raised on a spear or a lamp waved back and forth, he had no idea. He prayed harder for the ship to move, just to start its great roaring slide into the sea.

'This is *praetorian* business,' he heard Paullus say.

There was the sound of a scuffle and both Cormac and Malvo tried to turn away from it. They were too late. The massive bald figure pushed past a legionary too low in rank to force the issue. Cormac and Malvo came face-to-face with Paullus as he stood there, his mouth open in astonishment.

'I have to take the gangplank in!' the legionary growled at Paullus.

The bald man had one foot still on it as he stared. He rubbed a hand on his jaw, the light of understanding dawning. Not a miracle to see them alive, but a crime.

Paullus looked from Cormac to Malvo and back again. He nodded, as if to himself.

'You should tell the father . . .' he began. Those were the words he had prepared and he faltered. Neither Cormac nor Malvo spoke as their world broke to pieces around them. Paullus dipped his head again. 'Tell him his son died well. Tell him we tracked those savages to their village, killed them all and burned it to the ground.'

He tossed a golden locket through the air and Cormac caught it.

'He'll want that, I don't doubt,' Paullus said.

Cormac could only stand like a stone as Paullus turned his back and went down the gangway. The legionary called a curse after him as he and his mates pulled it onboard.

Cormac and Malvo went to the edge of the deck as the galley began to move, faster and faster until it crashed into the sea with a great burst of white spray. They saw Paullus standing on the shore in the growing gloom, his expression unreadable.

'Why did . . . ?' Malvo muttered.

He stopped as Cormac put a hand on his arm. There were too many ears to listen on that deck, as well as the dead. The truth was they couldn't know. Perhaps Paullus hadn't wanted to see them tortured and impaled, or meant it as a reward for how they'd fought. He would have read the stacked gabions, heard the reports of the legionaries who'd come too late. Perhaps it was just a moment of kindness, amidst all the cruelty and blood.

Cormac saw the sail raised. The wind was for Gaul and though he knew captains didn't like to move at night, the sea was calm and it was just a little way. The dead had to be taken home.

As they went out onto deep waters, he thought of the blue-stained men who had come onto a beach to defend their land. Some of them had been killed there before they'd retreated. The rest had been slaughtered in their homes when Roman soldiers came looking for vengeance. Cormac felt a chill that had nothing to do with the sea wind. He was the one who had mentioned auxiliaries being carried off. He'd been thinking quickly, trying to account for the numbers of dead not matching those Paullus had left to fill gabions. It had seemed a solution at the time, but the result . . . the result had been men, women and children butchered in reprisal. A village of his own people burned. By the gods, if this was the coast where he'd been taken up, perhaps his own village.

He felt his stomach cramp and leaned over the edge of the deck at a dangerous angle to empty it into the waves below. Malvo grabbed the back of his tunic as Cormac heaved and spasmed, spitting and weeping in the growing dark. He had been a slave once. He was free then, but they had made him something harder than he had ever asked to be. He almost wished Paullus hadn't shown that extraordinary moment of mercy. Cormac longed to fight, to lash out against all the pain and grief he had known.

He felt better when he had nothing more to spill. He and Malvo sat by the body of Gaius Perca, marked with a leather tag on a cord. Rome was efficient, Cormac thought coldly. A machine of war, but ordered and recorded, down to the last boot and name. It was also his home, whether he wanted it or not.

The camp in Gaul wasn't completely deserted. Boats came and went from the shore, carrying messages and orders as well as the dead. Yet the army had moved on. When the wind blew, it felt like a place of ghosts, a dead city. Hungry dogs yapped and wagged if they saw anyone alive, with gulls calling overhead. It felt abandoned after the noise and life of the legions. Cormac just wanted to leave it behind.

He had scrawled a permission from Centurion Titus Livius to be there. It was one name Cormac knew would not be appearing at his shoulder. He and Malvo took possession of the body of Gaius Perca as it was laid out on the dock. The toll of the dead had been heavy and of course there were scribes there to record the names and legions of each of the fallen.

Cormac winced at the sight of funeral pyres. Like golden tents along the shore, a dozen of them roared that night, surely visible across the water. He supposed it did not feel right to burn men on a foreign shore. Gaul was Roman land, after all, with no sea their spirits could not cross to go home.

After services too brief to be worthy of the name, the ashes would be put into urns for return to family tombs. Grieving relatives would be given something of the man they had lost, as well as part of two or three others burned alongside him. Cormac shook his head, looking back at the wrapped body waiting on the cart. Having his servants on hand had kept Gaius Perca's mortal remains from the fires. Malvo had made a great fuss about treating their master's son with dignity, scorning the offer of a mere urn.

There had been no trouble finding the cart either, not in a place where forty thousand had passed through just days before. Cormac had been offered his pick. Perhaps the legion factors had wondered at his insistence on the sturdiest they had, Cormac didn't know. He'd turned down a light cisium cart drawn by a pair of mules, and instead found a grain-hauler that was a few years old and built of weathered oak. It would carry a good weight on their sombre journey.

In the darkness, he and Malvo made a last sweep of the shore thereabouts, checking there was no one watching. They set to then with spades, digging through the spars and charred beams of a warehouse shed that had burned.

'If someone comes, we are burying our master in Gaul, as he always wanted,' Malvo said, panting.

Cormac shook his head.

'In sandy ground? We're lucky no one's found the others . . .'

He paused as his fingers touched something beneath the surface, something that did not move like stone. He recoiled as he felt the give of flesh, his hand running over what was clearly a face.

'One of them here,' he hissed, shuddering. 'Where did you bury them again?'

'Let me light a lamp and I will *tell* you,' Malvo whispered back.

Cormac just grunted and felt around. He could not tell if the body was that of the centurion or one of the poisoned legionaries. He felt a twinge of guilt at that. They had not hurt him, not really. They'd just been summoned from their beds to guard a cart and then been killed. He slapped himself on the face to sharpen his thoughts. He hadn't made them drink the poisoned wine! In fact, he'd pleaded with them not to take it. They had got what they deserved . . . He closed his eyes, pleased Malvo couldn't see him shaking. Perhaps it was working with men like them: on the sands, at sea, on the shore of Britannia. He *knew* the legionaries, better than he ever had in Rome. Just marching a hundred miles through Gaul and stopping every night to eat and rest and repair old kit had brought that about. He didn't *want* to know them. He didn't want to think of them as men at all. Yet he did – and he felt a weight press him down, one Malvo didn't seem to feel.

His hands had been moving as he worked, like eels sifting the sand. He'd found a dozen pieces of strong-box metal, but there was no pattern to it. The sea could have rushed up and disordered the spot he remembered. He supposed he was lucky the bodies hadn't already been exposed. Yet . . . He paused.

'Here,' he called.

Malvo was beside him in a moment, plunging long fingers into the sand alongside his. Cormac heard his friend grunt as he found the depression.

Like the shingle in Britannia, Cormac could feel beads, rough and cold. He raised them up, but the moon was hidden and he could see nothing.

'We don't have any sacks,' Malvo said.

He was up before Cormac could reply, moving to the cart. Cormac groaned to himself as he understood, but there was no time to go searching an empty camp. The body of Gaius Perca had been wrapped over and over in thick cloth. Malvo unrolled his shroud without ceremony, spilling the Roman onto the sand with great heaves. It was not dignified and Cormac did not look at the stiff figure as it lay there. He took a large piece of cloth as Malvo hacked it free with his knife, tearing strips from another edge.

Together, they worked by feel until their fingertips were sore, collecting every misshapen droplet they could find. The sea had shifted some from the central spot, the movement of waves washing the sand smooth. Yet they found those too once they understood the pattern in the dark, collecting each one and dropping it into the rough bags they made. There were more than Cormac could believe, endless handfuls of the things. Somewhere, a legion scribe would be going mad once he understood an entire pay chest had been lost. Only the chaos of the invasion had made this possible, Cormac thought. Otherwise, the theft would have been discovered already. He recalled the softness of the features he'd touched in the sand and felt gorge rise in his throat. That damned poisoner meant they would be hunted eventually. Cormac didn't know how the praetorians would find them, but he suspected they'd never stop looking for men who had vanished with a chest of legion silver, especially when they found the bodies. He wondered briefly if he and Malvo could carry the corpses to the funeral pyres, but there were witnesses there. No, they had to leave them.

'Any more?' Malvo said by his ear, making him jump again.

His friend's voice was awed and Cormac understood why when he rose and looked into a cart filled with fat sacks of the beads. The moon was rising, which seemed right. There was more weight in those crude sacks than he could believe. A legion's silver that had chilled as it fell, waiting in the sand for their hands. Cormac shook his head, realising he had stood stunned for too long.

'What about . . . him?' he asked, indicating the body.

'Leave him,' Malvo said.

He was not a man of sentiment, Cormac knew that. It was what he had expected, but he clenched his jaw.

'He was brave, Mal,' he muttered.

'And now he is dead. Come on, let's get moving.'

'No, I think we should take him. It doesn't feel right to

leave him here. Someone will wonder why we left him – maybe find the others as well.'

Malvo clenched his jaw, but he didn't climb onto the cart seat. The horses were steady enough, nags of strong build and broad shoulders that could take the weight.

'Fine,' Malvo said angrily. 'Take his feet.'

Together, they rested the body of Gaius Perca on the sacks. Cormac could not have said why he did it. He had smoothed sand over the faces of dead men just moments before as he and Malvo tried to cover the marks of their presence. Dignity for the dead meant nothing, or perhaps everything, he was not sure. It was either some vital part of a life, or it didn't matter at all.

Cormac climbed up to sit by Malvo and took the reins, slapping the backs of the team lightly to get them started. The animals snorted as they took the weight, but they dragged the cart round in a great arc and then up onto stone roads leading away from the shore.

Cormac glanced back to where funeral pyres burned. No voices called in accusation or outrage after them. He and Malvo were free. They could go anywhere with what they had in that cart. They could live like senators in Greece or Hispania.

'We'll stop in the next big town,' Cormac said. 'Someone will take a few of those beads for coins. We can hire a place to lie low, until they stop looking for us.'

'You think they'll look?' Malvo said.

He touched the hole in his cheek, always aware of how memorable it made him. Cormac noticed, of course. He missed nothing.

'They will when the bodies are washed into view, I'm sure. We can wait it out in Lugdunum, maybe. I'll get you a hooded cloak – or you could just grow a beard. While I learn how to stamp coins. A few months, Malvo.'

'And after that . . . we are going back to Rome?' Malvo asked softly.

'*Yes*, we are going back to Rome!' Cormac said firmly. 'There is nowhere else. We have scores to settle, Malvo. We're rich men now! They'll never see us coming.'

Cormac bowed, as he believed men of Syria or Jerusalem did when they traded in Rome. Malvo stood glaring at the moneylender, offended that Cormac had said he spoke no civilised tongue.

The shop was not on one of the main streets of Lugdunum. That part of the small Gaulish city looked to have known better days. The crossing stones had even been stolen from the street outside, no doubt finding some other use in the hearths of local taverns. Cormac had let Malvo pick the road, relying on his friend's oldest instincts. It did not seem to have been a good choice.

They watched as the moneylender weighed thirty of the beads on tiny scales, breathing through his nose in silence, adding slender pieces of iron in reducing sizes until the thing was perfectly balanced and still as a stone. The man made a note of the weight, then brought out what looked like a glass vase, inscribed on one side with a series of lines. Cormac stared in interest as the man filled it with water to a long mark, then dropped the beads in, one by one. Peering at it from all angles, he noted exactly how far the level rose.

The moneylender saw Cormac's concentration and smiled, sensing a mind like his own.

'Archimedes,' he said.

Cormac nodded.

'I've read of it, but never seen it done. The crown.'

The moneylender bowed his head, pleased. Malvo looked from one to the other, but it was as if they talked a different language and he could not ask.

Cormac noticed his friend's confused expression and realised he could not explain without continuing the fiction that his 'master' spoke only the language of Syria. Neither of them knew a word of that tongue, of course, which would make bluffing almost impossible.

'So . . . you weigh the silver beads,' Cormac said, 'then find their size by the water they displace – as Archimedes saw when he climbed into his bath . . .'

'I have always assumed that was just a story,' the moneylender said. 'The idea of a philosopher running naked down the street, crying . . .'

'Eureka,' they said together, smiling. The moneylender shrugged.

'If there is lead in these beads, the weight divided by the volume will not match the figure I have for silver. That is how Archimedes proved the king's crown was gold and not some base metal, without having to melt it down.'

Cormac wiped a prickle of sweat surreptitiously as the man consulted a ledger. There had been gold in the praetorian chest as well as silver. Though he'd tried to find only silver beads, he was not certain they were pure. He'd expected a moneylender down on his luck would not look too closely, or ask questions. That might have been a mistake. Perhaps such a man had to be even more careful than his wealthier colleagues.

'That is . . . correct,' the moneylender said at last. Cormac breathed again. 'You'll understand I cannot give you the same value by weight, of course. There is art in stamping and forging the metals. A mint will take half the value in labour alone.'

'How fascinating,' Cormac said. 'Is there such a place in Lugdunum?'

'There is, of course – under imperial licence. If there were not, I could not take these crude drops from you. Lugdunum is no backwater, my friend.'

'My master is a wealthy man,' Cormac said. 'If you will accept the first few beads as a gift, I think he would like to see where real Roman coins are made. To see beads of Syrian silver being given the face of emperors would be a great privilege. Surely the skills are priceless.'

He saw the man check the beads once more, then the figure in his ledger, confirming his calculation of their worth. Thirty had to be a month's wage and no small bribe. Nor were they corrupted, which was more than could be said for many of the coins that passed through his hands.

Cormac smiled as he saw the man waver. While he waited, he listed the tools he would need. A workshop, hammers, an anvil, an iron forge, tongs . . . The one thing he could not easily make were the iron dies that bore the image of an emperor. With two of those, he could turn all their melted beads back into coins. He would need a jeweller's set of files, he thought – and some coins to copy. Malvo could swing the hammer, once they had bought, made or stolen what they needed. Cormac smiled as the moneylender nodded to him, taking the opportunity to bow again. They were back.

23

The house of Gaius Perca was not at all what Cormac had expected. He and Malvo had prepared themselves for a rung of society second only to the senate. They wore garments of good cloth and Cormac rode a fine new gelding alongside the cart Malvo drove. More, they had hired four guards to protect them on the road. Most of the fortune remained in the house in Lugdunum, but Cormac had a pouch of gold he liked to touch and count. It had not been easy separating it from the silver, but the yellow metal drifted down when it was all melted together, settling on the bottom.

Perhaps it mattered that he and Malvo had dug for that shine in the deep earth for years. It meant something to them both, knowing how much blood and sweat had gone into it. Together, the guards would keep them safe on dangerous roads. Those men believed he and Malvo were wealthy merchants and appearance mattered.

More importantly, they could not leave the body of Gaius Perca any longer. The house in Lugdunum had a basement about as cold as a grave, but the smell was growing worse each day, filling the rooms above like nothing on earth.

Cormac had made the decision when he started to dry-heave during his evening meal. They had made barely a fifth of the beads into blanks and finished coins, but there was no help for it. Gaius Perca *had* to be taken home. With wet cloth over their faces, they'd taken another two days to bury all the tools and dies in the basement, smoothing the earth floor back so there was no sign. Then they wrapped the body in fresh layers of cloth, covering the brown stains that seeped through. The smell of death was a memory of war for them both. It made it hard to keep food down when the wind blew towards them. Malvo said the cart would need to be burned.

The scribes of Legio II Augusta had listed his city of return on the tag they'd attached to his body. Ravenna, in the north – a seaport of marshes, with half the buildings built on piles of wood over water. It did not seem especially wealthy at first sight. Cormac wasn't even certain it was the right place until he reached the outskirts and asked for the family of Gaius Perca.

At her kitchen table, his mother stared at the locket Cormac had given her, turning it over and over in her hands. It seemed, in all the confusion of the invasion, the announcement of her son's death had never been sent. Cormac had expected to hand over the body for some fine family tomb in marble, to be thanked, perhaps rewarded, then go on his way. Instead, he and Malvo had destroyed a woman with the news.

'Is his father here?' Cormac murmured after a time.

She shook her head.

'Long dead. Gaius was all I had. You say you saw him die? Tell me about it. Tell me what he said to you.'

Cormac winced as he rubbed his jaw. He had already described the last moments of her son to her, but the words had not penetrated her grief. She shook her head at intervals as if something itched. He supposed he understood that.

'He came to retrieve some baskets we were filling with stones,' he said. 'He seemed very angry about us having them.'

She smiled.

'Yes, Gaius had a temper. He would shout and send the chickens flying when someone crossed him, making the most terrible oaths. But he would always say, "Mama, I will make such a fortune you will never go hungry again." I believed him. He was so beautiful, my son, my darling son.'

Cormac looked around him again. The little house on a piece of scrub marshland was not what he had imagined when he thought of a tribune's family. The young men who joined legions as one of the six were destined for great things, as he understood it. They came from wealth and influence, not . . . He saw a mouse running along an ancient beam, disturbing a thread of dust. It too was thin. Not this.

'I had expected some family estate,' he said.

'We had one once, before my husband went into business, the poor fool. He wanted to dig a great canal to the sea, to make Ravenna a city to equal Rome, can you believe that? You saw the marshes? The ground is just swamp around here. His bridge sank, his investors pulled out, he could not finish . . . He left us just this place. The Percas are still equestrians by blood, but you cannot eat a noble class, nor a good name. We found him hanging from a beam in the barn. Gaius found him.' She wiped her eyes, but tears spilled once more, running in the wrinkles of her cheeks. 'My son was determined to make it right, to restore all we lost. He swore to me he would rise to lead legions, to stand in the senate. He had such dreams! You should have heard him. I loved to hear him talk.' She began to sob softly, rubbing her thumb over the locket her son had worn. 'Now, that will not happen and . . . who will look after me, now?'

Cormac felt Malvo shift in the other chair. He looked up to see his friend glaring at him, guessing what was in his thoughts. Cormac had a pouch of gold in his pocket and he wanted to give it to her. He wanted to ease the awful grief he had brought to that place, that poor house on the verge of falling down around her ears.

Malvo shook his head in warning.

'I wonder, dominus, if I might have a word outside.'

'Not now,' Cormac said curtly.

Malvo crossed his arms, eyes cold. He did not completely abandon the role they had chosen, though perhaps he already regretted it. Cormac could play a young nobleman better than Malvo. Yet a servant could not argue with his master.

Cormac reached out and put his hand on the woman's arm. She could not have been much less than forty, though she looked older. Life had been hard on her and would be harder still without a son to help. Cormac wondered how long it would be before she too was found cold and still in that place, perhaps swinging from the same beam as her husband. He winced at the image. Her son deserved better, he thought.

'Domina,' he said. 'I have not told you everything . . .'

'I would like a word,' Malvo said. He stood up and the old lady looked at him in confusion, eyes wet and rimmed in red.

'Sit down or leave,' Cormac said, too roughly. His friend sat once more.

'Domina,' Cormac said, 'we only met your son on the last day. I saw him fight – and he was exactly as brave as I have said, or more so. He may have saved us both. Yet we were auxiliaries, not even from his legion.'

'But you brought him home,' she said. She pulled back her hand and he did not try to hold it. There was suspicion growing in her eyes, even fear. He worried she might start to scream for help and spoke on quickly.

'He deserved more than to be burned on the shore of Gaul, or so I thought. Honestly, my first concern was getting away. I'd . . . had enough of war, domina. Look, your son had a name and no fortune.'

He brought out the pouch and spilled gold coins onto the wooden table. Malvo groaned in disbelief. The woman's eyes widened and she put the locket down and picked them up instead, weighing coins in her hand.

'Domina,' Cormac went on. 'I do have a fortune – and I truly admired your son. I am a free man, I swear, though of no good line. I wonder if you might let me use his name. I would always treat it with the honour it deserved.'

She began to shake and rock, eyes wide. For a moment, Cormac thought she was gasping for air, but it was a sort of sob.

'For these? For these gold coins?' she said at last. 'I know he would be telling me to take them.' She nodded. 'Very well. I cannot refuse. You pay my poverty, young man, whoever you are. I know I could not stop you using it.'

'Perhaps,' he said. 'But as I said, he was a brave man and he loved you, that much is clear. I would like to honour him.'

She held out her arms and Cormac embraced her. Malvo got up in a temper and left, shutting the door too hard. Cormac kissed the woman gently on her forehead. There would be hard words with Malvo later, he had no doubt. He had paid a fortune in gold for a name marked as dead on the records of Legio II Augusta. That was a problem for another day. Yet Cormac felt it was right. He'd killed and robbed and suffered for those coins. Some of that pain washed away as the mother of Gaius Perca sobbed in his arms.

PART THREE

AD 44

24

Rome. It endured, but was never really the same. Cormac had left it wearing chains, back when Caligula was still trying to be a good man. *That* Rome had died with the young emperor, only to be remade in turn by Claudius. Massive aqueducts stretched overhead, casting shadows on clean, rebuilt roads. New facades and temples and columns and statues had risen on every corner. Cormac tried not to stare as he rode through streets he hardly recognised. He was mounted on a gelding any tribune of the eques class would admire, a mount as fine as he had ever known. Money was not about ownership, he reminded himself, but the labour of others. He could not remember where he had learned that, though it had stuck.

He looked to Malvo, who rode an ass alongside. His friend wore a deep hood then to keep his face concealed, looking somewhat like the shadow of death as he stared fearfully around. Guards jingled along in pairs behind them both, ready to protect master and servant from the touch of beggars. Cormac raised his eyes to the sky in frustration. He had *told* Malvo not to peer about in that guilty way! They had both learned to ride in Gaul, but Malvo detested horses. He said they looked at him. As a result, his friend had refused a mount more suited to an eques, or even the servant of one. They had funds to buy a herd if they'd wanted, but Malvo seemed happier in his servant role, mute and glaring. The ass he rode was his compromise, like the cloak he wore. He had taken Cormac's suggestion and let a beard grow for the first time in his life. Even in the mines, they'd had a barber to shave those who wanted it. They were not savages. The result hid the hole in his cheek, with tinted wax to fill the missing nostril. Cormac was pleased enough with it.

In some ways, Malvo was a weakness in his new role, a crack in a fine pot. Yet he would be weaker still without him, Cormac was certain. Of course, if anyone recognised Malvo, they might wonder if his companion was another face from the past. Cormac clenched his jaw, feeling exposed as he rode. No, he would *not* look down. Men of his new social class expected the whole world to look away first.

At the foot of the Quirinal hill, he saw a new acquaintance waiting for him. Martinius Cesca was a short and somewhat fussy fellow, neat and quick in his movements. Cormac had employed the factor to seek out a house to rent in the city, one suitable for a wealthy young eques from Ravenna.

Cormac tried to seem calm as he passed a street wall he certainly did remember. It was like going back to his childhood, to stand on the Quirinal – and of course nothing seemed to have changed there. Except him.

It had been Malvo's suggestion to rent a place close by the Silanus property. Cormac had resisted at first while Malvo talked of hiding beneath the feet of the ones who hunted them. It was definitely the last place Senator Decimus Silanus would expect to find them. Yet it was another risk. Cormac wondered if a man could lose himself in pursuit of danger, like the ones who drank wine every day, until it suddenly drank them.

He reined in before an iron gate, dismounting and following Cesca into a well-tended garden. Someone else took the horse and donkey as Malvo followed. He assumed so anyway. Gaius Perca was a man used to having servants, after all. Cormac stopped. No, all right, he wasn't. He couldn't help going back and making sure his horse wasn't being stolen. He turned and then nodded in relief when he saw two lads bringing both animals in through another door. Cormac brightened. He had a stable!

He trotted once more along the path to catch up to Malvo and Cesca, the factor showing the house he had procured for them.

'Ah, there you are, dominus. There are three bedrooms above, with shutters over the windows installed as you asked. The atrium is large and collects rainwater from the roof. There, you see the shallow pool. Lined in lead, dominus . . . There are also bathing pools, one a cold plunge – though that is smaller than the owner led me to believe.'

Cesca flushed and Cormac waved a hand.

'It's no matter. I prefer to use the Balneae when I am in Rome.'

'Of course. Would you like to see the stables?'

'I think I can find them.'

Cormac eyed the silver ring he saw glinting on the man's finger. A freedman, rising in the world. Well, he was trying to do that himself.

'I will need staff, Cesca. House and stable servants, cooks – a sword trainer.'

He saw Malvo look up at that and wanted to tell his friend to keep his face in the hood. The beard really had grown thick, like a hedge poking out. Cormac was serious though. The violence in Gaul had shown him swordsmanship was a skill he needed. Malvo may already have had the knack, but Cormac had almost been killed because he couldn't block and lunge with any special talent or quickness.

'The next slave market is in three days, dominus,' Martinius said, scratching his jaw. 'It is the largest in the city and held once every quarter. I would be happy to act as your agent, of course. We'll find anything you need there – and there are slave quarters in the basement here. Enough for forty men and women. I believe I am a fair judge of quality, if I may say so, dominus . . .'

'If you choose them for me, you will expect to add to the purchase price? I am to be gouged again just to have staff?'

Cesca looked embarrassed, but he nodded.

'A fifth part is usual for the factor, dominus. I do know the slavers and the tricks they use. The drugs that make a slave bright of eye only to have him die the following day. I can find you a staff, one that will be the envy of your friends.'

Cesca sensed the young master's mood change as Cormac took a step to loom over him. There was an anger there that surprised the young factor. He could not think what he had done to deserve it. Cesca twisted the ring on his finger with his other hand, a reminder to them both of his freed status. He could not be struck, even by an eques, not without consequences.

Cormac saw Malvo watching and worked to master his emotions. He was playing a role, he reminded himself, a scatterbrained young eques spending family money on luxury and entertainment. The feeling of rage that had risen at the talk of slaves had sprung from nothing, tearing his deception to rags. Cormac knew he was glaring from the way Martinius Cesca trembled and glanced at the gladius on his hip. For now, of course, the threat was mostly bluff.

With a huge effort, he made himself smile. Let Cesca think he was one of those mercurial sorts who frightened the ones who served them.

'A tenth part, Cesca,' he said. 'Or I will find someone else. And I want to see each deed of sale, with your tenth added and properly accounted. I do not object to a man being paid, but I will not be made a fool. Is that understood?'

'It is, dominus, by Jupiter it is. I would never dream of . . .'

'Leave me now, Cesca. If the market is in three days, I have much to do before then.'

The factor dropped to one knee rather than bow, still feeling he had ground to make up with this irascible young nobleman. Cormac waited until he had left, until they were completely alone. He turned to Malvo then.

'This is *next door* to the Silanus house! When I agreed to the Quirinal, I didn't mean next door!'

'Right at their feet,' Malvo said with a grin, throwing back his hood. 'They will never look for us here.'

Cormac groaned. The Malvo he had known first in Rome had changed over the years. He supposed he had as well, but it was more obvious in his friend. Where he had been cautious once, Malvo was now reckless. Where he had feared retribution and pain, he now feared nothing at all. His faith had grown in Cormac, despite the years they had spent in the mines. Cormac swallowed. He was not sure that confidence was deserved, or whether he even had it in himself. Still, they'd spent months in Lugdunum planning for this – and they had a house. True, it was a house where he could look over the wall of Senator Decimus Silanus, but perhaps Malvo was right. No one would expect him to be sipping cool drinks on the Quirinal a dozen yards from a man whose family had owned him. Not that he had anyone to make the cool drinks, he thought.

'I'm going to have to buy slaves, Mal,' he said.

His friend shrugged. Malvo had known poverty and violence from a young age, but he'd never been owned. He'd never been burned by a man to satisfy the law.

'Get experienced ones then, ones who know how to run a house. Don't be soft on them, either. They'll steal us blind if you are soft.'

Cormac chuckled, then broke off as he saw the sun was low in the sky. The days were still short in the second month. He needed to reach the temple of Saturn before it closed to worshippers and supplicants of all kinds. He reached into a pouch at his waist and produced a silver ring. It was a plain thing, but Cormac had made it him- self in the workshop in Lugdunum. It was made from silver beads he'd melted and cast himself. He rubbed the thing with his thumb, then stripped off the cloak and toga, revealing a simple belted tunic underneath.

He looked at Malvo, then held out his hand for the sheaf of papers. He was irritated to see his fingers tremble. This was his world! The temple of Saturn held the aerarium, the treasury. Next door was the tabularium, the record house of the whole empire. It was part of the Capitoline hill, with the massive temple to Jupiter just above on the slope. He swallowed. That was the problem, perhaps. The edge of the forum was a sacred place, with gods looking down on all he would do. Watching while he lied.

He took the vellum sheets Malvo handed him and the two young men nodded to one another. They had left Rome as boys, but returned as hard and dangerous men. It had become a joke between them to say it, but it didn't seem quite as funny when his hands were shaking.

'Good luck,' Malvo said.

The tabularium was a huge building alongside the temple to Saturn, with its own entrance. That hallowed ground for scribes was a place Cormac had once dreamed of entering, gradus scriptorum in hand, a free man. Well, he was sort of free, Cormac thought. His sentence of ten years in the mines *might* still have been in play, he was not completely certain. Or it might have been annulled when the praetorians took them to be auxiliaries. It was not the sort of question he could ask.

He was panting slightly as he stood beside the columns of the temple. In there was the treasury of Rome, the house of coins – and for him, the heart of the city. Cormac had never stepped across that threshold, but if things went well in the tabularium, it too would play its part. As Gaius Perca, he could exchange bags of silver coins for the sort of notes he had once dared to forge. Now, they would be backed by true metal, as good as coins themselves.

The thought was a light one, though clouds were dark overhead and a drizzle was falling. The day was fleeing before the night. The streets were clearer than usual as people hurried home to warmth and a meal and the embrace of loved ones.

He did not envy them. He had become a wolf, Cormac reminded himself. Wolves did not have warm arms and a loving wife, or children . . . Well, he supposed they did actually, or there would be no new wolves. The image broke apart in his mind and he loped up the side steps to the record house.

'It's starting to rain out there,' he said to the young man at the desk.

The fellow nodded pleasantly enough, raising his eyebrows.

'We're closing in just a moment, I'm afraid. Are you here to see someone?'

'I am expected, I believe. There was a letter sent ahead? From Legate Aulus Plautius?'

There certainly was. Cormac had both written it and paid a messenger to take it from Ravenna to Rome.

'Ah yes, I remember that one,' the young man replied.

He held up a finger and left his chair, heading into back offices. A white-haired version of him returned, as if passing through that door somehow aged a man. Cormac assumed they were father and son, or perhaps grandfather and grandson.

'We did have a letter from Aulus Plautius, yes. A recommendation. You must be . . .'

'Gaius Vitreus Gallus Corvus, yes,' Cormac said with a smile.

The old man's white eyebrows came together.

'A Gallic crow of glass?' he said.

Cormac blinked. He had chosen the scribe's name and minor family carefully, but he hadn't expected anyone to challenge it as quickly as this. He was fighting a sudden urge to run when he saw the old man was grinning. Cormac relaxed.

'It is a family name, dominus,' he said. 'Inherited from my father and his. Most call me Corvus – the crow part.

'I am teasing you, lad. I am Manus Flaminius Felix, though I am neither a priestly hand, nor especially lucky. Hmm-mm. Call me Felix, boy. You will need a sense of humour if we employ you here.'

'*If*, dominus? I was led to believe there would be work waiting for me.'

'Then you were misled, my boy! Legate Plautius is certainly a man of influence and fine family, that is true, but I cannot teach, do you understand?' The old man peered at Cormac as if seeing him for the first time. 'In truth, you do not look like a scribe. If I'm being honest, you look more like the sort of man Plautius might send to kill someone. Hmm-mm. I hope that is not true!' The scribe chuckled as the younger version of him resumed his seat. 'Don't you think so, Manius? I said he looks the sort to kill someone. Hmm-mm.'

'I, er . . . I do have my gradus,' Cormac said. He handed it over and the old man read it as if he had never seen one before, running his hand over each line until Cormac found himself sweating, certain he would be denounced. Yet it was just the man's fading sight that made him peer so closely. Felix nodded, satisfied.

'Passed in Lugdunum, I see. Rather later than most, but still. I hope the provinces maintain the standards expected in the tabularium of Rome! Come, come. I will test your skills. How well do you know your Horace?'

Cormac smiled, he could not help it.

'His father was a freed slave,' he said, holding up his hand to show the silver ring. 'I have always held the son in the highest esteem.'

The old man chuckled, a pleasant sound as he led the way back from the public area to a vast archive. Cormac tried not to stare as he passed shelves that stretched to the high ceiling, reached by precarious-looking ladders. There were hundreds of men working there – and at least a few women, dressed in stolas of severe cut.

'I used to dream of working here,' Cormac said.

The old man looked at him quizzically, hearing the truth in his voice. He did not seem displeased.

'It is not a bad life,' he said. 'Without us, Rome would grind to a halt in a single day. Legions would go unpaid, debts would be forgotten, marriages would vanish into air! Though perhaps a few husbands might thank us for that, eh? Hmm-mm. No? Not married yourself, I see, or you would have understood the humour. Humph. We are the record-keepers of the empire, my boy. There is always work here.'

They stopped at a desk while Felix sparked a little oil lamp. Cormac wondered if they had ever had a fire in that place of wood and vellum and resin papyrus. He didn't think it was a question he should ask, not before he had been accepted.

'This section is where the service of all our noble legions is recorded. It is updated each month, for all twenty-eight. The records must be meticulously kept, or men might never be released from their term and paid what they are owed. For today, I would like to see your hand, young man.'

Cormac prevented himself from holding out his hand,

understanding in time to avoid another 'Hmm-mm' from the elderly Felix. He seated himself to demonstrate his writing and then rose immediately as a woman turned the corner, bustling towards him with a great sheaf of vellum in her arms.

Cormac stood back to let her pass, noting the frown on the old man's face.

'Cornelia,' Felix said in greeting.

'Felix,' she replied.

The old man bowed his head and Cormac copied him. She was rather striking, he thought, with a fine arched neck and dark eyes that flashed. He imagined attractive women always moved at speed, so as not to tempt men into beginning a clumsy conversation.

She stopped, a pace beyond them both. Slowly, she turned. Cormac caught the scent of whatever oil she dabbed on herself and was transported back to a schoolroom and a previous life. He felt his stomach creep.

'Good evening, domina. I am Gaius Corvus. First day.' He smiled, keeping his face perfectly blank as she narrowed her eyes.

'First day if he can read and keep a good hand, or first and *last* day,' Felix added.

For all the man's cheerful disposition, Cormac doubted he would allow a lower standard, no matter who had asked him to find a job. He had no idea what Felix suspected – that this Gaius Corvus was a son born to some mistress of the legate, or just a favour to a family friend. Rome ran on such things, which was his reason for sending the letter, sealed in wax and written in a good hand. Ink was his skill, Cormac reminded himself, his life's blood.

Cornelia peered at him in the dim light, seeing a

broad-shouldered young man with hands that were well used and strong, at least compared to most of the scribes in those stacks. In turn, she saw his gaze snag on the wedding ring she wore on her left hand. She smiled at his disappointment then.

'You seem familiar,' she said. 'Have we met?'

'In Gaul, perhaps?' he said lightly. He had been sixteen, he reminded himself, glimpsed and forgotten, before six years of hard labour. His jaw was different, his frame made strong by hard work and little food. He was no longer a slender youth. As Felix had said, he looked the sort who might be sent to kill a man.

'Still . . .' she said. 'Oh, it will come to me, I'm sure. Until then, Cormac.'

She turned on the spot, her stola skirts swishing. He stared after her in horror, realising she had used his real name. Had she even noticed? He waited for her to return in a rush, but the path between the shelves remained empty.

The old man didn't seem to have heard. With the tufts of white hair in his ears, perhaps that was not too surprising.

'Come, come, boy. There is no time to flirt with the ladies. The day is spent – and if I am not satisfied, there is no point coming back tomorrow! Sit, sit. The, er . . . Twelve Tables, if you will. Begin with the . . . fourth and keep writing until I tell you to stop.'

Cormac took up a reed and used the tiny phial of water to mix a paste of ink. He took a deep breath. She had known his name. She had known his name.

He began to write.

'*Si membrum rupit, ni cum eo pacit, talio esto . . .*' It was the doctrine of revenge and it suited him well.

25

Cormac paced up and down the end of the garden, as far from the Silanus property as he could get. That was one disadvantage of lying right under their feet! He could not talk through plans with Malvo with the chance of some Silanus servant stopping on the other side of the wall and listening to every word. Money was more than labour, it seemed. It was also privacy. Spent like a fool, it was privacy's lack.

He glowered at Malvo, his friend sitting in the shade and drinking something made of lemon and white wine with shavings of ice. The spring day was warm so the mush melted quickly, but Cormac could not begrudge it to him. Bringing an ice block down from some mountain fastness under cloth was an expensive business. The thing was only a part of its original size by the time it reached the city. It sat then in their basement, still wrapped in cloth and disturbed only when Malvo went down there to scrape more ice for his drink. It caused less trouble than the women Malvo brought to see it. There had been a lot of drunken laughter down there the previous two evenings. Malvo seemed to have a knack for finding them, at least when the wine was flowing.

Cormac paused, gripping his hands behind his back and twiddling his thumbs. He didn't mind his friend satisfying a few appetites. In fact, he envied him. They had been six years in the mines, after all. Yet somehow Cormac remained apart, cold and untouched and miserable.

The slave auction was the following day and he was already dreading it. The coward's way was to stay at the house and let Martinius Cesca make the purchases. Some part of him wanted to. A wealthy young eques might care little for his household. Yet he found it drifting into his thoughts at odd moments. He had been sold in such an auction, on some grubby dock in Gaul. He had to see what it was like.

'Is that third cup to your taste?' he asked Malvo.

His friend heard the bite in his voice and frowned, sitting up.

'I don't know why you have to be so sharp. You have the job in the stacks, don't you?'

'In the tabularium, yes. That old boy Felix is decent enough, I have to admit. I wasn't expecting to hear my own name though! What if she remembers me? All of this . . .' he gestured to the garden around them, remembering to lower his voice, 'all this goes away, Malvo. Understand?'

Malvo was watching his friend. An amused light came into his eye.

'This woman . . . is she pretty?'

'What does *that* matter? She knew my name! Everything we planned is in danger.'

'Right. Is she pretty though? It feels like you are avoiding the question.'

'Fine. Yes! Not that it matters. She wears a ring. A woman in her twenties will have a husband at home, I don't doubt. Probably half a dozen brats as well.'

'So she *is* pretty? Interesting.'

Cormac stopped his pacing and grinned at Malvo's innocent expression.

'She is not one of your tavern women, Malvo. She is a complication, one I don't need. I need the job in the tabularium for two things and two things only.' He held up his fingers to count them off and did not see Malvo do the same behind his back, enjoying his ease in the spring sun.

Cormac kept his voice low, though only the horse and donkey could have heard them.

'One, I need to find where they keep the gradus records. I can add something to the stack there. There has to be a copy in the official record, or someone will always be able to trip me with a search.'

Malvo touched a second fingertip. He was lightly drunk, which he knew was a mistake in the afternoon. It would lead to headaches later and having to go for a nap, but he was determined to take a little time off. There was a woman who liked him in the Golden Hand. They called her 'Lovely Di' and he'd thought she might be in that night. Cormac frowned at his new friends like some vigile, but there was no harm in it. Malvo had carried a burden of fear for a long time, just waiting for the hand on his shoulder that would mean they were done. He deserved a little female affection, Malvo was sure. It didn't hurt that Cormac had made him a metal piece for his cheek, shaped like a mushroom and painted black. With the help of oil and some discomfort, he had worked the smaller part through the hole. It was invisible in his dark beard, but that wasn't why he loved it. No, for the first time in his adult life, he could drink and eat without holding his face, or worse, dribbling food. He had not explained to Cormac what that meant. He assumed he knew, as he knew so many things.

'And two!' Cormac said. He glared at his friend then, sensing the man's drunken amusement.

'Two . . .' Cormac went on, 'Gaius Perca served with Second Augusta as a tribune. You and I know he's dead, but here I am giving his name to our silver. I need to find those legion records and change them – how, I have no idea – so I don't find myself accused of using a dead man's name.'

'With his mother's permission,' Malvo said, making a mash of the words as his voice slurred.

Cormac shook his head.

'She cannot help with this. I have to explain how a dead man was sent home, but somehow lives. A Gaulish healer who saved him, perhaps? One of those followers of Christ? The key has to be in the records. Whatever is written in there *is the truth*. It doesn't matter what anyone else says. The tabularium is the heart of Rome. It will let me be Gaius Perca, or Gaius Vitreus Gallus Corvus.'

'But not . . . at the same time,' Malvo replied.

Cormac sighed as he glanced over.

'You should not drink in the day, my friend, seriously. It makes you . . . it does not sit well with you.'

'I have found white wine mixes well with the lemon and . . . thing. Ice.'

'Really?'

'Try it.'

Malvo held up a cup and Cormac sipped from it. The wonder of cold wine on a hot day was not lost on him. He nodded.

'Very well. I will try a cup. But no singing tonight, Malvo. Understand? I don't want our new neighbours complaining about us to the vigiles.'

Malvo closed one eye. He was trying to wink, but could not seem to open it again.

'No singing,' he agreed.

Cornelia sat at a little cedar table in a corner of the building she and the other scribes called the stacks. She read under the light of a tiny lamp, its flame protected by a sheath of clear glass. Old man Felix was more terrified of fire than anything. He made scribes sign out those lamps, then return them at the end of each shift. The penalty for failing to do so was dismissal – leaving one burning untended would earn a lashing in the public forum as well. Cornelia glanced over her shoulder yet again, fancying she heard some scratch or settling of pages. There was always a chance of someone wandering down there, though she had chosen a spot where there was not much reason to do so. The tribute records of the Greeks were a maze, stretching back room after room, to the time of Julius Caesar and further, to the Republic.

Cornelia looked up again, like a mouse disturbed in some guilty thing. She suspected there were no unknown corners to Manus Flaminius Felix, but at his age, he could not resist the urge to sleep after lunch. It had left her with enough time to find what she needed, settling in this private spot to scan line after line of tiny lettering. This particular scribe could have been Felix himself, for all she knew. There were no gaps between words and hardly any space left between lines, all to save space and money. The text was a block and hard to decipher in the lamplight.

What was interesting was the lack of a birth record for Gaius Vitreus Gallus Corvus. She'd had to guess his age, of course, but she had the lists for three full years either side of twenty-five. Scribes had recorded every free soul born to the empire in those lists, with a place of birth and names of both parents. Felix had told her the new recruit was from Gaul, which narrowed it down . . . but there was nothing in the records. Every Roman citizen had their name collected and copied in Rome, reaching the tabularium months after their birth. She supposed there were a few country folk who didn't inform the local aediles when they had a child, but if they ever hoped to hold an official position, they had to be part of the lists she held. She shook her head in wonder. It had to be him.

His name had come to her when he'd said 'Corvus'. No, she'd thought, not that: Cormac. Even then it hadn't meant anything to her in the moment, not really. It was as she left the stacks and walked home it had come back: a face from a different life.

She touched the wedding ring that graced the fourth finger of her left hand. If it was true that a nerve ran from there directly to the heart and source of all love, her gold band felt none of that warmth. Her husband Fulvius had gone away in the night, taken by a fever that entered from a simple cut. Her parents still pressed her to marry again, but she had his wealth and was in no hurry to pass it to the care of another, not that year. Only her mother's wet-eyed need for grandchildren would bring her to an altar – and so far, Cornelia was enjoying a freedom she had neither planned nor expected.

With care, she gathered up the sheaf of lists and snuffed the lamp, plunging that part of the stacks into darkness. If she fell and broke her ankle, it would be Felix's fault, she thought. Yet if anyone even suggested lamps on the darkest corners, he would talk of the great fire of Alexandria, begun by accident and becoming a loss so great the world would never know the full extent.

So. The young man with the broad shoulders and long hair was *not* a scribe from Gaul, whatever he was. Records were sometimes delayed in their return to Rome, but not for twenty years. He had worn a silver ring, Cornelia recalled – the mark of a freed slave.

She frowned to herself, tying her hair back as she walked. The stacks stretched into the distance, a vast maze she had learned to navigate. There. Eleven shelves up. Ladder. Count by touch. Hold the papers carefully in one arm, trapped to her side. Lean in as you climb . . .

She put the sheafs back in the exact spot where they could be found again. A faint rumble from Felix's back office assured her the old man was still sleeping. She had time and the mystery was an itch she had to scratch. The boy she remembered from the schoolroom had been light in his wit and manner, given to smiles and laughter. He'd always entered and left with a sullen boy . . . a Silanus? It had been a long time ago.

She began to doubt herself as a flood of memories returned. The one who called himself 'Corvus' was nothing like the boy she remembered, not beyond a faint resemblance. He was taller, with hands scarred like a soldier. His hair was tied back and would hang to his shoulders if he undid that knot. She wondered what that would look like.

She was not certain, but there was still that finger scratching at memory, saying it was him, it was him . . .

Felix snored in his office nearby, mouth open and eyes half shut as was his way. Cornelia bit her lower lip as she considered. She bowed her head as another of the scribes came bustling past on some errand. She felt his gaze on her, perhaps as a woman, but also as a busy scribe coming across a colleague who seemed to be doing nothing. He would be reporting that idleness to Felix, she had no doubt, not formally, but in some casual remark about how she didn't seem to be very busy that day.

She clenched her fists as he swept past. Such a bustling fellow he was, with his important work! She raised her eyes for a moment. The truth was, there were a hundred things she could be doing. Felix had a list of families intent on tracing their lineage. Whenever the scribes had a free hour, they were meant to return to those and fill the time. 'You are not paid to be still' was the phrase Felix used, a dozen times a day.

She cocked her head as the snoring choked off, then resumed. Old men in charge were not held to the same standard, it seemed. Go. She set off down a corridor between high shelves, stepping round ladders like a dancer. Freed slaves were named as well, she recalled. Every document of manumission was copied to the imperial records – and Cormac was an unusual name. If it was him, she could find it, she was certain.

She smiled as she halted in a new section, looking up and up. Sheafs in vellum and papyrus were there, alongside wax slates, even lead tablets with names scratched on them. There was an index, she saw in relief. If he had been freed, anywhere in the empire, he would be listed there. She swallowed as she realised what a large section this actually was.

26

The Forum Boarium was on a piece of open ground between the Capitoline and Aventine hills. With the river Tiber at its back and a stream of boats dropping and collecting wares at all hours, it was the port of Rome, where goods of empire met their markets. On most days, there was some sort of cattle sale, with animals sold for meat or milk, whether oxen, sheep, pigs, goats or chickens. In the early mornings, those went to the highest bidders in vast numbers, led away for slaughter or loaded onto boats to some further destination. Those markets cleared by noon and even the manure was collected by street boys and sold in buckets to those with vegetable gardens.

Cormac stood with Martinius Cesca as the sun rose and the slave market opened. From massive pens along a temple wall, the first ones were taken out in chains and prodded forward, climbing up steps to a section like a stage. Bidding was instant and noisy, a cacophony of voices driving the price up. Cormac clasped his hands behind his back and tried not to look horrified. This was meant to be a world he knew.

Malvo had wanted to come, but this was a very public place and Cormac felt less recognisable without him. He had done everything he could to disguise his tall friend, but if he came across someone from their past with Malvo beside him, Cormac was certain they would point and say his name – and all they had planned would shatter like a glass jug.

He had never stood in the forum boarium before. None of his trips to the school or Silanus holdings had taken him past that point and as a slave himself, he'd had no reason to see men and women bought and sold. He wondered if these were considered better quality, good enough for a block in the sacred city.

He swallowed, trying to look calm though he could feel sweat dripping. He wore a tunic of fine white linen to his knees, with a robe of dark red over one shoulder. A silver clasp held that in place and of course his gladius sat on his hip as always. Apart from the missing purple stripe of a legion tribune and a shirt of mail, it was what Gaius Perca had worn on their only meeting. Cormac was that day an eques, his family line second only to the senate. He needed a household while in Rome and he was there to choose the best with his factor. He kept one eyebrow slightly raised at all times, as if the entire business was beneath him.

He had not expected to feel a surge of anger, making him want to fight. The moment he had strolled into that open space with Cesca and looked up, he'd known he should not have come.

A thousand men, women and children were chained in the pens there, in coffles twenty or thirty feet long. They had been brushed and cleaned by slavers to fetch the best price. Yet they looked grim to Cormac's eye. Some of them were naked, the better to display strength or beauty. Others wore loincloths and shivered in the dawn cold.

Cesca looked to him in slight confusion, not yet understanding this hot-headed young master. The factor had a list of the ones he wanted on a wax-covered slate. He had been busy earning his commission the night before, scouting good stock and speaking to a dozen slavers before the sun rose. Most of those sold would be worked to dropping in tanneries or vineyards far from Rome. The ones Cesca wanted were more experienced, men and women who might be trusted to run a household. The trouble was, they commanded higher prices for that reason. A man to carry bricks would always be cheap; one to tutor children could cost as much as a racehorse.

'One from our list is coming up now, dominus,' Cesca murmured.

Cormac nodded, staring at a middle-aged woman shoved onto a makeshift stage. A crowd had gathered, of course. This was Rome and the sales were public entertainment as well as a market. When the woman was stripped to the waist, the crowd jeered and called comments, trying to outdo one another in crudity or laughter. It brought a bitter taste to Cormac's throat, rising like heat. He remembered rotten fruit thrown by these same people, or those like them. At least the slavers and their guards would thrash anyone who threw something at one of the slaves. Slaves were valuable, after all.

Cormac signalled to Cesca as the woman's price reached six hundred denarii. Cesca bid eight hundred and was outbid in turn as the price reached a thousand.

'I thought you said the prices would be low after the invasion,' Cormac hissed.

'Dominus . . .' Cesca raised his hand and nodded to twelve hundred. 'They are! This is half the price it was in Cicero's day. If we get an experienced housekeeper for less than two thousand, it will be a very good morning. Fourteen . . .'

The auctioneer accepted Cesca's bid and another man shook his head, making a mark on a slate much like the one Cesca held. Some factor for a senator or wealthy merchant, Cormac understood. It was the same as any cattle market, though with more weeping.

The stunned-looking woman was draped in a robe and led away.

'Did we not buy her?' Cormac asked. 'Where is she going?'

'To be checked by the market doctor, then tattooed with your name,' Cesca said. 'Is it not that way in Lugdunum?'

Cormac considered his answer. He did not want to arouse the factor's suspicions, but he brimmed with questions.

'My father used to see to purchases, before he died,' he said. 'I have not visited an auction before.'

'Ah, I see. I was wondering why you looked so . . . Dominus, I am happy to explain or describe anything to you, of course. That last was one who used to work for the Aemilii family. She was sent to auction after thirty years of service, so she knows her way around a household. She was cheap at fourteen hundred, dominus, seriously. It is partly the new slaves coming in from Britannia, but also her age. I imagine she has bad eyes or something. Still, she will have a few good years, if the doctor passes her as fit.'

'Do we trust their doctor?'

Cesca looked pleased with himself.

'I have it in hand, dominus. My own man will be there to check for fevers and the like. There was a woman a few years back, a cook. She cost a fortune, but her memory was vanishing. She wasn't even that old, but she couldn't remember half the recipes she was said to know. I had to involve a praetor to get her purchase price back, but I did it. I will not be robbed, dominus, don't worry.'

'I don't want her tattooed,' Cormac said. 'In fact, I don't want any of mine marked. Make that clear to the slavers, or the auctioneer, if you would.'

'Branded then, dominus? Some of those on this list will have brands or marks from before, of course. I could have a new brand prepared, if you have a family or a legion symbol . . .' He stopped when Cormac held up his hand.

'No brands, either.'

He rubbed a spot on his chest, as Cesca had seen him do often in their discussions. He wondered if the young eques had a bad heart.

'Some sort of owner's mark *is* usual, dominus . . .' Cesca saw Cormac flush and went on quickly. 'But I have heard and understood. No new marks. Very well.'

He consulted his list and bid quickly on a pair of trained guards, two brothers from Sicilia. For that, he had to bid four thousand denarii, until Cormac wanted to tell him to stop. The pay he had stolen from the praetorians was a vast sum in most circumstances, but renting a house and buying slaves for it was clearly going to be ruinous. Cesca was spending his funds like water and the list on his slate was still long.

'Don't overpay,' Cormac growled. 'I will not be robbed.'

'Of course, dominus,' Cesca said. He looked irritated for the first time, a little tired of this angry eques from the country who knew nothing and yet sought to control everything. Still, the commission would be sweet. Cesca was happy to run up the price when he was adding a tenth for himself. That was simply common sense.

Cormac said nothing more as his factor bought another eight men and four women for the household, for a total of thirty-two thousand, six hundred denarii. Cormac decided to call it a day. He and Malvo had ended up with a fortune so great they hadn't been able to imagine spending it in a lifetime. He'd had no idea how buying expensive slaves would eat into it. They'd arrived in Rome with two hundred and ten thousand denarii – over eight thousand gold aurei by value. Some had been lost in making dies and stamps – and sheer wastage when melting metal and dribbling it into moulds. Cormac sweated at the thought of all that and wondered when he would regret handing over a pouch of gold to the mother of Gaius Perca. It had seemed the right thing to do in exchange for her son's name, but he was watching Cesca bid as if money meant nothing and the memory of his generosity began to sting.

Cormac stood still as a boy was shoved onto the podium. He had been beaten, that was obvious from the swollen eye and bloodied lip. The boy was shaking as he looked onto a baying crowd, all bared teeth and amusement at his expense. Cormac felt a wisp of memory, of standing in a place not unlike this one, a bruised sky in the distance and strange words being shouted. He'd understood nothing then.

'Fresh from the campaign in Britannia, strong as an ox. Young enough to be trained and right sharp!' The slaver's description was a weak attempt to sell the battered-looking boy.

Cesca saw Cormac's sudden attention and groaned inwardly. Not one of those, he hoped. They were bad for business.

'I have the last on our list coming up, dominus – two Spanish horsemen. They'll do well in the stables, or we'll sell them next quarter. Not everyone works out . . .'

'How old is that child?' Cormac asked.

Cesca made a pretence of peering as the bidding began.

'It is against the law to sell one younger than ten, dominus . . . so we'll say ten. In truth though, he might be a bit younger. Nine? Or twelve and small for his age, it's hard to tell with the savage races. They should have stained him blue for the sale, for comedy or as an exotic. I've seen that done.'

'Bid on him,' Cormac said.

Cesca made a pretence of checking his slate once more.

'No call for a boy, dominus, not to run a house. You'll start tongues wagging if you buy a child you don't need, if you follow me.'

'I am not interested in what the gossips say,' Cormac snapped. 'Bid for me. No, I'll do it myself.'

'My commission is still a tenth,' Cesca muttered mulishly.

It would do as a cover, Cormac realised. Let Cesca think he was tight with money, or poorer than he pretended. That had the added benefit of being true. He could hardly say the boy reminded him of himself, that he felt stained by the very place he stood and he was desperate to do one good thing before he had to leave and vomit.

'He's not on your list,' Cormac said. 'If I bid myself, I will pay no share on his price.'

Cormac raised his hand and the auctioneer spotted him. The man's gaze drifted to Cesca to see if it was legitimate. The factor gave a sullen shrug and the auctioneer brightened visibly, sensing the sort of tension that had made him very wealthy.

'One thousand,' the auctioneer said, starting high. He plucked another bid from the crowd, though Cormac could not see a hand raised. 'Twelve hundred there . . . do I have fourteen?'

'Fourteen hundred,' Cormac confirmed, nodding his head.

Two other buyers consulted their lists, including the one Cesca had beaten to a few of the better lots over the previous hour. That man was flushed with irritation and raised his hand, nodding sharply. The auctioneer smiled as bids came in, quick as birds, back and forth between those two sides of the marketplace.

Cormac did not look at whoever was bidding against him. His gaze was set and cold as he kept his hand up, not bothering to lower it. Cesca leaned in.

'Dominus, he is running up the price.'

'I know,' Cormac said.

Cesca looked at him without understanding.

'Is he . . . a competitor, dominus? Have a care he does not ruin you.'

Cormac glanced at his factor, seeing a flustered young man, quite out of his depth. He could not explain. Gaius Perca would certainly not have explained.

'Four thousand,' Cormac confirmed.

The auctioneer was leaning on his rostrum, relaxed as he beat bids from the air with his hand. Back and forth.

At six thousand, the other bidder was beginning to

sweat. Publius Arminius had only joined in to teach an expensive lesson. If he left it too late, he'd be the fool. Yet Cesca's client was still bidding. If the man was a pederast, perhaps he would ruin himself. Of course, if he had been hired to break one Publius Arminius, he would pull one last bid and the whole city would be laughing.

'Do I have seven thousand, two hundred . . . ?'

The auctioneer was looking at him, Publius realised. Silence settled on the crowd like warm air. If he nodded yes and was left with it, he would be Rome's idiot. His name would be mocked in all the taverns for trying to run up a sale and losing a fortune. He looked across at the young man standing with Martinius Cesca. Cesca he knew, but the client was a stranger . . . He looked like an army man, a thug more than a member of the nobilitas. Well dressed though, with a sword on his hip. Publius Arminius hesitated and the auctioneer leaned closer over his rostrum.

'I need to hear a bid . . .' the auctioneer said.

His disappointment felt personal, but Publius shook his head. The man's face fell further.

'You're sure? Seven thousand is the bid against you . . . No? Very well.'

The auctioneer looked to Cormac, pointing with one stiff finger. In truth, he was more than pleased. It was a huge price for a boy who didn't even speak the language.

'Sold for seven thousand!' he said.

The crowd craned to see who had paid so much, then settled back down for the next lot. Cormac felt a terrible tension leave him. He saw Cesca was flushed and realised he could offer to pay the ten per cent to smooth the man's ruffled feathers. No, he thought. Let the bastard swallow the loss.

The boy, of course, understood very little of what had happened. Cormac watched him taken off the raised area and cuffed on the back of the head when he tried to struggle. They had not yet beaten the will to resist from him. Cormac was oddly pleased about that.

'Dominus, may I ask . . .' Cesca began.

Cormac looked at him.

'I need a guard, one devoted to me. One trained from very young.'

Cesca looked dubious, but he had to accept it and bowed his head. He had filled his list with good stock that day, earning himself a small fortune. He could not begrudge a rich man's whim. He saw Cormac peering at the next coffle being brought up. Cesca checked his list, making sure he had not missed anyone else. No, he had his household – and a few above and beyond in case they lost any to illness. Disobedient or stupid slaves could be resold the following quarter, which was always the danger, of course. The best ones remained with their owners and were rarely sold. The system worked, as long as new crops kept coming in.

'That one,' Cormac said. He shook his head and chuckled. 'Bid for me, would you, Cesca? I don't want that fool over there running me up again.'

Cesca checked the list of names he had compiled. He vaguely remembered the one on the rostrum, but had dismissed him the night before.

'Dominus, he has to be sixty. Freed a few years back, then returned to slavery for debt and crime – and sold twice more since then. He will not be a reliable man, if you will accept my judgement.'

'Just bid for me, damn you,' Cormac snarled at him. 'Or will you lose your fee again?'

342

Cesca coloured. He was not used to being spoken to in such a way, no matter who this spoiled young eques thought he was, with his pale skin and growling voice! Was Cesca expected to cringe from his anger? This was Rome, not some piggery in Ravenna, or wherever he hailed from! Cesca summoned his dignity, standing tall.

'I believe our business is at an end,' he said coldly, deliberately omitting the 'dominus' that had graced his speech before. 'I wish you luck and I will send my bill.'

Cormac scowled. With Cesca involved, the other bidders could not have been certain he was the one interested. Now, they would know. He waved Cesca away, caring nothing for his irritation. Whatever had offended the factor, he would not have survived a day in the deep mine, with violence and the dark. Cormac didn't watch as Martinius Cesca stalked off through the crowd. He'd wait a long time for his bill to be paid as well, Cormac would see to that.

He raised his hand as bidding began again. It was noted immediately and he saw a little cluster of heads bow together as the previous antagonist consulted with his mates. Cormac groaned without moving his lips.

'Six hundred . . .' he said, nodding.

The auctioneer had spotted the same action and looked delighted. He positively beamed when that little group began to bid in turn, sharing the risk and glancing across at Cormac to make sure he noticed them.

On the little rostrum, Nartius stood before the crowd. He too had been battered black and blue, new bruises over old. His hair no longer swept back in oiled wings as Cormac remembered him. He had aged badly, with new wrinkles from the life he'd known since leaving the Silanus estate. Cormac remembered him best from the night Silanus had pressed irons to his chest. Nartius had tied him then, holding him still while questions came, over and over. He still woke with that memory on bad nights. It had taken something from him and he had never recovered it, not in all the years since.

It seemed Nartius had fallen on bad times, just as he had. To be sold back into slavery was a hard punishment. For it to be the third or fourth time meant he had fallen to the lowest ranks – the slaves no one else wanted. Cormac knew his price would usually be low, just a few hundred. He might work a year or two in a mine, though even that was unlikely. At his age, he should have been in some gentle role, enjoying his last few years before the last sleep.

Cormac hesitated. He had not expected to feel a whisper of pity, not in that place. His first instinct had been to buy Nartius simply to cut his throat. He'd come back to Rome for revenge, after all. Nartius would have made a fine beginning. To suddenly feel sorry for a man he considered his enemy surprised him . . .

'One thousand, two hundred . . . ?' the auctioneer was asking. The competitors looked worried and Cormac saw his long pause had rocked their little group. He took a moment to smile at them. He even half-turned away just to let them know he could leave them with the price.

Without Cesca as his shield, Cormac was forced to play the part: a reluctant lover, tempted to come back for one last bid and no more . . .

'And two hundred . . .' he said at last, as if the words surprised him.

The auctioneer turned quickly to the group, but the

damage was done. They thought they were the ones being fooled and shook their heads like gulls, mute as stones.

Cormac waited as the auctioneer tried to tempt them back. He made sure he smiled and clenched one fist in triumph as the man cried 'Sold!' once again. Let them worry he knew something they didn't, the bastards. They had cost him a fortune.

Nartius was led back to the doctors and the money men round the back. Cormac bit his lip at the thought of the sum he would have to fetch by sundown from the temple of Saturn. Slave markets preferred gold and silver to notes on lenders, he knew that much. All the trouble he had taken to deposit coins there would be undone.

He smiled into the morning light, closing his eyes and enjoying the warmth. He and Malvo had come back to destroy their enemies: Nartius, Pugio, the magistrate Gracchus, the vigile Terentius ... and of course the Silanus family. If they achieved that, it would not matter if every last coin was spent. Cormac could settle down then to life as a scribe.

He found he had been staring at nothing as the sale went on, though his part in it was over. The sale officials were standing nearby, making sure he did not vanish before he had arranged to settle his debt. Yet he didn't move, didn't care what they wanted.

For years, he'd kept alive the idea of putting all his struggles behind him, of one day becoming a scribe and working in silence, with the hiss of the reed and good vellum. He'd pictured Malvo at work in some shop or other, visiting each other's houses and families, living a life of peace and contentment, so long denied them both.

In that place, with the stink of slaves in his nostrils, he

suddenly realised it would not be enough. He'd wanted two things – a simple life and all his enemies in the cold ground. No, he wanted more than that. They had made him a slave and they had freed him, but it was all from their hands. That wouldn't do, not when it came time to face his ending. If he ever married, or if his children asked how he had come to Rome, he would say he was from a land far away, but that he had always been free, whether he had known it or not.

He realised he wanted what he had seen in Senator Decimus Silanus. He wanted other men to fear his wrath, to worry if he even frowned at them. He wanted them to hear thunder as he walked. He wanted to rise in the senate and have them fall silent just to hear him speak.

He felt lightness in his chest at that, a new strength of purpose. No one born a slave could stand in the senate . . . so *that* was what he wanted. They had plucked him from a slave pen like the one he faced that day. They had brought him to Rome and made him think he had just one purpose, to write their words. Being free was not enough, he understood that. He would take back the power they held over him, or he would see the city in flames.

Cormac waited in a room of cool grey marble, veined in such a way that revealed its origin in the mountains of the north. Only the best had been used in the treasury of Rome, of course. The surprise had been how cramped it was. In his imagination, the house of coins had always been vast. Yet it was the record house next door that made it seem small. Gold didn't take up half as much room as scrolls, he supposed.

Malvo had been summoned from the house on the

Quirinal, once Martinius Cesca had ceased to be any use. The factor had vanished from the slave sale and not yet reappeared. Cormac swore he really would make Cesca wait for his commission, not least because young sons of the nobilitas were notoriously slow payers of bills. It fitted his role to make the man wait, but he would also enjoy it.

It might have been distressing so see how small a bag of gold over forty thousand denarii represented. Cormac had never held such a weight in his hands. At twenty-five denarii to a single gold piece, he watched one thousand, six hundred and forty aurei counted out with enormous care in the temple of Saturn. The huge statue of the god overlooked worshippers in the main temple, while treasury business went on in the side wing. There was no conflict between commerce and prayer, not in that place. This was the beating heart of the city – one of the few spots in the world where a man could count out almost two thousand aurei and act as if they did it every day. Which they probably did.

Cormac took one leather bag while Malvo took the other. Each of them grunted slightly at the weight. It was about the same as a sword and shield, so not beyond them, though it seemed heavier. One man alone would have been vulnerable to any thieves willing to try their luck.

It was certainly too much to carry openly on the street, even with Malvo beside him. Cormac accepted the offer of aerarium guards. The treasury had a vested interest in keeping clients safe and so employed a private force of ex-legionaries for that purpose. Cormac had no qualms passing his bag to one of those, though it had to be more than the man would earn in a lifetime.

Malvo walked at his back with hood raised and head

bowed, as had become his custom. In comparison, Cormac walked with shoulders back, confident as any eques of Rome. He had heard the gossips were more than a little interested in him as fresh meat, this young man from Ravenna who seemed to have wealth, but no wife or household. Well, he had begun to put that right.

He and his little group walked back to the forum boarium, ignoring the stares of passers-by. As a result, Cormac did not see Cornelia coming out of the tabularium, her face turning idly to see who was around, then standing very still as she recognised him. She faded back into the portico entrance, all thoughts of lunch forgotten.

Those were *treasury* guards walking with Gaius Vitreus Gallus Corvus, she thought. She glanced at the building they had left, then rushed across, too quickly to find a moment of common sense and think twice. A mere scribe did not hire guards, not a scribe who worked in the tabularium, anyway. They were not poor, but neither were they rich. He had even walked differently!

She settled herself as she entered the temple, dropping to one knee to give honour to the god whose statue watched from on high. Saturn was father to half the pantheon of Rome, just about. Men who could not have children sometimes came to pray there, she knew.

Hurrying down the side aisle, Cornelia reached the open door that led to the treasury, nodding to the guards on duty. She stopped at the pale marble counter that separated the public area from the vaults beyond. She had never crossed that line, but she'd never needed to.

'Cornelia! You are early, aren't you?'

Cornelia smiled prettily. She was, but she could only shrug.

'You know Felix! If anyone yawns, he sends them off on some task or other. Any records for the stacks today?'

'Always, always,' said the young man.

Cornelia knew he was interested in her, or perhaps the wealth her first husband had left in her care. She didn't usually play up to it, but she was flushed with interest that morning, unaware of how it enhanced her beauty and the effect it had on a treasury clerk.

'I'll take them now then,' she said lightly. 'To get them copied. No rest for a scribe.'

'Of course, Cornelia,' he said. He brought out a sheaf of vellum, alongside scrolls all tied together like a honeycomb. 'Here, I've made these ready. I hoped you would be the one to come in. In fact, I wondered . . .'

'Perfect!' she said. She was not quite oblivious to what he was saying, but sensed she needed to cut him off. It was common for men she met to show some sort of interest in her, as if time alone was an aphrodisiac. She didn't let it annoy her, however. For the most part, they were sweet.

She took the papers into her arms almost greedily, pressing them to her bosom and making the treasury clerk wish he could be among their number in that moment.

'There'll be more tomorrow,' he called rather mournfully as she left, but she did not hear him. She had the records of all transactions that day. Somewhere among them would be another piece of the puzzle. She went out into the spring sunshine and looked across, to where the man she was tracking had vanished from sight. Felix would be pleased she had taken the time to collect the day's records for the copyists, she thought. She just had to make sure she got a good look at them first.

27

Cormac was in a part of the stacks he had no business visiting. He had prepared an excuse of getting lost or turned around if anyone appeared, but in the main he hoped it wouldn't happen. He wanted to be in and out and back at his desk with no one the wiser.

Over the first week, he had worked diligently and well for Felix. He'd taken one day off to visit the slave market as Gaius Perca, careful to make up the lost time with extra shifts. There was always enough work, he'd discovered. Just copying senate speeches alone was a constant and unending chore.

He climbed the ladder quickly, reader's lamp in hand. It was a finely made little thing with a flame under glass. He froze as one of the rungs creaked, then shook his head, irritated at himself. The mind played tricks. High up in the stacks, there was no one to disturb him, not as far as the eye could see.

He could not shake the sense of being watched even so, unless it was his guilty conscience. He told himself to focus. The stacks were never perfectly quiet, he'd learned that much already. Perhaps ninety men and women worked like bees in that ancient building. Yet he might not see one, not if he stayed in one place and kept his head down. Of course, old man Felix might appear anywhere, usually muttering as he walked. Yet the chief scribe liked a nap after lunch. While Felix snored, a subtly lighter mood could be seen in the other scribes. Cormac had heard laughter and light talk, until the old man arose to patrol once more. They were like children in the presence of a magister then, smiles fading, settling back to their given tasks.

Cormac frowned as he wiped dust from a label, reading a name. Wrong place. He had to go down and push the ladder along the row to get it where he wanted. He winced at the squeak, but the sound was common enough. There were twenty-eight legions in the empire, but many more recorded there. Like men, it seemed legions too could die, with much older names retained as part of the long history of Rome. Some were marked with a red ribbon wrapped around the first leather volume, like a wound. Cormac itched to browse those dead names and battles fought, sometimes centuries before. If he had time, he knew he might have sought out accounts of the battle of Cannae, where entire legions had been destroyed on one terrible day. He dared not. His fingers tapped their way along, then stopped. The official record of Legio II Augusta was under his hand.

Something scraped in the silence, like a heel turning on dust. Cormac froze. He was high above the walkways, clinging to the ladder like an insect on a bending reed. He felt that height suddenly, just waiting for someone to ask what he was doing so far from his desk.

No one appeared and after an age, he breathed again. There was no more time! He looked past older volumes from Spain and Gaul. Legio II Augusta had been active for a long time and those had gathered dust. Cormac looked to where newer, darker leather waited for his hand. Those binds had been opened more recently, he could tell: the records of an active legion.

With a breath, Cormac slid out a black calfskin bind from its brothers. His lamp rested on the shelf well enough, but cast only a narrow light. He had to lean flat on the ladder, hands through the rungs as he flicked pages. He saw a name in gold leaf of the current legate – Vespasianus. It was not one Cormac knew, or cared about.

He was consumed with the sense of someone coming and felt sweat prickle as he flicked page after page of perfect vellum, each covered in the tiniest black lettering. Every detail was there, from the number of spear-tips forged, to horses shod . . . to names of the legion tribunes.

He held the page closer to the light. There. Six of them. The 'tribunus laticlavius' was a privileged position. Whoever held it was destined for great things, a young man in his teens or early twenties . . . an eques with a good name but no fortune, perhaps. Cormac ran his hand over the name of Gaius Perca.

A voice sounded, almost making him drop the bind. It was followed by laughter and he held on, stiff as a board. A man was asking a question in one of the rows nearby. He thought he recognised the dry tone of Felix's grandson, busy on some errand or other, completely at ease in those surroundings. Cormac panicked. It was no secret the younger man would replace his grandfather when Felix retired or died. He would not ignore a scribe in the wrong part of the stacks, reading a record he had no reason to open. A scribe could be dismissed for breaking rules of privacy, Cormac knew that much.

He wiped sweat from his face and turned pages again, looking for . . . there. The lists of the dead. Emperor Claudius had returned to Rome months before, holding a triumph in the city to celebrate bringing an entirely new province into the empire. Cormac had heard he even renamed his son 'Britannicus' to recognise the vast achievement.

Legio II Augusta had lost some of its strength in the fighting, so it seemed. Cormac saw page after page of names removed from the payroll, each one sent to Rome to be copied into the official record. This was the source of all truth, the pages he held. If there was ever a dispute, this was the bind that would be opened, long after men's actual memories had faded. It was one reason Cormac had lied and forged and worked to get a job in the stacks.

Sweat stung as he blinked, trying to see in the dim light, turning each page and running a finger down every name.

He found it, stopping. Gaius Perca was listed as killed in action, along with the exact date. They were efficient, those legion scribes. Men's pay and pensions depended on their work, after all. Cormac swallowed, tugging the page out. He had intended to blot ink over it, to remove the name of Gaius Perca completely. He shook his head in frustration. This was the 'perfect' copy, made with pride – no errors allowed, no scratched-out names. He would have to copy the entire page like a piece of art, then put it back. He swore to himself as he shoved it inside his tunic, closing the bind and returning it to the shelf.

He blew out the lamp and took it up, though it stung

his hand with heat. He went down the ladder at dangerous speed, panting as he stood on the floor, the blessed,
steady floor. His shaking legs moved him away from
the place of his guilt almost by instinct, so that he was
hurrying along to the end of the row when Cornelia
stepped out.

'Oh! You startled me!' she said, though it seemed more
the other way around. She did not look startled. Cormac
forced himself to smile, though his heart had almost leapt
from his chest at her appearance.

'I'm sorry, I was looking for the . . .' He trailed off as
she waited, his excuse vanishing completely. Her eyes
were large in the gloom, he noticed. She used kohl around
them, as the women of Egypt were said to do. He rather
liked the effect.

'Looking for the . . . what? I know this part of the stacks
well. Perhaps I can help.'

'The . . . er,' he tried to remember what task Felix had
set him that day as his heart thundered and sweat made his
face shine. 'Sewers! The inspection record. Master Felix
wanted me to bring them out.'

'I see,' Cornelia said. 'Well, they are not here, are they?
These are legion records. The shelves you want are numbers thirty-two to six, over there. Come, I'll show you.'

'Thank you, I think I can find them,' he said.

She put her arm through his and he did not know
how to respond. He allowed himself to be towed along
beside her.

'It's no trouble at all. I'll show you,' she said. 'You know,
I was entering your name a little earlier. For you to receive
your first month's pay. Gaius Vitreus Gallus Corvus, that's
right, isn't it?'

He nodded and she made an approving sound.

'I wasn't sure I had it exactly right, so I went to check your gradus scriptorum. Six years ago, was it?'

Cormac nodded again, though he was beginning to feel a noose tightening around his neck. The young woman seemed rather an innocent, but he had placed that gradus scriptorum in the right binding himself. He didn't like the idea of anyone checking on it, not so soon. After all, there was no Gaius Vitreus Gallus Corvus, family friend of a legate and recommended for a scribe's job in the tabularium. The entire thing was a fiction and one he intended to abandon at the first opportunity.

'Interesting,' she went on. 'There it was, just as it should be, fresh as the day it was made.'

They came to a halt and he found himself facing a young woman whose perfume transported him back to an old schoolroom and a different life.

'In fact, do you know, the ink was so very fresh . . .'

He kissed her, suddenly and without warning, crushing his lips on hers and holding her head in one hand as he bowed her backwards. His other arm snaked round to support her weight. He felt hands come up to his chest as if they might push him away, but they stopped, like time and thought, curled into fists there.

It went on for an age. When they broke free of one another, he had to gasp for the length of time he had not breathed. Her eyes were huge and dark in that part of the shelves. She touched her lips as if he had bruised them or left a mark, then spun on her heel and fled. He did not follow her, but just stood, heart pounding, unsure whether she would fetch Felix, or perhaps a magistrate. He had made things worse, he realised. If she'd had suspicions

355

before, he had done nothing to relieve them. In fact, he had to have shortened his time in the stacks.

He left the section where records of sewers were kept, hurrying back to his little desk on the other side of the tabularium and relighting his lamp. No, he could not complete the copy there, not while Felix could come up behind him! He would have to remove the reference to Gaius Perca at home, then return it to the section for Legio II Augusta. Could he just destroy the page? No. He hesitated. Pensions and families depended on that record.

He had known those men, the ones who had died for Rome on a foreign shore. He'd seen their pyres lighting the night. He just needed to copy that list without the name he was using. All before that young woman recovered enough from her shock to have him sacked.

In darkness, Cormac knocked on the street door to his new home. It was swept open before him as the master was recognised. He passed a bowing young man and had to admit Cesca's choices were shaping up well. The household had settled in with some pleasure, which he could understand. At the point of sale, his new staff had to have feared a stint in the mines or much worse. To discover a relatively pleasant house with a young owner who expected nothing more than cleaning, food and care of his horses must have been a great relief to them.

Cormac frowned as he heard argument, growing louder as he passed through the garden. He sighed. The smell of rosemary was strong in the air. It should have been a peaceful evening in Rome.

The only two causing him trouble were the pair he had bought himself. He still didn't know what had possessed him to buy the boy. Oswin was an angry, battered creature, about as wary of his new owner as a wild fox. It didn't help that the lad spoke only a few words of Latin, though he seemed to understand more.

The other angry voice was Nartius. Cormac stood in the darkness of the garden, wondering again why he had risked everything he and Malvo had achieved. What had he been *thinking* to buy the seneschal from the estate? Cormac was still unsure. On the first night, he'd waited to see recognition flare in the older man. Nartius had kept his gaze down and never once met his eyes. He really had aged badly, jowls sagging loose where they had been fine and plump. The years had been hard on the man. Perhaps it had been pity that made Cormac buy him. He raised his eyes to the night sky, remembering his new oath. A man on the path to power had no place for pity.

In the kitchen, something crashed. It sounded like someone had thrown a pot, the noise going on and on, iron spinning on a tiled floor. Cormac winced and went in.

Nartius had the boy up against a kitchen beam, held in one hand with the other drawn back. Cormac took in the scene and growled, a sound more animal than man. They both froze and Nartius let go of the boy as he registered the presence of his new master. There was something terrifying in the massive figure in the doorway, standing with fists clenched and a look of fury. Nartius stood with head bowed.

Cormac saw blood on Oswin's lip and in that moment he itched to draw the sword on his hip and kill the one who had hit him. He'd felt blows from Nartius himself and he could hardly see for rage. Yet he was not a boy any longer. His anger was a fearsome thing and he had killed men before. Like blood on heated steel, it had tempered something in him.

'Why did you strike the boy?' Cormac asked softly.

'He doesn't listen,' Nartius replied. He spoke to the floor and it was hard to remember the smoothness of his arrogance before. His hair had grown thin so that the scalp showed, where once it had been two dark wings, shiny with oil. 'Dominus, I can run a household for you, I swear. I've done it for a Silanus. I can do it for you as well. But the boy will not do as he is told. If you just leave me to it, I'll get the best from him.'

Cormac let something slide away, the tempering, the control. When he'd been a boy, he'd dreamed of one day being big enough, strong enough to beat Nartius, to really hurt him. All he could see was the man he had been. All he could hear was his voice, sneering, kicking him awake. He drew the sword and Nartius made a sound of terror as Cormac crossed the room.

The boy scrambled to get out of the way as Cormac grabbed Nartius and put him up against the same massive post. The blade was wickedly sharp. He held it across the throat of the seneschal.

'You won't hit him again,' Cormac snarled into his face, showing his teeth. 'I forbid it. Say it for me, Nartius.'

'I won't, I *swear*, d-dominus. P-please . . .'

Nartius was holding perfectly still, terrified of the blade that pressed his skin, the iron that could slice his life away in a quick movement. Cormac saw resignation in his eyes and felt suddenly sick. This was not the tormentor of his childhood, the petty bully who had kicked or cuffed him a thousand times. This was a whipped dog, a man beaten once too often. A man made to fear the world.

'Ah, damn it,' Cormac said. He lowered the blade. 'Who am I, Nartius? Come on, you know me. Say my name.'

'Master Gaius Perca, dominus . . . p-please, I was just trying to get the boy to understand his work.'

'The boy is not your concern, Nartius. Look at me. Tell me my name.'

The man met his eyes for an instant, the gaze sliding away as hard experience had told him was safest. Cormac nodded when Nartius looked back suddenly, close enough to see the pupils shrink. Nartius' mouth opened in amazement.

'You're dead,' he whispered. 'Or in the mines. It can't be you . . .'

'But it is, Nartius. I have come back to settle scores.'

Cormac looked up as the kitchen door opened. Malvo had heard the raised voices and come to see what was going on. He took one look at Nartius' shocked expression and groaned.

'It's you as well, isn't it?' Nartius said. 'The beard, but . . . I remember you.'

'By the gods, you told him?' Malvo demanded. 'Then he's dead. He'll give us up.'

He drew a knife from somewhere in his robes and Nartius saw his own death in the action. He held up empty hands as if to fend off an attack.

'I won't, I swear. Please don't . . .'

With a wail, he ripped open his tunic, showing a series of brands and tattoos on the flesh. He had been burned many times, either to mark him for a new owner, or on return to the slave market. Cormac winced when he saw one of them wept blood and pus, fresh and painful.

'I'm not the man you knew,' Nartius cried out. He

seemed to feel the exposure of his torn tunic and held it together with his fingers.

'The man who fell in with Pugio,' Malvo said.

Cormac scowled. This was not the way he had imagined it. Nartius was a proud and dangerous enemy, not this blubbering man, covered in brands.

'He gave me no choice,' Nartius sobbed. 'I had nothing else. No one wanted me! Then Pugio sent me to steal coats and the vigiles took me up anyway. I was a slave again, just a month after you went to the mines. Please don't kill me. Let me run, at least.'

'Does Pugio still live?' Cormac asked.

Malvo rolled his eyes.

'Cormac, he can't be trusted.'

'I can,' Nartius said. 'I swear on my soul I can. Before all the gods, I give you my oath. I will not betray you. I have no . . . no more fight in me. Please. Please.'

He sank to his knees, broken. Out of sight, Malvo mimed cutting a throat, asking the question. The boy Oswin watched all three with wide, dark eyes, turning from one to another. Cormac wondered how much of this he could possibly understand. He shook his head in answer to Malvo and his friend swore, crossing to the kitchen board to cut an apple into pieces with the knife he still held.

'We've killed other men, Nartius,' Cormac said quietly, 'and we're not finished. Do you understand? I just wanted to work once, to live a quiet life. They wouldn't have it. I met a praetor who wanted me whipped to death for speaking up for myself. A vigile who wanted my life ruined in a mine, if I survived at all. I've been burned and beaten and chained up and made to fight more times than I can remember. Men like Pugio? Like Silanus? They took *everything* from us. From you too, Nartius. So tell me. If you had the chance to bring them a little justice, wouldn't you do it? Why should we let them live in peace?'

'I won't betray you,' Nartius said. 'I swear it on Jupiter, on Apollo . . .'

'On Janus,' Cormac said.

Nartius nodded, pale and resolute.

'I swear it on the god Janus.'

'My patron, Nartius, the god with two faces. He sees the ones who creep up on him. He sees them coming.'

He put out his hand and Nartius took it, allowing himself to be drawn up. He trembled still, in reaction to his terror. Yet he looked at Cormac in awe. The man who loomed over him looked like the sort to lead a battle charge, not the young scribe he remembered from the estate.

'You've grown up,' Nartius said softly.

Cormac nodded.

'I have.'

The boy was still looking from one to the other. Cormac glanced at him.

'How much do you understand?' he asked.

Oswin shrugged.

'A little,' he said. 'You kill him. Now no kill.'

'Yes,' Cormac said. 'Now no kill. What about you though? What am I going to do with you?'

The boy held out his hand for the gladius. Cormac turned it over, passing it hilt-first. He had to know if Oswin could be trusted.

'You should know, boy . . .' he began.

Oswin lunged with it, stabbing Nartius in the side with the point. He did not have the strength to make it deep and Nartius was scrambling away, yelling in fear. Malvo was still cutting his apple and so it fell to Cormac to snatch the weapon back.

Oswin was grinning at the spill of blood on the stone floor. He laughed as Nartius dropped to one knee, pressing his hand to the wound in shock.

'You no sleep!' Oswin said to him.

Cormac frowned.

'Look at me, boy,' he said.

Oswin looked up at him. The boy's face was a mass of bruises, fading yellow and purple, old and new. His lip had been split and one of his eyes was stained red. Yet he returned the gaze with delight at having stabbed someone.

'Not him,' Cormac ordered. 'Understand? Say it.'

The boy looked up at the one who owned him. They were all the enemy, Cormac could see that in his expression.

'You're mine, son. And so is he. So he won't hit you – and you won't stab him in his sleep. Say it, or we're done.'

Oswin held his gaze for a beat, then nodded.

'No hit . . . no kill in sleep.'

'That's it. No hit, no kill in sleep.'

Cormac realised he would have to keep an eye on the boy for a while even so. The threat of anyone being killed as he slept was enough to ruin a few nights, perhaps for all of them. Oswin was a savage, but he was quick and he understood when to stop fighting. That mattered. It meant he could be trained.

'So, gentlemen,' Cormac said, 'I don't know how long we have before someone knocks on that door. It could be a week from now, or six months, but if I drag myself up, the chances are, they'll pull me back down. They want everyone in his place, helpless, while they have all the power.

Still, I know how they work now. I thought for a while I would be content to hide myself, warm and safe in a shop, writing wills and selling speeches.' He chuckled, but it was not a pleasant sound. 'Instead, I'm going to make them afraid. A few months, a few years, it doesn't matter, I see that now. I see through their rules, their laws – their money! I'll rise so high they can't touch me, or I'll go down in flames like Icarus.' He smiled. 'And if that's the way it comes out, I'll take as many with me as I can.'

Though still pressing his wound, Nartius was wide-eyed at what he saw in the three of them. Malvo nodded, his trust in Cormac absolute. Oswin grinned like he'd found a silver coin, understanding the sentiment more than the words.

28

On the street of Capua, Malvo looked across at Nartius, wondering if he could really trust the man. For all he'd suffered, Nartius still had an air of superiority that made Malvo's hackles rise. Cormac had encouraged the seneschal to become his old self, buying him a new belt and tunic and a shave at the barber. What hair Nartius had left had been oiled and swept back once more.

Malvo had watched him grow in confidence, losing the hunted, battered look he'd worn on the sale block. Still, Cormac had told a few stories of Nartius back in the mine camp. Malvo had long considered the man as a name on the list. It meant standing with him in a strange town was a peculiar experience. If Cormac hadn't been the one asking, Malvo would never have gone along.

Malvo glowered as Nartius nudged him, dropping his hand to the dagger hilt that showed above his belt. One thing was sure, Malvo owed this man no loyalty. If the old fool ever betrayed them, Nartius would feel that blade between his ribs before Malvo ran.

Nartius was not subtle, jerking his head to catch Malvo's attention. Malvo glanced at the carriage, the one they had marked the day before. It drew to a halt, not twenty paces from where they stood across the street. It was the third time they had seen it, establishing a pattern, though of what they were not yet sure.

That was all Cormac had asked of them. He'd found the address in the record office, with details of staff, pension paid, everything. It seemed the man who had wanted Cormac whipped to death, who had sentenced them to ten years in the mines, had prospered in the years since.

From the tabularium in Rome, Cormac could plan a campaign. He still needed feet on the ground, Malvo understood that much. In role as Gaius Vitreus Gallus Corvus, Cormac had to be at work in the stacks just after dawn, earning trust and a small wage. It meant it was Malvo and Nartius who'd rented a cart and pair, then travelled two hundred miles down the Via Appia to a city neither man knew. They were strangers there and Cormac had judged correctly that either one alone would be helpless. Together, they may have bickered and annoyed one another, but at least they could stand on street corners without looking like spies or informers. So Malvo hoped, anyway.

'What will you have?' the vendor asked.

She was a middle-aged matron with grey hair drawn back and fastened with a clip of mother-of-pearl. Her husband crashed about in the tiny kitchen behind, while she served the public from an opening in the wall. It was perfectly placed to watch the house across the road. Malvo had been pleased with himself when he'd joined the queue. A man in a line could stare at anything he wanted, or just chat idly with a friend. Cormac had taught him the importance of seeming innocent.

Nartius nudged him again, taking his attention from the shopkeeper to snatch a glance at a young woman stepping out of the carriage. Malvo had already seen her, of course, he just hadn't been so obvious about it. The lady looked up and down the street, like a doe sensing a wolf. Malvo was glad the passers-by hid him then. He smiled appreciatively.

'If you don't order, you'll have to step aside. There are people waiting,' the vendor said loudly.

She was already looking past this stranger with the black beard and hood. Some of her regular crowd were there and she exchanged a look of apology with them. Yet there was something unnerving about the hooded man, so she did not take the orders they called out, not while he still loomed.

Malvo jabbed a finger at one of the pictures painted on the wall. It seemed to have fish in it and he liked fish. Fried in oil until the skin bubbled, then wrapped in flatbread with some sort of local green herb. He paid two copper asses for two of them, watching as the woman expertly made them up and passed them across. She looked flushed and already weary, wiping sweat from her forehead with the back of her hand. He supposed the morning rush was her busiest time. Others heading off to work stood with bowls on the raised pavement, eating with spoons tied to rings on the wall. As each one finished, they let the spoons fall and set the bowls on the counter, moving swiftly on. It was all very civilised and Malvo ignored the glares of those he'd forced to wait. He had no idea if there were vigiles in this town, or some group like them. Looking at the fine clothes of the people, he supposed there had to be.

In their absence, a gang like the one he had known could have made a fortune.

Stepping away, Malvo bit down on the wrap, crunching little bones and picking out a larger one he tossed into the gutter. Nartius began to devour his, and there was nothing suspicious about two men standing on a kerb and eating breakfast. It might have been why Cormac had sent them both, or because he didn't trust Nartius either.

Across the road, the carriage trundled away, leaving the young woman before a door Malvo and Nartius had watched for four days. As Malvo flicked a scale from where it had caught between two teeth, he saw her raise her right foot behind her, bending the knee until she could reach back and free some stone from her sandal. It exposed a length of fine calf and he could not look away for a moment.

She sensed his scrutiny, of course. All women seemed to know when they were being watched, at least in Malvo's experience. Men were rather more oblivious. To his embarrassment, she looked over her shoulder and saw him in his dark cloak and hood, munching a fish roll like a village idiot. Malvo stopped chewing, holding his breath.

'*Look away*,' Nartius hissed at him.

Malvo turned his head in the hood, though his gaze stayed on her. He thought she smiled then, though it was lost as she approached the street door. The praetor – no, the ex-praetor – was a lucky, lucky man, Malvo thought.

'She saw us watching,' Nartius said glumly.

'We're just men, staring while she fixed her sandal,' Malvo said. 'I think . . . yes, I think she probably has that happen a lot. It's nothing to one like her.'

With the door to the house safely closed, Nartius finished his fish roll with some smacking of lips.

'It could still be a daughter,' he said, wondering if Malvo would buy him another.

They had spent almost a week observing the home of the one who had sat as magistrate six years before. For that particular year in Rome, Gaius Gracchus Aemilianus had sentenced many men and women – to be whipped, enslaved or executed, depending on the crime and his whim. According to the records Cormac had found, the man seemed to have relished his position, producing more and harsher verdicts than anyone else had managed for years. His reward was being made governor of a city within reach of Rome, along with an official residence listed in the tabularium as an imperial property. His role as praetor may have lasted only a year, but well-connected men clearly moved on to more permanent positions, at least if they were favoured. Gracchus had survived the years under Caligula, after all. He had to have friends.

Malvo cracked his knuckles as he thought. As governor of a city, Gracchus had guards and high walls to keep him safe. Cormac had only sent the pair of them to gather information, to look for weaknesses. The truth was, there didn't seem to be any. Gracchus always moved with guards, perhaps aware of the ill feeling that sometimes followed those who had once sat as judge and jury. The title of praetor came with rewards, that was obvious. It also brought some risk.

Since their arrival in Capua, Malvo and Nartius had haunted every move Gracchus made, from observing his official residence to standing outside banquets and festivals, the governor enjoying music or poetry while they watched in bored frustration. His main interest was the gladiatorial ring. He seemed to follow those bouts with the same enthusiasm some men brought to the racing teams in Rome. Malvo knew he was over there that morning, to watch the practices.

The governor's house came with a full complement of slaves, of course, so that there was no chance to sneak in and surprise him in his bed, not that Malvo could see. That would have been suicide and Cormac had told them not to make a move until they had described everything to him, safely back in Rome. The job was almost done, with not much to show for it. Only the young woman was a diversion for them. She . . .

Malvo saw the door open and turned quickly, hurrying away. He had a sense for danger he'd developed on the streets at a young age. It moved him on before he'd made a formal decision. Nartius stumbled with him, though he looked back in the sort of guilty fashion Malvo had trained himself out of. Still, he could not help asking.

'Is it her?'

'Yes. The carriage driver has spotted her. He's coming back. Could still be a daughter?'

'No . . . a daughter would have known Gracchus was at the amphitheatre. A mistress, though, stealing a little precious time away from her husband? She might not.'

The amphitheatre was the pride of Capua, four floors high and faced in marble – better than anything in Rome, so the locals said. It lay a short walk from where they stood, just a mile south on a straight road. Recent experience suggested Gracchus would be there for the morning, then enjoy a lavish lunch. Would the young woman know to find him there? Would she dare to, under the gaze of

Capua's noble classes? Or would she return home, disappointed? Malvo watched the carriage move away on the stone street, the wheels rattling between the kerbs and crossing stones.

'We should follow her,' he said.

Nartius groaned.

'My back protests,' he said. 'As does my hip.'

'Tell them to keep their thoughts to themselves,' Malvo growled. 'Keep up.'

Ahead of them, the carriage turned a corner, negotiating a crowd of workers waiting to cross. As soon as it vanished from sight, Malvo began to lope along. He was no great runner, but he was twenty-three years old. If he absolutely had to, he could run all day.

The carriage was heading south, sure enough, towards the amphitheatre. Gracchus loved the sport with a rare passion, the only thing about him Malvo could appreciate. In Rome, it might have been the behaviour of a serious gambling man, but in Capua, Malvo did not know if that still applied. It would all be reported back to Cormac, but first . . . he had to see where the young woman was heading. He smiled as he heard Nartius puffing along behind.

The carriage was in no great hurry and Nartius was still just in sight when it pulled up at the Circus Capua. Malvo was breathing well enough when he saw it stop. He knew he was recognisable, that was the problem. He needed the beard and hood to keep his lopsided face from being the only thing people recalled. Yet it too could be remembered – beards were still rare in Roman towns. He frowned, wiping sweat as the sun grew warm.

The young woman climbed down from the carriage once more, helped onto the road by her driver. Malvo dared not go any closer, so sat on a stone bench like the old men, watching from the shadow of his hood.

Nartius came up after a time, heaving for breath and so red-faced Malvo thought he might burst his heart or suffer one of the strange ailments where a man's face sagged.

'Be my eyes, would you?' Malvo muttered. 'She has marked me once already.'

He waited as Nartius squinted down the road.

'A man has come out – a big fellow. He is . . . he is embracing her.'

'A friend, a brother?' Malvo asked.

Nartius snorted.

'Not the way she holds his face to kiss him, no. A husband or a lover. He has the look of a fighting man.'

'Walk past them,' Malvo snapped. 'Quickly – hear what you can. Go!'

Nartius made no more objection and trotted across the road, slowing to pass the couple. Malvo risked a glance, sighing as he saw Nartius continuing on, vanishing into the distance. They had both been seen, he thought. They would both be remembered. Yet it was a risk he'd felt he had to take.

It was another hour before a low whistle raised his head. Nartius had circled round on back streets and approached from the other direction, acting about as suspiciously as anyone Malvo had ever seen. He understood what Cormac meant when he said he despaired.

Together they walked back at a more reasonable pace. They had taken rooms above one of the shops near the governor's house. It was past noon and both men were footsore and hungry once again.

'It was her husband,' Nartius said. He seemed delighted

about something and he chuckled. Malvo considered strangling him a little. Just enough to make a point, not to death.

'Will you make me ask?' Malvo said at last.

His companion looked hurt, but he went on.

'He had taken a wound to his arm and so ended his practice early for today. Nothing serious, but I heard her asking if he would get it stitched by the doctors. He said he'd need sour wine and a poultice, but he wasn't worried.'

'So . . .' Malvo prompted, though he had already leaped ahead.

'A gladiator. And she is his woman. He is a dangerous-looking creature, Malvo. He glanced at me as I passed.' He shuddered, recalling the moment. 'I felt it like the touch of the grave.'

Malvo grinned to himself. A man of violence, with a woman who visited a lover while he practised. There was a chance to impress Cormac there, to bring him vengeance like a thunderbolt sent from Rome. Malvo could be Cormac's agent, his right hand – the sword that would strike on his behalf.

Nartius saw his smile and shook his head.

'Cormac said to come back when we had something we could use.'

Malvo turned to him.

'Unlike you, Nartius, I am a free man. You and I are here now, aren't we? Who knows if the opportunity will return? By the time we go back to Rome, it might be lost. No, I know exactly what to do.'

Cornelia reached up with her left hand and patted her own right shoulder. She *had* him. She took a moment to enjoy the satisfaction, to straighten it all out in her mind. He had not made it easy! Only eleven large sums had been removed from the aerarium on the day she had observed him leaving. The order of them was not important to the treasury clerk, so they had all been shuffled together. That meant tracking each one down by name and amount, eliminating them one by one. It helped that most of the men involved were over the age of fifty. She had looked up every record, finding dates of birth and where they lived. She'd made her own list then, crossing them through with her reed pen as she dismissed them. Two more had required gold enough to fill a cart, the amount itself elim-inating them. They were marked with the ring seal of the imperial household and she'd dropped those like they were hot. Still, the search had become a game, especially for the last three.

Gaius Perca was the name, she was sure of it. She had two more to check, but he was about the right age and he had served as tribune with Legio II Augusta in Gaul. The young man who called himself Gaius Vitreus Gallus Corvus claimed to be from Gaul – and he had the look of eagles about him, she was sure of that. The Gaius she knew did not resemble the usual sort of scribe, not in the stacks anyway. Her man had the look of a soldier.

Gently, almost reverently, she brought a page of vellum to her lips and kissed his name. She would still investigate the final two, but she was certain.

'Cornelia!' a voice said behind her. 'You will mark the page! What girlish nonsense is this to be kissing vellum in this hidden corner?'

She gave a shriek and almost threw the page into the air, so deep had her concentration been. She turned in shock to see the one she feared most, who surely held her fate in his hand at that moment.

Old man Felix practically bristled with indignation at what he had witnessed. His face was red with anger as he drew the page from between her thumb and finger, examining the list of names. She sat frozen rather than resist, just staring as he bent his eyebrows to the page and peered at the letters. All but three names were crossed through and she saw he was mouthing those, committing them to memory.

'What is this foolishness? On best vellum, too? Have you any idea of the cost of such a page?'

'I meant to sand it clean again, Master Felix, when I was finished. It was just to hand while I was looking up some names. It was . . . just the treasury list.' She swallowed in fear as he looked up then.

'The list that some men in this city would give their eye teeth to see? The list of wealth moving each day? Please tell me I have not placed my trust in you only to be betrayed, Cornelia! Who paid you for these names?'

Cornelia felt her throat dry as she realised how serious the situation was. What had been an idle game had become something that could see her dragged before a praetor and condemned. She tried to speak. There could be no more lies under that cold gaze. Did she have to tell all? The prospect made her cheeks burn.

'Master Felix, it was . . . a personal matter. I thought I saw a man I knew out in the forum, coming from the treasury. I used the record to check the names, just to see if I was right. It had nothing to do with the sums involved, I swear it on the gods.'

She could feel tears sting her eyes as he looked on her.

The old man was a gentle presence on most days, but all sign of that had vanished. His gaze was empty of pity as he regarded the quivering young woman at the table.

'You have worked here for, what, three years?' Felix said. 'And before today, I have been pleased with your labours. There are some who say women are a distraction to the scholars, but I have found them diligent and careful. I cannot say the same of all my male scribes!'

He settled himself onto a second stool, sitting across from her and lacing his fingers together on the table.

'I will give you a chance, Cornelia, to make me believe there is an innocent explanation. If you cannot, I will have to end your employment this day. It would then be my duty to report your actions to the court – and your fate would be decided by others. It would be out of my hands, but it would be just and fair. Do you understand?'

She nodded, tears streaming.

'Very well,' he said, gesturing to the pile of sheafs and wraps she had assembled. 'Convince me.'

She began to tell everything she knew, weeping all the while.

29

Capua was a beautiful city. Barely a dozen miles from the sea, it had grown wealthy on trade and closeness to Rome. Spelt grain grew well in the black earth there, harvested and transported on the Via Appia to be made into bread for the capital. The auctions too were famous, with vast sums changing hands as farmers brought in their crops. More, there were bronze foundries that gleamed like Vulcan's forge, hammers ringing to produce statues of Aphrodite and Athena, Jupiter and Apollo. Those were sold as far away as Syria and Gaul, with the profits returning to Capua.

Beyond those trades, it was still best known for its gladiatorial school – and the stain on its reputation from a century before. The great rebellion of Spartacus had begun in Capua. Those slaves had threatened Rome herself before being destroyed by elite legions. The survivors had been crucified in their thousands along the same Via Appia. Most of those rough posts had been taken for firewood in the decades since. A few remained as broken stubs on the side of the road, surrounded by shards of old bones, whitened by time and sun.

Malvo could have paid a boy to deliver the note, he knew that. He could have told Nartius to do it as well, if he'd trusted the man. Instead, he had Nartius off buying food for them to eat that evening, while Malvo watched the side entrance to the arena. It was a simple plan, he reminded himself. Cormac always said those were the best kind, without too many things to go wrong. Malvo panted slightly as he stood there, breathing through his mouth like a dog. He and Nartius had checked Governor Gracchus was in his house after a night spent carousing with a few friends. The man would sleep late and with just a little luck, the gladiator Andronicus would find him in bed and utterly helpless.

Malvo grinned at the thought. He had asked the staff of the arena about the best fighters. It turned out this Marcus Andronicus was unbeaten that year, a terror on the sand. Malvo's only regret was that he would not be able to witness the man's righteous rage when he came for the governor.

Malvo still remembered the praetor's disdainful expression as he'd stared down on the line of chained men in court. Though years had passed, it could flash into his mind's eye and make him twitch. That moment had burned itself into his memory, like the irons Cormac had described. It raised a rage in him to be so overlooked. It was as if the man who had sat in judgement raised himself on those he sentenced, like surly stepping stones.

'I will watch them carry the bastard out,' he murmured as he stood there. He knew Cormac would ask if he had

377

seen the body. That was part of it, but he truly wanted to witness the destruction of the praetor.

His thoughts broke apart as the door opened. The first two times had been staff from the arena, but Malvo drew in a sharp breath when he saw it was Marcus Andronicus. He hurried across the little road as the gladiator leaned on a wall to stretch. By the gods, he was a fine specimen! Taller and much broader than Malvo, the gladiator wore a white tunic that left legs and arms bare, showing a mass of scars and muscle. There was a bandage around his right bicep and a legion tattoo on a forearm.

Andronicus clearly retained the instincts of a trained man. He looked up and down the road as he stretched his legs, ready to begin his daily run. He spotted Malvo's approach immediately and turned to face him. This was not a man who could be surprised.

Marcus Andronicus stood relaxed as Malvo drew up, one foot back and right knee slightly bent. In perfect balance, the bigger man was suddenly ready to attack or defend from a blow.

Malvo swallowed and tried to remember what he was meant to say. He halted with one foot raised on the kerb so that he stood a head below the man watching him. He saw the gladiator held up a single flat palm. It felt like running into a wall and Malvo could only wonder at the authority in a simple gesture. The gladiator had signalled for him to halt and so he had.

'That's close enough,' Andronicus said, his voice low and hoarse. He was shining with sweat after sword train-ing. The man smelled of wild animals, as if he had been wrapped in a bear pelt. Malvo had to summon his courage to reply.

'You are Marcus Andronicus?'

'I am.'

'I have a written message from my master. Private and personal, dominus. Of the most serious matter.'

The gladiator gestured for it to be handed over. Malvo noticed the man's right hand rested on a knife hilt on his hip, ready to draw. He lived with violence, always ready for it. Perhaps he had enemies, or betting syndicates who might see value in hobbling the favourite before a bout. The fight game was ruthless enough, Malvo knew. Careers were short, though there were few deaths on the sands. Yet wounds took their own toll and crippled men would starve.

Malvo held up both of his own hands, showing he held no weapon. Slowly, he withdrew a piece of vellum from his belt, folded and sealed with a wax coin. 'Andronicus' was written on it – and Malvo could not help looking at the name as he handed it over. It was not a good hand, not really. The letters were badly spaced, so that some of them bunched and then left an odd gap in the middle of the name. Nor was it quite straight. Yet he had written them and that made them a wonder. Cormac had taught him painstakingly over six years in the camp, using a stick to mark the muddy ground, then a bit of board and a piece of lead. Overseer Farix had helped when he saw, offering his own suggestions. It was Malvo's achievement and he was proud of it. It was true Nartius could write in fine style, with loops and a neatness Malvo could never match, but this was his. Cormac would hear he had written the note and he would clap Malvo on the back.

'If you wish, I can read it for you,' Malvo said.

Andronicus looked up at him with the sort of expression Malvo remembered from the praetor. With a jerk, the gladiator snapped the seal and opened the single page. Malvo held his breath as the man's eyes moved back and forth. There were only two lines, but they caused a deeper flush to come to the one reading them, as if his skin was fired brick.

'Do you know what is in this?' Andronicus growled.

He held it up and waved the page at Malvo as if he was trying to strangle it. Malvo saw rage building and shook his head.

'My master said it was urgent, but that is all I know, dominus.'

The man grunted. He turned on his heel and hammered his fist on the door he had come through. Malvo blinked as it opened and Andronicus vanished inside. The governor's house was a mile to the north. As the gladiator disappeared, Malvo breathed in understanding. Of course. Governor Gracchus had guards. He had staff and friends staying. Andronicus would know that. He was fetching his famous swords, perhaps the armour he wore on the sand. It would be a terrifying spectacle and Malvo resolved to hurry along with him, to be close by when the magistrate had his guts spilled like a trout.

A scream sounded, stopping Malvo's breath. He looked up and up at the windows cut in the high walls, trying to find the source. Four storeys of white stone shimmered in the heat of summer. A man's voice rose in anger above where Malvo stood, accusing, building in volume and speed. Other men's voices joined in, calling for peace. Malvo swallowed a lump like an apple core trapped in his throat. He had not known she was there, not that day. He went to the street door and leaned inside, trying to see what was happening.

He saw stairs, with mules being led around the ring of sand. The grooms had stopped their labours at the sudden commotion. Malvo hesitated, exchanging a glance with the one who had opened the door for Andronicus.

'This isn't for the public,' the man began. 'You should go round . . .'

Malvo stepped past, relying on his size and glower to intimidate.

'I'm with him,' he said, bounding up the stairs two at a time.

He could hear a woman's voice rise to the heavens as he reached the top. Malvo froze when he saw she was there, gold-haired and beautiful in her fury. None of the arena servants had shared her name with him. Whatever it was, she was yelling at Andronicus as he held her in a grip she could not break. One block of a hand was buried in her hair, gripping the base of her neck. She wrenched and scratched at that grip, but he stood like a wall.

'Let me go!' she shrieked.

'I'll let you go *when you deny it*,' Andronicus roared.

His voice was a weapon and she flinched, leaning away. Malvo too froze at the pain and rage he heard. She tried to stand straight, glaring at a man twice her weight and strength.

'You were never home!' she said. Tears came into her eyes and Malvo was close enough to see them spill down one cheek. 'I am *sorry*!' She began to sob and her husband let go where he held her. She staggered back a step without his strength to hold her up.

In that instant, he struck out, punching her in the

stomach. The air whooshed out of her and she dropped as if her legs had been kicked away. Malvo winced as she hit the ground hard, lying there. Andronicus stood over her, panting as if he had come back from one of his runs or a bout on the sand. That golden expanse gleamed through the openings behind the pillars, the air rippling with heat.

Four other men came rushing up then. Dressed in loose belted tunics, they looked like younger versions of Andronicus and they moved with speed and certainty. Two of them gripped Andronicus by the arms and he reacted with sudden violence. Like a bullock feeling the rope for the first time, he threw his weight back and forth, sandals scraping the ground. He began to howl, a great ragged shout of pain and grief as they dragged him away.

Malvo found himself drawn to the figure that lay on the ground. She was curling up, he saw, pulling in her legs. One of her sandals had been torn from her foot, so that her toes were bare. She made a groaning sound, whispering words to herself as she held the place her husband had struck.

'What can I do?' Malvo said.

He reached for her, thinking he would help her rise. She seemed unaware, blind with pain or betrayal. She tried to stand and as she took her hand from her stomach, he saw the palm was red with blood. Andronicus had not punched her, as he'd thought. His blade had been in his hand.

She moaned as she saw the blood pouring into her lap. Somehow, she had the strength to sit up, but it pooled across her skirts and Malvo could only stare in horror as she looked in wonder at her wet hands. He'd wanted the governor to be killed, not this young woman. He'd wanted

Cormac to be pleased with him. Instead, everything had gone wrong.

Two women came running then, with a man who made even Andronicus look small. He exclaimed in shock when he saw the wound, scooping the young woman into his arms like a child and running with her to wherever wounds were tended.

Malvo wondered if she could be saved. Surely a place where men fought for the entertainment of crowds would have good doctors. He wanted to follow, but he was a stranger there and he could sense eyes on him as the arena staff began to wonder who he was and what part he had played. He backed towards the stairs. When someone called out for him to stop, he leaped down the last steps and out into the sun, wincing at the brightness.

Nartius had laid out an evening meal by the time Malvo returned. The older man was worried, having spent a day alone in Capua with no news.

'Thank the gods! I was beginning to think you'd been arrested and taken up!' Nartius said, pouring a cup of wine.

Malvo looked exhausted and sunburned from standing too long in the street. He accepted the cup and drank it dry, more from thirst than any other need. Nartius refilled it with water and Malvo sank that in a few gulps, holding it out again.

'Where have you been?' Nartius said as Malvo began to eat. 'They are talking of a murder at the arena. The governor hasn't stirred from his house except to sit in his garden and drink wine. What happened to our plan?'

'That gladiator killed the plan, that's what happened!' Malvo retorted. 'I thought he would go and find the man his wife was seeing. Instead . . . he killed her, Nartius. She would not deny it, so he just killed her. In front of me, just about. He stabbed her in the stomach. I waited hours to hear if she had been saved, but they were useless. I thought they would be good with wounds, those people! But I saw her brought out, wrapped for the tomb.'

'We're back at the beginning,' Nartius breathed, frowning. Cormac had ordered them both to come home, to report all they learned. That mattered less to Malvo, he assumed. Less than a man who was Cormac's slave, purchased at auction. For this disaster, Nartius feared being sold again, or killed to keep his mouth shut. He chewed one lip as he thought.

'Will Andronicus be sent to trial?' Malvo asked suddenly. Nartius shook his head.

'For what? Killing an unfaithful wife? After she admitted it in front of witnesses? Of course not. Even if he were not famous, there isn't a judge from here to Rome who would condemn a man for that.'

'He should be,' Malvo growled. 'He should be nailed up for what he did.'

'Don't be a child,' Nartius snapped.

'I am the one who told him, Nartius. It's not childish to think I played a part in it. I did.'

'Though he might have found out next week and done the same thing. What matters is that the governor has not lost a hair on his head. Your plan failed.'

Nartius had moved to the window to look across the street. Above the shops below, it gave a good view of the governor's home and gardens, which was why they had chosen it. Nartius shook his head in frustration as he stared out.

'I hope you will make it clear to Cormac where the blame lies, Malvo. I advised against it and I have more to lose than you.'

'Don't worry, I'll take the blame,' Malvo said irritably. 'I played my part.'

'Is that . . . ?' Nartius said suddenly. He gestured to his seated companion. 'Come to the window. Tell me that isn't Governor Gracchus leaving his fine home.'

Malvo stood with a scrape of his chair, peering round Nartius into the afternoon sun.

'It is him, I'm sure of it.' Malvo would have known Gaius Gracchus anywhere. The years of soft living had added a little flesh to the governor, but it was still the man who had sentenced him to ten years in the dark, with violence and death risked every day. The man was alone and Malvo felt an overpowering desire to race after him.

Nartius sensed his outrage, holding up an arm to block any sudden move to the door.

'Where is he going, without any guards, Malvo? Take a breath and ask yourself that.'

Malvo peered again at the man striding down the street. Gracchus wore a sword on his hip, he realised. He walked stiff-legged as if in a rage. Malvo turned wide-eyed to Nartius and the slave nodded.

'He is going for revenge. He is going to attack the one who killed his mistress.'

'Then it's not over. Come on, we have to see this,' Malvo said. 'If we go now, we can get ahead of him.'

The listless weariness had vanished as new purpose flooded in. Nartius didn't argue, but clattered down the wooden stairs to the street, already breathing hard and struggling to keep up with the younger man. The sun was low in the sky and the day was hot, but like Malvo, he had to see it play out.

A thousand paces is not a great distance to get ahead of a marching man. Malvo lost Nartius as he darted into an alley, heading to the arena side entrance. By the time he reached it, he looked back to see Gracchus coming round the last corner. Malvo hammered on the door, willing it to open.

The same servant showed his face, scowling as he recognised Malvo.

'You again? I told you before, this is not for the public. Go and . . .'

Malvo held up a silver denarius. The man's expression cleared and he made it vanish, stepping back to allow the stranger entrance. There were always scouts and fans gathering to see gladiators train. It was one of the chief entertainments in the city and news of the violence earlier that day would not hurt their ticket sales. The story was already being repeated all round Capua, in every barber's shop and bath-house. There was even a rumour that the governor was the lover in question, though at least two other men had been accused, with gossip spreading faster than truth.

'Is Andronicus here?' Malvo asked.

The servant jerked his head to a figure leaning on the rail and looking out onto the arena sands. The man was lion-like in the setting sun, lounging with a power and strength most would never know. He was close enough to have heard his name, but Andronicus did not react. There was grief in him, Malvo saw, a heaviness of stance as he rested his head on muscular arms. There was an amphora of wine by his feet as well. The stopper had been removed and it lay on its side, clearly empty. He could hear steps approaching on the other side of the door and he faded into the gloom to observe.

The same servant grumbled as he answered the knock a second time. He stood back as Gracchus entered. He too had been drinking, Malvo saw immediately. He was dull-eyed with wine, stumbling slightly as he passed the threshold. His hair had whitened in the six years since Malvo had seen him in court, in a different life. Yet it was the same man. Malvo shrank into his cloak and tugged at his hood so that only his beard showed.

'Where is he?' Gracchus demanded. 'Where is Andronicus?' The voice had all the peevish arrogance Malvo remembered.

Andronicus turned then, seeing the man who had come in. Malvo watched him take note of the sword Gracchus held, the blade bared as he threw a scabbard aside. It was like watching a child attack its father, but Andronicus only watched him approach, head low, eyes dark and gleaming under heavy brows.

Gracchus made a sound of rage and lunged. Malvo watched the gladiator begin to block and then stop himself, his arm dropping to his side. Everyone present stared as Andronicus let the sword through. It chopped up into his ribs and he gave an animal grunt, almost a cough. In his fury, Gracchus drew back to hit him again. Malvo found himself rising from his seat as something changed. Andronicus reached out and gripped the governor's arm, holding it steady. Though blood poured, spattering the ground, he took the blade from his attacker, then gathered up the governor's toga in one massive fist.

The two men looked at each other for a long moment. Gracchus struggled to break the hold on his clothing.

'Arrest him! Put him in chains,' the governor shouted. He could see a seething anger in the eyes of the gladiator. For the first time, Gracchus began to be afraid.

'I'll sentence you myself,' he snarled. 'I'll watch justice done.'

The gladiator looked at him with red eyes.

'Share it with me then,' he said. He showed his teeth, whipping the blade across the governor's exposed neck. Blood sprayed and Gracchus clung to him in astonishment until his legs buckled and he collapsed in a sprawling heap.

Andronicus stood panting as he threw the sword down. His own wound poured in great gouts, though Malvo was not sure he even felt it. The big man turned once more to stare out over the sands. Someone was yelling for physicians, but before they could come, the gladiator slumped. The blood slowed and with no more warning, he too dropped, eyes staring at nothing.

Malvo just breathed for a long moment. He touched his hand to his mouth and his vision blurred. The one who had sentenced him to the mines was dead, but it had not gone the way he'd thought it would, not with a young woman killed, along with her husband.

The door to the street had been left swinging and Malvo went out, blinded by the sun. Nartius was there and he could not speak to him as they walked away, not then.

30

Cormac found Oswin a calming presence in the household. As another of the staff rekindled cooking fires from the night before, he set up wax slates and bone pens on the kitchen table, ready to teach the boy his letters. It was a satisfying process and Oswin would smile whenever he saw he had pleased the one who owned him. Each morning, Oswin scowled in concentration as he copied curves and straight lines, then said the names out loud as Cormac pointed to them. His progress had been quick – much faster than Malvo, as Cormac recalled.

At the same time, Cormac found himself talking to the boy, perhaps because Oswin could only cock his head and work on letters, without much understanding. It would come, Cormac reminded himself. In the meantime, he could talk without having to worry about revealing too much to his audience.

He glanced up as one of the kitchen slaves laid a spoon by his bowl. Cormac bit his lip when he realised he had not been completely aware of food being made. It was going on around him, and like a real eques, he had let it happen without thought. The idea troubled him and he sat frowning, cracking his knuckles. A man became his mask, it seemed.

As he picked up the spoon at last, he heard voices coming through the garden, voices he knew. Cormac put aside his thoughts and signalled for two more bowls as Malvo and Nartius entered. A single glance showed a more subdued pair than he had expected. He'd sent them away to get used to one another's presence and Cormac could see at least part of the awkwardness had vanished. Yet they were downcast. His stomach sank at the prospect of bad news.

'Good evening, gentlemen,' he said, indicating chairs at the table. 'Would you like to eat first or tell me now?' he said. 'Come on, sit, both of you.'

They drew up chairs and Malvo glanced at Nartius, then at the kitchen slave. He at least had not grown up with staff listening to every private word.

'Would you leave us, Els, please?' Malvo said.

The matronly woman jumped as if she'd been pinched, lost in her own daydreams. She nodded and vanished, closing the kitchen door behind her.

'As bad as that?' Cormac murmured.

'Judge for yourself. Gracchus is dead.'

'What? How? I told you to *watch*!' Cormac snapped. 'Did you . . .' Even in their own home, he dared not say the words.

Oswin looked from one to another, eyes wide. The two men had brought anger in with them like a cold breeze. The little boy was worried and confused.

'It wasn't us,' Nartius broke in. 'Not really.'

'All right, Nartius, I'll tell it,' Malvo growled.

Cormac saw the older man shrug and nod. They had learned to trust one another, it seemed. He'd been right about that at least.

'Gracchus had another man's wife as his lover. A gladiator's wife. So . . . I let the man know about the affair. I thought the fighter would go to Gracchus and cut his head off. Instead, he killed his wife in front of me.'

His face twisted and Cormac's heart went out to the pain in him. He'd seen Malvo kill without a second thought, without a sign of regret or sorrow. Cormac hadn't really known regret was in him until that moment. Yet Malvo was hunched and wretched with it, his guilt like an odour.

'Gracchus tried to arrest him,' Malvo said, after two long breaths. 'He went for that gladiator with a sword in his hand – and I think the big man let him. They both died. I'm sorry we didn't come back and report first, Cormac, all right? You might have found a better way. I'm sure you would have. I won't make the same mistake again. Neither of us will.'

'It sounds like . . . you don't need me to tell you anything else,' Cormac said. He *was* furious with them, but he understood the bond they shared. He'd wanted that, however it had come about. As for the magistrate, Cormac looked inside himself, but there was no regret, except that he hadn't seen it. If Malvo had gentled, perhaps Cormac had hardened.

'He took six years from both of us!' Cormac reminded him. 'Six long years of pain and misery. I'd see a hundred of his sort in the gutter and step over them all without looking down! It's done, Mal. There's no point moping about something we can't undo! Cheer up! I never said it would be easy, did I? I'm only sorry he never knew it was us.'

Malvo nodded sharply. He pressed the edge of his hood against his eyes for a moment to soak up a glimmer of brightness, then cleared his throat.

'And you? What did you manage while we were away?'

'My job in the stacks, for one. Though I think I may be suspected. I can't seem to go anywhere now without the old man turning up and checking my work, or his grandson, or that Cornelia woman.' His gaze became softer as he said her name, making Malvo snort.

'Still playing with fire there, I see, but you were to watch Pugio.'

'And I did,' Cormac said, stung by the note of criticism. 'In my evenings, Oswin and I walked your old neighbourhood by the south gates. You know better than most that he doesn't show himself on the street, not where vigiles might see him.' A slow smile spread and Malvo matched it.

'But you found him anyway,' Malvo breathed.

'I found him,' Cormac confirmed. 'Or at least I guessed where to hunt for him. I saw half a dozen cockfights with no sign of your man. I watched boxers battering each other bloody. Then on the fourth night, I saw Pugio entering a fine gambling house down by the Circus.' Cormac smiled more widely then, pride showing. 'Like you, I took a risk, to see inside, to get the lay of the place. It cost me twelve denarii, but your man was there, throwing dice and losing even more than me.'

'Good,' Malvo said. There were only a few in Rome who might recognise the two of them. Pugio was one, as was Terentius of the vigiles and, of course, more than one

Silanus. While those men lived, neither Cormac nor Malvo could ever know peace.

'Pugio next, then?' Malvo said. He saw Cormac's expression become more thoughtful. 'Cormac?'

'Hmm? Definitely. Pugio next. This one is for you. There is something else, though, that I've been working on while you were away.' He glanced at Nartius and the older man looked suddenly wary. 'I suppose it depends on what you have to say to me, Nartius, in some ways. It's something I have wondered about for a long time. From a different life, I suppose.'

'Dominus, I swear,' Nartius said. 'Ask and I will tell you anything.'

'You swear? You are my slave, Nartius. If I had a question for you, it would be my duty in law to put you to torture, would it not?'

The older man rubbed his forehead as sweat appeared. He was remembering hot irons held to Cormac's skin, searing him. Cormac waited while the man's fear grew, saying nothing. He owed him that much.

'You were on my list as well, Nartius,' he said softly. 'Not so very long ago.'

'Dominus, I . . . I didn't know anything then. I'm sorry. Please, whatever it is, just ask me.'

'Let me vouch for him,' Malvo said, surprising them both.

Cormac looked from one to the other and was pleased. He nodded.

'Very well. It was about the death of the old master, Nartius. Senator Silanus thought I was the last one to see his brother. But someone had laid him out when I came home – and that has rankled with me for a long time. So, Nartius . . . was it you?'

393

The old seneschal said nothing, but after a hesitation, he nodded slowly. A line of sweat drifted from wrinkle to wrinkle down one cheek. If it itched, Nartius did not move to wipe it away.

'I slept in the room next to his and I thought I heard him . . . there were sounds. When I went in, he was still moving.'

His gaze had turned inward and Cormac could see he was remembering terrible things.

'There was a smell in the air,' Nartius went on, 'a bitterness I thought I knew. I cannot be sure with the years since, but I know I thought then it was hemlock. I picked some from a verge once, by the road. You remember Sophia from the kitchens? She slapped it from my hand and told me to remember it, or it would kill me the way it had killed Socrates. That was the smell in the master's room that day.'

Cormac slumped in his chair, a great tension going out of him. He had not known he bore the weight until it was suddenly gone.

'Thank you for telling me,' he said. 'Though it means they did kill him . . . and set us both free in the act. How strange that something so evil could produce any good at all.'

He saw Nartius wince and realised they had not both come free through the years since that day. Cormac nodded, making a decision. He turned to Oswin and pointed to the wooden dresser he used as a desk. The boy leaped up with all the energy of youth and went across to it.

'While you and Malvo were away,' Cormac said, 'I thought about what would happen if I fail. Malvo and I accept the risks in what we are doing. I do, at least. If I am taken up by the vigiles, or put before a court, well, I will not complain or wish I'd taken a different path. This is my path – and I will walk it without regret. But that ending, whenever and however it comes, should not fall on anyone else. I don't think I'd want that on my conscience. So I have prepared documents, Nartius, making you once more a free man. Along with your bill of sale, they are not forgeries. They should hold up if anyone ever questions them, whether I am condemned or not. At this moment, I am your owner under the law. It is my right to free my slave, no matter what happens after. Do you understand?'

Nartius crumpled as he sat across the little table. In the lamplight, he looked older, shaking as if a fever had him. Oswin brought back a piece of fine vellum, real stretched calfskin with lettering bold and black. The boy handed it to Cormac and he slid it across the table to the man named on it. Cormac waited for Nartius to read the whole thing, then slid a silver ring across the polished wood after it.

'You'll need this as well,' he said, 'so that people know.'

Nartius' eyes filled then and he dropped his head as he wrestled the ring onto a finger. It was just a simple band of silver, but it meant the world. Cormac knew that better than anyone.

Oswin cleared his throat then and Nartius looked over at him, staring at the sheaf of papers he still held, all sealed with coins of dark blue wax. The newly freed man looked at Cormac in confusion.

'If I die, Nartius,' Cormac went on. 'Not before, mind – I need a staff! If I am taken though, I know I can trust you to distribute these manumussions, for my household. I would not like to go to the grave owning them, if you understand me. Will you hold them till then? I still need you to run the house, though for a wage. I'm hoping you will agree to those terms.'

'If you answer one question, I will,' Nartius said. He had recovered from his first reaction and he took the sheaf of papers from the boy without looking at them.

Cormac nodded, warily.

'Ask,' he said.

'Is Malvo holding a knife at this moment?' Nartius said.

Cormac glanced aside, but Malvo raised both hands empty. Nartius breathed in relief.

'So I am truly free to refuse? To leave?'

'That is what freedom means,' Cormac said softly. 'I would not deny it to you. If you wish to leave, leave. I will find another way, perhaps start again in another city.'

'There are no other cities,' Nartius said with a grin. 'There is only one. Very well. I will run your household, Cormac – as a free man. Perhaps we should discuss my pay. With all my experience, I am not a cheap hire.'

Malvo cursed and Cormac chuckled.

'Very well. I can pay you . . . eight denarii a month, as well as room and board.'

Nartius rose and put out his hand, to Malvo and then to Cormac.

'That is more than fair,' he said. His voice broke with emotion and he laughed in embarrassment. 'Oswin, fetch a jug of wine, would you?'

The boy looked blank and Nartius sighed, pointing.

'Jug, boy. Jug! I think we should toast my new employer.'

'A cup, but no more,' Cormac said. 'Unlike you two, I am expected at work tomorrow morning.'

'If you think they suspect you, perhaps it is time to drop "Gaius Vitreus Gallus Corvus",' Malvo said seriously. 'You could send him on a long journey, or have him die of a fever, left safe in a pauper's grave.'

Cormac looked at something they could not see, a smile playing on his lips. Malvo groaned when he saw that.

'There are a couple of things I want to do yet, before I give him up. I have removed Gaius Perca from the list of legion dead. We still need that young cockerel, the eques who opens so many doors. You see the value? Every soul in Rome passes through the stacks in the end – at birth and death, along with anything they do in between. I cannot give that up, not until I am certain it is no more use.'

With dawn pale gold across the forum and its temples, Cormac was part of the bustling crowd passing across the vast space, all heading to work, worship or some part of the governance of Rome. Praetorians stood guard on corners and the night shift of vigiles were heading back to their barracks with prisoners on a chain. Cormac kept his head down when he saw those, though it was from a different life.

He felt like a bee entering its hive as he reached the steps to the tabularium. He stopped for a moment to appreciate that massive building – part of his dreams for as long as he could remember. For all his talk of revenge, there was a part of him, a small part, that he knew could just have vanished into the stacks and never come out, burrowing into those oldest volumes like the tiny weevils they sometimes found. Old Felix made the scribes clean every surface with vinegar when that happened, until he was sure the infestation had been destroyed.

Cormac smiled. Inside that place was work he knew, work he was good at. He had learned the names of every man and woman in there, warming to some and disliking others. If on previous days he'd felt a cold breeze blowing, he had to assume it had something to do with kissing Cornelia. For all he knew, they had been seen, or she had said something about it to the old man. It was a problem he had yet to solve, but his mood was still light as he passed between the outer columns. This was the house of records and he was becoming a master there. There was satisfaction in that, a deep and honest joy that surprised him for mattering as much as it did. He was *good* at something – and no one could take that away from him. On fine days, he could pretend it was his life in that place, that he had no worm inside, aching for power and authority. Other men dreamed of gold and horses. He dreamed of the senate.

Beyond the first doors, a queue of citizens had already formed, ready with whatever they needed to check or confirm or have copied out. Felix was there, looking troubled. He saw Cormac enter and immediately began to move around the counter, bent on interception. Cormac strangled a groan. The man had a way of raising errors that took up half a day. Even his explanations took an age and there was nothing to do but nod and agree, until he was allowed to leave – with his own work still to do and less time to get it all done. The way the old bastard was bustling round to stop him, he wondered what time he'd manage to leave that night. Cormac was working on a plan to have Pugio taken up by the vigiles, but it had to be perfect. The man had both wealth and friends. There was every chance Pugio would call in some favour and be back on the streets with blood in his eye, hungry to find whoever had tried to cross him.

Malvo had wanted to just stick a knife in his ribs, but Pugio always had a couple of blockish-looking men nearby and the gang master was no fainting flower himself. No, if . . .

398

'Master Corvus!' Felix said, his voice louder than usual.

He took Cormac by the hand, gripping and pumping it as if in welcome. The old man was perspiring, Cormac noted. Perhaps he was not long for the world.

'Master Felix,' he replied politely. 'Are you well? I'm still working on the aediles list you asked for. If I have a free hour or two this morning, I'm sure I can finish it.'

He caught a flicker of movement in the door that led past the public waiting rooms, into the stacks themselves. Cormac glanced over and saw Cornelia there. His smile died as he saw she had been crying. She stood with one hand to her lips, the kohl around her eyes smeared.

'Cornelia?' he said. Without thought, he started to go to her, only to find Felix still held his fingers in a vice.

'Cornelia was told not to show herself,' Felix snapped.

His expression was thunderous and Cormac could only blink in confusion.

'May I have my hand back?' Cormac asked. 'If you wouldn't mind?'

'Mind?' the old man said, his voice hardening further. 'Oh, I mind *very much*, Master Corvus. I mind that you entered these hallowed buildings with black evil in your heart – and no true name! I mind the damage you have done – and you may be assured I will root out every last part of it, whatever you came here to accomplish. On my oath, I will find it all!'

Spit had gathered as white froth in the corners of the old man's mouth. He had swollen and turned almost purple, with pale patches on his cheeks. Cormac had heard such a pattern described but never seen it. He wondered if the chief scribe was going to suffer an apoplexy.

With a jerk, he pulled his hand free, easily overcoming

the old man's strength. Felix rubbed those fingers in his other hand, his face full of reproach. He leaned in suddenly, making Cormac want to recoil.

'I told them I wanted a moment to myself, to look you in the eye, to see if I could read the treachery in you. I see it, whoever you are! You disgust me.'

Cormac swallowed nervously as he heard the tramp of sandals behind him. He knew that sound all too well from his time in Gaul. He turned slowly to see soldiers blocking the light. There was nowhere to run, except into the stacks themselves. He saw Cornelia was still there, tears streaming. His mind raced, but he said nothing, though the old man trembled in bitter triumph.

A hand clapped on Cormac's shoulder, a weight and authority that almost buckled his knees. The queue had gone utterly silent as the citizens of Rome watched the scene play out. Cormac turned to look up into the helmeted face of a legion officer. His eyes picked out the symbol on the man's breastplate. As he was in Rome, he'd expected praetorians, but it was a different legion that had come for him.

'Gaius Perca? Tribunus Laticlavius of Legio II Augusta?' The optio did not wait for Cormac to nod, though he seemed to note the way the blood drained from the younger man. 'You are under arrest for deserting your legion at time of active service. In accordance with your rank, you may appoint an advocate to speak in your defence. You will be tried by a council of legion officers. When you are found guilty, the sentence of death by impalement will be carried out immediately.'

Cormac felt another soldier grip his wrist and pull it behind him, links of a chain clinking in the perfect silence. He heard Cornelia sob and shook his head. He could not claim to be Gaius Vitreus Gallus Corvus, he was sure. That name was burned, or they would not have come for him. Yet he could not die for the sins of another. Gaius Perca had not deserted . . .

He groaned to himself. He had removed the name of Gaius Perca from the list of men killed in action. It meant he could use the name, but if anyone ever checked, they would not find a record of a young man lost in Gaul. No, they would think they had unearthed a deserter. Cormac glanced at Felix, seeing the way the man still shook in reaction, overcome with indignation.

Cormac took a deep breath. There were too many ways to go wrong. He'd tried to see them all, but there he was, being chained, with just one way out left.

'I am not Gaius Perca,' he said. 'I have never served with Second Augusta. I am no deserter and you have the wrong man.'

'Told you,' one of the other soldiers said. 'I remember Perca – and this isn't him.'

The optio scowled. He leaned in close to Cormac, so that their noses touched.

'There was a bit of a debate about that, son. A right huddle of lads. You see, Perca had only just joined Augusta, then – gone, some said, killed on a beach in Britannia. That was the way I was told it, anyway. That would have been the end, too, if the chief scribe of Rome hadn't watched one of his own staff entering the treasury and putting the name of Gaius Perca to funds in and out. He searched the legion records for you – and the list of dead men, better men than you or me. No Gaius Perca there, son.'

Cormac saw Cornelia close her eyes. He wanted to embrace her, to tell her it was all right, but he was chained and helpless. He knew very well the old man had not seen him. His eyes were useless at more than a few yards anyway. No, it had to have been her.

'Nonetheless, I am not him,' he said, raising his chin.

The optio smiled and it was a horrible expression.

'When the news came, our legate heard about it, about a deserter – or one using the name of a better man. "Be certain," he said to me. The punishment for desertion is worse, do you see? Ever seen a man impaled? It's slow, and it gets worse and worse. I've heard men say they wouldn't wish it on their worst enemy, but I would, son! That's exactly what I'd wish on him.'

'I am not Gaius Perca,' Cormac said.

The optio shrugged.

'So I asked myself, how can you be certain? Perca was only with Augusta for a couple of days – and in the confusion of the crossing to Britannia, well, you were there. You remember how it was. But there was one who would know. I just had to bring her with me.'

The man jerked his head and the wall of legionaries parted as an old woman was brought forward. The mother of Gaius Perca was clearly terrified. Cormac's heart sank as he saw her confidence.

'Just speak the truth and you can go free. All right? Is this your son?' the optio asked her.

'Yes,' she said, looking Cormac proudly in the eye. 'That is my son, Gaius Perca.'

He had paid her very well, he remembered, as he was dragged away.

Historical Note

The Silanus family came very close to imperial power. Junia Claudilla was married to Gaius Caesar – Caligula – but died in childbirth. The famous monster of Rome only really came about *after* that bloody day – scenes I have written in the book *Nero*. Claudilla's father, Senator Marcus Silanus, died either at Caligula's hand in the birthing room – my preferred version – or as a forced suicide shortly after.

I wrote this book to run alongside some of those events – from Tiberius, to Caligula and Claudius – though from the perspective of a freed slave, a condition and social class that is endlessly fascinating. I have more often favoured the viewpoint of caesars, kings and khans, but all men and women face hard decisions – and those choices can mean as much as the fate of Gaul to them, perhaps more.

Note on names: The Silanus family used very few, repeated over and over through the generations. 'Marcus Junius Silanus' was annoyingly common, passed from father to son. 'Decimus' and 'Gaius' also pop up more than seems quite fair to this author. It is true that a Marcus Junius Silanus was also engaged to Claudius' daughter – and that the engagement was broken off by Agrippina. We know

now that she wanted her own son Nero to make that bond, securing his rise and her own.

Note: The castration of slaves was legal until AD 83, under Emperor Domitian. He issued a 'senatus consultum' decree, forbidding the act on pain of vast fines, up to half of the owner's wealth. It has to be said it did still go on, so that in the second century, Emperor Hadrian doubled the penalty and added restrictions on condemning a slave to death without submitting the decision to a city prefect for approval.

Those examples are telling, but they tended to be rare events. Freedmen were valued at all levels of Roman society, right up to the ones advising Emperor Nero. It was common practice for a Roman master to either allow his slaves a day to earn on their own behalf, or to pay and give bonuses for their labours, so that in time, they could buy themselves free. It was not uncommon for entire households to be freed on death by a benign master. In addition, Emperor Claudius decreed formal manumission for slaves abandoned in their final years or for ill health. In short, Roman slavery was a mixture of horrors and perhaps surprising compassion.

This book opens in AD 37. It is my intention to mirror some of the timeline of the Nero trilogy – though telling a completely different story. In researching that emperor, I became intrigued by the concept of freedmen and freedwomen – including ones like the father of Horace. Or Nero's minister, Phaon, who was hugely wealthy, yet was born a slave.

AD 37 is four years after the death of Christ in Jerusalem, then in Roman-occupied Judaea. It is the year Tiberius was smothered by Naevius Macro – with Caligula either helping or giving the order. As I said in the foreword, it is also the year Nero was born to his mother Agrippina – just sixteen years before he becomes emperor.

Note on baths: The details of thermae in Rome are from a number of sources, including an incredibly well-preserved one I visited in Pompeii. I added in some of my own experience visiting a sauna in Finland, though not the fact that I passed out after swimming in the Baltic and then heading into the hottest room. Having measured my length on the tiles and still quite naked, I was shaken back to consciousness by the head of the Russian Orthodox Church in Finland at that time.

Note on keys: Though locks existed before this in Egypt, the Romans were the ones who really developed the technology. They used key rings and bronze keys to turn mechanisms, usually raising a bolt or bar on the inside of the door. As with so many things, the best surviving examples come from Pompeii and Herculaneum and are astonishingly complex devices for the period.

The Praetorians are an interesting force in imperial Roman history. Originally, they were four and a half thousand strong – deliberately and symbolically one cohort fewer than all the other legions. Under Tiberius and Caligula, their number was raised to somewhere between six and nine thousand men: the same number of cohorts, but each one allowed up to 1,000. They were always much better paid than other legions – up to three times normal, as well as bonuses on special occasions that could be a year's pay or more. It would have been a good life in Rome and it was rare for them to be called to war. When it came to the AD 43 Britannia invasion force under Legate Aulus Plautius, Emperor Claudius did arrive after a journey from Rome by sea and then overland. It is unknown whether Agrippina and her son Lucius were with him.

The most detailed source is still the Greek, Cassius Dio, who described the invasion well over a century after the actual events. Taking him at his word, Emperor Claudius was not in that original invasion fleet, but came later, when Aulus Plautius requested his presence. Claudius then remained in Britain for two weeks, before returning home. His praetorians would have marched with their emperor and rather than get bogged down in arrivals and departures, I put them in the pre-invasion force. I haven't found a reference to them in Cassius Dio, but Claudius took on British tribes with forces he had brought with him, independent of Plautius. As a separate matter of interest, lines in Suetonius confirm the presence of not one but two future emperors in that army – Galba and Vespasian.

Some guesswork is required, but the invasion force would have been around twenty thousand legionaries, with around the same number of auxiliaries. To transport forty thousand men – and four elephants! – would have required a huge fleet of around eight hundred ships. It was to be Claudius' greatest achievement and resulted in the title of 'Britannicus'. The senate awarded it to the emperor, but it became his son's name, just as 'Germanicus' had been earned in previous campaigns. I have described it in more detail in the trilogy *Nero*, *Tyrant* and *Inferno*.

Note on mules: This hybrid of a mare and an ass was used in ancient Rome to pull a carriage known as a 'cisium' – a light, fast thing capable of running fifty miles in nine or ten hours. Mules are longer-lived than horses and stronger than asses, with greater endurance and frankly better and less obstinate natures. Charles Darwin once said they were a rare example of art outdoing nature.

Nero was said to shoe his favourite mules in silver, while his second wife Poppaea shod hers in gold. Yet they often went without horseshoes of any kind, having very tough feet. The ass, or donkey, was introduced to Britain along with rabbits as a food crop in the Roman invasion of AD 43 – the earliest records of mules come after that. With 63 chromosomes compared to the 64 of horses and 62 in donkeys, they were almost always infertile, though there have been very rare exceptions. Yet they cannot establish a line and so breeders always need to return to donkeys and mares. Both Emperor Vespasian and President George Washington bred them.

It is true there were gold mines in Gaul, worked by slaves and free men at this period. Julius Caesar brought so much gold back from his conquest of Gaul that he devalued the currency by an entire third. It was brutal work with a good chance of drowning, suffocation or being crushed in a fall. I have tried to describe it as faithfully as I could for the period.

The treasury building in Rome was indeed built in a wing off the temple to Saturn, by the forum. As an older god of wealth and agriculture, that makes some sense. Only the magnificent columns at the front survive today, but are worth visiting. The 'aerarium' literally means 'house of copper coins'. Next door was indeed the tabularium, the records archive of the empire. A little way off from both is a building on the site of the ancient Tullianum or 'Carcer' prison, later known as the 'Mamertine'. There is a church today on the spot where both St Peter and St Paul would have been held before execution. A couple of the original cells are still there to be seen. From the word 'carcer' we get the word 'incarcerated', still in use today.

Note on tribunes: A legion would have had six of these, usually from the equestrian class, which was a rank below senate families. Though often appointed, the tribune rank was above centurion in authority, with a senior and a junior man in the six. The 'tribunus laticlavius' was in his late teens or early twenties, a very young noble out to complete a year of military service with honour and so secure a glittering career in Rome.

This story of vengeance and a freed slave ends here with disaster. The second part will take us into the reign of a new young emperor: Nero. That young man has the world at his feet and his mother at his side. It is a different age – and perhaps Cormac is the man to take advantage.

Conn Iggulden, London, 2024